Adven... ready to face danger...
or embrace desire

CHARLES MILLER—Ruthless business tycoon amassing a fortune from a young and growing land. He was driven by dark passions and a burning hatred for his closest kin.

STEPHEN MILLER—Charles's bold and brash twin brother. He chose to live the dangerous life of a frontiersman... and to love another man's wife.

ELIZABETH STODDARD—Raised by the maverick Eli Stoddard, closest friend of the great Mohawk Sachem Aaron Brant, no one could tame her spirit... or keep her from the side of the man she loved.

CREE WOMAN—Married to a brave, half-blood warrior until renegades brought tragedy to her world. She alone had the courage to save a white man's family and a young man's soul.

PÈRE ANDRÉ—Defrocked priest and boisterous trapper of the North West Company. He fought and loved with an unexpected fierceness... for a reason only he knew.

THE CANADIANS
From Hudson Bay to the Manitoba Plains, they brought an exciting future to a brash untamed land

Bantam Books by Robert E. Wall
Ask your bookseller for the books you have missed

BLACKROBE—The Canadians, Book I
BLOODBROTHERS—The Canadians, Book II
BIRTHRIGHT—The Canadians, Book III
PATRIOTS—The Canadians, Book IV
INHERITORS—The Canadians, Book V

THE CANADIANS
by
Robert E. Wall

V
INHERITORS

BANTAM BOOKS
TORONTO · NEW YORK · LONDON · SYDNEY

INHERITORS: THE CANADIANS V
A Bantam Book / June 1983

ISBN 0-553-23303-3

Published simultaneously in the United States and Canada

Bantam Books are published by Bantam Books, Inc. Its trade-
mark, consisting of the words ''Bantam Books'' and the por-
trayal of a rooster is Registered in U.S. Patent and Trademark
Office and in other countries. Marca Registrada. Bantam
Books, Inc., 666 Fifth Avenue, New York, New York 10103.

PRINTED IN THE UNITED STATES OF AMERICA

H   0 9 8 7 6 5 4 3 2 1

For
My father-in-law and mother-in-law
Stephen and Stephanie Palasek

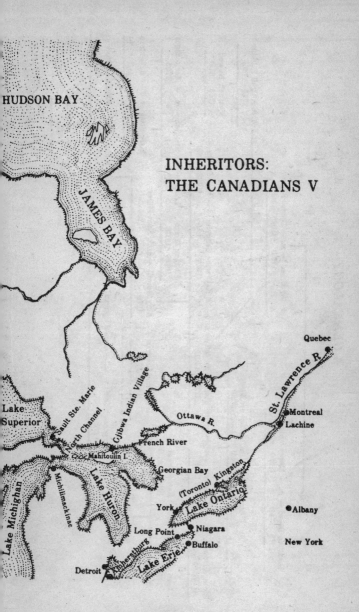

HUDSON BAY

JAMES BAY

INHERITORS:
THE CANADIANS V

Quebec

St. Lawrence R.

Lake
Superior

Sault Ste. Marie

North Channel

Ojibwa Indian Village

Ottawa R.

Montreal
Lachine

French River

Manitoulin I.

Georgian Bay

Michilimackinac

Lake Huron

Kingston

(Toronto)

York

Lake Ontario

Albany

Lake Michigan

Long Point

Niagara

Buffalo

New York

Detroit

Amherstburg

Lake Erie

A GENEALOGY

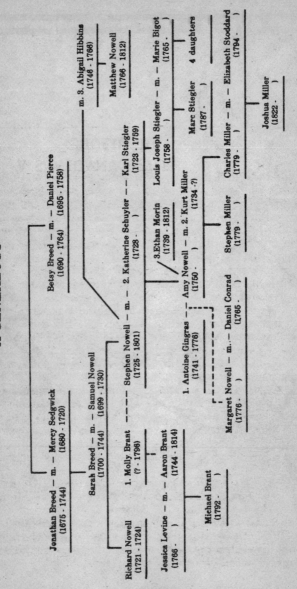

Jonathan Breed — m. — Mercy Sedgwick
(1675 - 1744)   (1680 - 1720)

Sarah Breed — m. — Samuel Nowell
(1700 - 1744)   (1699 - 1730)

Richard Nowell
(1721 - 1724)

Jessica Levine — m. — Aaron Brant
(1766 -)   (1744 - 1814)

Michael Brant
(1792 -)

1. Molly Brant — — — — Stephen Nowell — m. — 2. Katherine Schuyler — — Karl Stiegler
(? - 1796)   (1725 - 1801)   (1728 -)   (1723 - 1759)

Betsy Breed — m. — Daniel Pierce
(1690 - 1764)   (1695 - 1758)

m. 3. Abigail Hibbins
(1746 - 1766)

Matthew Nowell
(1766 - 1812)

Louis Joseph Stiegler — m. — Marie Bigot
(1758 -)   (1765 -)

Marc Stiegler   4 daughters
(1787 -)

3. Ethan Morin
(1739 - 1812)

1. Antoine Gingras — —   Amy Nowell — m. 2. Kurt Miller
(1741 - 1776)   (1750 -)   (1734 - ?)

Margaret Nowell — m. — Daniel Conrad
(1776 -)   (1765 -)

Charles Miller — m. — Elizabeth Stoddard
(1779 -)   (1794 -)

Stephen Miller
(1779 -)

Joshua Miller
(1822 -)

PROLOGUE

September 1813

The sun burst through the early morning grayness, touching the sails with gold. The wind was light, and *Detroit*, a three-masted ship built at the Amherstburg yards and just launched and rigged, glided through the rolling waves of Lake Erie. In her wake sailed her sister ships—the smaller *Queen Charlotte* and the brigs and schooners *Lady Prevost*, *Hunter*, *Little Belt*, and *Chippewa*.

Charles Miller, lieutenant of the Provincial Marine, had sailed the waters of Lake Erie for most of his life. But this voyage was different. Never before had he sailed to war. The British had only one purpose now: to find the American fleet, which had left Presque Isle in Pennsylvania, and to destroy it. Upper Canada, west of Niagara, could not be held without control of Lake Erie, and the gains made at Fort Detroit last year would be squandered if the Americans were not found and destroyed immediately.

Lt. Morse, Charles's colleague in the Provincial Marine who had sailed with him in the old *Nancy* ferrying Brock's men to Detroit, shared the watch with him. Captain Robert Barclay paced the quarterdeck. His one empty sleeve—trophy of his long Royal Navy career—was pinned to his coat.

"The bloody wind is fickle this morning," Barclay said half aloud.

"Aye, sir," responded the helmsman instinctively, although it was clear that Barclay had not been addressing anyone in particular.

Both Charles and his companion kept to their side of the quarterdeck, trying to give the privacy that was traditionally allowed the captain on the quarterdeck, but Barclay wanted to talk. He walked over to his subordinates.

"This will be the day of decision, gentlemen," he addressed them.

"Aye, aye, sir," they both responded together.

"All these months of worry and work and of scarcities—they all stop today. The enemy fleet is out and we will find and destroy them."

"It has been difficult, sir," offered Morse.

Barclay chuckled bitterly. "That is a considerable understatement. Building a fleet in the godforsaken wilderness with no iron foundries, no seamen, importing everything from Montreal to Kingston by almost nonexistent roads. It has been a nightmare. And now, even though we've put out to sea, I've only a handful of experienced seamen. We British are used to better. We command the world's oceans, our ships have won every major engagement since the first American war, and here we find ourselves contested for control of this little lake. But we'll win again. We outgun them, gentlemen. Our cannon don't have their weight but we've got the range. We'll fight them at a distance. So long as we have the weather gauge." He glanced up at the sails. "The damned wind."

Across the lake was the vague outline of the American shore. The sky was now a pale blue, and the sun on the port side gave a welcome warmth, driving away the chilly dawn air.

From the mast above came a shout. Charles looked up. The inexperienced seaman in the crow's nest was pointing ahead. Charles raised his glass in the direction the sailor pointed. There were islands off to the east. Yes, and clearly now sails were emerging, distinguishable from the gray outline of the land itself.

"Put in Bay," he said aloud. He himself had often anchored his schooner at Put in Bay during storms.

Barclay reached for Charles's glass. Morse held it up for him as he put it to his eye and then steadied it with his arm.

"The islands, sir, there's a good anchorage there," said Morse.

"The American fleet is coming out," said the captain. "My esteemed opponent, Commodore Perry, has erred. He's coming out of the anchorage directly to face me. He's giving me the wind. We shall beat him."

Morse had his glass trained on the American fleet.

"There are nine of them, sir, and only six of us. Even odds, I'd say, for the Royal Navy."

Barclay handed the glass back to Charles.

"This battle will be won or lost, gentlemen, by our two ships and their two brigs."

The fleets continued to approach each other. The breeze was slight and their progress was slow. Barclay remained on deck. The guns of *Detroit* and the other ships were run out; sand was scattered on the decks, and a hot breakfast was ordered for all hands.

Charles's body felt clammy. He could feel the sweat trickle down his sides under his coat. He was unsure if it was the effect of the hot September sun or just plain fear. He had never been more frightened in his life. He tried to steady himself. He thought of his family, attempting to calm his nerves. He thought of Elizabeth, who loved him, of her brother, Michael, seven years younger than he but already a veteran of Queenston Heights. He thought of Michael's father, Aaron Brant, once a legendary warrior, now a broken invalid. None of them had been found wanting in the face of battle. His own twin brother, Stephen, was fighting on the other side—and damned by all, but no one said anything against his courage. Every male in the family had been tested by war. Even his mother had faced the loss of her husband with extraordinary courage. Now it was his turn. His mouth was dry and he couldn't swallow.

"Damn it," shouted Barclay, "the wind is changing."

Charles broke out of his daydream and glanced in the direction of the ensign that had been nailed to the mast. The wind had shifted and now came from the southwest. Now the Americans sailed with the wind, and the British-Canadian fleet would have to await their assault.

Captain Barclay slammed his hand down on the green wood of the quarterdeck railing; it cracked with the snapping sound of a sharpshooter's rifle. Several veterans on the gun deck actually ducked at the noise.

Barclay looked at the damage with an amused grin. "If a one-armed man can do that with his hand, imagine what Perry's carronades will do." He turned to face the two Provincial officers and saw their look of concern. He clapped Morse on the shoulder. "No matter," he continued. "The Yankee ships will be no stouter. But we have a new factor with the wind change, gentlemen. Our guns will still out-range theirs but we can't stand off and pick them off one by one from afar. They'll be able to close. We must damage them so badly that by the time they're within range with their carronades they'll be too devastated to fight. Lieutenant Garland!" Barclay called out for his first lieutenant. "Join me please on the quarterdeck. Morse, Miller, thank you, gentlemen. Your knowledge of the lake has given confidence to all of us. You may now go to your gun crews."

Charles and his friend descended the stairs to the gun deck. Morse was commander of the portside guns; Lieutenant Inglis of the Royal Navy had charge of the starboard side. Charles's task was to assist the commander whose side was most heavily engaged. With the Yankees sailing directly toward them from the southeast and Barclay turning his fleet to the southwest to pick up the wind, it was clear that Charles would be joining Morse on the port side.

The lake was calm, with almost no roll. The sun was hot. Most of the gun crews had stripped to the waist and tied pieces of cloth about their heads to keep their hair and sweat out of their eyes. Charles envied them. His officer's coat felt heavy and dreadfully conspicuous.

He could see the American ships clearly now. One of their brigs was surging forward toward *Detroit* while her twin lagged behind.

"That will be *Lawrence*, Perry's flagship." Barclay's voice broke the deathly silence aboard *Detroit*. "It is a vessel, my lads, named after an American captain who was defeated and killed off Boston by our own *Shannon*. Let that be an omen."

The crew of *Detroit* cheered. Barclay waved his hand. Charles tried to cheer too, but his throat felt so constricted that only a hoarse rasp emerged. This was all madness, standing exposed on an open deck while across the water of his lake, his beloved Erie, other men approached, determined to blast his ship out of the water and to send him, Charles Miller, to the bottom to feed the fish.

The fleets continued to converge. On the quarterdeck, Barclay signaled his cabin boy, who raised a bugle to his lips. The lonesome cry reached out over the calm water toward *Lawrence*, which inched along through the blue-green water. The bugle call was Morse's signal. He dropped his raised sword, and his first gun belched flame and lurched backward against the restraining ropes. Charles moved forward to the railing to watch the shot fall.

"Short," he yelled, his voice high-pitched and unrecognizable even to himself.

Wedges were placed under the gun to raise its elevation.

"Fire," Morse screamed.

This time the shot struck the railing of the Yankee flagship, sending deadly foot-long splinters flying in all directions.

"Continue to fire all portside guns," Barclay called out.

Charles lowered his sword and the five guns under his command thundered as one. Smoke and the acrid smell of gunpowder filled the air about him. He could see spars on *Lawrence* crash onto the deck.

"Too high, Mr. Miller," yelled Lieutenant Garland, who stood on the quarterdeck next to Barclay.

"Dislodge those carronades she carries before she can get into our range."

Charles bent down and sighted each of his guns. *Lawrence* continued to approach. Her guns were still silent, still out of range, but her very approach, silent and unalterable, sent shivers through Miller.

He screamed out, "Fire," once again, and for a second time the roar of the cannon crashed into his ears and the smoke and stench filled his lungs. He coughed and tried to swallow; his lips were dry and cracked when he shouted. Now his guns no longer fired in volleys. The gun crews swabbed out the muzzles, rammed home the cartridges of gunpowder, and placed the heavy shot into the tilted muzzles and touched the powder holes with a slow match. Each cannon roared as it was fired, and the crews began all over again. White splinter marks appeared along the bow and starboard hull of *Lawrence* but still she came on, while the rest of the Yankee fleet seemed to hang back.

The eight guns on the port side of *Queen Charlotte* opened up on *Lawrence* as well. The American ship was taking heavy damage now but still she came on.

Then *Lawrence* veered. At first Charles thought she had had enough and was breaking off, but suddenly the world about him came apart. Hot metal seared the air, splinters of wood smashed into metal with a clang and into human flesh with a sickening dull thud. Men screamed and blood sprayed in all directions.

Charles felt the breath knocked out of him and he fell to his knees. He looked about, dazed. One of his guns lay on its side, dislodged from its carriage. The gun captain lay beneath it; his mouth was open. Charles knew the man was screaming but the roar of guns drowned out the sound. He looked himself over, expecting to see blood seeping from some open wound. But he was untouched. The gun crew lifted the cannon with a lever and dragged the broken body of their comrade from under it. He had ceased his screaming and soon disappeared, dragged below deck to the mercy of the surgeon's pitiless knives and saws.

Detroit's port guns continued to fire. Charles rose to his feet. His sword had been knocked from his hand and his hat was missing. He knew he should be giving orders but his crews were firing, paying no attention to him. He knew that *Lawrence* would fire a second volley any minute now. The thought paralyzed him. He heard his name called. It was Garland.

"Get your guns under control, Miller. The enemy is still too far off for blind shooting. You must sight your guns. You..." The rest was drowned out again as the decks of *Detroit* were ravaged by grapeshot. Men screamed and cursed. Charles looked for some place to duck, to flee, to leave this horror behind him. But he could not move, no matter how much he wanted to. The sand on the deck had been dyed red with blood. Men oozing gore staggered aimlessly on the deck.

George Inglis grabbed Charles's arm and shouted into his face. The roar of the guns had deafened Charles; he could not understand what the English lieutenant was saying. His eyes followed his comrade's pointing arm toward the quarterdeck. It was a shambles. The helmsman was crawling down the stairs, dragging his leg behind him. His breeches had been torn off, and his wounded leg was attached only by sinew.

Inglis moved toward the helmsman, yelling at an uncomprehending Charles to take command of the starboard gun crews. Charles followed his fellow officer toward the quarterdeck. The helmsman tumbled the last few stairs to the gun deck and fainted, lying in his own blood. Garland, the first lieutenant, lay in a heap against the railing. He was dead. Barclay lay at the base of the wheel, propped against it. He was conscious, but from his thigh blood trickled down his leg and into his boot.

"Inglis, take command," Barclay croaked, "while Miller

here takes me below to the butcher. If he can stop the bleeding in time, I'll return to the deck to finish off the Yankees. They've hurt us but we've hurt them worse. Signal *Queen Charlotte* to work her way in close and keep firing."

Charles lifted Barclay in his arms. The captain wrapped his one arm about Charles's neck and was half carried, half dragged down the stairs to the main deck.

"It's just a scratch, lads," Barclay called out to his men, who stared at him with anguish and fear. They could not have heard him. The roar of cannon drowned out his voice, but the fact that he addressed them inspired some with confidence that he would soon resume his command.

"As soon as the surgeon digs the ball out, I'll be back up to give the Yanks the drubbing they deserve. Keep the guns firing."

He called into Charles's ear, "Get me below fast, Miller. I can't have the men disheartened looking at me."

Below decks was even more terrifying to Charles. Men lay about in dark corners, rags tied over their wounds to stop the bleeding. At a low table, lit by a lantern held high above his assistant's head, the ship's surgeon grimly sawed through the thighbone of a screaming sailor pinned to the table by four of his comrades.

"It's the captain," called out one of the wounded.

The surgeon glanced up from his grisly work and with his quick eye discerned that Barclay's was not a mortal wound. He continued to cut through the bone.

Charles laid Barclay down on the floor and covered his ears with his hands, not only to drown out the screams but also to blot out the hideous thunder from the decks above.

"Go back to your command now, Lieutenant," Barclay said to him. "You're needed on deck."

"But someone must stay with you," protested Charles.

"I have an appointment with yonder surgeon, Miller. I'll need no one to help me keep it. He'll see to that."

Charles hesitated.

"That's an order, Lieutenant," Barclay said through gritted teeth. "Your concern for me is misplaced. Do your duty."

Charles stepped back out of Barclay's line of vision. It was not concern for his commanding officer that had made him hesitate. For all the horror found below the water line, at least here no grapeshot clanged against metal. He was afraid to go back up into that hell.

He saw the surgeon carelessly fling the leg he had been working on onto the gory floor. His victim had fainted at last and would not feel the searing flame that cauterized the stump of what had once been a powerfully muscled limb.

The surgeon looked over at him quizzically.

"Are you hurt, Lieutenant," he called up to Charles.

Charles shook his head and pointed toward Barclay. The captain had been dozing and the surgeon's question had awakened him.

"Is Miller still here?" he called out. "I must protest to you, sir. I can't see you, but if you remain below I'll press charges of cowardice in the face of the enemy against you."

Charles had no choice now. He climbed the stairway leading back to the gun deck. George Inglis, with a new helmsman, stood fearlessly on the quarterdeck. Lieutenant Garland's body had been removed. Lieutenant Morse, his hat and coat removed and his white shirt sticking to his soaking torso, was personally shifting one of the great guns back into firing position. He waved at Charles. Charles went to Inglis's position on the starboard side. So far no guns on the starboard had been fired, and its crews were being used to replace casualties on the portside guns.

Miller caught sight of *Lawrence* for the first time since returning on deck. He was astounded. She was a mere hulk, lying still in the water, but her guns flashed and her metal tore holes in *Detroit*'s sides. Suddenly the crew of *Detroit* cheered loudly. The commodore's flag on *Lawrence* was coming down. The Yanks were surrendering. Then a small boat pulled away from *Lawrence*'s side, making straight for the second American brig, which was so far untouched by any British fire.

Inglis yelled to the marksmen to get into the riggings and fire at the retreating boat.

"That's Perry and he's escaping," Inglis shouted.

"The coward," screamed Morse. "His ship has surrendered. He can't leave it."

Charles stared incredulously at his friend. It was as if they were playing some sort of game and someone had broken the rules. What kind of game was this, a game that tore limbs from bodies and scattered brains and blood about the deck?

"Not true," Inglis shouted. "He's changing flagships in the middle of the battle." He pointed at the Stars and Stripes that still flew from the stumps of what had once been *Lawrence's* masts. "The Yanks haven't given up yet, lads. Pour it into them."

The cheering grew louder when the form of Robert Barclay, supported by two surgeon's assistants, reappeared on deck. The captain, his face pale from pain and loss of blood, again waved to his crew. He was carried back up to the quarterdeck and, holding onto the rail, reassumed command of his ship and his fleet.

As soon as the second American brig took aboard the American commodore, it began to inch forward toward *Detroit* and *Queen Charlotte*. *Detroit's* sister ship had taken an equal beating and had signaled that all her senior officers were dead and that the ship had fallen to the command of the lieutenant of the Canadian Provincial Marine, as inexperienced in war command as Morse or Miller.

As Charles stared out at the American fleet, he saw the calm surface of the lake ripple. The American brig and its escorting gunboat seemed to leap forward.

"The wind's picking up," shouted Morse.

Barclay gripped the rail with his arm. "Inglis," he shouted. "He's going to try to split our line and cross the *T* and rake us. We can't have it. Damn it, I'll not have the enemy pull a Nelson on me. Bring her about and bring the starboard guns to bear on the American. What is she called?"

"It's *Niagara*, sir," said Inglis.

"A good name. We'll keep it after we take her. After all, Niagara is British soil and a British river, or at least it will be when this war is over."

The American gunboats, up to that moment, had been lagging far to the rear, but now they came into range with their heavy guns and opened fire on *Detroit*. Barclay looked around for his smaller vessels and signaled them to drive the Americans off. But *Chippewa*, *Little Belt*, and *Lady Prevost* had been driven off by their American counterparts and had run to the head of the line to escape the American fire. *Hunter* lay dead in the water, her crew decimated by *Lawrence's* brutal pounding earlier in the engagement.

"Keep those guns firing," Barclay screamed above the shouts of his men. "Helmsman, bring us about."

Suddenly out of the smoke *Queen Charlotte* loomed. An experienced officer could have avoided collision but none remained on *Queen Charlotte*. The two ships crashed into each other with a sickening wrenching of timbers and a whine of taut rigging and a ripping of canvas.

"Try to disengage," called Barclay, who had been knocked to the deck by the collision. He knew they were in mortal danger. Unless he could untangle *Queen Charlotte* from his flagship, only *Detroit's* battered portside guns would be able to fire on *Niagara* as she crossed his line and rake both of the ships from stem to stern.

Charles watched *Niagara's* approach with an almost fatalistic fascination. She seemed to fly across the tiny waves. Barclay was back on his feet. Charles felt Morse grab his arm. He stared blankly into the wide-eyed face of his friend.

"Charles, all your crew's to the port side. The starboard guns are useless now. Help me."

Morse's last plea was punctuated by a shove that sent Charles toward the stern and rear portside guns. At that moment, grapeshot loosed by the American schooner *Caledonia* raked the quarterdeck of *Detroit*. Barclay screamed as a ball struck his shoulder. Then he stared at the wound. His good arm, his only arm, was he to lose it also? Blood rushed down his side. Inglis grabbed the wheel from the helmsman.

"Take the Captain below," he ordered.

Barclay was slipping into shock. In the far recesses of his mind the realization that he might lose this battle was suddenly dawning.

"Fight her" was all he said as the helmsman helped him below to face the surgeon again.

And now as *Niagara* sailed through the British line, her guns, both port and starboard, fired at once. She seemed to be lifted out of the water by the power of her broadside. Her metal tore into the crippled *Detroit* and *Queen Charlotte*. Shot passed over Charles's head. He was about to order his crew to fire when suddenly the gun was dislodged and tumbled onto the crew servicing it. The hiss of hot metal burning into flesh seemed to chase all other sounds from Charles's mind. Again *Niagara's* guns flashed. Charles opened his mouth and screamed as he saw Morse's lower body torn from his torso, his legs quivering uncontrollably on the deck. It was more than his mind could stand. He reeled away from the chaos on the gun deck and tore down the stairway. Below decks, men lay all over the blood-drenched floors. He dropped down among them, sobbing, his chest heaving. He could feel vomit rising in his throat. He retched and gave up the hot breakfast so thoughtfully provided for them all before the slaughter began. He lay there, not moving, lying in his own puke. He did not even notice the quiet when Lieutenant Inglis waved the white handkerchief. Barclay's ensign had been nailed to the mast and could not be lowered.

I

Winter 1815

The village lights flickered in the valley below like tiny jewels displayed on black velvet. The fir trees loomed above them and then blocked their view. As they rode, the bells of the horse's collar jingled. The driver had hunched so far down into his raccoon coat that from the passenger's viewpoint his hat appeared to be sitting on his fur collar.

Elizabeth Stoddard Miller reached for her husband's gloved hand. It was hard to get used to the name "Miller." She had added it only twelve hours earlier at the church of Notre Dame de Bonsecours. Charles Miller, who had been staring at the snow-covered branches above him, turned to look at his new wife as her hand touched his. His woolen toque covered his ears and the back of his head, but in the front his blond hair, wet and dark with melting snow, drooped into his eyes.

She had so much to tell him—so many plans she wanted to share. She had hated every moment of waiting. She recalled her impetuous request when she was only sixteen and had asked him to sleep with her. She had been guileless and innocent. Her father, Eli, had told her the facts of life and she wanted to test her new knowledge. She remembered Charles's outrage, and even now, three years later, her face, unseen in the dark, flushed with humiliation at the memory of it. She reddened even more at the memory of Stephen Miller's mocking falsetto. Her husband's twin brother had overheard her offer and Charles's rejection. He made it clear that he would not have rejected her. She blotted Stephen's leering grin from her mind.

For three years she had waited impatiently for the war with the Americans to end and for Charles to return. She had suffered through the defeat on Lake Erie and Charles's

1

capture. Then the war had ended, and everyone returned to the lines they had held before the hostilities began. Nothing was changed by the war except the people. Charles's stepfather, Ethan Morin, had been hanged for treason by the British for leading a Canadian-American legion against the forces of the Crown. Charles's mother, Amy, had been in Montreal for the wedding. She sat with her mother, Charles's grandmother—the ancient and benign Katherine Schuyler Nowell. But Amy was not benign. She snapped at everyone who addressed her, especially her well-meaning French-Canadian half brother, Louis Joseph Stiegler. Amy lived with Louis now, away from her sons, angry at Charles for not siding with his stepfather and angry with Stephen for fighting at his stepfather's side and ending up in exile on the other side of the Canadian border. Elizabeth thought of her own foster father, "Father Thomas" Aaron Brant. He had returned from his last battle a cripple, his heart damaged beyond repair. He had died in Mother Jessica's arms late in 1814 at night while the rest of the house in York village slept. And Charles himself had been changed by war. He refused to discuss it but she knew he had been through hell.

But it was time to forget all that ugliness. The Americans had returned behind their borders. They were at peace.

"That's the village up ahead," Elizabeth cried out. They would spend their first night together at Ste. Ann in the inn.

"Tell the driver this is the place," she cried excitedly. "Speak to him in French, Charles."

"I don't speak French," he responded in amazement.

"Well, he'll miss the inn."

"Not damn' likely, missy," said the driver over his shoulder in wretched English. "I have my hunger and so does the *cheval*."

"Sir, watch your language in front of a lady, my wife."

"My excuses."

"Charles, be still," said Elizabeth.

He glared at her and fell silent. The horse and sled glided through the village streets until they came to the inn at the river's edge. The waters had turned to ice earlier in the winter, making a natural bridge from one island to the next. Tomorrow they would cross.

The sled came to a halt in the inn's courtyard. It was late but the innkeeper appeared at the door, his lantern held high.

"Mr. and Mrs. Miller," he called out into the blackness. "We've been expecting you. I have a supper all laid out in your room."

The innkeeper's wife, her dressing gown clutched about her and her lace nightcap perched precariously on her head, stood behind her husband and squinted nearsightedly out into the courtyard.

"Now there," she called out in French, "where's the bride?"

Charles stepped down from the sled into the shin-deep powdered snow. He reached out and offered his arm to Elizabeth. Instead of stepping gracefully down from the sled and onto the drop step, she allowed herself to fall into his arms. He caught her clumsily and was knocked back and almost off his feet.

"Elizabeth," he hissed at her, "behave like the respectable married woman you now are and not like an impetuous girl in pants."

She glared at him but then forgave him mentally. Nothing was going to ruin this night for her. Not even Charles's foul moods. She slid her arm through his and walked with him into the inn.

The first floor of the Hotel Ste. Ann consisted of one large room. A giant fireplace occupied the back wall. Chairs were piled on top of the large oak tables so that the innkeeper's servant could sweep up the evening's debris. The glow of the dying fire in the hearth struck the chairs, casting exotic shadows against the log walls. Elizabeth shivered and moved closer to Charles's side.

"It's a bit grim in here," she whispered.

"You're right," he responded.

"Follow me," said the innkeeper, holding up his lantern to light the dark stairway to the second floor. As they reached the landing they were both startled by the striking of a giant clock, a grandmother's keyhole clock that reached from floor to ceiling; its chimes were strangely unmelodious and seemed to clunk rather than chime.

"I'll stop it if it bothers you," the innkeeper offered. "My wife and I are used to its chiming and ticking all night, but some folks dislike it."

"Don't bother," offered Charles. "My wife and I are exhausted. We shall not hear a thing tonight."

The innkeeper swung open the door to their room. It was small but cozy. A coal fire burned brightly in the small

3

hearth, throwing out a generous warmth. A small table, covered with a homemade linen cloth and carefully set with pewterware and glass, stood close to the hearth. The innkeeper took a match from the hearth and lit two candles that sat in pewter candlesticks on the table. The meager light they gave seemed to make a cheery room even more cozy.

Elizabeth threw off her heavy coat and dropped it on a maple deacon's bench that stood against the wall next to the doorway. She spun around to make her skirts spin out and then she collapsed onto the quilts that were piled high on the giant bed. She seemed to disappear totally as she sank farther and farther into the down.

Charles watched in dismay, but the innkeeper merely laughed. "My wife brought them from Sorel when we were married and first came here to Ste. Ann. You'll be warm and comfortable in them tonight. Monsieur Miller, I have a beautiful duck for you and your wife. This is a stupid duck, mind you, *très stupide*. It did not know enough to fly south with its cousins in the fall. I shot him some days ago and hung him up to season. My wife has prepared him for roasting and she has her finest cherry sauce for basting."

"That sounds irresistible," responded Elizabeth.

"Only the best for our returning heroes. Your cousins in Montreal, the Stieglers, have informed me that you were with Barclay at Lake Erie."

Charles stiffened at the mention of the battle.

"What of it?" he asked sternly.

"A gallant battle, sir, unfortunate only in its outcome. But I hear you are exchanged only now that the war is over, that you refused the Americans your parole, that you would fight them again and so they held you to the peace. You are a brave man, sir. I salute you."

Charles stared straight ahead. His lips began to tremble.

"They say that Barclay will never have the use of his one remaining arm. The court martial exonerated him completely. By the way, one of the seamen aboard the flagship lives here at Ste. Ann. Would you wish me to make contact with him for you?"

Before Charles could answer, Elizabeth interrupted.

"Enough talk of the war. Innkeeper, my wedding feast, the duck and cherries, be quick about it."

The innkeeper bowed in her direction and backed out of the room.

4

Elizabeth clapped her hands together in delight but she stopped when she saw the stricken look on her husband's face.

"Charles, what is it?"

He shook his head. "War talk. It brings back terrible memories. I have no desire to meet with any veteran of that day."

Elizabeth rushed to his side and pulled his head to her bosom. "I know, my dearest. We'll mention it no more and we'll see no seaman here in Ste. Ann."

Charles was trembling. The memories of that day would never leave him. He had learned on that day that he could not trust his own courage. He had run and hidden. None of the others had. Yet what he had done was sensible, rational in the face of madness. Sensible or not, however, the shame had lodged deep within him and ate away at his confidence.

They dined in silence, washing down the duck with a bottle of French wine. After dinner Elizabeth climbed into the great down quilt. Once under the covers, she slipped out of her travel clothes and lay waiting for her husband. He sat staring into the remains of the cold fire in the hearth.

"Charles," Elizabeth called, "come join me."

"In a second," he responded, but the second turned into a minute.

Elizabeth, in impatience, left the bed and stood before her husband in her chemise, blocking his view of the embers. He did not notice, at first, but when he did, he looked up at her in shock.

"It's not proper for a lady to parade around in her undergarments."

"I suppose it is proper, though," she responded, "for a husband to fail in his duty to his wife on their wedding night."

"What are you talking about? You simply must learn a wife's role. I am not Eli Stoddard or Aaron Brant. I'll not indulge your whims."

"Is it a whim to want your husband, the man you've loved and waited for for over three years and whom you've married this morning, to stop sitting like a eunuch, staring at a fire on his wedding night?"

"And where in God's name did you learn about eunuchs? Proper women do not speak like that."

"I learned about eunuchs from the same place I learned

5

about malaria, yellow fever, and mandrake weeds. From Eli Stoddard's medical books. My father is a doctor."

"The man should have kept them locked up."

"I'm surprised you didn't say he should have kept me locked up. Is that what you are planning for me?"

"You know what I mean, Elizabeth. You're too impulsive, you always have been."

"Is that what's keeping you from coming to bed?"

"No, I was just thinking."

"It's not a time for thinking, it's a time for feeling."

"I don't like my feelings," Charles said with some bitterness. "I don't like myself very much."

"But why?"

Charles did not answer, but the distant stare came back into his eyes.

"Oh, not that again," said Elizabeth aloud. She took her husband's hand in hers and tugged. She regained his attention, and he smiled at her and rose to his feet in response to her pull.

It was late. The old clock on the landing had clunked three times. Elizabeth could not sleep. First of all, she had bled badly and had stuffed linen between her legs. It had been painful and, if she were honest with herself, not very pleasant. Charles had been clumsy. It was almost as if he had never been with a woman before, or at least not a woman he should try to please. He lay next to her now, snoring lightly. He tossed about frequently. His sleep seemed punctuated by periods of frightening dreams when his body stiffened and his legs and arms went rigid and low moans escaped from his mouth. It had happened shortly after he had fallen off to sleep, leaving her awake and disgruntled. She had thought to wake him but his moaning stopped and his limbs relaxed. She let him sleep on and then it had happened twice more during the night. She felt sorry for him. He had suffered terribly during the war, that was clear. He seemed aimless, distant, and yes, frightened, even if the last manifested itself only at night while he slept. She would have to do something about his fears. But first she would have to do something about his lovemaking. Women had whispered to her on her wedding morning that she should bear up under it all, that men had their beastly side, which women had to cater to, but Jessica had told her that it was beautiful and pleasurable in time,

6

while Eli, who of course was a man, spoke of sex as God's second-best gift to mankind. The first was, of course, the British monarchy. Elizabeth was determined not to be cheated out of this second divine gift.

They crossed the ice in the morning and drove across one island and then crossed more ice to the western shore of the river. The sled raced on west and south toward Kingston. On their left the St. Lawrence was solid, an easy crossing into New York. Charles stared at the river. He had been silent all day. His face was red and wet with the cold wind. Finally he broke his silence.

"That's the whole source of our troubles over there," he said, pointing to the New York shore. "It is a disease—the American disease, their damned self-confidence, their assurance that they will win, that all will fall before them, that only they are brave."

He had become very agitated and almost rose to his feet in the sled. The driver looked around to determine the cause of his sudden outburst.

"Well, they don't always win. We beat them in the last war. We stopped their 'easy walk through Canada.' We have the same borders we had before the war. And we'll maintain them forever. Never again must we be vulnerable to them. Our towns must become forts; Kingston must have a citadel. So must Halifax and Quebec. The St. Lawrence here is a border. It is vulnerable. Our shipping must move through water routes solely under our control. We must build canals and we must command the lakes. It may take my life to do it, Elizabeth, but I have found a goal worth working for. I'll devote my life to making Canada safe."

And by that he meant that he would make himself safe.

II

York, Spring 1821

Jessica Brant stormed through her kitchen, sending her cook and cook's helper fleeing out into the dining room.

"The woman has no couth whatsoever," said Jenny, the cook, her Scottish accent distorting the word *couth*, which Mary, her helper, could not have understood even if she had known the meaning of it. "The mistress has no place in the kitchen. She should give me the menu, take my advice on it, and then eat it."

"It's her infidel background," suggested Mary softly. The cook's helper was from Ulster and thought that Jews were the pope's disciples. "And they say that her husband was a red Indian."

"Mr. Brant? I knew him only after his illness. He was weak and docile. He didn't look like any savage to me. For God's sake, the man had blue eyes. I've heard those stories about him, but they say he was the son of a baronet in New York so he came by his wealth and his position honestly, but how he came to marry a Jewess is beyond me."

"Jenny!" Jessica called.

"She's got the voice of a banshee," said Mary.

"Jenny, you and Mary come back in here. The kitchen must be cleaned from top to bottom. I want every bit of old food thrown out. Easter is coming. It is a new beginning. The whole family will be here. Where are you two?"

She swung open the door to her dining room and spied the two women. "There you are! What are you standing around for? Get back in there and get back to work."

The two women looked at each other, shrugged their shoulders, and moved back into the kitchen.

"First she throws us out and then she orders us back in," whispered Jenny.

Jessica had her work clothes on. She intended to give the house a thorough cleaning, just as her Aunt Elizabeth had swept the house bare in the old days back in New Hampshire. She caught a glimpse of herself in the wall mirror. She stopped and looked again. There were strands of gray in her black hair now and she had definitely thickened in the middle. But her complexion was still good. Aaron would have approved. The thought of her dead husband saddened her. She was alone now. Her Aunt Elizabeth had died years before, then her father, and now Aaron.

She shook her head. She was not alone. She had her son, Michael, thirty-three years old, unmarried, surely a confirmed bachelor. He should have a wife and she should have grandchildren. But he was too busy in the Assembly, too busy with his law practice to listen to a mother's pleading. And then there was Elizabeth, her adopted daughter. And Charles, Elizabeth's husband. They had been married now for six years. Jessica knew her daughter. The calm that seemed to envelope her was a façade. There was a storm brewing there. Too much quiet between Elizabeth and Charles and no children to bind them.

And then there was her third child, the ninety-one-year-old Eli Stoddard. He had entered her life in the first year of her marriage back in Montreal, the arch-Loyalist. He had moved into her house after Aaron died. He said she needed a male protector. But she knew that it was loneliness. He needed to be near their shared daughter, Elizabeth, who now lived just down Bay Street from Jessica's mansion. She and Charles had moved into the old house on Front Street when they first arrived in York. But Charles's Canadian company had proved so successful that after two years he and Elizabeth had moved to the new house.

Jessica laughed aloud once, as she always did when she recalled Eli's offer of marriage. He said it was improper for a widow and a single man to dwell in the same house together. To this day she did not know how she kept a straight face when telling him that, as attractive as he was, she could not dishonor Aaron's memory by an early remarriage. He never raised the issue again but he had moved in anyway.

That was the whole family. Charles's mother—Jessica's sister-in-law, Amy—lived in Quebec with the French branch of the family—the Stieglers. Charles's sister, Maggie, had married Daniel Conrad and now lived with him in Boston.

10

Charles's twin brother, Stephen—well, no one knew where he was.

Eli came down the front stairway, probing each stair with his walking stick. He would admit nothing, but his eyesight was fading.

"Jessica?" he called out when he reached the bottom. "What is all the infernal cacophony about? It sounds as if we were infested with unlactated bovines."

"It's spring cleaning, Eli," she responded.

"After that infelicitous news, I think I shall depart to Front Street."

Front Street was his euphemism for his favorite saloon, which, it was true, was on the lakefront. Jessica worried about his going there every day. But she realized that it was silly to worry about a ninety-one-year-old man developing a drinking problem. He had not developed one yet and was not likely to. She knew he went there for the male company. Michael was never home nor was Charles. Eli had only Jessica, Elizabeth, and these maids to talk to. He missed Aaron almost as much as Jessica did.

"Be home for dinner," she ordered.

He stepped out onto Bay Street and turned right. He crossed King Street and continued his slow walk, using his stout cane as a support. It was a beautiful spring day. The ice had left the harbor, and although there were occasional patches of dirty snow left in the shadows of buildings or bushes, the sun was warm. A film of sweat broke out on his forehead but was cooled instantly as he approached the lakefront with its refreshing breeze. There were boys throwing rocks into the lake, trying to make them skip. One boy was trying to teach his young puppy to fetch a stick from the water. But his pup had no retriever blood in his veins. He would watch the stick longingly, his tongue hanging from his mouth. The boy would feint with his arm and the dog would make a false start for the water and then quickly recover and jump at the boy's leg expectantly. Finally the stick went flying through the air and struck the harbor water with a smack. The dog went into the chilly lake up to his chest and then stopped as if colliding with an invisible stone wall. He turned his shaggy head and sad eyes back toward this pitiless monster who abused him "as not a fit mutt whatsoever."

*   *   *

11

The saloon, Meachum's Alehouse, was doing a booming business. It had stood here for over three years now. Yet Eli wondered about its future. The Presbyterians and Methodists were after Meachum and his establishment. Eli had fled Presbyterianism early in his life when his uncle, Jonathan Edwards, had attempted to drag him off to the College of New Jersey at Princeton. He had resisted Presbyterians then and he would resist them now. The only good thing about the papist Irish was their respect for whiskey.

As he pushed open the door, his nostrils were struck by the odor of beer and pipe tobacco. There was a fire in the hearth, which was not needed, but Meachum, the tavernkeeper, either had not noticed or ignored the heat. But his patrons could not ignore it. The aromas of tobacco and beer were occasionally overcome by the acrid smell of human sweat. Eli had spent much of his winter by Meachum's hearth. But not today. He found an empty chair by the window looking out into the alley.

Meachum's daughter Virginia came over to him. Never was there a more misnamed child. It was bruited about York that she had slept with every available male in York village between the ages of sixteen and sixty and had now turned her eyes toward Kingston.

"What would you have today, old man?" she asked as she pushed her light brown hair back off her forehead.

"Child," he began. Then he noticed her low-cut bodice, which left little to the imagination, and corrected himself. "My, you're no child any longer. Miss Meachum, I've had a mug of that hot rum every day all winter without variation. Why does it cross your minuscule mind that today of all days I would desire a substitute libation?"

The girl started to laugh. "Someday I'm going to find out what all them words mean, old man, and I'm going to slap your face."

"I'm absolutely palpitating with anticipation," he mocked her. "Now bring me my rum."

The girl wiggled away across the room toward the taps. She sidestepped, too late, a group of men who sat by a round table opposite Eli's window seat. A large hand smacked her behind with a resounding crack. The girl literally jumped into the air.

"You bloody pig," she cursed the man. "Touch my arse again and I'll cut your hand off."

12

A toothy grin broke across the hairy face of a large blond man.

"If that's the only part of me you damage after last night I'll thank the merciful Lord," he laughed.

The men with him broke into lewd laughter.

The girl continued on her way. On her return with Eli's rum she made a wide detour to avoid the blond man and delivered Eli's drink still rubbing her rear.

There was something familiar about the blond man. Eli felt he should know him.

"Now, where were we before I became distracted by Meachum's virgin, who I suspect is blushing now, although in a very invisible way?"

Again the men laughed.

"You were saying the Yanks won the war," said the slow-witted blacksmith, Michaels, whose shop had accidentally burned to the ground when the Americans had set fire to the public buildings of York. "Seems to me that would be pretty hard to claim, seeing as we took their capital, Washington, and burned it."

"Now, by your logic," said the blond man, "we Canadians lost. They took our capital, the village of York, and they burned the government houses."

The blacksmith looked befuddled for a moment and the blond man continued.

"The war ended when the Yanks kicked the stuffing out of us on Lake Erie and Lake Champlain and finally when Andy Jackson whipped our asses at New Orleans. The British quit right then and there. The Yanks beat Wellington's best men. The men who whipped Bonaparte in Europe got their asses kicked by Jackson and his Tennessee boys and that was enough for old loony King George and his sissy Regent son. They got their ministers, prime ministers, chancellors over to Belgium and signed a peace for fear the Yanks would send old Jackson and his hell-raisers up north to take Canada right away."

"That wouldn't have been so bad," said John Montgomery. He had arrived in Upper Canada just after the war broke out and still spoke with the nasal twang of the western frontier. He had been a known American sympathizer during the war and had been placed under house arrest right after the American raid on York.

"I don't like what you fellows are saying," said Michaels, the smith.

"And it's right that you don't," chipped in Eli, who had

13

finally placed the blond, bearded man. "The scoundrel you are speaking to has no right to refer to himself as a Canadian since he spent much of the war in an American uniform."

The blond man looked over at the old gentleman.

"Well, I'll be damned! It's Stoddard," he exclaimed, spilling some beer on his pants.

"Yes, sir, you will almost certainly be damned since your morals are second only to your tidiness."

"Old man," said the blacksmith, "are you saying this man is a traitor?"

"There were extenuating circumstances," replied Eli, "that might have led even me to sheath my sword. But I never, sir, would have turned it against my king and country."

"I think he said you're a traitor," said Michaels, who slammed his massive right fist into his open left palm. "And I think I am going to bust your goddamned head open."

The innkeeper came swooping down onto the scene.

"Not in my tavern, gentlemen. There's an alley outside for that sort of thing."

By this time the blond man and Michaels the blacksmith had squared off, and a crowd had gathered about the table.

"Let's go into the alley," said the smith.

"After you," said his opponent with an exaggerated bow and a wink in Eli's direction.

The crowd went whooping out the side door.

"There's going to be a fight," someone yelled. "Michaels is going to break some more bones."

Eli stood on his bench and threw open the window. He would have a perfect ringside seat. The two combatants were already in the alley and the spectators had formed a ring about them.

Michaels stripped off his shirt and bared his enormous torso. The blond man followed suit. Although his muscles were well developed, he had clearly led the easy life in recent years. His belly had a decided bulge, and a bit of flab hung over his belt.

Montgomery, the American sympathizer, joined Eli in the window. He looked at both of the combatants as they circled each other.

"Michaels will kill him," Montgomery offered.

"I'll take that wager," said the old man. "What do you say to a pound note?"

"Too steep for me," said Montgomery.

"A shilling, then," said Eli.

"You're on."

Eli had no confidence whatsoever in the blond man's fighting ability, but he could not abide Montgomery and could not consider even being on the same side as the American sympathizer. He ignored totally the fact that he had accused his "champion" of being an American traitor.

The blacksmith grew tired of circling and lunged at his opponent. The bearded man stepped to the side lightly, and Michaels crashed into the crowd of men ringing the alley; they shoved him back to his feet. The smith once again stalked his opponent. Again he lunged and missed, but this time, as the blond man stepped aside, his foot went crashing into Michaels's crotch. The smith grabbed himself with both hands and let loose with an enormous fart.

"Christ, Michaels," one of the crowd yelled, "is that what you use instead of bellows?"

The crowd howled at the joke. But Eli watched the blond man's look of consternation as Michaels straightened himself up.

"The man must have cast-iron balls," yelled Montgomery from the window.

The blond bearded man attempted to strike Michaels in the face with his fist, but the smith caught the blow in midair and grabbed his foe's fist in his own. It seemed dwarfed in the enormity of the smith's hand. The "traitor" tried to pull away but could not. Suddenly Michaels, moving with uncharacteristic swiftness, pulled his foe toward him and grabbed him about the chest. He began to tighten his massive biceps. The blond's face went pale, then started to turn red. He was being squeezed to death. The crowd grew silent. They knew that Michaels was angry and none dared interfere. The blond-haired man was as good as dead if Michaels didn't drop him.

"Michaels, it's over," yelled Eli. But Michaels wasn't listening to any old man.

Eli stretched out the window as far as he could reach. He raised his heavy walking stick high above his head. It came crashing down with a hollow sound atop the blacksmith's crown. Michaels's eyes rolled upward. He dropped his opponent and fell to his knees. Then he fell in a heap on the ground.

Eli turned to Montgomery.

"Men with iron balls are prone to weak heads. They are both out cold," he said. "Neither wins."

"You old skinflint," said Montgomery. "*You* knocked Michaels out. Not your man."

"You're no gentleman, sir, if you squabble over a shilling," said Eli as he dropped the coin in question onto the table.

As Montgomery picked up the coin and left the window, mumbling to himself, the loser entered the tavern and staggered over toward Eli.

"They told me you konked him one."

"Damn' right I did," responded Eli. "A shilling is a shilling."

"I saw *you* pay off."

"Well, Stephen Miller, you are family, even if you are a bloody traitor. My precious Elizabeth is married to that twin brother of yours. A hard man, Charles Miller."

"They got hitched? Well, the girl had been planning for that for a long time."

"Where are you staying?" asked Eli.

"I'm sleeping around."

"No doubt," said the old man. "Do you plan to reveal yourself to the family? Is it safe for you to be in York? Didn't they sentence you to death back at Detroit?"

"I was kind of hoping they had forgotten all about that and let bygones be bygones. There was a war and I had my reasons."

"Well, my friend," chuckled Eli, "let's hope that is the case. Every young man must sow his wild oats, even if his wild oats consist of murder and treason and other minor issues."

Stephen grinned at the old man. Hearing him carry on like this reminded him of the good times before the war.

Charles replaced his teacup of fine white porcelain in its saucer. He stared at the tiny violets that dotted the cup without really seeing them. He was startled when John Sutherland, his secretary, opened the door to his office.

"I've this month's statements for you, Mr. Miller, sir."

"Leave them on the desk," said Charles, picking up his cup once again and finishing his tea.

Sutherland did not offer to fix another cup. He knew his mentor's prescriptions about moderation in all things. Sutherland suspected Charles became constipated whenever he drank too much tea, or so his moods would indicate. The young man was convinced that the maxims Miller proclaimed loudly really had less to do with abstract morality and more to do with Miller's needs.

Charles pushed the cup away and rose from the maroon leather chair and walked to a heavy mahogany desk, which dominated the room. The desk had only one sheet of paper on it. The rest of its richly polished top was clean. Sutherland had seen to that. Miller disliked clutter. When he finished one topic, everything pertaining to it was neatly filed away and the next papers brought in. "Cluttered desks make cluttered minds," he said continuously.

Sutherland, who had attended the local church school, hated clichés but could ill afford to say so. The school's recommendation of him to Charles Miller had led to one of the most important attainments of his life, his position as secretary to the head of the most important shipping firm on the lakes, the leading supporter behind the dream of bypassing the St. Lawrence rapids at Lachine and the building of the canal to join Lake Erie and Lake Ontario.

Sutherland's mother bragged to all her neighbors about it. Miller shipped most of the manufactured goods that went from Montreal west to the farms of Upper Canada. He had ties with the great North West Company and was one of its directors.

Charles sat down at his desk with a sigh. He dismissed his secretary. He was weary. He had been up late into the evening working in his office. Then he had argued with Elizabeth. He hated it when she complained about his lack of attentiveness. She must understand that he was a busy man. Last night she had even berated him for not making love to her more often. No other man had a wife who complained about such things. She even seemed to relish her times with him. It was an obscenity. It upset him so that he found it more and more difficult to perform, and the greater the difficulty, the fewer the times he allowed himself to be trapped. He didn't need sex, at least not that kind. The moaning and the passion, it all embarrassed him. They were approaching middle age, at least he was. They had no children. That was unfortunate. An infant might keep Elizabeth's mind off other things. They would keep trying until a child was conceived, and then he would be free.

He picked up the paper on his desk. It was the report of the North West Company's expenditures and profits from the sale of furs. He glanced at them absentmindedly at first, but soon he became absorbed. The old company seemed to be still strong, even if it had lost many of its resources after the Ohio Country was closed to it. Astor and his associates now controlled that world. The company, operating from Montreal, would find new sources in the West.

Charles studied the figures more carefully. He frowned. Then he rose from his desk and walked to the rosewood wall cabinet. He pulled open the doors and reached for a marbled green-and-white ledger book. He turned over several pages impatiently until he found the figures he was looking for. He picked up the ledger in both hands, walked slowly back to his desk, and studied the company papers again. He sat down, lost in concentration. Suddenly he slammed the ledger shut with a loud bang. Sutherland opened the office door and glanced at Charles Miller with concern.

"Is everything all right, sir?"

Charles ignored the question. "Sutherland, how much North West Company stock do I own?"

"I can't say for sure, sir, but you are a major shareholder."

"Begin proceedings to sell it off in small amounts at a time."

"Yes, sir. Should I sell it all?"

"Yes. It is time I began to diversify. And, Sutherland, begin today to inventory all our warehouse holdings."

As Sutherland closed the door behind him he gave his employer a quizzical look. But Charles did not notice it. He was already lost in thought. He was amazed that the company would try such a thing. He was amazed that he had almost missed it.

As Sutherland went into the outer office, he walked to his accountant's table. There was something wrong with the North West Company's report. He was sure of it. He had invested his savings in the company as well. If Charles Miller was dumping North West Company stock, then John Sutherland would follow suit. He had accumulated a pretty nest egg for himself and his mother by watching Miller's activities, and it was clear now that Miller's activities would require even more careful watching.

Charles glanced at his gold watch. He would be late for dinner at the Brants' house if he did not hurry. Jessica was strict about her Friday night meals—a hangover from her Hebrew past. It troubled Charles that his wife had been raised by a Jewish woman and that the man she called her brother, Michael Brant, was half Jewish and a quarter Mohawk. Elizabeth was not, of course, related to either of them by blood. And he had insisted that Elizabeth join him in the Anglican communion. They attended church every Sunday.

He was startled by Eli's booming voice from his outer office.

"Kill the fatted calf. The prodigal son has returned."

Charles opened the door and stood face to face with his brother, Stephen.

"Hello, mate," said Stephen, holding out his large and calloused hand.

"Where in God's name did you turn him up?" a startled Charles asked Eli.

"I discovered him dwelling in Meachum's house of sin on Front Street, drinking, fistfighting, no doubt wenching, all the things you would never think to do and one of the reasons your brother has always been more interesting than you are, Charles."

"Doctor, I am enjoined by the fifth commandment to honor you, as my wife's father. But I suspect that I could remember that my wife is your foster child, not your real daughter."

Charles took his twin brother's hand and shook it.

"You've changed," he said. "We used to look very much alike. There are some who say that twins share the same soul but I doubt it. We share nothing now, not even looks."

"Ah, Charlie, all I did was grow a moustache. It's you who's changed. You've gotten thinner and I've put a few on around the middle."

Eli was still sputtering over Charles's remark. He was accustomed to pampering and was so old that everyone indulged him. And it was clear that both Eli and his brother had been drinking all day.

"Come, Father Eli," said Charles, placing his hand on the old man's shoulder, "forgive me. But you're really quite free with your own tongue, and every once in a while it does you no harm to receive a bit of your own medicine."

"I'm the doctor, young man, only I dispense the apothecary's wares." Then, pointing at Stephen, "I thought I'd bring this . . . American . . . home to dinner."

Charles could just imagine Jessica's reaction. He turned to his brother.

"How's mother?" he asked.

"How did you know I've seen her?" Stephen asked.

19

Charles reached over and fingered the gold locket and chain that Stephen wore about his neck.

"Great-grandmother Nowell's locket. The last time I saw it, mother was wearing it. I gather she finally decided which one of us was worthy to wear it in her place. She never will forgive me for not joining you in attempting to rescue our stepfather."

"Well, brother, you're wrong. Our mother didn't pick either of us. She gave it to our sister years ago. Neither of us ever noticed it. Our sister, Maggie, sent it to me. She's married to some Washington fellow named Conrad, the congressman. Seems it just reminded her of all of us Millers and Nowells. She doesn't have very much use for any of us. But you're right, I did see mother in Quebec before I set out for Upper Canada. She gave me the last portion of my share of Grandfather Nowell's estate."

"If I know you, boy," interrupted Eli, "you've squandered it away already."

"Not at all," responded Stephen. He patted the slight bulge in his middle. "My gold is all right here in my belt."

Charles's eyes widened. "This is a relatively safe town, Stevie." He reverted to his brother's childhood nickname. "But you must be a fool to carry money like that around on your person. I have a safe in this office. You're welcome to use it."

"This gold is all I've got in the world, brother. It stays in my belt."

"Suit yourself," said Charles, shaking his head. "I must go home. Eli, I assume you intend to invite my twin brother to our Friday evening meal at Jessica's."

"Of course," said the old man, "we only stopped to pick you up."

Charles closed the office door behind him. "Sutherland, I'm leaving. Close the office and go home," he said.

"Yes, sir," responded the clerk, annoyed that his employer had never introduced him to his brother.

"You never answered my question," Charles said to Stephen as he opened the outer door. "How is our mother?"

"She's well," said Stephen as they stepped out into the street. "She browbeats Uncle Louie and his wife and runs the whole estate on Isle d'Orleans. The entire Stiegler family is bullied by her and they love every minute of it and they love

20

her. But, as remarkable as she is, she's ordinary compared to Grandmother Nowell."

"I believe I've met that girl," interrupted Eli.

"Girl!" laughed Stephen. "She's eighty-six years old, a mass of wrinkles, yet her voice is as soft and sweet as your Elizabeth's."

"Eli told you we've married?"

"Didn't think you had such good sense. My opinion of you, brother, has improved, even if she is a mere child."

"She's of ripe age for bedding," argued Eli, "and if your brother had gonads in his scrotum instead of cotton batting, I'd have already achieved my long-awaited status as foster grandfather."

"Sir," said Charles angrily, "that matter is none of your business."

"None of my business," yelled Eli, his eyebrows arched and shocked. "Why, if you weren't family I'd challenge you to a meeting on the field of honor."

Stephen started to laugh loudly. "I'd like to see you on the field of honor, old man, walking sticks at twelve paces." Again he shouted with mirth.

"Don't belittle my stick, you silly piece of anal refuse," shouted Stoddard back at him. "I doubt very much that you'd be alive at this moment if it were not for my stick."

"That's the house on the left," interjected Charles as they turned up Bay Street.

It was a three-story white clapboard house with dark blue, almost black, shutters. About the property line ran a low white picket fence. Eli poked open the little gate with his fabled stick. He bowed and allowed the brothers to pass by him. They walked up the gravel walkway. On the blue-black front door hung a highly polished brass knocker shaped in the form of an eagle—of Napoleonic Empire design by American craftsmen. Under the eagle was a brass plate that read, "Aaron Brant, Esquire." Jessica Brant had not removed it after her husband's death and she never intended to.

The door swung open and Mary, the cook's helper, stepped aside to allow the three men to enter.

"The mistress is on the warpath, Mr. Eli," she whispered. "She's been a regular tyrant all day and now she's had to delay dinner."

"Tell her we'll need only five minutes to dress for dinner. And tell her to set an extra place. We have a guest."

21

Great tears welled in Mary's eyes. "Ah, I could not do that," she cried. "The woman will feed me to the devil."

Just at that moment Jessica burst through the double doors separating the dining room from the hallway. She wore a dark blue high-waisted dress. Her black hair, now streaked with white, was pulled back and tied in a bun. Her black eyes still sparkled, not with mirth at this moment but with anger.

"Charles, Eli, how nice of you to come even if you are thirty minutes late and sunset is at hand."

"Madam, it is you Hebrews who make a fetish out of the sundown," responded Eli.

Charles walked to her and attempted to kiss her cheek, but she pulled away. As she did, she caught sight of Stephen.

"And who is this?"

"Forgive me," said Charles. "I'd forgotten you never met."

Jessica walked over to Stephen. "It's not necessary to tell me who this man is. One would have to be blind. The eyes, the hair, that straight Anglo-Saxon nose. It must be like looking in a mirror, Charles, except for the moustache and the fat."

"Fat?" responded Stephen.

"Well, plump anyway. You're Stephen Miller, Charles's twin. It's good to meet you. I feel I know you. I've heard so many stories."

"I have explanations for them all."

"They are not all bad," answered Jessica.

"You're hiding good news about this lad," offered Eli. "Come out with it. His reputation could use some help."

"His mother told me how he came to his stepfather's defense. That was noble, if foolhardy."

Charles stepped back. A look of pain crossed his face. The compliment to Stephen was an implied criticism to himself. No one noticed his reaction.

Jessica pushed Charles and Stephen toward the door.

"Go change," she said. "I've a beautiful spring lamb, which is almost ruined. Hurry."

Stephen resisted her shove. "I've nothing to change to. I own only what I'm wearing."

"Eli," she said, "take him to my room. Aaron's suits are still in the cupboard. Let him wear one of those. They are a bit dated, but he is about Aaron's size. Please hurry."

Elizabeth sat staring at Stephen Miller dressed in "Father Thomas"'s clothes. She had always called Aaron Brant by that

22

familiar name because Eli had called him Thomas. Now here was this blond stocky man sitting in "Thomas"'s clothes but looking every bit like a healthy Charles. She could not help comparing the two brothers. Charles was sickly and drawn. His hair had become stringy and thin. He looked older than his forty-three years. In contrast, Stephen was muscled and had a ruddy complexion. He appeared no different from the way he had when she last saw him six years ago. In fact, he looked younger than her thirty-three-year-old brother, Michael, who now always wore the dark clothing of the legal profession. Michael sat directly across from Elizabeth, carefully spooning his last bit of soup into his mouth. She looked back and forth between the twins until she noticed Charles staring at her. From the look on his face she realized that he knew precisely what she was doing. And he knew she found him wanting.

"Cousin Miller," said Michael Brant to Stephen, "what brings you back to Canada?"

"The lad worries about his position," interrupted Stoddard. "Michael's afraid someone will discover that his sister's brother-in-law is a traitor."

"You have such a way with words, Eli," said Jessica.

Michael looked embarrassed. "I don't regard you as a traitor, Miller. I gather we met on the field of battle at Queenston Heights. The American soldiers I faced there were brave men. My father said you chose the American side out of conviction. I did the same thing—but for Canada."

"The problem is that my brother was raised a Canadian, as I was," said Charles.

"Enough politics," said Jessica forcefully. "Mr. Miller, tell us your plans."

Stephen smiled his big grin, flashing his white and even teeth.

"I haven't any—except to get some work."

"Charles," said Elizabeth with some excitement, "he could work for you. Then the whole family would be together here at York."

Before Charles could respond, Stephen shook his head.

"I can't stay put in a town."

"Well then," said Eli, "employment with the North West Company is the thing. Charles, you're a stockholder. Do right by your brother."

23

Charles was about to say that employment with the North West Company would be only temporary work when Mary entered the dining room carrying a platter of roast leg of lamb surrounded by potatoes.

"Michael," Jessica addressed her son, "pour the wine."

Mary placed the platter on the center of the great dining room table. Eli rose and picked up the carving knife to begin slicing the meat.

"Your years in medicine come in useful," laughed Stephen.

"There's not much Doc can't do," Michael chimed in as he went from place to place and poured the wine.

"Your maid is extraordinary, Mrs. Brant," Stephen commented. "You had a place setting awaiting me so quickly."

Jessica smiled and said nothing. It had not been for him at all. She always set an extra place at Passover.

"Charles," Elizabeth asked, "you didn't respond to Eli. What about a job for Stephen with the company?"

"I think it could be arranged," Charles said thoughtfully. There was much that could be arranged for his brother.

Elizabeth placed the whale oil lamp on the walnut nightstand by her bed. She set the stepping stool in place and climbed up onto the bed. She fluffed up the pillows and leaned back against them. On the nightstand was a copy of Mr. Defoe's *Moll Flanders*, which she had found in her brother's library just a month ago. She had been amazed to discover anything other than legal books in Michael Brant's study. She was savoring the career of Moll, even though she knew Charles would be shocked to see her reading it. He was so proper, even moreso than her lawyer brother. There was little chance of discovery, however. They slept in separate bedrooms and his visits were few. She dragged the book into her lap, a wrinkle crossing her brow. She realized that she enjoyed the exploits of Moll so much because she had no exploits of her own. She had given up all her youthful, wild ways—her sense of freedom. She recalled stowing away on Charles's ship dressed as a boy. She remembered being Isaac Brock's water boy as they crossed Long Point, and she recalled how Father Thomas would shake his head in despair when she came to the family meal dressed in her brother's pants. It was a rebellion against what her parents expected a girl to be. Yet she had given up all that rebellion out of love for Charles. Her frown deepened. She had gained very little.

She rarely enjoyed her husband's company in this bed and it would be an impropriety to go to his.

There was a soft knock on the door. Elizabeth shoved *Moll Flanders* under the covers. The door opened and Charles peeked in.

"Are you awake?" he asked softly.

Elizabeth smiled. She had complained to herself too soon.

When Charles saw that she was sitting up, he stepped into the room.

Elizabeth was immediately disappointed. He had his coat on.

"I have to return to my office," he said. "I have some work that has to be done before Monday and then I must lay out the next week's work for Sutherland. I'll be sailing for Montreal on Monday."

She looked at him in surprise.

"You can have your father come over and stay. I'm sure Jessica could use a brief vacation from the good doctor."

"Eli won't be there himself. He's traveling on one of your ships to Newark to a political meeting of some sort."

"A man his age should stay put."

Elizabeth smiled. "I think he also knows when Jessica needs a vacation from the good doctor. I'll move in with Jessica while the two of you are gone."

"Fine," said Charles turning his back to her to leave.

"Don't work too long," she said to him as he left.

He didn't hear her. The door closed and Elizabeth stared out of the window at the blackness of the night. She extinguished the lamp and continued to stare. Finally she turned over onto her stomach. She flinched when she felt the hard edge of *Moll Flanders* dig into her.

Charles walked down Bay Street toward the lakefront. Meachum's tavern was still alive with lights. He could hear drunken singing coming from the one large taproom. He turned at the corner and ducked quickly into the back alley. He waited in the shadows at the back door of the tavern. The door opened once and a brilliant shaft of bright light pierced the darkness. Charles pressed his body hard against the far wall of the alley. He could feel the roughness of the clumsily sawed clapboard against his bony back. Meachum, the tavernkeeper, appeared outlined in the doorway. He tossed what he had been dragging out into the alley. It was a drunk. The ejected patron rose to his feet.

"I'll piss on you, Meachum," he said.

"You'll have to have something to piss with first, you dumb shit," yelled the innkeeper as he slammed the door.

Suddenly the alley was again in darkness and shadows. The ejected patron rose from his feet cursing. He stumbled and crashed into Charles. He gasped in fright as his hand touched the unexpected human form. Charles moved aside.

"What are you, some sort of cutthroat?" yelled the drunk. "Well, you'll get nothing from me. Meachum, that son of a bitch, he got it all first."

The drunk staggered past Charles and down the alley to the street.

Charles's tensed muscles relaxed. He waited in the darkness. He heard a commotion outside in the street.

"Watch where you're going," he heard the drunk yell again. He thought he saw a shadow duck into the alley but there was no further motion. His mind was playing tricks on him. He was alone. The voices from the tavern began to subside. He heard Meachum yell to Ginny as he went out the front door, locking it behind him. They'd clean up in the morning. She was to make sure she showed up on time and she was to be sure she locked the back door. Five more minutes passed. Charles was sweating despite the night chill. The tension had built up within him to an unbearable level. The alley door opened again but this time no light emerged. He could see her shadow begin to step through it.

"Ginny," he called out.

"Oh, no, not you," she replied wearily. "I'm tired. It's been a long night. I'm not up to your games tonight."

"Please," whispered Charles. "I have the money. I know you can use the money."

Greed overcame weariness rapidly. "All right, come in."

Charles followed her quickly through the door of Meachum's tavern.

"Strip," she ordered. "I haven't time for a long drawn-out session. Where's the money? Put it on the bar."

She opened a locked cabinet with a key she wore around her neck. Charles handed her the gold piece. She bit into it expertly and then placed it in a leather pouch inside the cabinet. From inside the cabinet, she withdrew a leather strap.

"I said strip," she said roughly to Charles.

"Yes, Ginny," he said meekly.

"What did you call me?"

"I mean, yes, sir."

Charles had removed his coat. He unbuttoned his shirt rapidly but his fingers trembled with excitement and he fumbled over the buttons. Ginny raised the strap and cracked it against the seat of Charles's pants. He winced.

"You know why you have been sentenced to this punishment, sailor, don't you?" she said, following the ritual.

"Because I am a coward, sir," he said as he bent forward.

III

York, Spring 1821

Elizabeth enjoyed the opportunity to spend time with Jessica and Michael. Early spring chills had given way to warmer days and occasional soaking rains and a glorious outburst of color as the flowering shrubs and bushes burst into life. She sat in the covered porch at the back of the house enjoying the afternoon sun. Mary had served tea to Jessica and Elizabeth. Michael would return within an hour and Eli was due home tomorrow. Charles would come later in the week. Jessica had invited Stephen to dinner and he had agreed to come. Jessica was disturbed, however, that Stephen had agreed only after she told him that Elizabeth was staying with her and would be present for the meal.

Elizabeth had laughed when her mother told her of her suspicions. She was secretly flattered, although obviously she could say nothing to Jessica about it.

They sat quietly sipping tea, enjoying the sound of a bee exploring a new flower. Jessica was crocheting. It was to be a cover for the dressing table in her bedroom. She looked over at Elizabeth staring off into space.

"It's hard when they go away," Jessica offered. "Harder even than when they stay at home."

Elizabeth smiled.

"My Aaron was only away a very few times in our years together. I hated every one of them. The last time, I knew something would go wrong. I just didn't know what. During the war, I feared for Michael and I feared for your Charles. I never thought it would be my Aaron who would fall victim. He was too old to fight." Tears came to her eyes. "Why do I get sloppy at quiet times like these?" She reached into the sewing basket and pulled out a delicate lace handkerchief. She blew her nose softly into it.

"Mother," Elizabeth reached over and touched her hand.

29

"I'll be all right," Jessica sniffed. "It's so good to have children when you're in pain. They can be such a comfort. You and Michael have been wonderful, far better to me than I was to my own father."

Elizabeth had heard the story of Levine the peddler and his opposition to Jessica's marriage many times. She had always felt that it was the old man's intolerance that had been at fault and not her mother's lack of devotion. But the mention of children upset Elizabeth. She wanted children of her own and Charles was doing very little to make it possible.

Jessica saw the look on Elizabeth's face and knew instantly what it was that troubled her.

"It will come in time, child," she said. "I had to wait for Michael. The waiting is hard, but when it comes and you feel the life inside you, a part of your own body and yet separate, a new person, there is nothing like that feeling in all of the world. And it will be yours."

"When, mother? When?"

"Patience," responded Jessica.

"Patience never fathered a child," said Elizabeth angrily. "And at the rate he is going neither will Charles Miller."

"Elizabeth," said Jessica, shocked by her daughter's outburst. "It could be you."

"I'll make that judgment," responded Elizabeth, "when my husband gives me the opportunity to conceive. But, damn it, I'm going to have to get the opportunity."

Jessica was accustomed to her daughter's strong language in the past but it had been years since she had heard an outburst like this. Charles Miller had tamed her, domesticated her, but if he doesn't make her a mother very soon, thought Jessica, it will all have been in vain. The signs were clear. The old Elizabeth was still alive under the skirts and petticoats, still vibrant, ready to emerge. There was a knock on the front door. Jessica stood up.

"That can't be Michael," she thought aloud. "He wouldn't knock."

Elizabeth followed Jessica through the front parlor to the hallway. Sutherland, Charles's clerk stood, hat in hand, in the hallway.

"What is it?" Elizabeth asked.

"Mrs. Miller," he stammered.

"Something is wrong with Charles," Elizabeth proclaimed calmly.

Jessica was awed by her daughter's calm.

"No, ma'am, it's Mr. Eli. I've just had word from *Tecumseh*, Mr. Stoddard's ship. Mr. Stoddard had some sort of attack. They had to leave him at Stoney Creek."

Elizabeth's face went pale. The door swung open and Michael Brant entered the hallway. His dark eyes took in the scene immediately.

"What's wrong?" he asked.

"We don't know," responded Jessica. "It's Eli."

"Mother, I must go to him," Elizabeth cried.

"You can't, ma'am. He's down the lake at Stoney Creek and we have no means of transportation."

"What about the ship that brought word?"

"*Tecumseh*? She only dropped anchor. They've already sent her on the way to Kingston."

"What about Stephen?" interrupted Michael. "He could take you. He's a master boatman and he's traveled all the lakes by canoe. He could take you to Eli."

"Michael, I'm not sure Charles would approve," said Jessica.

"I don't give a damn," stated Elizabeth, now near hysteria. "I'm going to Eli. Find Stephen Miller, Michael." She ran out of the room.

"Michael, you need not go looking for him. He's due here for supper," said Jessica.

Elizabeth dug her paddle into the murky lake water. The sun had set, but still her brother-in-law pushed on. She was close to exhaustion but she didn't want to admit it.

It seemed like days rather than just a few hours ago when she had fled her mother's house in Stephen's company. Jessica had tried to stop her. When that failed, she had tried to talk Elizabeth into taking Michael with her. But Elizabeth knew her brother's strengths and weaknesses. He loved her and would do anything for her but he—the son of a Mohawk warrior—had become so civilized that he could offer no aid on a hard-driving canoe trip. He barely remembered how to handle the musket he had fired six years ago at Queenston. She refused to take him. She had fled from the Brant house to her own house, where she changed into her old pants, which she had kept in a locked trunk in the attic. If she had not been so frightened, she would have been pleased to note that they still fit.

Stephen purchased the canoe on the waterfront with money he had taken from Sutherland. Charles would have to reimburse his clerk. She thought of Charles returning home to an empty house, but despite a glimmer of guilt, she dismissed him from her mind. They set out with three days' worth of provisions that Stephen had also obtained on the dock.

That had been five hours ago. In that time they had traveled far. They would arrive at Stoney Creek tomorrow.

"Stevie," she said, turning back to look at him in the rear of the canoe. He flashed his smile at her. His face was red from the sun and exertion. He had removed his linen shirt to keep it dry. His muscles rippled with each stroke. His body was so like Charles's, yet her husband seemed shriveled compared to his brother.

"We have to land," she said finally. "I can't go on very much longer."

Stephen nodded and turned his paddle to steer the bow of the craft toward the shore. The canoe struck rock below the surface just offshore and nearly capsized. Stephen jumped out and steadied it. He pushed the craft through the waist-deep water. With a great foolish grin he looked at his shirt so neatly folded and dry on the bottom of the canoe.

"So much for comfort," he said as he shoved the canoe toward shore.

Elizabeth stepped out onto the dry land and Stephen came sloshing up beside her.

"We'll need some dry wood for a fire."

"I'll find some," offered Elizabeth and took off toward the woods.

"Don't go far off," he yelled. "I don't want to have to go looking for you."

By the time Elizabeth returned with an armload of wood, Stephen had unloaded the canoe and relaunched it. She saw him about thirty yards offshore, his fishing line trailing behind the craft. She piled some of the dry wood together with sticks and dry leaves left over from last autumn. She poured a bit of gunpowder from Stephen's horn and struck a flint next to it. The powder flared and the leaves and sticks caught fire. Elizabeth continued to feed the flames. Before long she heard the cracking of dry wood and knew the fire had caught.

Stephen arrived onshore. He glanced at the fire with a nod of approval, then he took his knife from the sheath, cleaned the fish, impaled them on sticks, and placed them over Elizabeth's fire.

After they had eaten, they sat huddled before the flames. Stephen shivered. The air was chilly. He took a bottle of rum from his gear and sheepishly offered it to Elizabeth. She shook her head.

"Go ahead," he urged. "It will warm you."

"I don't like it."

He shrugged, pulled the cork with his teeth, and took a long gulp. He sighed as he felt the sweet warm liquid inflame his throat and belly. He looked over at her.

"How are you going to explain this unchaperoned trek into the wilderness to my Puritan brother?"

"What do you mean?" she said defensively.

"Well, you know he'll raise a stink. Perhaps you should have waited until his return. We should at least have taken your brother with us."

"Michael? Don't be silly. His father taught him everything and he has worked diligently to forget it all. He is so thoroughly a town dweller now that asking him to leave his law practice is like asking him to stop breathing. Michael had a Jewish mother and a Mohawk-English father. But I have no doubt that his basic nature is Jessica's. He'll always favor the town."

"You're avoiding mentioning Charles."

"My husband will understand why I rushed to Eli's side in his hour of need. For all I know Eli could be dying or already dead." She started to sniffle.

"I'm sorry," said Stephen. He knew the depth of her feeling for the old man but he had great doubts that the unbending Charles would understand. He should never have taken her on this journey. But, damn it, she had needed someone to take her and he was the only one who could. She looked very beautiful sitting by the fire. The flickering flames played on her face, highlighting her cheekbones and reflecting in her eyes. He truly wished that she had fallen in love with him and not Charles all those years ago. It would have made a difference in his life. Maybe he would now own the great house on Bay Street and a fleet of ships. He smiled. No, Ethan, his stepfather, still would have been hanged and he still would have blamed the British bastards for it. Even for the love of Elizabeth he doubted that he could have done anything different. He wrapped his warm woolen blanket about his body.

"It's time to sleep," he announced. "If we begin at dawn we can make it to Burlington tomorrow."

Elizabeth followed Stephen's example and grabbed the edges of the blanket she sat on and pulled them tightly about her. The old buffalo robe that Jessica had insisted she pack with her, a prized possession of her dead husband's, was folded in quarters. Despite the smell of old campfires and camphor it would make a comfortable pillow for her head. She lay down, watching the fire's tiny flickers. She could see Stephen's chest move with the regular rhythm of sleep. She saw his handsome face in repose, the smile wrinkles about his eyes softened. She wished he'd shave his moustache. She tried to imagine what he would look like without it, but then the stern face of her husband appeared before her drooping eyes. She turned her back to the fire and fell asleep.

"What do you mean I could have been dead or dying? You ventured into the wilderness seeking confirmation of rumor?" shouted Eli as Elizabeth stood before the old man's bed in a Stoney Creek cabin. He was pale as the white sheets that he had pulled up about his face to cover his body from the prying gaze of the female, even one he regarded as his own daughter.

"Mr. Sutherland told us you had been removed from Charles's ship and that you were in Burlington."

"I'm not sick," said the old man, shaking his white head vehemently. "Who is that behind you?" he said squinting out of his ancient eyes.

"It's me, the traitor, old man," answered Stephen with a grin.

"You traveled with him, that lecher? Bend down to me, girl."

Elizabeth obliged.

"Did he touch you?" the old man asked.

"Not once," said Elizabeth. "What's wrong with me?"

"It is not a joking matter," scolded Eli. "Now I'm going to have to get well rapidly to accompany you back as a chaperone."

"I thought you weren't sick," joked Stephen.

"I wasn't. Now I am. I am sick of smart-aleck remarks from young men whose brains are so located as to provide excellent cushioning for a hard chair. Elizabeth, leave me. I need to dress and this scoundrel will have to help me."

Elizabeth looked quizzically at Stephen.

"Don't look to a stranger to see whether or not you should obey the demands of a parent."

Stephen nodded to his sister-in-law. "He's a feisty old goat," he said. "I think he'll survive a canoe trip back to York."

"Damn right I will. Thank Mistress Bridges for her hospitality toward me, Elizabeth. The woman took me in sight unseen, a very charitable act. Then she damned near killed me with her wretched gruel for breakfast, for luncheon, for evening repast. Gruel—warmed-over vomit is what it tastes like."

"How would you know?" asked Stephen.

"Stevie," Elizabeth admonished.

"No, let the man mock me. It will only increase my ire and increase my blood. I need more blood in my brain. You see how pale my face is?"

"See how lucky I am?" Stephen countered. "My blood hasn't so far to travel to reach my brain."

Eli let loose a shout of laughter.

"Oh, Miller, how could two brothers be so different? Charles is a dried prune compared to you. Elizabeth, my love, you picked the wrong man to live with."

Elizabeth gave the old man a withering look.

"Sorry, my love," he said. "I have no desire to grieve you. Charles is a good man."

He had misunderstood her look. She had not been angered by his attack on her husband but rather by his suggestion that she had chosen wrongly between brothers.

She slammed the door as she left. As soon as she had gone Stoddard seemed to shrink in the bed. Stephen walked to his side and pulled back the bedcovers. The old man sat up with Miller's assistance. Stephen pulled the yellowed nightshirt up over Eli's head. His old body was bony and emaciated yet his belly protruded. Stephen had seen that phenomenon only once when he had stumbled into an Ottawa band that had run out of food in a terrible northern winter. The starving children had bellies like that. There was a stale smell about the old man's person.

"You've been lying to us, old man."

"Deductive reasoning worthy of an Aristotle, Miller."

"How sick have you been?"

"I was rowed halfway across the River Styx before the boatman recognized his mistake and returned me."

"Are you going to make it?"

"I've no choice, boy. I wasn't fooling about my hostess's food. If I don't get back to Jessica's house I'm done for."

Stephen dressed the old man hurriedly and threw his Indian blanket as a shawl about his shoulders. Then he picked him up in his arms.

"Old man, we're going home."

He pulled open the door and stepped into the front room of the cabin. Mistress Bridges was leaning over her stove.

"Mr. Miller, Mrs. Miller tells me you'll be taking your father-in-law back now. I've made a bit for a travel packet of food."

Stephen was confused by her form of address. Then he realized that their names had confused the woman into mistaking that he and Elizabeth were husband and wife. But there was no mistaking what she was cooking on her stove— another pot of gruel.

"Get me out of here," yelled Eli when he saw the pot.

Elizabeth opened the front door, took the bundle of "goodies" from Mistress Bridges, and led the way down to the lakefront through three or four cabins that constituted the village of Stoney Creek. Stephen laid Eli gently in the canoe. Elizabeth sat in front and grabbed her paddle. Stephen placed one leg in the stern and then shoved off. The stern dipped heavily into the water and then the bow shot out into the lake. Stephen's paddle dug into the water deeply and then he turned the blade, pointing the bow northeast toward York.

As they paddled, the spring sun grew very hot. Gradually the pallor of Eli's face gave way to a flush of the sun and fever. Elizabeth turned frequently to feel his face. She would bring her paddle inboard, take some cool lake water, and place it on his brow. She looked at Stephen and shook her head. Panic was gripping her. The old man was much sicker than he had first admitted. The terrifying fear that he might not make it home began to gnaw at her heart. She renewed her paddling.

Stephen saw the fear rising in her.

"Elizabeth," he called.

She turned around, at first startled by the sound of his voice.

"He would have died in the tender clutches of Mistress Bridges. We have to get him back to Jessica. She will nurse him back if we can reach York in time."

Elizabeth merely nodded that she understood.

36

"That means we keep right on going through the night for as long as we can hold out."

They continued to cut through the mild ripples of the lake. Stephen had stopped only once and that was to remove his heavy shirt. He was sweating heavily, and he would need a dry shirt when the sun set and the night chill descended. Elizabeth stopped every half hour or so to offer Eli a drink of water and to cool his face. But by midafternoon the old man was delirious. He called out to friends and acquaintances long gone from this world. Elizabeth's cheeks were wet with tears when she realized at one point that he addressed Father Thomas, Aaron Brant, his best friends.

They ate their supper while they paddled. Blisters developed on the palms of Elizabeth's hands. Soon the blisters broke, and the pain of the festering sores moved up into her wrists. She dared not let go of the paddle because she knew that if she did she would not have the strength or the courage to grasp it again. Stephen called to her, but she ignored him and dug the paddle into the water.

Stephen knew that Elizabeth was in desperate straits. But he had been the one who told her that time was a factor for Eli. To stop or to ease up was to her now a form of betrayal of the old man. He looked down at Eli's reddened face. He had placed their belongings in such a way that the bundles shaded the old man's face.

Suddenly he heard a thump and then a wretched scream. His eyes darted from Eli to Elizabeth. He saw her paddle float by. She clutched for it and missed. Her eyes darted in every direction. She was in a panic. Stephen saw Elizabeth's hands, raw and bloody.

"Holy God," he muttered. "Elizabeth, stay put." He was afraid she would try to stand and follow the paddle to the rear. She obeyed him.

He tilted his paddle and the bow of the craft responded instantly. A few strong strokes brought him to the floating paddle. He scooped it up out of the water. Elizabeth reached for it, but he placed it on the bottom of the canoe by his side. She looked at him with desperate eyes.

"I have to help. I love this old man, Stephen."

"Then tend to him," Miller responded. "I'll do the stroking." The canoe was moving forward again. Stephen could see Elizabeth's agony. Her hands were hanging at her sides.

37

"Drag them in the water. It's still cold enough to numb them after a time," he ordered.

She obeyed and grimaced as the cool water touched the fire in her hands.

Eli moaned once and started to turn.

"Keep him quiet, Elizabeth," Stephen called to her. "Can you hold anything?"

Elizabeth nodded.

"There's that grub the old woman gave us."

Elizabeth pulled at the wrapping of Mistress Bridges's bundle with her fingertips. She uncovered a loaf of stale bread and an earthenware pot of cold gruel.

"That's disgusting," Elizabeth said.

Stephen started to laugh. "The old man was right," he chuckled. "She doesn't know how to fix anything else. We were right to get him out of there."

Stephen continued to paddle alone as the afternoon wore on. The sweat had flowed down to his beltline and soaked through the upper portion of his buckskin pants. Elizabeth had fed Eli some of the cool lake water but he had refused both the bread and the gruel. Now she grew sleepy. She curled herself up in the front of the canoe with her neck resting against Eli's leg.

Stephen powered the craft by himself. The heat of the sun had lessened as it dropped lower in the sky. It still struck his back but soon it would lose its height and he would need his shirt. The girl was asleep. She had exhausted herself, he thought, for old Eli. Eli had rescued her as an infant and made her his own. He had indulged her whims, spoiled her, they all said. But it could not have been so bad. She clearly returned his love for her. Her blistered hands were proof of that.

He looked into her sleeping face. Too bad nothing had happened last night. He had wanted something to happen. He had wanted something to happen ever since he had first met her at Amherstburg during the war. He sensed that she had wanted it too. But it was too late to do anything now. The old man had to be brought to York. The trip might kill him, but to leave him behind without medical care and without the love of those who cared for him would have killed him more surely.

Eli Stoddard, despite his advanced years and illness, was a lucky man. He was deeply loved. Stephen doubted if anyone

38

but his mother loved him. He had no children that he knew of and his sister in Washington barely knew him. His father and stepfather were dead, and he was sure his brother, Charles, disapproved of him and now merely tolerated him.

The setting sun was now beginning to color the sky behind him. Still he paddled. He was beginning to feel chilly now. A slight breeze arose and rippled the surface of the lake. He stopped and allowed the craft to proceed forward with the force of momentum. The canoe glided softly. Stephen reached for his shirt. It stuck to his wet torso but it would dry rapidly in the breeze. He looked toward the orange and purple sky. There were clouds blocking his view of the sun. He became nervous. The breeze picked up and the lake's surface became choppier. If a storm came up, all chance of returning to York this night was finished. Rougher waters would make traveling more difficult or even impossible.

Eli and Elizabeth still slept. His muscles ached. He longed to reach calm water and end this journey. He grunted now each time his paddle dipped into the water.

Night descended rapidly. He had to work harder now against the waves. The bow of the canoe banged into the surf, sending a spray back into Stephen's face and wetting the sleeping forms of Elizabeth and Eli.

Elizabeth was awakened by the spray. She sat up and looked about. A look of bewilderment crossed her face. She had fallen asleep on a sunny calm day and awakened at night with the lake churning.

She started to reach for the paddle by Stephen's side but her face broke into a spasm of pain from the blisters on her hands.

"Don't try anything," Stephen yelled at her. "Cover the old man's body with your own."

"Maybe we should head for the shore and wait it out." She yelled now to make her voice heard above the sound of the waves beating against the birch bark.

"No chance. I've seen these storms last for days. He wouldn't make it then. Our only chance is to run before it, back to York."

At that moment a great gust of wind blasted at their backs. Off to the west, lightning streaked through the black night, illuminating Elizabeth's face for a split second. Stephen saw fear there but no panic. Her only care was to cover her father and to keep him dry.

39

Time came to a halt for Stephen. His shoulders and arms worked like a machine. The paddle stabbed into the waves, worked its way to the rear of the craft, then twisted slightly to keep the bow toward the east headed for home.

Elizabeth called out, "We're taking on too much water."

"I can't help it."

"How much longer?" she asked.

"Can't tell."

"How do you know where we're going?"

"I don't," he yelled at her. "Right now I'm letting the wind take us. It's coming from the southwest and driving us northeast, and that is where York lies."

She was afraid what would happen to them if they missed York harbor. But he knew what her next question would be.

"I don't know where it is, Elizabeth. I can only rely on my own instincts."

Then he was silent. The angry waves were driven by the wild wind at his back. Suddenly the wind stopped. The canoe slowed its pace but still bounced from wave to wave toward the northeast. He sat back on his haunches. He did not know Ontario as he did Huron and Superior or even Michigan, but his instincts were usually right and they told him to make his move now. If he was wrong, Eli was a dead man. He decided. He twisted the paddle and the canoe turned due north. Now the waves caught the canoe broadside and water splashed over the side.

Elizabeth looked up at Stephen. Enough inactivity, she thought. She picked up the earthenware pot and emptied Mistress Bridges's gruel into the water. Then, despite the excruciating pain in her hands, she began to bail the accumulating water out of the canoe.

Stephen smiled at her. She was a brave woman.

The going was slower now. The force of the wind tried to turn the bow away from the shore. Stephen had to use all his strength to keep it pointed north. A dark form loomed ahead. Stephen exhaled with relief. He recognized it as one of the islands in York harbor. They passed it and instantly the swells declined in size. Stephen no longer had to paddle so hard.

"I think you've done it," Elizabeth called out. "Stevie, we've made it home."

Stephen hadn't the strength to respond to her shout of glee, but he could not stop paddling. He would not until the canoe was sent gliding onto the landing beach at York at the old Toronto Carrying Place.

Eli slept soundly in his own bed. Jessica sat in the corner of the room, her chin resting on her chest. She started awake with a snort. She looked around the room, surprised by her own snort and relieved to realize that no one was present to hear except Eli. His rough breathing indicated that he could not have heard anyone. The enamel-and-gilt clock on the mantelpiece struck twice. Jessica yawned and rose from her chair.

She bent over Eli. His fever was still with him but it had gotten no worse. The doctor had bled him and placed suction cups on his back. She shuddered. Had Eli known that she had called in one of his rivals, he would have risen from his bed out of sheer orneriness to refute his diagnosis. She pulled the yellow woolen blanket up to his chin. She herself had trimmed the edge with yellow silk. She loved the feel of it and every night she would rub two fingers along the edge as she fell asleep. But tonight she would not sleep and she had placed her blanket atop Eli's shivering body.

She was startled by a pounding on the front door. None of the servants would hear it. They slept in the attic. She picked up an oil lamp from beside Eli's bed and went out into the hall. Stephen Miller was asleep in the guest room down the hall. She pitied his exhaustion. She would not awaken him. She went down the stairs to the foyer of the house. Again the pounding. This time she heard her name called and recognized the voice of Charles's clerk, Sutherland. She unlocked the heavy oak door. Sutherland stepped aside and allowed a dripping Charles Miller to enter the house.

"Mother Jessica," he said, "is Elizabeth here? She was not at home when I arrived."

"She's upstairs in her old room."

"Sutherland tells me she took off with my brother. How could you allow it?"

Jessica chuckled. "No one stops Elizabeth when she makes up her mind on something, and just let something involve Eli and forget about allowing anything."

Charles was thoughtful for a moment. "How's the old man?" he asked.

"Ill, but the doctor expects him to live. Old polecats have tough meat. Elizabeth, the poor baby, is exhausted and her

41

hands are all blistered from paddling. The doctor had to cover them with salve and bind them."

Charles looked disturbed for the first time.

"I'll spend the night if it is all right with you," he said to Jessica.

She nodded and Sutherland quickly handed Charles the cloth bag he carried in his hand. Then the clerk departed into the blackness beyond the glow of Jessica's lamp. She closed the door.

"You know Elizabeth's room," she said as she ascended the stairs. "I'll spend the night watching Eli."

Halfway up the stairs she turned around. "I feel better now that you're back. It was like the few times that Aaron was away from me. The family is leaderless without its head. Your brother is a good enough fellow but you are the steady one, Charles." Then she continued to the top.

The weariness of her step was obvious to him. He knew he should offer to sit up for her, but he too was exhausted. He walked down the hall to Elizabeth's old room after whispering good-night to Jessica. He opened the door with a light touch. The window was open and the sound of the rain filled his ears. The draft caused by the open door stirred the lace curtains and he felt a cooling breeze strike his face. Elizabeth stirred. Charles set his cloth bag on the floor beside the bed. He went to the open window and closed the wooden shutters. He took off his coat and tossed it across the back of the desk chair.

Elizabeth sat up and pulled the covers around her neck.

"Charles?" she asked. In her own mind the image of the man with the yellow hair, the strong sun-reddened shoulders came into view.

"You were expecting someone else?" he asked.

She smiled. "I did not know you had returned."

"I arrived this evening. Sutherland told me you hadn't returned. So I came here."

She moved to the right side of the bed and patted the empty half with her bandaged hand.

"Come on in. It will be like the old days before separate bedrooms."

Charles blushed but the darkness of the room hid his embarrassment. He was amused by her remembering the old days when they had made love so often. He removed his pants and neatly folded them along the seams and placed them next to his coat.

"Jessica tells me Eli is holding his own," he offered.

"The doctor said he'd live."

Charles took his nightshirt from the carpetbag and threw it over his head. Then he climbed into bed next to Elizabeth. She snuggled up next to him and placed her head on his chest.

"I've missed you," she said.

"I've only been gone a few days."

"You've been gone a lot longer from my bed," she responded.

"Elizabeth, we are not children."

"Nor do we have any."

Charles turned away from her. But she touched his shoulder with her bandaged hand. He turned over onto his back again and once more she rested her head on his chest. Her hand moved down to his stomach and lower.

"I'm sorry," she said. "There can't be much finesse to lovemaking when you've only fists wrapped in cotton."

But it did not take finesse to get a response from Charles. He was soon aroused. He sat up in the bed and pulled the nightshirt up over his head and threw it onto the floor. He leaned down and kissed Elizabeth on the lips. She responded by opening her mouth and allowing her tongue to slip between his slightly parted teeth. He pulled his mouth away from her. He always did that, she thought, whenever she showed any initiative. She relaxed and lay back against the pillow. It would be the same as it always was. She felt him trying to enter her. If she was patient it would be over quickly, particularly if she tried to think of something else.

IV

York, Summer 1821

Charles turned from the ledger books. He was sure now that the North West Company was in grave trouble. It was time to invest his money in the Hudson's Bay Company, its great rival, and it was time to think of supplying the settlers in Upper Canada rather than trading in furs. Montreal would still be Canada's greatest port when free of ice. But its days as hub of the fur trade were numbered.

Sutherland knocked at the door.

"Mr. Stoddard to see you, sir."

Eli pushed past the clerk. The three months since his illness had restored his health but not his old vigor. His face was drawn and the skin at the top of his head seemed to have shrunken and his bony skull threatened to protrude through it. His white hair hung to his shoulders from the sides and the back of his head. It was stringy and none too neat. His face was drawn and his eyes bulged.

"Father Eli, it's good to see you getting out of the house."

"Why?" asked Eli.

Charles was taken aback. "Because... because you are Elizabeth's father and I am sure it will please her and me."

"I'm not her true progenitor, as you well know. I serve in the rarely appreciated role of guardian. And although I am sure it will please her, I have no reason to believe that you will be affected by it in any way at all."

Charles stood up at his desk. "Eli, I have no intention of being abused by you."

"And I have no intention of abusing you. I've come to settle my estate."

"That's normally done after you're dead, Eli."

"Well, I was almost deceased. It frightened me to think I had not provided for my Elizabeth. I'm not rich, but every-

45

thing I have must go to her. I've had a lucrative practice here at York and few expenses. Jessica has taken no rent, although God knows I've offered often enough. But Thomas's wealth through his father was enormous and Jessica needs nothing. But all her wealth will go to Michael. Elizabeth must have something of her own."

"Under the law, sir, anything you leave her will come to me as her husband."

"That is precisely what I've come to discuss. I have a piece of paper I want you to sign. It leaves all my wealth to Liz and cuts you out."

"Why should I sign such a paper? It would deny me my rights as a husband."

Eli smirked. "Elizabeth tells me you don't exercise those rights very often or very well."

"She said what?" Charles's voice rose in disbelief.

"Calm down, boy. She tells me everything. She always has. Why does that come as a surprise to you? And don't try to divert me. I want her to have my wealth. And if you don't sign it, I'll spread the word around York that Charles Miller is impotent."

"That's . . . that's not true."

"I know, at least not exactly, but the whole town will believe me. I'm a doctor, don't forget. Of course, you could prove me wrong by standing on Bay Street exposing yourself. But that's about the only way you could do it."

Charles was angry now and with anger came calm.

"Give me your paper. I'll sign."

"Now you're showing your God-given gift to man—reason."

Charles took Eli's handwritten will from the clawlike hand of the old man. He read it through quickly. He picked up his quill and signed. It was a worthless piece of paper. Everyone but Eli, stubborn old Eli, who moved along paths that only he could fathom, everybody but Eli would know it was worthless.

He handed the signed paper back to the smiling man.

"Good. Now, Charles, I wish you to remain calm. I went through this charade because I don't trust you. You've always been a narrow-minded prig. This will leave Elizabeth my estate for her lifetime. Then it will pass on to the heir of her body. I wanted my money to go to your children without you controlling it." The old man started to laugh.

Charles was convinced that the fever had finally destroyed his mind.

"Eli, Elizabeth and I have no children."

"You're about to. She told me that too."

Charles looked at Eli in some confusion.

"So you see, my story about your impotence would never have been believed. Your wife is three months gone. In a few months she will be large with child. I, of course, will deliver it. I could not have made a charge of impotence stick—unless of course I spread the rumor that somebody else did the job for you. But no, that would have cast aspersions on Elizabeth. But the fact remains that you, Charles, will have a son or a daughter. I would prefer a granddaughter. And I'm sure that is what it will be. And my granddaughter, who will be named Ann after my mother, will inherit all my wealth on attaining her majority. I think of it as her dowry, Charles."

"Elizabeth is pregnant?"

"That's the way it normally happens, unless, of course, you plan to hatch an egg and produce my granddaughter in that revolutionary manner."

"Why didn't she tell me?"

"How should I know? She came to me when she suspected and I told her she was. Then I drew up this blessed paper and came over to see you."

Charles felt a sense of relief float over him. Naturally Elizabeth would seek the opinion of her doctor before telling him her suspicions. It was Eli who had acted rashly, telling him before Elizabeth could meet with him in private and reveal the news to him. He was sure she would tell him tonight.

"I must go now, Charles," said Eli.

"Good evening to you, sir," said Charles politely.

"I'm glad you're taking the deceit so well, Charles. After all, Ann will be your daughter and independence should be a mutual goal."

The old man was outrageous. Still, thought Charles as he closed the door behind him, the paper was next to worthless. He would be named trustee of his wife's estate no matter what Stoddard's paper said. He would have to worry about it in twenty-one years, when his child came of age, provided Elizabeth was not alive. What guarantees did any of them have that they would be living in twenty-one years?

Sutherland entered without knocking.

"I couldn't help but overhear Dr. Stoddard, sir. He is really quite loud. I'm very happy for you and Mrs. Miller. She must be ecstatic. Three months ago she thought she faced the loss of her dear father and risked public condemnation for improper behavior by rushing off into the wilderness with your brother to aid him. And now three months later she not only has her father and her reputation intact but you will both be bringing a new Miller into the world, and after so many years. Again, sir, congratulations to you and Mrs. Miller."

Charles thought Sutherland very bold. His remarks were out of character for him.

"Thank you, Sutherland," he said looking at the man quizzically. "You may go now. I won't be needing you anymore this evening."

"Thank you, sir," said the clerk, "but I'll be a while. I have a great deal of work to complete before I can go."

The clerk left the room. Charles rose from his desk and turned to look out his window toward the back of the Bay Street properties, including his own home. His first response to the news of Elizabeth's pregnancy was surprise. He had always assumed that he was sterile. It had never crossed his mind that the trouble might be with her. But Elizabeth's pregnancy put that fear to rest. He turned away from the window and sat back down at the desk.

Sutherland's words came swooping into his mind. "My brother, she was away with my brother in the middle of the wilderness," he said aloud. His mind began to work rapidly. Suddenly he became suspicious of her desire to get him into bed that very night. He shook his head, as if to get rid of a thought too painful to contemplate. But then he knew. He had been right. He was not man enough to father a child any more than he had been man enough to fight the hostile invader. If Elizabeth was pregnant then Stephen was responsible. He felt his eyes filling with tears. He straightened up in his chair. He would not cry like some little boy. He would maintain his dignity—always. He rose and went to the wall cabinet. On the lower shelf he kept a bottle of whiskey and a set of fine cut-glass tumblers. He poured himself a healthy shot and downed it in one gulp. The heat in his throat and stomach took away the threat from his eyes.

"I will always keep my dignity," he said aloud.

*   *   *

Since her visit to Eli, Elizabeth had been bursting with the news. She had known deep inside she was with child, but she had skipped months before and had raised her own hopes before, only to have them dashed the next month. But never before had she skipped two months. And now Eli had confirmed it. At last she and Charles would be parents. It would bring them closer together. She was sure of it.

He is late, she thought as she walked through the dining room of their house. She had set the table with a fine lace tablecloth, her best wineglasses, and her finest china. Hers were not as nice as her mother's. She laughed aloud. How far she had come toward domesticity. As a girl she would not have cared a fig for china or stemware. All she had worried about then was keeping up with the accomplishments of her brother, Michael, by riding and shooting better than he.

The new cook, Ginny Meachum, peeked into the dining room. She saw Elizabeth alone and then she backed out into the kitchen again. She was not much of a cook, but Charles liked her work. He also paid her extraordinarily high wages, Elizabeth thought. This evening, under Elizabeth's explicit instructions, she had prepared a roast for dinner. It was not to be overdone. But Charles, simply by staying away, would get the gray, tasteless meat that he loved so well.

She heard the front door open and close.

"Charles," she called out. There was no answer. She walked from the dining room into the front hallway. He stood with his back to her, placing his walking stick in the stand before the eye-level mirror. He looked at her reflection in the mirror and their eyes made contact. She could see the pain in him and it frightened her.

"Charles?" she called out again.

He turned to face her and it was as if a mask had fallen into place. There was no pain in his eyes now. There was nothing in them.

"Yes, Elizabeth," he answered.

She looked at him in confusion. Why had he hidden his feelings? Did he always do that? She had always thought of him as a quiet man—a man in charge of his emotions. But she had never thought of him as a man who suppressed his emotions. Suddenly in that one look in the mirror she felt she had seen inside his soul and she had seen torment.

"What's the dinner?" he asked.

"A burned roast," she responded, still distracted by what she had seen.

"Now, Elizabeth, our cook is a fine girl."

"Yes, I know, but she comes quite expensive."

"I'm starving," he said to change the subject. "Let's get to the roast."

He took her by the hand and led her into the dining room.

"My, my," he exclaimed, "what is the occasion? Everything good we own is displayed before us."

"Nothing special," she responded. She shook off her worried mood and began to join in his teasing tone.

They sat down at the table. Charles poured the rich red Burgundy wine into the Waterford glasses. He held one up to allow the light from the candles on the table to catch the patterns of the cut glass and to send shadows against the far walls of the room. The candlelight revealed also the rich redness of the wine.

"It is fortunate for me," said Elizabeth, "that my husband is one of the richest men in York. I have such lovely things and such good wine."

She sipped hers. Ginny Meachum entered the room with the meat on a platter.

"Ah, the good roast," said Charles lightly. "Here we go," he said as he took up the carving knife and started to slice the pieces of meat for both of them. A few moments later Ginny returned with fresh corn and peas from the kitchen garden.

Charles helped himself to a small portion.

"I see you're determined to keep your figure, husband, unlike your brother."

At the mention of Stephen's name the same look came flickering back into Charles's face.

"My brother and I are not much alike."

"Nonsense, you're twins."

"I mean in personality," he responded. "Speaking of my brother, I found him the kind of position he has wanted. It is with the North West Company, as a voyager on the lakes. He'll be gone for half the year hauling goods to the Ft. William on the way west."

He stared at Elizabeth and she felt uncomfortable.

"He's left already for Lower Canada. No time for goodbyes. I advised him to put his share of the family money, the money my mother gave him, in the North West Company stock but he has refused. I will keep it in my safe. It is a foolish move. The old trade is doing so well and the company reports are outstanding."

Elizabeth nodded in agreement but without much interest.

"I have invested in the company for Eli and for Jessica and Michael also."

He continued to ramble on about investments, almost as if he were trying to convince her. Yet he knew she knew very little about such matters.

Finally, in desperation, Elizabeth interrupted him.

"Charles, I'm pregnant."

He stopped speaking for a moment. "I know," he said finally.

"How?"

"Eli."

"Oh, damn him," she said in disappointment. "How could he ruin my news? Are you happy?" she asked him.

"Should I be?"

"We've tried for years, Charles."

"I assumed we would continue trying and I suspect we would have but for a little help."

"What do you mean?"

"Come now, Elizabeth. I've suspected for some time that I could not sire a child. On the other hand, you were alone some nights with my very persuasive brother. How well you chose. People will exclaim how much the child resembles the father even if the father is not the father."

Elizabeth sat gaping at Charles.

"What are you accusing me of?"

"Was he good, Elizabeth? Better than I?"

"You bastard," she said softly—so softly he could barely hear her.

"Let us keep up the ladylike pretenses at least, Elizabeth, if you please."

"Charles, I have never been unfaithful to you. Never."

"Then how are we to explain the embarrassing presence of this little nipper, or if Eli is right and it is a girl—my lord, what is the feminine for nipper? I don't know, is it a nip-ess?" His voice oozed sarcasm.

"How can you say these things to me?"

"Please, Elizabeth, drop the act. You've been lusting after my twin since you first met him. It must be a temptation for a woman to see if identical twins are identical in

51

every way. I'm surprised you have not used the claim that you thought it was me all along."

Elizabeth stood up in her place.

"I'll not be spoken to like this, Charles Miller. I am your wife and I deserve your respect."

But Miller was beyond maintaining his dignity. He was consumed by jealousy. And had consumed too much whiskey and wine.

"Sluts don't get respect," he said.

Elizabeth picked up her wineglass and threw its contents in Charles's face. Stifling a cry, she dashed from the room and out the front door of the house toward her mother's. Most of the early evening strollers had disappeared from the Bay Street sidewalks. But even if the street had been at its busiest, Elizabeth would have seen no one through her tears. She found the walkway to the great white house almost by instinct and pounded on the door.

The maid, Mary, swung open the door and Elizabeth nearly tumbled into the hallway.

"Mary," she said, "get my mother!"

The Irish girl stared openmouthed and unmoving.

"Get my mother, you silly little bitch," she said, slapping the girl across the face.

"Yes, Mrs. Miller," the girl cried and ran out into the kitchen looking for the cook.

"Stupid child," Elizabeth said, holding back her own tears. She climbed the flight of stairs to the first landing. Her mother's door was already opening. Jessica had heard the commotion below. Elizabeth rushed into her arms.

"This is a personal meeting, Charles," Jessica said as she sat in Miller's private office the next morning. "I don't believe it necessary for Mr. Sutherland to be here."

"Personal or not," responded Miller, who sat behind his great desk, "I believe you plan to cost me money and Sutherland is my bookkeeper."

"I am trying to save your marriage. Does your clerk run that for you too? I almost wish he did. He might have done a better job."

Miller's lips tightened into a thin, unnatural smile. He nodded to Sutherland.

"You may go."

The clerk began to move slowly toward the door. To

Jessica's astonishment, it was clear that he was reluctant to leave.

Jessica sat silent for some moments after Sutherland had closed the door behind him. She was trying to gather her thoughts. It was Miller who spoke first.

"So save my marriage. I'm waiting."

"Charles, you have given mortal offense to my daughter and I am not sure that I can save your marriage."

Charles rose from his chair and came around to the front of the desk.

"I am sorry," he said. His tone softened and the sarcasm seemed gone. "I love Elizabeth. I always have."

"Then why in God's name have you insulted her so and at such a moment?"

"I have not insulted her unless to speak the truth is to insult. I am sure she was seduced by my brother on their trip to Burlington."

"That is an outrageous charge. What evidence do you have?"

"Her pregnancy," he responded.

Jessica was clearly embarrassed. Her face flushed red. But she was determined to push on.

"Was it impossible for you to have fathered the child?"

She meant to question the time and the frequency of their lovemaking. She was struck by his response.

"I've known about my sterility for some time."

Jessica's face went even more crimson but she persisted. "How?"

"That's my business."

Jessica was sure now that Charles's mental balance was at stake.

"I am forced then to choose between my daughter's claim to innocence and faithfulness and your unsubstantiated claim of sterility. I believe it is your jealousy of Stephen, your brother, that has given rise to this crisis—not any impropriety by my daughter. Beg her forgiveness and bring this—this farce to an end."

"My wife may return to her home anytime she wishes. I have not cast her out." He swallowed hard. "She and the child will be welcome."

"Charles, my boy, she'll not come back without an apology from you and the acknowledgment by you that the baby she carries in her womb is yours. Even then it will take all my

53

powers of persuasion to get her to return home. She has already consulted Michael on the legal questions."

There was a soft knock on the door and Sutherland poked his head through.

"Please forgive the interruption, sir, but the letter you've been waiting for from Montreal has arrived."

Charles looked in annoyance at his clerk. He opened his mouth to speak and then closed it again, saying nothing.

Sutherland continued to stand in the doorway.

"Mrs. Brant," Charles addressed his mother-in-law formally, "I have no more to say to you. Please tell my wife what I said to you."

Jessica wanted more time to argue with Charles but she was not going to do it in front of a third party. Why would this clerk not go away and mind his own business? She rose and walked to the door.

"Please consider my words, Charles," she pleaded, then she left, ignoring Sutherland.

Charles returned to his desk, dropping wearily into his chair. He picked up his ink pen and began to doodle absentmindedly. He looked over at Sutherland.

"You mentioned a letter."

"There was no letter, sir. I just thought you might want an excuse to end the interview."

"That was thoughtful of you," he said rather bitterly.

"Thank you, sir," said the clerk. He turned to leave the room.

"Oh, Sutherland!"

"Yes, sir,"

"I expect the old man will be pounding on the door next. I don't wish to see him."

"As you say, sir."

"Thank you. And Sutherland—"

Again the clerk hesitated at the door.

"Be a good fellow and bring me the family account books."

"They're already in your drawer."

"Are they really?" asked Charles, the sarcastic tone returning to his voice. "You must be reading either my mind or my mail."

Sutherland lowered his eyes and remained silent.

"Will that be all, sir?" he asked finally.

Charles was already poring over the ledger book and

ignored Sutherland's question. The clerk closed the door quietly.

Charles had wished to avoid this confrontation but Michael Brant made it impossible. When he informed Brant of the family losses, the lawyer had insisted that Charles meet with them all and make a settlement with his wife, Brant's sister.

Now Jessica Brant and Elizabeth, whom he had not seen in two weeks, sat across from him in the parlor of the Miller house. Sutherland hovered in the background, shuffling through the papers that Charles had had prepared.

"Mr. Sutherland," said Jessica. "I hope Mr. Miller did not handle your investments too. In that case you would be as broke as he is."

"Oh, Mr. Miller is quite solvent."

Elizabeth looked up, startled by Sutherland's words.

"You mean Charles impoverished everyone but himself?"

"Madam," Sutherland responded, "Mr. Miller made the wisest investment he could make. He was a very diversified man and has not suffered as much as others, but his losses in the North West Company were considerable."

"And yourself, Sutherland. How much did you lose? You didn't answer my question," said Jessica, who now thoroughly disliked the man.

The younger man blushed. "Mrs. Brant, I'm an employee. I don't have the kind of capital it takes to invest."

"It's hard to think of you as an employee," responded Elizabeth. "You're more like Mr. Miller's right arm."

"You flatter me, madam," said Sutherland.

"Well, Charles, what is the total?" said Jessica. "Are Eli, Michael, and I all wiped out?"

"I'm afraid so," said Charles casually.

She almost could have sworn he smirked when he spoke.

"It's not quite that bad, Mrs. Brant," Sutherland corrected. "Your house has been sold to the firm. You, of course, may remain by paying rent to Mr. Miller."

Elizabeth held onto Jessica's arm. "You're making my mother pay rent?"

Charles merely shrugged his shoulders and looked away.

"The old man," continued Sutherland, "although it is awkward, he can remain by paying rent to your mother."

"What do you mean by awkward?" Elizabeth asked.

"Well, there could be talk."

"Mr. Sutherland, Eli is ninety-one."

Sutherland looked embarrassed. It was not appropriate to be having this discussion with a lady, especially his employer's wife. Jessica remained in stunned silence.

"Charles, I have no doubt that Michael with his law practice will soon be on his feet again but you cannot expect him to support Elizabeth," said Jessica.

"Don't be upset. I'll take care of everyone. You will have to be frugal but I'll guarantee the necessities," Charles said.

"All of Father Thomas's money gone? All the Nowell estate squandered?"

Charles's temper flared. "Squandered is hardly the right word, Elizabeth."

As quickly as he became heated he again became calm. "And after all I too have suffered severe reverses."

"The family will have to tighten its belt," offered Sutherland. "I've offered Mr. Miller the possibility of lowering my wages. He has been so generous to me over the years and there is only my mother and me to support."

Charles did not volunteer any indication of whether or not he had accepted Sutherland's offer.

There was a knock at the front door. Elizabeth rose to answer.

"Ginny can get that," offered Charles.

"Ginny is obviously sound asleep someplace else," Elizabeth said, rising to open the door. "I was always after you to hire someone else. You could hire two servants for what you pay her."

She opened the door and faced Eli Stoddard and her brother, Michael.

"Elizabeth," said Eli firmly, "we've come to speak with Charles."

"Come in. He's in the parlor."

Eli leaned heavily on his cane and followed Elizabeth through the doorway and into the parlor.

"Charles, Mr. Sutherland," he said, "I've come with my lawyer to learn the full extent of what has happened."

"Mother Brant." Charles ignored Eli. "You must know how sorry I am. The North West Company in which I have invested the family wealth has had a series of unforeseeable losses and has failed. Nothing can be salvaged. Its trade facilities have been turned over to the Hudson's Bay Company."

Stoddard made a strange, nervous sound in his throat.

"It would seem to me, Charles, that it would have been

better to invest in the Hudson's Bay Company," he said finally.

"That is a matter of judgment. Unfortunately, we made the wrong one."

"*You* made the wrong one," interrupted Jessica. "We trusted you as the man of business and you failed us."

Charles sat back in his chair, his face flushed with anger or embarrassment. It was impossible to tell from his demeanor which emotion he suffered.

"Mrs. Brant, I've already told you that your house is safe," offered Sutherland.

"Well, at least we won't be in the streets," said a subdued Eli.

"The rent will be minimal. Just enough to support the company's costs."

"What company? What rent?" said Eli in amazement.

"Why, Mr. Miller's trading company. It has purchased the house from Mrs. Brant's creditors. Mr. Charles has generously decided that she and you, Mr. Stoddard, may remain there. All you'll have to do is pay a minimal fee."

"Well, I'll be damned," said Jessica, finally coming out of her silent shock. "That house is mine. Aaron left it without debt."

"I'm afraid that since you gave Mr. Charles power of attorney and since your losses were so extensive, the liens against the property had to be honored. But we salvaged it so that you will not be disturbed in your last years. Mr. Charles is willing to sign a lifelong lease with you for the house."

"Mr. Charles be damned," said Jessica.

"That a girl," piped up Eli.

"I trusted you, Charles Miller, and you betrayed me," she shouted.

Elizabeth went to her mother's side and took Jessica's hand in her own. Jessica pulled away. Then she saw the hurt look in Elizabeth's eyes and she quickly hugged her adopted daughter. Eli joined the two women.

"I've heard enough," he croaked. His ancient voice had grown weaker with the years. "I believe some nefarious deed has been done here to deprive these women of their patrimony. I smell the unctuous fumes of greed and foul play."

I shall have to use my grandchild's patrimony to salvage all of this:

"You invested in the North West Company too, Eli," said

57

Charles "—I hope you divested." All could see from the look on Eli's face that he had not.

"I will not live in a house that is not mine," chimed in Jessica.

"Mother, you have no other place to live," said Michael.

"You have your law offices. There are several rooms. We'll move in there. Eli and Michael will take one room and Elizabeth and I will take the other."

"Mrs. Brant," said Sutherland, "this is all unnecessary. You can be quite comfortable in your old house. No one wishes you to move. Isn't that right, Mr. Miller?"

Charles still sat slumped in his chair. He did not respond to Sutherland's statement. He merely stared at the group of people on the other side of the room—his family, his wife, his mother-in-law, his wife's foster father, his wife's brother. If only his own brother had been here, the moment would have been complete. But Stephen's money was in his safe. It struck him as amusing that the irresponsible member of the family was the only one who had never turned over his life's savings to the keeping of Charles Miller. He looked over at Sutherland, who sat anticipating his response.

"Let them live wherever they wish," he said wearily.

Elizabeth looked at him in shock.

"Charles, please!"

"What do you want from me?" he said loudly. "This family is a pack of wild mules. Maybe it is all that wild Indian and that wild Hebrew blood. You can never rely on them to do the proper thing. Live in a wigwam for all I care."

He rose from his chair and stormed out of the room.

Jessica turned on her heel. She took Elizabeth's hand and took Eli by the arm. The old man seemed to straighten up. Michael followed behind. They walked down Bay Street arm in arm until they reached the old Brant house.

"Eli, Michael, we must pack," said Jessica. They stood together before the large blue-black door.

"Eli, your pocket knife!"

He handed it to her. She began to work with it on the brass nameplate. The house no longer belonged to the family of Aaron Brant. His name must not be attached to it.

After they had left, Charles returned to the parlor, where Sutherland sat alone. He jumped to his feet when Charles reentered.

"I'm sorry, sir," he said.

"Don't be. They'll all come to their senses."

Sutherland said nothing. He had only meant to apologize for being caught sitting at his employer's writing desk.

"Perhaps we should distribute my brother's money to Elizabeth. It's only fair he should help support her."

Sutherland grew flustered. "I don't think that would be legal, sir. He gave the gold to us for safekeeping."

"I suppose you're right," said Charles, "but it doesn't seem right that my profligate, degenerate brother should be the only one to escape unhurt from this mess."

Elizabeth could not bear to watch her mother pack her life's belongings. She could see the tears welling in Jessica's eyes but the older woman would not let them flow. Elizabeth blamed it all on herself. If she had not fought with Charles he never would have allowed the house to be disposed of and he would have considered her mother's feelings more.

The answer was obvious to her. There was only one way to stop all of this. She had to go back to Charles. She had to accept his slurs with the knowledge that she was innocent. Then her family—her mother, her brother, and old Eli— would be left in peace.

She could not tell Jessica or Eli. They would only try to stop her. And so she simply walked out the front door and back down the street to her own home. She hesitated as she drew near her own walkway. The memory of Charles's accusations burned deep inside her. It pained her still. The venom that poisoned him frightened her. But she had to go forward. She hesitated. Should she ring the bell or just walk in? It was her home even if she had run from it. The door was unlocked. She pushed it open.

"Charles?" she called.

There was no answer.

"Ginny?"

Again no answer.

She walked into the parlor. Charles's writing desk was open. There were papers lying scattered on it. Perhaps Ginny had left a note indicating where she might be, or perhaps Charles had left her a note. She went to the desk in search of the papers. Most were tallies of figures, something to do with this morning's family confrontation, no doubt. But one page struck her eye: the initials S.M., with a large sum of money written next to them. But her eyes widened when she saw the words next to the sum of money. "Dead—C.M. inherits."

The paper fell from her hand. Was Charles so degenerate, so desperate, or so full of hate that he would try to harm his brother? She could not believe the man she loved could kill for money. But for jealousy? She did not know. Nor did she believe she knew who Charles Miller really was. Even her love for him, so unquestioned only days ago, was now clouded. But one thing was clear. Stephen was in danger.

She was startled by what sounded like a stifled scream coming from the wine cellar below the stairs. She was frightened now. She never went down there. Charles always took care of the wine himself. But she could not leave now. She went into the hall. She could hear only the ticking of a wall clock as its pendulum swung back and forth. She opened the cellar door slightly. Now she could hear it. It was like a thud followed by a grunt. She stepped inside the doorway and went down two steps. Her eyes adjusted to the gloom. Charles was bent over a wine barrel and Ginny the maid raised her arm and struck the master a powerful blow on the buttocks with a strap. It sounded more like a crack now than a thud. Elizabeth stepped back in horror and the wooden stair on which she stood creaked.

Ginny looked up and gasped when she saw Elizabeth. She dropped the strap, which landed on the cellar's dirt floor. Charles looked around him in annoyance and he too caught sight of his wife. He stood up and with difficulty tried to conceal his obvious arousal. Ginny panicked and ran up the stairs, past Elizabeth, and out the cellar doorway to the hall. Charles picked up the strap and held it out to Elizabeth.

"Perhaps you want to take her place," he said. "It only works when a slut does it."

Elizabeth gasped. She could not believe Charles was doing this perverted thing. He was mad. He was capable of anything. She did not know this man. She turned and ran, following the route of escape taken by the maid. She had to warn Stephen. He was in grave danger at the hands of a maniac. But how to warn a man in the midst of the woods of Canada. She would find a way even if she had to warn him herself personally.

V

Lachine to Sault Ste. Marie, Summer 1821

Stephen Miller downed another ale. It was the only thing he had in common with his supposed colleagues, the French-speaking voyageurs of the rivers and lakes. He knew their trade. He had trapped on Lake Superior and wintered at Mackinac and traveled beyond Sault Ste. Marie for Mr. Astor, but these men had traveled beyond Grand Portage and some had even been to the Athabasca country. Stephen felt alienated in their presence. He could hold his own in a canoe, but he would be a novice on this journey.

It was ironic, he thought, that to begin his journey to the north and west he had to come east. But the St. Lawrence and Ottawa rivers were the inaugural points for the trek to the west. Neither York nor even Detroit was used any longer. The North West Company stayed clear of the American border in their trail to the northern fur country, where the fattest and thickest beaver furs were to be found.

Stephen had traveled all the way to Quebec City to see his mother before returning to Montreal and Lachine for the start of his new job. He would never forget the visit to the farmhouse where his mother and grandmother lived together. The old lady, her face now a mass of wrinkles, sat on the porch looking across the river at the falls. Neighbors would drop by to chat with Amy and be brought to the porch to pay their obeisance to the great lady—the mother of Monsieur Louis Joseph, the great man of Isle d'Orleans, and the woman who had wiped the brow of the great Montcalm as he lay dying. She was also the wife of the lieutenant who lay buried in the churchyard—Monsieur Louis Joseph's father and some said Montcalm's illegitimate son. No one had the courage, of course, to ask the old lady any questions and so no one was really sure of the answers.

The group of village folk visiting the farm were shocked when Stephen approached Grandmère, impudently kissing her atop her head. They were even more shocked when the mass of wrinkles that was her face broke into a huge smile, revealing her still straight white teeth. Then the Anglais sat and spent the entire afternoon joking and laughing with the old lady.

Later in the day as the sun began to set behind the great hills of Quebec, Louis Joseph, Katherine's son and Stephen's uncle, arrived. He was a huge man with broad shoulders and a narrow waist. But the protruding belly indicated that his skinny, sharp-faced wife had not failed in her duties in the kitchen. He greeted Stephen warmly, embracing the man by kissing him wetly on both cheeks. He gave the same greeting to his mother, who seemed to like it. But when he tried to kiss Amy she pushed him off. He backed off quickly, twisting the ends of his huge gray moustache nervously. Louis Joseph always treated Amy warily.

Amy finished her cooking in the kitchen. She could afford help and Louis Joseph's people took care of the farm and any heavy housework. But Amy enjoyed cooking for Katherine and herself. Having her son with her, even if only for a brief visit, pleased her. She sat down in the straight-back wooden chair next to Katherine's rocker and patted her mother's hand softly.

"Tell me, Stevie," she addressed her son, "what has Charles cooked up for you?"

"It's nothing big, mother, just something I've always wanted to do, to take a canoe into the wilderness, to go where I have never been before and see things few white men have ever seen."

"I hope you come home with your hair," said Katherine, her voice cracking.

Amy was amazed how much Katherine resembled in look and in sound her own Aunt Margaret, and she had now almost equaled her aunt in years.

"Mother," Amy said, "since the war things have been quiet with the Indians. The Iroquois tend their farms and live in houses just like us."

"He's not talking about going to places where you find tame Iroquois."

"You're right, grandmother. I want to meet up with the western tribes. Occasionally when I was at Mackinac I'd meet an Indian from beyond the woodline. He'd tell me about miles and miles of grass with rolling hills that looked like ocean waves. I want to see all of that."

"I'd rather sit here in my rocker," said Katherine. "It's always been the same," she continued, staring off into the distance and addressing no one in particular. "The men always go away and we wait for them. Sometimes they return, sometimes they don't."

Amy, whose bitterness was always near the surface, interrupted her mother.

"You were luckier than most," she said—meaning luckier than she herself had been. "At least one of your men returned to you—my father. And you were with him until the day he died. None of mine ever returned to me."

Louis Joseph looked uncomfortable standing against the porch rail. He knew she would be thinking of Antoine Gingras, her first love, drowned in the St. Charles so many years ago during the American Revolution and drowned because he had come to bring Louis Joseph home. The man needed to change the subject.

"Stephen," he said, "you may run into my scoundrel son, Marc, on the trail. He still leads that life instead of returning home to me and maman."

"Marc and I are old friends, sir. It will be good to see him again."

"Well, I have some messages you must give to the boy. Come into the house and I will write them down for you."

"I have to get on with cleaning up," said Amy as she rose from her straight-back chair and followed the men into the house.

The sun was almost completely gone now, its golden rays piercing the sky as it fell behind the hills of Quebec. But Katherine insisted on remaining in her chair commanding the river. She was alone. Why was she always alone? But deep within her she knew her loneliness was almost over. Her ancient eyes strained toward the great river. There was a tiny speck out there struggling against the current of the channel. It grew larger. It was his canoe. He was coming for her finally. She became confused. Which one would it be? Then she smiled. The same confusion sixty years later. The canoe was larger now as it approached her landing beach. She rose from her chair to get a better view. She felt so much better. So much younger. Her knees no longer sent lightning fire up her legs from her arthritic joints. The sun was so bright, so glaring, it was shining in her eyes, creating a halo effect on the landing beach. Who was it that was coming for her? She squinted. Again her face broke into a smile. It was them, both of them, but not as they were at the end—they were boys. The tall one with the blond unruly hair and the muscles seeming to want to bulge from the confines of his jacket, and the dark quiet one with the lost look on his face and the brilliant blue eyes marred only by the white line that ran through the brow and lid. They laughed and joked with each other as they walked up the beach toward her. She had to go and meet them. She flew from her porch into the golden sunlight to join them. Her joy was complete. Both of them had come for her.

Stephen found her sitting where they had left her. He returned to the house to break the news to his bitter mother.

Stephen's daydreaming was interrupted by the face of Marc Stiegler, his younger cousin. He was bearded and dark-haired, small and wiry like his mother. He resembled his father not at all.

"Is that all you Anglais pigs are good for, sitting on your ass and drinking beer?"

"Marc," Stephen shouted. He rose and grabbed the smaller man in a bear hug. Both of them were laughing.

"Eh, break it off," said Stiegler. "The others will talk. They'll say we can't even wait to be on the trail before we're doing such things. They will send the priest to talk to us."

"Keep me away from priests," said Stephen.

"No fear from this one!" Marc laughed. "Innkeeper!" he yelled, "I'm dying of thirst. Give me a mug of the piss you call beer in this place."

The owner none too graciously slammed a pewter mug on the table, splashing some on Marc's buckskin pants. The voyageur did not notice it.

"I saw your father in Quebec and he had some messages for you," Stephen announced.

"I know," said Marc, his eyes rolling upward as if imploring heaven. "Come home to your dear maman and myself; give up your life of sin and grovel in the ground raising turnips. My father sets great store by turnips. He says plant them and improve next year's crop of everything. Dump cowshit, horseshit, turnipshit on anything and it grows. You'll never get me to go back there. Not ever again."

"You heard then that our grandmother Katherine passed on?"

Marc was silent for a moment. It was clear he had not heard the news. Then he smiled.

"Let's hope that when it is our turn, cousin, we will have lived as long and as good a life as she lived."

An enormous gray-haired, gray-bearded man with arms like small tree trunks came up behind Marc. He was dressed in fringed buckskin pants and a brown woolen shirt. On his head he wore a broad-brimmed felt hat and about his neck he wore a wide orange kerchief. Next to him stood another huge man, a younger version of the older man. The older man spoke to Marc in French and stared at Stephen. Marc responded in French and the large man reached out his hand to Stephen. Stephen offered his and suddenly found himself yanked to his feet. The man's huge mitt was about his bicep. His other hand thumped Stephen on the chest. Then the fist went crashing into his belly and he doubled over in pain. He steeled himself for the next blow, which was sure to come crashing into his exposed face. He looked up when it didn't come. The man had backed off and stood smiling at Stephen and grinning at the younger giant at his side.

Miller made a fist and went toward his assailant.

"No," Marc called out, "Stevie, this is Père André, the priest. Don't hit a priest. It's a sacrilege."

"What the hell was he doing to me?"

"I was testing you," said the priest in heavily accented English. "See if you strong. If you can trail the *canot de maître* up the Ottawa takes muscles. Beyond that takes..." He tapped his skull. "Since you listened to Marc and not strike one with tonsure and bring down the anger of the Lord, I think you have both muscle and brain. But to go beyond Fort William and Rainy Lake, that takes..." He pointed to his crotch. "We see about that later."

Stephen started to laugh. "This is a priest?" he said to Marc.

André did not wait for the voyageur to respond.

"And a damn good one despite the bishop, whose balls dried up under his cassock when he was sixteen." As he spoke his good humor left him and his face became flushed.

His fist came down on the table with all his might and the table gave way with a splintering of wood.

"Here, *mon Père*," said Marc, handing the priest Stephen's ale.

André's face broke into a smile. Marc leaned over to Stephen and whispered, "Never mention the bishop to him. If he brings it up himself give him a drink or run for cover."

"Now, *mon ami*," André said to Stephen, "a friend of skinny Marc is to be mine. A cousin, his blood is my blood. I can be a good friend. With me at your side you'll never have to want for absolution. You steal because you have hunger and André forgives you. You get drunk, I fix that. You fornicate with a squaw and get the pox, I fix up your soul."

"Can't you do anything about the pox?" asked Stephen in a tone of mock surprise.

"Of course," said André, "I cut your cock off." He took an enormous shining knife out of its sheath. "But everybody tells me they prefer me to take care of their souls."

"I understand," said Stephen, "but I'm a Protestant."

"So, I also cut the cocks off Protestants."

"I'm converting," said Stephen.

The three men started to laugh, as did the man who had accompanied André, although it was obvious that he spoke no English and he shared only their mood. Stephen looked quizzically at Marc and then at André's companion. Marc shook his head as if to say, Don't ask who he is.

The innkeeper looked with dismay at his table as he brought Père André his ale.

"Don't fret," said the priest in French. "Put less in the curé's collection plate next Sunday. We all work for the same company." He laughed loudly at the joke and swallowed the ale with one gulp.

"Another ale for Père André," shouted Marc Stiegler.

The priest broke into a song. Soon all the other voyageurs in the tavern took up the melody. Only Stephen remained silent. The French words were a mystery to him but not the rhythm of the song. He could tell it was a paddling song, sung to help fight against white water or to help the paddlers through the monotony of crossing the lake.

Another round of ale was brought. Père André finished this mug in the same fashion he had finished the first—in one giant gulp. He was on his fourth with no effect showing. The young man stayed at his side, ignored. The singing and drinking continued. Tomorrow they would leave civilization and would not return until just before fall. They would make the most of this night.

Stephen rose from the table after his fifth mug of ale. His bladder badly needed emptying.

"No kidneys," shouted Marc over his singing as Stephen signaled to him his call of nature. He went out the back door of the tavern and walked into the alley. The stench told Stephen he had found the right place. He undid the lacings on his leggings and began to let loose a stream of urine that splattered against the wood of the tavern wall. The tension in his bladder had begun to ease when suddenly he sensed somebody behind him. He tried to tuck himself back in. He had always found it difficult to urinate in the presence of another. He started to turn when he felt an arm about his neck and the point of a knife against his ribs. He knew he would be dead in a few seconds. The only thought that crossed his mind was that an alley urinal was a hell of a place to die. Then there was a thud and a moan, and just as suddenly as it appeared, the arm and the knife point disappeared. Stephen turned to see Père André wiping blood from the blade of his wicked knife. Directly behind him was his cousin Marc. At his feet, life draining from his face, was a man Stephen had never seen before.

"You're lucky, *mon ami*," said the priest, "that your cousin and I had the same need to make piss. Where did this scum I have just sent to his just reward in hell's fire come from?" He made the sign of the cross over the assassin. "Why did he want to kill you? You look harmless enough, even if you do piss on your pants."

Stephen looked down at himself. In his hurry to rearrange himself he had wet himself a bit. But he was more concerned about the dead man at his feet.

"Did you flash some gold inside?" Marc asked.

"No," Stephen responded.

"Well, these thieves will take any opportunity," André said.

Then they stepped back into the tavern and joined the party. Someone would notice the corpse the next morning.

They left Lachine at first light. The current of the St. Lawrence was swift here. The men paddled against the current in giant canoes almost forty feet long. Each canoe held ten men and almost four tons of trade goods and people.

Père André was a *gouvernail*, or rudder man, and he stood balanced in the stern of the craft, his nine-foot paddle determining the direction of the canoe. Marc was the *avant*, standing in the bow, searching the water for rocks. His giant paddle could be used to ward off the ripping granite that lurked so frequently just beneath the fragile skin of the birchbark.

Stephen, as a new man, sat in the rear along with seven others. Behind their canoe seven other identical craft followed. The *gouvernail* of the second canoe was Père André's giant companion.

The spring waters of the river were high, and Marc had little work to do. The heavily laden craft moved rapidly against the current. Before long they reached the tip of the island of Montreal and the village of Ste. Ann. Beyond were white water and rapids. Père André steered the craft to the dock on the riverfront. He shouted in French. Marc translated for Stephen.

"We unload here."

"What do you mean? We just got started."

"We unload half. We cannot pass the rapids with a full load. Don't worry, my friend, you'll get used to loading and unloading."

They unloaded and then reloaded the canoes with half the previous goods. Now Marc earned his pay. He fended off rocks and yelled directions to Père André, all the while standing precariously in the bow. The rapids sent waves and spray swirling past the canoe while the craft made slow progress against the current. Stephen was exhausted and tense when they emerged into the smooth waters of the Lake of Two Mountains, a broad area where the Ottawa River joined the St. Lawrence.

He sat back on his haunches. The sweat was pouring off of him. Once again André steered the huge canoe to the shore.

"What now?" Stephen called to Marc.

"What else? We unload and then we return to Ste. Ann. A swift ride through the rapids and then we load everything we left behind and make the trip up the rapids all over again."

By now Stephen was convinced he preferred trapping to the life of a voyageur. He hoisted the ninety-pound packs of trade goods and supplies and one by one laid them at the river's edge. The underbrush hid the packs completely. The woods here, with no civilization about, ran right to the water's edge. Wearily, Stephen returned to the canoe. The second canoe had arrived. The giant *gouvernail* spoke to André and then shouted at his men to unload. The return trip, however, was exciting and fast. They flew through the white water at a speed Stephen found exhilarating. Once they returned to Ste. Ann, however, the long slow journey was renewed.

They camped that first night at the Lake of Two Mountains. Marc was in charge of the food for Père André's crew. He passed Stephen a bowl of beans and salt pork. This would be their diet for almost the whole trip west.

"How do you feel after the first day?"

"Exhausted," was Stephen's response.

"Well, turn in. Don't sit around singing with the others. Tomorrow it gets worse."

Stephen rolled himself into a blanket. His eyelids felt heavy. He stared across the fire at the outlines of his companions. They did not loll about the fire. Several had overturned the great canoes and were examining their delicate hulls for rock tears. Stephen could smell the pungent odor of pitch and he knew that some tears had been discovered and would be instantly repaired.

He watched Père André teasing Marc as his cousin threw wet grass on the fire to make smoke and drive off mosquitoes. Then the priest walked over to the young *gouvernail* of the second canoe. He patted the young man on the knee and offered him some tobacco. The younger man looked up at the priest with pure devotion. Then André walked past him and joined the crew in the canoe repairs. Stephen, with drooping eyes, watched the young man through the smoke's distortion. He wondered where he had seen such a look in a man's eyes before. As he drifted off, he remembered. It had not been in human eyes. It was the look a puppy gives to its master.

The twelve miles of the long Sault were worse than anything Stephen had ever suffered in his life. All he could remember about the trip was unloading and reloading. They poled the craft where the bottom was shallow and firm, and where it was not, they tracked. This last effort meant beaching the canoe. Then the paddlers, all except the bow and stern men, harnessed themselves and dragged the canoes upstream, tripping and falling in the shallow waters along the river's edge. Then Père André would yell again and they would haul the canoes to the shore, sometimes to reembark but more often to unload, trek upriver, and then return with the second half.

At last they were through with the rapids but still the Ottawa flowed past them. For another sixty miles they paddled. Each stroke was exhausting and reminded him of his journey to return Eli to York, except that trip had been in a light Indian canoe, not one carrying a load of eight thousand pounds. Once again Stephen heard the dreaded sound of falling water. As they approached, he realized this would be different. The sound grew louder until it was thunderous and drowned out even Père André's voice. The canoes again put in to shore. Once again the paddlers jumped into knee-deep water but this time Marc and André joined them. The canoes were beached. Stephen collapsed on the riverfront. They had come so far this day.

"Tougher than trapping, eh, my friend?" yelled the priest over Stephen's panting form.

"Off your ass," Marc screamed at him. "We have to portage."

Stephen soon found himself nearly bent in half carrying one hundred and eighty pounds and semirunning up the mile and a third to the top of the falls. He laid down his burden and returned to the shore for another hundred and eighty pounds. This way the entire contents of the canoe was brought above the fall line. Finally, with four men carrying it, the giant canoe, weighing almost six hundred pounds, was hauled to a new landing beach above the falls, reloaded, and relaunched. Once again Stephen paddled on the Ottawa.

Marc smiled back at his cousin.

"This time you're the veteran," said Stephen. "Unloading, poling, trekking, all of them are easier than a portage."

"That's why we do them instead," laughed Stiegler.

The days went by. They left the Ottawa for the Mattawa River and eleven more portages. They entered Trout Lake, Lake Nipissing, and the French River. Finally, through one of the many channels of the French River they entered Georgian Bay.

Now Stephen felt at home, out in the broad expanse of the lakes. It was not very far to his old haunts at Mackinac. They followed the north channel behind Manitoulin Island. The sun was hot in the late afternoon, and several of the paddlers had removed their shirts despite the mosquitoes and flies. By now each man gave off an aroma of sweat and campfires—a

70

natural insect repellent. Marc stood lazily in the bow. The hum of insects was everywhere. The giant firs along the island shore were reflected in the pondlike lake and off in the distance a loon called its lonely cry.

The shout from their left, from the island, startled Stephen. Canoes, small Indian ones, came swiftly across the water toward them.

"Ojibwa," Père André shouted.

Stephen reached for the gun by his side.

"Put it down, Anglais, the Ojibwa greet us in friendship."

Then the priest steered the craft toward the Indian canoes.

"We take ourselves a break tonight, eh, *mon Père?*" the paddler ahead of Stephen yelled.

As soon as the Indians saw the voyageur canoe head toward them, they reversed their craft and headed back toward the island. They entered a small bay. The shores of the bay were dotted with Indian huts. Women and children crowded about the giant canoe as soon as they landed. The voyageurs were surrounded by young women who poked at their trade goods and supplies with curious fingers.

Père André waited for the other canoes to land and then he stripped off his woolen shirt. He pulled out a cloth bag from within the bow of his canoe and removed from it a black cassock, which he threw over his head. A long series of black buttons ran up the front. By leaving all of them in place except the last ten the voyageur leader was quite easily transformed into a curé.

The girls lined up in front of the priest, as did all the voyageurs except Marc and Stephen. Père André joined the hands of one girl with one voyageur, looked up into the deep blue afternoon sky, and closed his eyes. Then he smiled at each couple and spoke in Ojibwa and French to each.

"What the hell is he doing?" asked Stephen.

"Joining up," Marc said. "Aren't you going to get yourself a squaw?"

Before Stephen could answer, a delegation of blanketed and feathered warriors and sachems walked across the village clearing toward the canoes and landing beach.

"Here's where we pay up," said Stiegler. He reached into the canoe and produced a keg of cheap French brandy. Père André, holding a huge wooden crucifix in his hand, walked

71

toward the men. They all bowed their heads before the great chief Jesus and his shaman.

"*Mes enfants*," André called out.

The Indian men knelt for a blessing.

"I have joined your women and my sons together. The great Jesus will bless this union for my brothers. He grants you this gift of some muskets and some brandy."

Great grins crossed the faces of the Ojibwa. One chief reached for the keg that Marc was rolling behind André. The priest grabbed the sachem's forearm.

"First you must confess your sins."

He stood while one by one the warriors spoke to the sachems, who spoke French to the curé. André then made the sign of the cross and the warrior was given a cup of brandy. The wooden bowls into which the brandy was poured were jealously guarded with both hands as the warrior sought the comfort of the council lodge. The lodges of their women were already occupied.

Stephen watched this in amazement.

"I'm no Catholic," he said finally to Marc, "but if he's a priest, I'm the pope."

"Oh, he's a priest. At least he was one. But he's a voyageur first. He converted this tribe to Jesus ten years ago. Every spring and summer they provide us with a night's fun and we bring them trade goods."

"Looks to me like you bring them whiskey."

"We have to bring them whiskey but we also bring them their powder and ball, their sewing needles, their iron pots, their steel knives, all the trade goods that have made their lives bearable. Are you partaking or have you suddenly gotten yourself a wife or a girl you're going to keep faithful to?"

For one fleeting moment the image of Elizabeth flashed through Stephen's mind. He smiled at the irony of it all. He was the one who always took what he wanted. Only he had never wanted anyone. Not for more than a few moments of pleasure at least. Now he wanted. But the one he wanted was beyond his reach—his brother's wife.

"Yeah, I'll partake," he said after some silence.

"Then get yourself joined."

"I'm not going through that farce. It's for you superstitious Catholics."

Stephen walked away from Marc but Stiegler followed him.

"Don't ignore Père André, Stevie. He knows what he is doing."

Stephen saw a young girl standing alone next to the priest.

"Shit," he said under his breath, and walked boldly toward André. He took the girl's hand in his and grabbed André's and put it on top of their joined hands.

"Ah, my Anglais friend has the balls blue from so many days with only a paddle to fondle. Go with God, my son."

Stephen was tempted to respond to the reprobate but realized it would be of little use. Instead he tugged the girl's arm, almost pulling her off her feet.

He checked himself. "I'm sorry," he said. She looked up at him in fright but the tone in his voice caused her to smile.

"Where can we go?"

She merely continued to smile.

He pointed to his crotch and then began to look around as if lost.

She suddenly looked very troubled. She reached out with her hand and patted him.

"Hey, what are you doing?"

On making contact with him she again smiled.

When he realized the source of her relief he started to laugh boisterously.

"Poor kid, you thought I meant I had lost my pecker. No way."

She took the initiative and led him toward a hut on the other side of the village from the landing beach. She pulled back the skin-covered entryway of the hut. Stephen bent down and entered.

The smell struck him first. The aroma of smoke was everywhere. The smell of worked leather and the sweet scent of grease and bear fat. He sniffed at the girl who entered behind him. She smelled the same, smoke and the sweet scent of grease. She imitated him. Her face came only up to his chest level. He could tell that she did not like the scent that came from him.

"Sorry," he said aloud, "but I've done me a powerful lot of sweating with no chance to get rid of the stink."

She motioned him to follow her. They went back outside the hut. Behind them by the shore was an even smaller hut. The beach was itself unsafe for landings for it was strewn with rocks of various sizes. There was smoke rising from the second hut. Stephen had to bend practically in half to enter it. Suddenly he could not see or breathe. The air in the hut was stifling. A fire pit sat in the center of the floor. It was filled with black rocks, some of which actually glowed red from the heating. The girl grabbed at his shirt.

"You can't do it in here," he said uncomprehendingly.

"Hell no, it's too hot."

He removed his shirt anyway. The sweat poured off him. She grabbed next at his leggings. He removed them and stood before her naked. To his chagrin she retreated from the hut. Now he was truly confused. The girl returned with a pot of water. She had removed her deerskin dress while outside. She was difficult to see in the gloom of the hut but Stephen could make out the outline of her firm breasts. She poured the water on the rocks. Instantly the hut was filled with the hissing steam. His face was dripping. His back and chest were covered with droplets of sweat. Even in the twilight of the bathhouse he could see the fresh droplets run down his belly, removing stale sweat, dirt, and grime and leaving a path of white amid the surrounding brown.

He went to her side and placed his hand on her bare rump. She pulled away from him. The steam was so heavy that he could barely catch his breath. The heat had become unbearable. All the pores in his body were open and he was wet from the nape of his neck, where the blond hair stuck like glue to his skin, down to his shins.

Stephen reached for the girl again but this time she raced from the hut. Before Stephen could respond, he heard a splash and a yelp of delight mixed with pain. He stepped out into the late afternoon sun. It blinded him after the gloom of the hut. He saw her standing knee-deep in the lake water. Her arms were wrapped about herself. She shivered. The breeze off the lake made him shiver also, although he knew it was a warm one.

"What the hell," he exclaimed and ran, splashing water in all directions. The girl ducked away from him. He whooped and yelled as the chilly waters of the lake enveloped his body. He dived underwater and then broke through the surface.

"Damn it, that's cold!" He stood and then stumbled as his bare feet gave way against a sharp rock.

The girl giggled, then ran out of the water. Stephen followed her, stumbling and tripping and cursing at the sharpness of the rocks on his feet. She ran toward the first hut. He was aware that other couples were watching them and laughing. He followed her into the first hut again. She sat naked on the floor, wrapped in her blanket. Her small but firm breasts heaved up and down with the exertion of the running.

Stephen smiled at her. He took the blanket she handed to him and wrapped himself in it. The girl stretched her small body along a gray wolfskin. She lay there provocatively. Stephen could feel himself stirring. He opened the blanket for her to see. She smiled at him. Stephen knelt down on the wolfskin. The girl took him into her hands and began to stroke him. It was true what the priest had said. It had been a long time. Her touch turned his chill to fire. Waves of pleasure ascended his spine. When he could bear it no longer he took her by the shoulders and pressed her backward against the floor of the hut. She seemed so small and frail. Her body sank into the fur. He lay on top of her and seemed to engulf her totally. She reached around his back and stroked his buttocks. He entered her and groaned. It had been a long time. Too long.

The stillness of the night was broken only by the buzzing of the mosquitoes and the soft swish of the lake waves against the rocky shore. Stephen's chest rose and fell almost in time with the waves. The moonlight poured through the opening in the roof of the hut and bathed the face of the Ojibwa girl who lay at Stephen's side.

A shadow slithered along the bare ground, then bent in half against the side of the hut. The man who cast it stepped out of the moonlight into the shadow cast by the hut, merging his own image with it. He listened carefully at the entryway. The rhythmic breathing of the woman and the light snoring of the man reassured him. He raised the skin of the entryway with his left hand while his right hand reached for the knife at his side. The blade flashed in the moonlight as it was raised in the air. The man allowed the entryway skin to fall back into place after he stepped into the darkness. He waited motionless as his eyes adjusted to the darkness of the hut. He knelt and began to crawl closer to the dark shapes in front of him. When he reached the feet of the man he rose from his knees to a crouching position, lifted the blade, and plunged it downward.

Stephen Miller awoke sensing danger. It was too late to avoid it. He turned to his side as the blade of the knife, originally aimed at his lungs and heart, tore into his left bicep, piercing it through and penetrating his side, cracking his ribs. Stephen let off a yell of fright and pain. The girl at his side sat bolt upward and began to scream hysterically.

Stephen grabbed the arm of his assailant but his attacker was quicker. He yanked the blade out of his victim and raised it to strike him a second time. Stephen's foot shot out and struck with numbing force into the attacker's belly. Automatically the knife hand went to clutch his gut. Stephen rose unsteadily to his feet. Blood gushed from his arm and flowed freely down his hand, dripping from his fingertips. He lunged forward and grabbed the attacker about the waist with his good hand, pinning his enemy's arms and the knife against his stomach. Then he lurched forward again and upward with all of his strength. His head crashed into the jaw of the assailant, snapping his head backwards. Stephen could feel his opponent's teeth crack and shatter against his scalp. He squeezed tighter and held on. He realized his assailant had gone limp in his grasp. Yet he feared to let go. The girl still screamed, and he could hear stirring in the nearby hut.

Finally the flap of the entryway was yanked back and Marc and Père André entered bearing torches. For the first time Stephen could see that the man he held was an Indian, an Ojibwa by his appearance. But he got only a brief glance. Blood flowed over his eyebrows and into his eyes, blinding him. The girl gasped and André spoke rapidly to her in her own tongue. Stephen released his grasp and the Indian fell to the floor of the hut, still out cold. Marc grabbed Stephen's arm. He pulled his woolen shirt off and tore it. He bound one piece about Stephen's upper arm, tying it tightly to stem the blood that gushed from the ugly knife wound. The bleeding from Stephen's side was slight.

"Who is the man?" André asked the girl in her own language.

She sniffed and looked away.

The priest pulled her to her feet by a handful of her hair.

"Watch it," Stephen cried out sharply, realizing that he was in no shape to defend anyone.

Père André spoke sharply to the girl. She shook her head and her eyes widened with fear.

Finally she spoke. André looked bewildered and turned to Marc and Stephen.

"She says the man is her husband," he said. "But she was

76

joined with Miller for tonight and for the rest of our stay. I don't understand."

The girl looked away in fear. André spoke to her again in a louder voice. Then he slapped her face.

Stephen was about to object but his eyes rolled upward and the blackness descended.

The pounding in his head was incessant and the pain in his arm was a burning throb. He was only partially conscious. Yet the paralysis of his tongue was fading and he knew if only he had the energy and wasn't so tired he could speak. Someone put a cool cloth on his forehead and removed the fetid warm bandage from his arm.

"I'm thirsty," he croaked, but it sounded like someone else speaking. He could not recognize the sound of his own voice.

"Some rum," someone said off in the fog beyond his eyes. "It will make him pee."

He recognized the voice of the priest.

"Just keep hot cloths on the wound and let him sip some lake water. It's more than cool enough."

He slipped back into the dusk of semiconsciousness. He seemed to be drifting. Once again he felt rough hands change the bandage. He did not know how much time had passed, but he was vaguely aware that it was night because somewhere behind his head a fire burned. He could feel the warmth of it and he could smell the smoke. There was a rasping sound in his ear. He was terrified that the rasping was in his own chest. He must be filling with fluid. He had once heard of someone drowning in his own fluid. The thought terrified him. Now it was happening to him. He struggled; maybe if he could sit up it would be better. But his limbs wouldn't move. He felt panic growing inside him. It was like being buried alive. He had to force himself to steady his nerves. The effort cleared his mind. He held his breath as he struggled to raise up on his right elbow. The pain shot through his whole body. He exhaled with a gasp and collapsed back again. He felt himself overcome with lethargy. But now he was more alert. The rasping sound continued. He held his breath and still it went on. He listened more carefully, recognizing the sound at last. It was the snore of his cousin Marc Stiegler. He smiled. He wanted to laugh at his own panic but he was too exhausted.

*   *   *

77

Père André stormed into the hut before Stephen or Marc was fully awake. The sun was up and sent shimmering waves along the top of the surface of Georgian Bay.

"Stiegler, you lump of moose dung. How long do you plan to lay on your ass pulling your prick?"

Marc raised his head and studied the priest.

"I have learned all my morning habits from you, Monseigneur."

André looked over quickly at Stephen and saw he was conscious.

"How are you feeling?" he asked, the mocking tone replaced by one of concern.

"Weak," answered Stephen. "And confused. What happened to me and why?"

"That's what we're about to discover. Can you stand, Miller?"

Marc reached under Stephen's right arm and began to haul him to his feet. He felt woozy. He stumbled but did not fall. His arm throbbed but the real pain shot from his cracked ribs to his shoulder. They walked out into the bright morning sunlight. Stephen followed Père André and Marc across the open village square to a hut larger than the others. Women and children stared at him and whispered to each other. They were no longer friendly, as they had been yesterday.

He followed the two other men into the hut. Once his eyes adjusted he could see a number of men sitting around a small fire. The hut was hot and the smell of unwashed bodies mixed with the pungent aroma of stale tobacco. Stephen's uneasy stomach rumbled. He felt nauseous and dizzy and wanted only to be free to go someplace else.

Père André found a place in the circle about the fire for the three of them. The men around the circle sat impassively, their expressions unreadable. Only occasionally did one move to scratch a groin or an armpit. Directly across from Stephen sat a large man. On his head a buffalo helmet with wide pointed horns sat precariously. He wore the rest of the buffalo as a robe over his shoulders. He was sweating and Stephen was sure he was uncomfortable. The regalia had to be a symbol of authority. His little acquaintance with Indians in the trapping he had done before the war had convinced him that they rarely discomforted themselves except for important reasons. He must be the boss, Stephen thought.

As if reading his mind, Buffalo Head began to speak in a

throaty, choppy language. At one point he raised his hand and the girl Stephen had slept with was led by two warriors into the hut. She was made to sit next to Buffalo Head. Finally the entryway was shoved aside again. Stephen's assailant, his eyes blazing in defiance and his head held high as if to ignore what must have been a throbbing pain in his mouth, stepped into the gloom. He looked about him, sneered when he saw Stephen, and sat next to an old man who made room for him and patted him on the shoulder.

Père André rose and requested permission to speak.

"I come to the council," he said in his French-accented Ojibwa, "to seek the reason why a warrior of this village would attack one of my men. We have come here summer after summer. We have entered the joining and our blood has mixed with yours. Why would a son of the Ojibwa attack a son of the company like a snake in the middle of the night? Is this what has befallen a great people that they now ape the behavior of the Sioux?"

There were murmurs throughout the crowd. The priest had given mortal insult comparing the Ojibwa to their hated enemy to the west.

The chief shook his horned head. It was clear he was angry and embarrassed at the same time.

He spoke rapidly to the girl. She lowered her eyes and looked away. Then he questioned the assailant. The young man almost spat out his words.

Père André leaned over to Stephen. "We have a problem. It seems the girl and boy were recently married. The boy was not here when we arrived. The girl didn't have his okay for the joining. She did it on her own. The boy has received no gifts."

The chief rose and smiled maliciously at André.

"It's a matter for our people," he said to the priest. "The joining was never there in the first place so it was not broken."

The young warrior gave a yelp at the chief's words. He rose quickly from his place, drew his knife from its sheath, and darted toward the woman. The blade flashed and the girl screamed. With quick upward strokes he sliced the nostrils and tip of her nose from her face. Blood spurted from the wound onto her mouth and chin. The girl ran screaming from the council hut. She was forever branded an adulteress among the Ojibwa.

"Jesus," said Stephen.

"Sit still," warned André. "Her husband can cut the balls off a man too, if the council has a mind."

Stephen stared at the knife-wielder. From the wild look in his eyes he knew André had expressed the young man's most ardent wish.

Buffalo Head spoke again and pointed toward Stephen's crotch.

André stood in outrage. "The man joined in good faith. I joined him. The only thing he owes the husband is whiskey."

Buffalo Head cackled and looked at the assailant. The whole council followed his example.

The young man could not afford to lose face. Among his people his honor had been restored by the mutilation of his woman. If he should refuse the white man's offer of a payment of whiskey they would question his motive. No Ojibwa would turn down a gift of whiskey, even from one who had slept illicitly with his wife. To turn it down would be a suspicious act and he had been warned to give rise to no suspicion.

He smiled at Stephen and held out his hand the way a white man did.

Stephen looked away in disgust.

"Take his hand," said André, "and count yourself and your future descendants lucky that he offered it. For a moment I thought we would all die here defending your testicles."

Stephen was contemptuous of the young Indian. He had been rough with women in his life but he had never harmed one. He realized that the priest was right, however. With a sense of some loathing he took the Indian's hand and shook it. He wondered where an Ojibwa would learn that gesture.

He rose and followed Marc and Père André out into the sunlight. There was no sign of the girl. Stephen wanted to find her, to help her.

"Forget it," warned Marc, "and don't believe that bullshit that His Eminence was giving off about dying to save your balls. If it became a choice between the trade goods for the company and you, he would have watched you roast on a spit with a stick up your ass and would have offered to help turn you over."

"You think so little of me, my son," quipped André. "But you know me well. Tell the crews to get ready to depart," he whispered to Marc.

"So soon?" answered Stiegler. "We usually stay a week."

80

"We have trouble here, lad. The Ojibwa who cut his wife's nose hasn't a jealous bone in his body. Not even whiskey would have calmed him. He was out for pure murder. Assassination. Somebody paid that boy to kill you, Miller, and I believe he will kill us all to get at you. By cutting her nose he has broken all ties with his wife. She's ruined. No one else will have her now. It would have been sufficient to send her back to her father and brothers. Now they want our blood and all the Ojibwa will join in just for the sport of it."

"The handshake puzzled me," offered Stephen.

"You noted it. There's hope for you yet," said André. "Right now the girl's family is furious with him. If I have this figured out, he'll turn them against us and they'll seek their revenge against all of us."

"How come you don't just turn me over to them?"

"Because, *mon ami*, you are a worker for the company and I need your muscle to take these goods to Fort William. I don't surrender any company worker unless I have to."

Marc stared at André. "You have before."

The priest laughed. "Let's just say I want to save Miller from assassins once again. It's becoming a habit with me. Besides, if they only wanted Miller—" He shrugged his shoulders. "But they will not be satisfied with just him."

Fog had fallen on the lake shortly after sunset. Banks of it had rolled down from the north coast from Lake Superior and enveloped Manitoulin Island. Stephen could not see beyond the reach of his arm. He lay beside his canoe, his boatmates at his side. André passed the word from voyageur to voyageur. The canoes were eased into the waters of the bay. Marc whispered to his crew to slip over the sides onto the floor of the craft. Sound would travel a great distance in the fog and they were convinced that their lives and their livelihood depended on leaving this village unseen.

André was the last to enter the canoe. He stood in the stern, and as Stephen and his companions dipped their paddles silently, he placed his long paddle at an angle and sent the craft swiftly out to the open waters of Georgian Bay. The only sound was the ripple of the water against the sides of the canoe and the slight gurgle made by the paddle in the water. André guided the way by instinct. He could see nothing, not even the first of the six canoes that followed his. Stephen could not paddle because of the wound in his arm.

His place in the canoe had been taken by another and he had been seated directly in front of Père André. The few fires that still remained in the village had disappeared after two paddle strokes. The canoe moved rapidly through the grayness. André could not know where he was going, Stephen thought. Yet the craft continued to move forward. No rocks appeared suddenly out of the gloom. Off to the right he heard a yell. André whispered a halt, and as word crept to the front of the craft the paddles were pulled in. They waited. A musket was fired and there was more yelling.

"Our friends have discovered our departure. If the fog lifts they will be on us. Now paddle, you bastards," he whispered.

The canoe surged ahead into the night. They paddled all night. They saw no signs of their companions nor did they hear anything more of the Ojibwa. With uncanny accuracy André steered the craft through the north channel toward Sault Ste. Marie and Lake Superior, where they were to rendezvous.

Toward morning Stephen noticed stars. He was surrounded by fog but above his head the sky was cloudless. With the sun's rising, the fog would burn off and they would see their destination. In turn they would become obvious to any pursuers.

Stephen pointed to the break in the fog above him. André merely nodded and continued to stare ahead, watching almost as if his gaze could penetrate the mist that covered the water's surface. The sky behind them grew brighter with each passing minute. Then the red rays of the sun rose above the eastern horizon and the fog turned a dirty gray. A breeze came up from the rear, scattering the mist into swirling billows of clouds. André turned to look back.

"Damn," he said.

"What is it?" asked Stephen.

"The bastards, they're like bats. They have followed us without seeing us."

Marc turned from the bow and called out to the others.

"The Ojibwa are behind us. About twenty-five small canoes. The whole bloody village is chasing us. One of the voyageur canoes is in sight behind us."

"Break out the sail," André ordered.

Several of the paddlers raised the great pole off the bottom of the craft and placed it in its notch. A square sail was wrapped about the pole. With the wind coming from the rear, they could run with it, skimming the surface of the lake. The Indians would be left far behind. André climbed over several companions and began to haul on the line that raised the sail. The wind caught the canvas and the canoe's speed increased as it surged forward.

The men in the canoe cheered and brought their paddles aboard. They were safe now. The voyageurs made obscene gestures toward the Indians and hooted in derision as their craft raced before the wind. But their elation was soon crushed. André, using his giant paddle, turned the craft about. The wind had blown off the fog and now all could see the length of the channel. Their sister craft lay dead in the water. Its mast, long unused, had snapped suddenly, and the sail had plunged into the lake, where it acted like a drag anchor. The Indian canoes were converging on it.

"Piss on them," yelled Marc. "They should have taken better care of their equipment."

"That's a company canoe, and those are our compatriots," said André. "We go to their rescue. If any man hangs back I'll skin his ass with a bullwhip. Let's move."

Stephen knew. They all knew who the *gouvernail* of the second craft must be. The ten canoe men dipped their paddles into the water in unison and the craft retraced its course back toward the Indians.

Stephen raised his musket in his aching arms. He could not paddle but he was determined he would take some braves with him.

The Indians closed quickly on the crippled voyageur canoe. Marc, standing in the bow, yelled at the other voyageurs.

"Cut away the mast, and start paddling."

The *gouvernail* of the crippled vessel climbed over his men, wood ax in hand, and began to chop. But suddenly, with his hand high in the air to bring down a blow on the offending mast, he seemed to crumple and fall. He stood looking dumbly at the head of an arrow that penetrated his back and came out between his ribs. He sagged at the knees and fell head first into the lake. Stephen heard a moan escape from André's lips. The first Indian canoe came gliding up to the company men. A musket was fired and the Indian canoe tipped, dumping the men into the freezing waters of the North Channel. Voyageurs cheered but a second and third canoe converged on them. Men rose in the great trade canoe to fend off the attackers. Several Indians leapt from their fragile craft into the company craft.

Stephen could hear war yells and screams. An Indian he recognized as the old man Buffalo Head had retrieved the *gouvernail's* body from the water and was quietly sitting in the stern of his craft, slicing the scalp from the dead man. Stephen aimed his musket and fired. The knife blade flew from the old Indian's hands as he grabbed his stomach with both hands. He fell backward and Stephen saw no more of him.

André's canoe was coming on swiftly now. In a minute it would be at the scene of the battle. But would a minute be in time to save their companions?

The Indians' canoes now completely surrounded the stricken voyageurs. Tomahawks and knives flashed in the early morning sunlight. Stephen had reloaded. He was the only one who could fire. His companions were feverishly paddling to cover the diminishing distance.

Again Miller fired. An Ojibwa warrior screamed and fell out of the voyageur canoe and into the lake. Now—too late—the Indians' attention was drawn toward these new attackers. André's speeding canoe was almost on top of them. The bow of the giant four-ton craft crashed into the fragile Indian war canoes and crushed them. Bodies went flying in all directions. Now it was André's men whose knives flashed.

Stephen saw the man who had nearly killed him and had sliced the nose from his wife's face. He was standing in the rear of the attacked voyageur canoe. His face was painted black and his chest and his hands were covered with gore. Stephen leapt from his place and landed on his hands and knees in the rocking, stricken craft. He kicked aside a tomahawk wielded by an Indian who lay wounded in the bottom of the canoe. He charged toward the rear and struck his attacker square in the belly with his head. The two men went tumbling from the craft into the water. The chill was numbing but Stephen reached for his enemy and grabbed his shoulder. He dived under water, dragging his assailant with him. His arm no longer hurt him. His anger, his need for revenge, and the numbing waters had stilled the pain. He reached to his side and pulled his knife from its sheath. The force of the water prevented a killing thrust. Instead he hugged his enemy's body close to his own. With constant pressure, he pressed the needlelike point of the knife through the Indian's

84

ribs, inexorably searching for his heart. The man struggled desperately to get away but Stephen held and pushed until he felt his blade penetrate the throbbing muscle in the man's chest. Then the Indian ceased struggling.

Stephen's lungs were about ready to burst when he broke the water's surface. There were bodies floating everywhere. To his left he saw André's canoe, the *gouvernail* standing proudly in the stern. The Indians had been broken. Those canoes that could escape could be seen scurrying back in the direction of Manitoulin Island.

They camped that night on the northside mainland. All the bodies that could be recovered from the water had been placed in the canoes and brought to shore. Now they lay stretched out, covered by canvas before open graves. Six men had fallen victim to the Ojibwa. Four bodies had been recovered.

André stood before the graves. His shoulders were stooped. His face had a gray cast to it and he looked suddenly older. Stephen and Marc lifted the body of the young *gouvernail*. Canvas covered his head, hiding the grotesque wound of an uncompleted scalping. Stephen felt some satisfaction that he had cut short the career of old Buffalo Head just as he was creating that wound.

The weight of the dead man and the depression after the excitement of battle was over caused Stephen's arm to throb with a burning pain. He nearly dropped his burden, but Marc steadied it. Slowly they lowered the body into the shallow grave. One by one the three others were also placed in their final beds.

André stood watching mutely. Tears flowed down his rough cheeks and disappeared into his gray-black beard.

"O God," he said softly, "receive our children into your comfort. Let them not be blamed for the sins of their fathers but be received into paradise. Mother Mary, take these children to your breast and, Blessed Jude, intercede for thy fallen and broken servant. Amen."

The voyageurs crossed themselves and began to shovel dirt into the graves. When they finished, identical wooden crosses were hammered into the soft dirt at the head of each gravesite.

André turned away and walked to the lakeshore. Stephen followed him with his eyes. The night was still. The only sound was the gentle lapping of the water against the rocks. The night's silence was then pierced with a shout of anguish.

Stephen, forgetting his wound, grabbed for his musket. The pain shot up his arm and he dropped the gun. Marc grabbed Stephen's shoulder.

"It's only André. Let him be in peace. He has much anguish."

"Were they—?" He was too embarrassed to finish the question.

Marc looked at him in surprise. "Is that what you thought? Of course not. What do you think André is? He's a priest. No, Mario the *gouvernail* was his son."

Stephen had never thought of that obvious relationship. It would explain their similar looks. He sat down by the fire, feeling guilty that he could have thought so badly of the priest and his dead son. Only after some moments did the irony of Marc's statement dawn on him. Priests, from all he knew about them, which was little enough, were supposed to be celibate. And they were certainly not supposed to have sons. The meaning of André's prayer became clearer to him.

André came back from the shadows and entered the light of the campfire after an hour. He walked to where Stephen sat. He collapsed with a sigh onto the ground next to Miller. He placed his hand on Stephen's shoulder.

"*Mon ami*, I believe I must give thanks to you for Mario's sake."

Stephen looked at André quizzically. "You don't have to thank me. I did nothing." He did not know what more to say. The priest's son was dead and there was little anyone could have done to save him.

"I mean when you got the Ojibwa chief and saved him from being scalped."

Stephen saw little comfort in the deed, but it was obvious the priest did.

"The Ojibwa and Sioux and other tribes believe that by mutilating a body they deprive its spirit of its parts in the hereafter. They will go to any lengths to recover the bodies of their dead and save them from mutilation. I would not want the lad to enter heaven without his hair. He had a good head of it, just like me."

Again the priest's eyes filled. Stephen found it strange that the priest shared the Ojibwas' belief.

"Because you do me this favor, I do one for you," André said. "Someone wants you dead. I think you must be a rich man. Assassins kill either for ideas or for money. The type that came after you were paid killers."

Stephen looked at the priest in astonishment.

"All my money is in the hands of my brother, my twin brother."

Now it was the priest's turn to look shocked. He crossed himself. "Either you have done a great harm to him or he is a very evil man."

"Charles has no reason to hate me. Although he is not my favorite relative, he's not evil either."

"I pity you, boy," the older man said. "I know of your brother. He is a director of the company and a very rich man. Greed can't be his motive. It must be hate. What have you done to him that he could hate you so?"

"I've done nothing. We took different sides in the war but that was years ago. If he'd wanted to kill me for that he wouldn't have waited till now."

The priest rose to his feet, leaning as he did on Stephen's shoulder for support.

"All I say to you now, my son," he flinched at the word *son*, "is watch your back. Even here, especially here, in the wilderness."

As André left the fire, Stephen's eyes fixed on a small bundle the priest had left behind. He unwrapped the leather strings that bound it together and stared in horror at the severed genitals of a male Indian. He had no doubt in his mind that old Buffalo Head had entered the happy hunting ground without any chance of partaking in the bliss of lovemaking.

VI

Fort William, Summer 1821

From Sault Ste. Marie, the canoes set out together across the giant inland sea of Lake Superior. Most often, when the wind was right, they raised their sails, but they never ventured far from the shoreline. On two occasions, dense white fogs descended and they were forced to paddle slowly, calling out to each other and traveling blind.

They made frequent stops along the rugged north shore of the lake. They rode out sudden squalls within the protective arms of the deep bays that dotted the rocky shore. Finally, three hundred miles from Sault Ste. Marie, they arrived at their destination, Fort William, at the mouth of the Kaministikwia River.

Stephen was lounging in the *canot de maître,* eating his ration of salt pork, when Marc, from his vantage point in the bow, let out with a war whoop as soon as the wooden-palisaded fort appeared on the horizon in front of him.

Stephen looked in vain from his spot in the rear.

"Don't worry," said Père André. "It is there, my friend. You must accept it like an act of faith. Unfortunately the sail narrows our vision as our weak intellects block a true understanding of the mysteries of faith. We will know them only when we attain heaven."

"I don't want to go to heaven, my good Father," said Stephen with some sarcasm. "I'm willing to settle for Fort William."

"After all we have been through," laughed the priest, "Fort William will seem like heaven."

The small brass cannon mounted on the walls of the fort blasted a greeting to the six giant canoes. Several of the voyageurs responded with shouts.

André gave the word to lower the sail. The voyageurs

broke out their paddles and in unison dipped them into the lake. They crested the long Lake Superior swells and went dashing toward the shore. At the last moment André twisted the giant paddle and the canoes moved into the quiet waters of the Kaministikwia, where the landing beach was located. With one giant surge the canoe ground to a halt, its bottom scraping against the sand. The voyageurs shouted and jumped out. The gates of the fort swung open and men and Indian women came running down. The voyageurs grabbed men and women alike in their arms and danced, while planting kisses on every available face. Stephen hung back a bit. Marc hauled a squaw by the arm and threw her into Stephen's arms. The woman smiled at him. She was enormously fat and Stephen's arms could not reach about her waist.

Père André came up behind them smiling.

"Shall I join you?" he asked with a boisterous shout.

Stephen pulled away from the squaw in fear that she might understand English or French. Both Marc and André laughed.

"Come, cousin," said Marc. "After all, it's been six weeks with only your hand for a companion. Even this large one must look good after six weeks."

"You forget the Ojibwa."

Almost instantly the joy of the moment was soured. A shadow seemed to pass across André's face. Both Marc and Stephen noticed it.

"I'm sorry," said Stephen. "I forgot about your loss there, my friend."

"There is no reason why you should not forget," said André. "Come, let us go to the fort and get drunk."

The one room in the company trading store served also as the saloon. The voyageurs crowded into it to obtain whiskey, brandy, and rum. There would be no one sober at Fort William this night. Stephen sat at a makeshift barrel-and-board table with his crewmates. Several of them had already passed out drunk on the gray-boarded floor of the store.

The storekeeper, a small man with the sharp features of the French but the swarthy complexion of the natives, clearly a half-breed, came over to Père André carrying a pitcher of ale.

"You'll need something to wash down your whiskey," he said in a strongly accented French that even Marc could not understand.

"Speak English," yelled André, "so my friend can understand."

"But I don't speak English, Father," said the storekeeper.

"No matter, you don't speak French either." The priest broke into a loud guffaw, grossly enjoying his joke at the storekeeper's expense.

"Never mind, Georges," André continued, clapping the storekeeper on the shoulder. "What is the word from the pemmican-eaters from the north? When will they rendezvous with us pork-eaters from Montreal?"

"There's been no word from Rainy Lake, Father. I'll bet it is those Scotsmen at the Red River. We company men have always said there would be trouble if farmers came into the northwest with their filthy sheep and cattle. It's buffalo country, not fur country."

"Lord Selkirk's Scotsmen have been joined by many of your Métis people, Georges."

"Not as sodbusters, Father. We are hunters."

"And you supply them with meat, without which the farmers would have to pack in their wretched bagpipes and go home."

"No doubt, Father, but the fact remains that the company men from Fort Chipewyan should be at the rendezvous spot at Rainy Lake and there is no sign of them."

The priest was quiet. "Can you have the small *canot du nord* ready for us?"

"We have seven."

"Tomorrow then, my friend." André switched to English for Stephen's benefit. "Tomorrow we trek to meet our comrades."

Pack horses carried the trade goods beyond the falls of the Kaministikwia where the smaller seven-man canoes were beached on the riverfront. Stephen had thought his journey over at Fort William, but he now found himself in the middle of another two-hundred-mile trip to where the waters flowed north. When they finally reached the land where the waters drained into Hudson Bay, the swift current carried them rapidly northward to Rainy Lake and the rendezvous camp. But there was no one to greet them. The northern comrades had not yet arrived.

André ordered his crews ashore and unloaded his canoes. The last of the salt pork they had brought from Lachine was devoured. There would be supplies for their return journey at Fort William. Fires were lighted in the night.

Stephen found Marc eating his dinner and sat beside him.

"What is the concern?" he asked.

"It's the farmers on the Red River. They have been inter-
fering with the trade for the past decade now, but the
northern canoes have never been this late before. They will
have a hell of a trek getting back to Athabasca and Fort
Chipewyan before the snows come. André used to work the
northern route. He has told me of those who failed to make it
back, frozen in the middle of Isle à la Crosse. If the Scots
interfere, it will mean a war, company men against farmers."

"Who's in charge out here? How can you have a war?
Governments have wars."

"No one's in charge out here. Oh, technically this is
Rupert's Land, the private preserve of the Hudson's Bay
Company, but Lord Selkirk, a Scottish popinjay, director of
the company, got himself a land grant and has brought his
bastards and his bastards' bastards over here to destroy the
trade and our way of life. Well, we North West Company
men don't recognize the Selkirkers' rights to the Red River
and their Fort Douglas. And we will not stand for their
interference. Some seasons ago they burned Fort Gibraltar,
our post on the Red River. We fought them with the help of
the Métis and killed twenty of them and chased their families
out of the Red River. But then Selkirk himself arrived on the
scene with reinforcements and brought them all back. Looks
like we're going to have to do it all over again. This is
voyageur country. It is not for farming. Everyone knows the
west and north here are not for farming. Not even a tree will
grow—just grass, miles and miles of grass and buffalo. It isn't
fit even for turnips. I didn't run away from the bloody turnips
on Isle d'Orleans only to meet up with them on the Winnipeg."

Stephen laughed. "You really don't like turnips."

"I hate the damned things."

Marc was about to launch into his antiturnip diatribe when
the silence of the camp was shattered by a musket from the
lake.

André ran to the shoreline and called out to the others in
French.

"It's them, the northern men, they've made it at last. Now
we can switch canoes and begin the journey home."

The northern canoes, carrying three thousand pounds of
fur each, landed on the lakeshore. The senior *gouvernail* was
a younger man about twenty-five bearing the unlikely name
of Christopher Douglas. Unlikely because he was clearly
Métis and spoke Cree as his first language and French as his

second. He was dark-complexioned with black hair and brown eyes, so brown they looked black. The man's eyes were the dominant feature of his face. As he entered the camp, arm and arm with Père André, the firelight struck his face and his eyes seemed to glow red.

The northerners greeted their southern counterparts affectionately as *mangeurs de lard*—pork-eaters. The northerners, who sustained themselves on pemmican, dried buffalo meat mixed with fat and Saskatoon berries, or on rubbaboo, a pemmican soup, were known as pemmican-eaters. It was clear that they regarded the southerners as softer and weaker men than themselves, even if only slightly so.

André introduced each of his men to Christopher Douglas, saving the crew of his own canoe for last. Marc knew the Métis already. Stephen shook his hand when he was offered it.

"And this is my friend Stephen Miller, the worst crewman in the lead canoe," said the priest, "but still better than any Anglais alive."

"I believe an Anglais can be good as a paddler only because you say so and you have received holy orders at the hand of the bishop."

Marc and Stephen's eyes both shot instantly to André's face. The hated bishop had been mentioned. To their amazement André only smiled.

"Miller," said Douglas in heavily accented English, "welcome to a very exclusive club. You must be very good if Père André rates you ahead of even one of his other crewmen in the other canoes."

Stephen smiled and acknowledged the compliment.

André took Douglas by the shoulders and again steered him to where he had set up his own bedding. They were soon deep in conversation. Stephen and Marc continued eating. Most of the northerners were eating pemmican and enjoying the trade brandy brought out from Fort William especially for the rendezvous. They broke into a paddling song, which everyone sang even while clenching pipes in their teeth.

"Something is wrong," warned Marc, staring at André and Christopher Douglas, who sat huddled in deep conversation. "Père André is so troubled about something that he failed even to hear the word *bishop*. Those two men are rivals. They respect each other for sure, but consult with each other? Never."

93

"Well, cousin," said Stephen, "if we were meant to know, we will. If not, why worry? I'm off to sleep. Tomorrow it's back to Fort William with the furs."

The landing beach at Fort William was again crowded with seven *canot du nord*, returning from Rainy Lake filled with beaver pelts, as well as the six surviving *canot de maître*. The voyageurs quickly transferred the pelts into the larger canoes and filled the empty space with provisions to get them to Sault Ste. Marie, where more salt pork and some wild rice awaited them.

Stephen worked in the late summer sun. The pelts were already bound in ninety-pound packs. With one great heave they could be hauled out of the northern canoes and placed in the larger lake-going vessels. Stephen was anxious to get the work done so they could get started on the long journey back to Montreal before the cold weather and ice began to block the waterways.

Stephen bent down to pick another bundle of pelts. He saw André's legs on the other side of the canoe. He glanced up and saw a troubled look on the priest's face.

"Anglais, come with me."

Stephen set the load down and followed the priest toward the fort and through the gates. André entered the storekeeper's saloon. Stephen followed him and stood dead in his tracks. Sitting at the table drinking a mug of steaming coffee was his brother's wife, Elizabeth.

"Liz, how in God's name?" He looked over questioningly at the priest.

"Come sit," André said. "Storekeeper, two more mugs of coffee."

Stephen fell into the chair and took Elizabeth's hand in his.

Elizabeth was determined she would not cry. She barely recognized Stephen. He was so hairy and so dirty. The smell of sweat and grease that came from his clothing was almost overwhelming. But when his look of bewilderment gave way to his flashing white smile of recognition, her resolve almost collapsed.

"Everything has gone wrong at home," she said, after sighing deeply to gain control of her emotions. "Charles has lost a fortune in investments. The entire family wealth is gone. He invested it all in the North West Company and the company has folded. Its assets are now in the hands of the

94

Hudson's Bay Company. My mother, Eli, and Michael are all living in Michael's law offices. Charles has gone mad. He has accused me—" She looked at André and stopped.

"Madam, you may make free to talk." He exaggerated both his bad accent and his bad grammar. "I be a Frenchman who speaks *anglais* bad and I be a priest. Every word you speak I already hear before."

She smiled, but she wished André would leave them alone. She wanted to speak to Stephen. She decided to ignore the priest.

"Stephen, I am pregnant and Charles claims to be sterile. He accused you and me of . . ."

"Now that is a sin I've heard of," interrupted André. "I can give you absolution."

Stephen put his hand on André's. "Please, friend."

"Anglais, I do not sit here because I have become an old gossip. What the lady says is known to me already. It is of great importance to both you and me. I make jokes because the moment is tense."

Elizabeth decided to push ahead. "He's gone absolutely mad, Stephen. Charles, that is. I think he plans to have you killed in order to get his hands on the money you left with him."

"Why kill Stephen," asked André, "when your husband already has the money? Why not just say it was lost like the rest."

"I never invested my gold. I put it in his safe and he gave me a receipt. And I gave the receipt to my mother in Quebec City before I left."

André whistled softly. "Now I begin to understand these attempts to kill you, Englishman. I too have received instructions. They were waiting for me here at Fort William with the storekeeper when we arrived back today. They come by the *canot bâtard*—the express canoe. The message from the North West Company says you are an agent from the Hudson's Bay Company and that I was to see that you did not survive the journey home."

Stephen suppressed his shock and smiled at his friend.

"I thought you were a good company man. Why are you telling me this?"

"If the lady is correct, then there is no more company. If you are an agent of the Hudson's Bay Company, then I may be working for you."

He said no more, but Stephen felt that André's loyalty to the company would have fallen before his debt of gratitude to Stephen.

"Elizabeth." Stephen turned anxiously to the woman. "How did you get into the middle of the wilderness?"

"I am still Mrs. Charles Miller. I came by Miller company ships to Detroit and then to Sault Ste. Marie and then by express canoe to Fort William. I kept one step ahead of my husband's messages to seize me and send me back."

"I think, madam, your brother-in-law is in great danger. Chris Douglas and I spoke of the rumors the Hudson's Bay people were spreading. The company is no more. We have arranged another rendezvous, this time at Grand Portage on the American side of the border. We will sell our furs to the Americans and then I offer my services to Mr. Astor's company. I will not work with the men of the Hudson's Bay Company. You and your cousin Marc can join me. I will split some of my share with you."

Stephen looked at Elizabeth. The expression of fear that crossed her face as André spoke distressed him.

"I have other responsibilities, André. I think I shall have to return to York and claim what is rightfully mine."

"Don't be a fool," retorted the priest. "You escaped assassination twice. But both times you were in the company of an entire group of voyageurs. And you were lucky to escape. You will never make it back to York alive. Every post on the lakes will be looking for you and hired assassins will follow your trail. You will never get home alive."

"You heard the lady: she's pregnant. I simply can't run away to the wilderness like you can."

"Ah, so you are the father."

"I am not."

"Eh, the English, so gallant, they do the right thing even when it is not the right thing."

He rose from the table and went to confer with the storekeeper.

"I won't go back to him, Stephen," Elizabeth said. "I had hoped he would relent with my mother and Eli if I went back to him. But I can't tell you what I discovered about him. When I realized he'd decided to kill you, I had to come to you. Michael can take care of mother and Eli, but you had no way of knowing what he planned for you."

Stephen played absentmindedly with his coffee mug.

"I can't bring myself to believe that Charles would kill me."

96

"Something has happened to him, Stephen," she said. "He is not the same man I fell in love with. That man was rigid and frequently ungenerous of spirit, but he was a noble man. Charles is not noble any longer. I won't let you go back there. Now that I've warned you, I can go back myself. He won't harm me."

He looked into her face, the face that had haunted his dreams since that night in the kitchen at Amherstburg. The lips that he had wanted to kiss that night in the woods on the way to Burlington. The body he had wanted to possess.

"Let's neither one of us go back, Elizabeth. Stay with me. There are women, Indian women, at the fort who could help you when your time comes."

"No, *mon ami*," interrupted Père André as he returned to the table. "You cannot remain here. The storekeeper knows the whole story. Soon it will spread all over the fort. They will find you here."

"What can we do?" asked Elizabeth.

Stephen looked at her and smiled. He realized that she had, in that remark, consented to be his—at last.

"We must make plans," he said. "What do you suggest, André?"

"You must come with me to Grand Portage, or so our friends will believe. I will arrange for you to have a small canoe. From there you will take the old voyageur border route to Rainy Lake, the Rainy River, and the Lake of the Woods. Chris Douglas will be waiting for you there. You will give him his share of the loot and he will lead you to the Winnipeg River and the Red River settlements. You will find peace there."

"You would trust me with your money, André?" asked Stephen.

The priest laughed. "Not with my money, my friend, I'll have that safely in my pocket. You'll have Douglas's money and his crew's money. I don't advise you to hold back on him. He comes from Portage la Prairie on the Assiniboine—a brief ride from the settlement—and he and his Métis are the scourge of the settlers. It would be good for you to remain in his good graces. Now will you two be going off together?"

Stephen looked at Elizabeth. She smiled back at him and nodded.

"Well, in that case even in the lady's condition one cannot

97

expect celibacy. I cannot expect it of myself and I have a vow."

He took Stephen's hand and placed it atop Elizabeth's. "You are now joined. Go in peace."

VII

Red River, Fall 1821

Stephen hated farms and his own was no exception. It stretched two miles back from the river yet was only two hundred yards in width. He and his neighbors each had the large acreage necessary for prairie farming, yet their homes were clustered in a long village on the shores of the Red River.

Stephen and Elizabeth were lucky. With his small portion of the furs he was able to purchase one of the older farms, with a ready-made house built from the trunks of the trees growing along the river. Newcomers had a hard time finding wood to build houses. Upriver Stephen could see the rebuilt fort, now called Fort Garry and under the command of the Hudson's Bay official. It was surrounded by the tipis of the Cree and the huts of some Métis. Some of the Métis were indistinguishable from the Cree and some of them were indistinguishable in life-style from the whites. He turned away from the river and looked over the flat country that stretched endlessly to the west. The short grass was sparse in early fall.

"Well," he thought aloud, "there is one consolation. We arrived too late to plant anything."

The previous owners had left an unharvested potato crop and he and Elizabeth had spent late summer digging up potatoes for the coming winter. The only meat they would have was the pemmican that Douglas had sold to them. It was enough to get them through a northern Michigan winter—he had experienced several of those—but he did not know what to expect in Rupert's Land. Nor did he know what to expect of a pregnant woman. Thank God for neighbors, he thought. Mrs. McAlistair, with five young ones of her own, lived next door. And on the other side was Ian Rowand, a Métis, and his Cree wife. They had three children.

Elizabeth came to the front door of their one-room house. She was going to haul water from the river again. The first time he had stopped her. It wasn't right for a woman of gentle birth to have to work so hard. She had reminded him that unless he planned to join her in the housework and neglect the farm, she could not rely on him to haul water every time she needed it. She would haul her own water, thank you, pregnant or not.

And she was decidedly pregnant. Her belly protruded and she could no longer wear the white sash that enlivened the blue work dress she normally wore.

"Soon," she joked, "I will have to give up wearing dresses and throw a flour sack over my head or borrow an Indian blanket from Mrs. Rowand."

Stephen watched her as she waddled down to the river. She was now more beautiful than ever. Her dark hair had taken on a sheen it never had before. Flora McAlistair had commented on how unusual that was. She had lost some of her hair in her last pregnancy, she lamented.

But Elizabeth's hair was never more beautiful. Her skin was smooth and her cheeks ruddy. Her hazel eyes sparkled as never before. She had developed a faint outline of hair on her upper lip, which embarrassed her. Mrs. McAlistair, again the oracle on matters of childbearing at Fort Garry, predicted a male child as now a certainty. She offered to take bets on the outcome, but such was her record that she had no takers. All it meant to Elizabeth was that she covered her face now whenever she went out in public.

Angus McAlistair, Stephen's neighbor, had become his good friend. He had been one of the original Selkirk settlers and had survived through sheer stubbornness, and through the multiple talents of his wife. He was a determined farmer and had plowed deep into the back country of his farm. He was unafraid of Indians or Métis, as he had been unafraid of North West Company men in the past. When all his neighbors had taken to boats on Lake Winnipeg to avoid company raids, he had stayed barricaded in his house. And he had survived.

But McAlistair's greatest achievement was his successful importation of five goats. Before long he had a small herd, which he penned in a dugout near his house. Stephen purchased a bred female from him. They would have milk and cheese this winter too. Angus McAlistair helped Stephen build a sod dugout of his own. They worked for three days. When they had finished, his other neighbor, Rowand, rode up on his Indian pony. He directed the animal into the dugout, hanging off the side of the horse and allowing it to enter. Angus stood staring at this swarthy horseman, his hands placed defiantly on his hips.

"Where the hell does that brazen fellow think he's going?" he said in his thick Scottish accent. "I don't trust them fellows. They are as wild as any Indians, even worse. An Indian has his tribal customs to keep him in check."

Rowand rode out of the shelter again without a word and galloped off.

That had been three days ago. They had not seen Rowand since. Stephen bent to pick up the basket of potatoes, the last of the harvest. The load was heavy, but before hauling them to the hut he could not resist surveying the place. He was proud of what they had done even if he had hated every moment of it. He had a house, a form of a barn with a nanny goat in residence. But most of all he had Elizabeth. He hated farming but he was the happiest farmer in Rupert's Land.

Elizabeth was returning with her large earthenware jug of river water. Stephen placed the basket of potatoes on his shoulders, emulating the way she carried the water. He waved at her with his free arm.

She stopped and waited for him to join her. As he reached her side he bent down and kissed her. Then they walked back to the house together. The house stood on a mound elevated above the riverbank. Stephen hoped the elevation would save them in spring runoffs, but he had been assured that no one in the settlement would be safe from the major floods should frozen ground and winter blizzards combine.

Behind the house the farm stretched out for two miles, or as his deed read, "as far as the eye can see on a clear day." The early evening sun bathed the sky in yellow and pink and turned the grassy rolling hills a rich gold. The plains were so different from anything he had ever experienced in his life. He was a woodsman, at home among the trees and underbrush. The thought struck him that his brother, Charles, the sailor, would have been comfortable with these endless vistas and hillocks of grass moving with the wind like cresting waves.

He put his arm around Elizabeth's waist.

"I can barely get it around you," he joked. "Is it the pemmican or the potatoes?"

"Don't tease me, Stevie," she pouted. "I hate being fat and ugly."

"Why should you care?" he said, withdrawing his arm and making ready to dart away. "You don't have to look at it. I do. It is a lot harder on me."

She frowned and he feared she might have taken his teasing seriously.

"I'm sorry," he said.

She sighed and lifted the pot of water from her shoulder and with one swift motion emptied its entire contents over his head. Squealing with glee, she dropped the pot and raced toward the house.

Stephen stood dripping water and sputtering. By the time he was over the shock, she had made it into the house and bolted the door.

"The little witch," he said aloud, brushing the wet hair off his forehead and out of his eyes.

He walked slowly up to the door. He placed his potato basket on the doorstep. He took a small checkered cotton cloth from the clothesline and dropped it over the potatoes. He took two potatoes and shoved them down the front of his shirt. Then he took his linen handkerchief, which was still wet with his afternoon sweat, and tied it around his head. He pounded on the front door calling out in falsetto.

"I'm Liz Stoddard. Me and my baby can beat any man, riding, shooting, or giving birth."

He strutted up and down in front of the unshuttered windows. One of the potatoes slipped from his shirt down into his pants.

"Oh, my goodness," he screamed, a high-pitched yell. "What have we here?" he said in an exaggerated basso, patting his crotch.

"Anything new would be an improvement," she called from the window.

"You've not complained up till now." He smiled.

"Not since I taught you that a man making love to a woman shouldn't act like a stallion mounting a mare."

"I don't know," he said in mock thoughtfulness, "none of my mares used to complain either. Let me in and I'll demonstrate."

"Are you demonstrating a man's technique or a stallion's? It would influence my decision."

"Let me see, if I say stallion I stay out here and get to pull my pecker. If I say man, well, then maybe something better."

"You're on the right path."

"Oh, I'll be a man," he said gruffly, pulling the handkerchief from his head.

"That's not quite the right tone. Somehow or other I hear animal noises."

He leaned against the rough wooden door and called out meekly, "I'll behave."

The door swung open. He whinnied like a horse and swept Elizabeth off her feet and rushed her toward the bed near the hearth. He pretended he was going to drop her on the bed but instead placed her tenderly on her back. He began to undo the buttons on the front of her dress.

"Stevie," she pleaded, "let's wait until after dinner. I've been working all day. I'll be nicer then."

"I suppose I haven't been working? We'll do it now and we'll do it after dinner again."

He had unbuttoned the last button and pulled the top of her dress away, revealing her full breasts. She was already taut with anticipation. He bent his head down and teased the rosy brown nipples with the tip of his tongue. Then he took the right breast into his mouth, sucking hungrily. She moaned with pleasure as he continued to play with her breasts, first one and then the other. She arched upward and attempted to push more of herself into his mouth. With her hands free she undid the buttons at her waist and began to wriggle from her dress. Stephen helped her, pulling the blue garment down to her knees. Then he raised his head and looked over her naked body, running his hands across her breasts and down to her swollen belly and lower.

She blushed.

"Don't look at me," she said, placing her hands across her belly in a feeble effort to hide the swelling there.

Again Stephen bent down with his mouth. He flicked his tongue into her navel.

She squirmed. It tickled. He laughed a soft chuckle. Then he bent lower and brought a totally different sensation to her whole body.

* * *

103

Stephen leaned back in the barrel chair. Elizabeth stood at the tub of heated water, washing the pewter plates purchased with the house.

"That was delicious," he said leaning over and patting her behind.

"I imagine it was," she said, "and so was the meal."

He laughed. "Yes, it's amazing what you can do with spuds and dried buffalo."

"Mrs. McAlistair says that every spring the whole settlement moves out into the prairies in search of the buffalo herd. Sometimes they are out there for weeks. Do you think we can go?"

"We don't have a wagon," said Stephen.

"The McAlistairs have two."

"We haven't a horse."

She looked crestfallen.

"And besides," said Stephen, "you'll have a little one rivaling me at your breast by spring. Do you intend to strap your baby onto your back like a squaw?"

She grew quiet.

"I'm sorry," he said. "Maybe we can arrange something."

"It's not the hunt," she said.

"What then?"

"You always refer to it as *my* baby. I'm afraid you'll reject the child and me eventually."

"It's my brother's child, Liz. True, he is my twin, so I guess I'm the closest uncle the kid will ever have."

She continued to frown but did not raise the subject again.

She went out the front door to a shed built as a lean-to against the house and pulled out four bundles of hay that had been bound tightly so they would burn as slowly as logs.

"It's getting cold at night now," she said as she reentered the cabin.

She opened the door of the old iron stove that stood in the converted fireplace and tossed two of the bundles inside. The flames rose high momentarily and then settled back down.

Stephen rose from the chair and walked to the bed. He stripped off his shirt and pants and then walked to the dresser on which stood a pitcher of water and a basin. He took the soap that Elizabeth had purchased from Flora McAlistair and scrubbed his face. Then he poured some water from the pitcher and scooped it up onto his face. He made a horselike sound with his mouth and lips.

"Be prepared, woman," he laughed. "You can't lock me out now. I'm already in."

He reached for the towel atop the dresser and then dried his face. Next he attacked his arms, armpits, and chest and finished with the lower half of his body and feet. When he had finished, he pulled back the covers of the bed and flopped down onto the straw mattress.

He watched Elizabeth as she fussed with the remnants of their supper and then as she followed his example and washed herself. She sat on the bed naked and Stephen raised the covers with one arm to allow her to slip under them. She shivered slightly and pulled her naked body close to his. He stroked her breasts. She turned on her side to face him and confronted the hardness between his legs. He entered her slowly and gently. He did not try the deep penetration he loved so much and which she enjoyed as well. He could see the slight look of disappointment on her face.

"No stallions anymore," he whispered in her ear as he moved into the slow rhythm. "I don't want to do anything that might hurt our child."

Her face broke into an enormous smile. She searched for his mouth then and kissed him deeply as if to make up with her mouth for the gentleness below.

The next morning at dawn Ian Rowand arrived at their front door mounted on his Indian pony. He had three more trailing behind him. Stephen was already up. He opened the door when he heard the horses pawing the prairie grass that grew between Miller's cabin and the river.

"Liz," he called behind him toward the bed where she slept, "it's Ian Rowand. Why don't you put on some coffee?"

"No need," said the Métis, "I've had my breakfast. I've come to seek your help, Miller. I want a dugout like you've got for your goats. Only I want one big enough for horses. If you help me build it I'll pay you with two of the three new horses that I got and I'll keep your horses in the dugout this winter until you can enlarge yours next spring."

Stephen was about to complain about Rowand's offer to pay—that really wasn't very neighborly. But then he remembered Elizabeth's excitement about the spring hunt and he kept quiet about neighborliness.

"That's quite a price to pay for a little bit of man's sweat," said Stephen.

Rowand jumped off his horse and went back to the others. He ran his hand down the neck of the roan that was the first in the string.

"These didn't cost me anything," he said with complete openness. "I stole them last night from a band of Cree."

Stephen became suddenly frightened. "Won't they follow you here?"

"Not likely. I could tell from their condition they had been stolen recently and driven east by the Cree. They'll think it's a Blackfoot party come east following their horses. The Blackfoot probably stole them originally from the Crow. It's all been going on for decades. They never think of someone like me cutting in on their little game. It's how I got my horse," he said, patting the rump of his own mount.

Stephen had already made up his mind that he would help Rowand. He wanted the horses and he wanted to go on the hunt next spring. He wanted fresh buffalo meat. He wanted to make his own pemmican. He wanted to wrap his wife and their child in a warm buffalo robe on cold winter nights. He would need Rowand's horses and the McAlistairs' wagon if this was to be possible. Out here in the west people helped each other. And he was glad to have neighbors.

The Fort Garry store was loaded with sacks of local dried buffalo meat and small bags of salt and sugar brought all the way from York Factory on Hudson Bay. Stephen needed everything and did not hesitate to use whatever money he had left over from the purchase of the farm. This first winter would be crucial. In the spring there would be fresh buffalo and crops. But the coming winter had to be survived first.

Angus McAlistair knew the winters. He had been through them before. Stephen followed him about the store, emulating his purchases but reducing his quantity. McAlistair had not only himself and his wife to feed but five growing children, two of them strapping boys.

Stephen saw a small buffalo robe lying on the counter. He walked over to it and hefted it in his hands. It would be just large enough to keep Elizabeth and the baby warm.

"How much?" he inquired of the clerk. He pretended not to hear the response. He made a fast calculation. He didn't have enough to purchase it without some serious bargaining.

He felt a hand clamp down on his shoulder. He swung around to look into the smiling face of Christopher Douglas.

"Well, Miller, isn't it? You were Père André's man."

The Métis's eyes seemed to dart about, first taking in the whole man and then picking him apart from head to toe, always evaluating, always judging.

"Douglas," Stephen acknowledged.

"Can I help you, friend?" the Métis responded. "I operate the store for the Hudson's Bay Company."

"Gone to work for the competition, eh?"

"I had little choice in the matter after the North West Company folded. By the way, have you heard from your priest friend?"

Stephen shook his head.

The Métis looked at the buffalo robe that Stephen still held in his hand.

"Here, let me make you a gift for old times' sake," he said. "Take the robe. It will keep that pretty woman of yours nice and warm this winter."

"I couldn't accept a gift," said Stephen.

"Nonsense," said Douglas. "They all took from Père André."

"What do you mean?" Stephen asked.

"It's my understanding," Douglas said boldly, "that some people are demanding an accounting of what happened and the punishment of the scoundrels who ran off with the last of the company's proceeds. The stockholders of the Hudson's Bay Company, who after all would have shared in the profits of the last rendezvous, are most particularly interested. And the villains most of them mention are a certain priest and a French-Canadian voyageur named Stiegler. But what I don't understand is that factors of the company like myself also get inquiries about a certain Mr. Miller and many strange instructions with reference to him. Since he was only a mere paddler, and a first-timer at that, I don't understand the special interest in him."

Stephen did not know what to make of Douglas's words. Was the Métis warning him out of concern for his well-being, or was he giving Stephen advance warning that he was coming after him?

"It's amazing," said Stephen, "that no one has cast suspicion on the pemmican-eaters."

"And rightly so," said Christopher. "We delivered our furs to Père André. And we have a signed receipt. It is the good Father who failed to show up in September in Montreal. Imagine, and him a priest of the church." He started to laugh. "Be my guest," he insisted. "Take the buffalo robe.

107

Keep that pretty girl warm. No one will be coming to Fort Garry about the matter until spring. Probably not until after the buffalo hunt."

Angus joined them and Stephen introduced him to Douglas. McAlistair's face seemed to darken when he heard the Métis's name.

"Ach," said Chris, "I see you've heard of me, McAlistair, and you heard bad things about me."

"How could I not? You and your crony Cuthbert Grant have plagued our people for years now. Your kind are, in fact, a plague bearing proud names like Douglas and dishonoring them."

Stephen was sure a battle royal was about to begin. But Douglas merely smiled.

"You're a bold man, Mr. McAlistair. You live isolated upriver from the fort with only two neighbors, and one of them is Ian Rowand, isn't it? I always thought he was one of my type. More than that, you curse Cuthbert and me in the same breath. One of us is sure to be captain in chief of the hunt next spring. You could end up with chips as your share of the hunt."

Angus made an angry noise in his throat. "Are you threatening me, man?"

Douglas merely smiled.

"Answer me, man. If you're not too much of a coward."

Douglas's face showed no emotion but his eyes narrowed to slits.

"Angus!" Stephen grabbed his friend's arm. But the older man pushed his hand off.

Douglas turned to Stephen.

"Don't forget, the robe is yours. You'll need it." And then he walked away.

Angus was still fuming.

"McAlistair, my friend," Stephen said, "you've made a dangerous enemy."

"The man's a viper," said Angus. "They're all vipers, these half-breeds."

"I've not found that to be true of Ian Rowand."

"I don't trust him either, Miller. Neither should you."

"He's our neighbor. We have to depend upon each other."

"You and I are both white men, Miller, even if you are one of those damned Easterners. We must stick with each other.

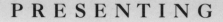

Enjoy the best of Louis L'Amour in special volumes made to last as long as your pleasure

As a reader of Louis L'Amour's tough and gritty tales of the Old West, you'll be delighted by The Louis L'Amour Collection— a series of hardcover editions of Louis L'Amour's exciting Western adventures.

The feel of rich leathers. Like a good saddle, these volumes are made to last—to be read, re-read and passed along to family and friends for years to come. Bound in rugged sierra-brown simulated leather with gold lettering, The Louis L'Amour Collection will be a handsome addition to your home library.

Silver Canyon opens the series. It's the memorable tale of Matt Brennan, gunfighter, and his lone battle against duelling ranchers in one of the bloodiest range wars the West had ever seen. After *Silver Canyon* you'll set out on a new adventure every month, as succeeding volumes in the Collection are conveniently mailed to your home.

Receive the full-color Louis L'Amour Western Calendar FREE—just for looking at *Silver Canyon*. Like every volume in The Louis L'Amour Collection, *Silver Canyon* is yours to examine without risk or obligation. If you're not satisfied, return it within 10 days and owe nothing. The calendar is yours to keep.

Send no money now. Simply complete the coupon opposite to enter your subscription to The Louis L'Amour Collection and receive your free calendar.

The newest volume...

The newest volume I placed on the shelf of my 8000-volume home research library was very special to me—the first copy of _Silver Canyon_ in the hardcover Collector's Edition put together by the folks at Bantam Books.

I'm very proud of this new collection of my books. They're handsome, permanent and what I like best of all, affordable.

I hope you'll take this opportunity to examine the books in the Collection and see their fine quality for yourself. I think you'll be as pleased as I am!

Send no money now–but mail today!

But the half-breeds, they will side with the Indians in any trouble. Now, no more. We have our provisions to purchase."

He stepped away from Stephen and began to haul his pemmican out to his two-wheeled Red River cart.

Stephen lifted the buffalo robe in his arms and followed the Scotsman outside. He found his neighbor whistling happily as he loaded the cart. All the tension of the meeting with Christopher Douglas was forgotten.

As they rode back home it was clear to Stephen that winter had come to the Red River. Billowing gray clouds were coming down from the north. Stephen watched them rush in, pushed by a wind so cold that he thought it would surely congeal the blood in his veins. He and Angus rode in the Scotsman's wagon pulled by Miller's two new horses.

"I'll bet," said the dour Scotsman, "that if you needed to take a piss that damn wind would freeze it before it hit the ground."

"I suspect that before you got finished," offered Stephen blandly, "the tip of your dick would be frostbitten."

"I suspect worse. It would freeze and fall off, all of it," said McAlistair without cracking a smile.

"I suspect you wouldn't notice it until spring," said Stephen beginning to smile.

"I suspect if it happened to you," said McAlistair, "your woman wouldn't even know it. She's plenty big enough now. Before long no more for poor Stevie Miller."

"Then that would make my life like yours."

The older man laughed. "Sure is cold," he said.

Stephen pulled his newly obtained buffalo robe out of the back of the wagon. He offered half to Angus. The cold had picked up moisture as it crossed Lakes Winnipeg and Manitoba. They were going to have their first snows and they would have them today.

They drove past McAlistair's farm and past Stephen's until they came to Rowand's.

Rowand's strangely quiet Cree wife, her hair tied in long braids and her whole body seemingly tightly wrapped in an Indian blanket, came out of the house to greet them. Behind her stood her three children. The two girls were replicas of their mother. Rowand's son stood behind his sisters. He stood bare-chested, as if to ignore the cold. The look of defiance in the boy's eyes indicated utter contempt for the white men. His body betrayed him, however. His entire chest was goose bumps and he occasionally shivered. The Cree woman spoke to her children in her own language. The boy, who looked to be about eight years old and certainly older than his sisters, moved forward to help the white men unload the provisions. It was clear that he did not wish to do menial service but it was also clear that he did what his mother told him.

"Where's Ian?" Stephen asked the woman.

She looked at him in silence.

At first Stephen thought she had not understood his question. But as Rowand stepped to the doorway of the house himself, it was clear that her confusion was seeing men, strong men, obviously virile men, like Stephen doing the work of women or boys.

Rowand was smoking a pipe. He stood as his neighbors hauled sacks of dried meat, salt, and sugar from the back of the wagon.

The woman tried to haul a huge sack. Angus jumped to grab it from her but she pulled away from him and threw it onto her shoulder with incredible ease. She gave the Scotsman a withering look of contempt.

When they had unloaded the Rowand provisions, Angus climbed back into the driver's seat. He was disgusted with these people and their peculiar customs. At his home men did the heavy work. Lord knew his wife was strong enough and worked from dawn to bedtime, but he'd never stand by and watch her haul hundred-pound bags. He clucked to the horses to get them moving again.

Rowand put his pipe down, and with catlike swiftness he leapt to the back of one of the wagon horses and with the pressure of his knees urged the two horses into a trot.

"What is it, Rowand?" McAlistair yelled.

The Métis turned around and flashed a smile at them. The horses trotted down the path. They passed Stephen's farm. Elizabeth stood in the doorway and waved. She had joked to Stephen that morning as he left that she was the only person at Red River who could stand in the door, keep her head and feet dry in a rainstorm, and yet have a wet stomach. She protruded greatly.

When they arrived at McAlistair's, the Scotsman began to unload his goods. He passed them from the back of the wagon to Stephen, who stood at the rear of the wagon and carted the sacks into Angus's house. He was younger than the Scotsman and he had never felt stronger in his life. McAlistair's teen-aged son, Jamie, and his ten-year-old, Andrew, followed by Flora, his wife, came out of the house. Jamie took a bundle from Stephen and disappeared into the house.

Rowand continued to sit astride the horse and watch the workers. When they had finished unloading, McAlistair got back up into the wagon.

"Hold it, Angus," Stephen called out. "There's only my stuff left and I've the smallest lot. You stay here. I'll drive the wagon home and bring it back to you tomorrow."

Angus looked up into the clouds. "You take the wagon home and I won't see it until spring. The snows are on their way. We'll not see prairie grass again until May. No matter, there'll be no using wagons with wheels again until the spring melt. Take it with you." He glowered at Rowand, who continued to sit astride one of the horses. "And watch your back," he added.

Stephen nodded at Rowand, who like a coiled spring immediately moved into action. He and the horses seemed to be part of the same creature. They reared slightly but then began to trot downriver again down toward Stephen's place. Elizabeth awaited them still. She ran to the door and opened it as the wagon pulled up into the yard. The first tiny flakes of snow began to fall. Stephen pulled the sacks of meat toward the back of the wagon. When he turned, he saw to his amazement the Métis standing, arms outstretched, waiting for a load.

"I thought Métis men didn't do this sort of thing," Stephen said.

"My friend, you must learn one thing about the Métis," said Rowand. "You can make no generalizations about us. The only thing a Métis will not do is what a Métis doesn't want to do. It amused me to make old Angus think me a lazy no-good lout. You know differently. I worked every bit as hard as you did on the dugout."

"There's no denying that," said Stephen while passing the sack to Rowand. Elizabeth held the door open while Rowand deposited his burden before the Millers' stove.

The snow was falling harder now. Rowand stepped back outside. He led the horses halfway between Stephen's house and the goat dugout. Then he unhitched them from the wagon. In an instant he had remounted one of them and led the other by the bridle.

"Run a line from the house to the wagon and then from the

111

wagon to the dugout. That way you'll not lose your way when you go out for some milk."

Stephen looked at him incredulously.

"Don't doubt me, Miller. I've seen men lost and frozen ten yards from their homes. The blizzards blind you. With a line you can feel your way."

He said no more, but rode away.

A sense of foreboding seemed to envelope both Stephen and Elizabeth as the Métis rode the horses home to the horse shelter at his farm. To both of them he seemed to be the last tie to the outside world and now he was gone. All that lay ahead of them was a Manitoba winter.

The winds seemed never to stop. They blew the snow in swirls that danced about the farmhouse, then came to rest in ever-increasing drifts. The rolling landscape was altered as the hills of drifting snow grew. The wood of Miller's house groaned in agony as the icy chill beat against it. The glass windows, so rare at Fort Garry, were coated with ice on the inside and it was no longer possible to look out of them. The ugly gray clouds continued to sweep across the sky on a mad dash toward the south, as if driven to flee this northern wasteland of ice and loneliness.

Stephen and Elizabeth had not ventured from the house in weeks except to milk the nanny goat. When the temperatures fell so low that Stephen feared the windows would crack, he relented and brought the goat into the house for the night. He had regretted it ever since. He still had not been able to rid the house of the stench. He hoped he would not be forced into that desperate a situation again.

He and Elizabeth went to bed every night with their clothes on and with whatever they could find piled on top of them. They kept the stove burning continuously, to the point that Stephen began to worry about having enough hay to burn until spring. They would be in trouble if they ran out, and they would need lots once the baby came.

Again he gave thanks for his neighbors. Not that he had seen any of them. But it was enough to see the smoke coming out of their cabin chimneys.

Stephen climbed the mound of snow, his milk pail in his hand, and pulled on the line that ran from the house into the heart of that snowmound. Somewhere buried beneath that hill was Angus's two-wheeled cart. When he reached the top he searched around for the second line that led to the dugout and the goat. He looked up into the sky. It was going to snow again. The clouds, black and low in the heavens, were moving in again from the west. Maybe these would pass them by. He shivered as the wind cut through his coat and penetrated through to his skin. When he had been a boy in Amherstburg he had often heard the locals say, "It's too cold to snow." He had believed it then but he would never again believe it. Not after a winter on the Red River.

Rowand's fire was sending off smoke. The wind had driven it his way. He looked upriver. He strained his eyes toward McAlistair's. Smoke curled lazily from the chimney at the Scotsman's place. He started to look away toward the dugout when a movement on the flat land behind McAlistair's caught his attention. He looked again. This time he could see nothing. Maybe it had just been his imagination, maybe it was a prairie wolf or some other stray wild animal. He remembered Angus's goats. Perhaps a wolf stalked the livestock. He retraced his steps back into the cabin. Elizabeth was still asleep. There was no point in awakening her. He picked up his old war musket and went back to his position on the mound of snow. Again he stared. There it was again. This time he was sure. Something had moved. There were several things moving from snowdrift to snowdrift. And they were not four-footed.

"Indians," Stephen said half aloud. They were sneaking up on the McAlistair place. They had to be Cree who had run out of food, he thought. The goats would be tempting targets.

"My God," he said, again half aloud. "So will my nanny and Rowand's horses—my horses."

He raised his musket to his shoulder and fired. The gunshot seemed to penetrate the silent whiteness and to echo endlessly. He knew his neighbors would immediately look to see its source. He removed his coat and waved it above his head. He pointed toward the prairie beyond McAlistair's cabin. A lead ball whizzed over his head. He ducked out of instinct. He was also an easy target for the enemy.

He saw Angus step out of his house in his long underwear. He followed Stephen's gesture and stood for some moments staring. Moments later, about twenty men came rushing from cover and started firing. Stephen watched in horror as McAlistair seemed to stagger and red blotches appeared on the white underwear. He sagged at the knees and fell on his face.

113

Stephen saw Flora come out of the house and try to drag Angus back in. As close as he was, Stephen could do little to help. The drifts cut him off from any chance of reaching the McAlistairs before the Indians did. He grabbed his lifeline and followed it, stumbling down the mound, tripping over his own feet, and nearly falling into the deep snow. He picked up the goat in the dugout and carried her back to the top of the mound. He looked at McAlistair's. Angus had disappeared and he could only assume that Flora had gotten him back inside. There were gunshots now, at least a dozen, but none were aimed at him. He followed the path back to his cabin.

Elizabeth awaited him at the door wrapped in her buffalo robe. Her eyes were wide with fear. He dropped the goat inside the house and slammed and barred the wooden door behind him.

"Stephen, what is it?"

"It's McAlistair. There's been some sort of raid. He's been hit. I have to go and help."

He realized his remark was stupid. How could he go there without leaving Elizabeth alone? He went to the window that opened toward Angus's farm but it was totally closed off by a snowdrift. He couldn't see, and the frustration of it turned to anguish and then to anger.

"Damn it, what can I do?" he shouted.

There was a pounding at the door. Elizabeth stifled a scream. She stood in the center of the room. Her robe had fallen down about her feet and she hugged her belly with her hands.

"Open up. It's me, Rowand."

Stephen removed the wooden bar from the door and threw it open. The Métis, rifle in hand, stood holding the reins of his horse.

"Angus is in trouble, Ian."

"I know. Mrs. Miller, can you ride in your state?" he asked. She nodded.

"Then up you go. Just let him have his head. He'll go right back to my place. My wife is waiting for you."

"I'm a good shot," she offered. "Do you have a gun there?"

"Yes," said Rowand, "it's a musket."

Again she nodded. She picked up the buffalo robe and pulled it tight about her.

Stephen walked to her side. He kissed her and then lifted her onto the back of the horse.

"Keep low. Don't give anyone a target."

She smiled at him. The fear had receded from her face but he knew it still gripped her inside.

"It's hard for me not to present a target, Stephen Miller," she said.

She kicked the horse and it began the short journey to the relative comfort of Rowand's dugout.

"Let's go," Stephen said to Rowand.

The two men crept from mound to mound of snow toward McAlistair's farm. The firing had stopped but all was not silent. There was a cracking sound. Stephen recognized it instantly. He raised his head above the drift. Smoke poured from the door of McAlistair's cabin and flames shot out of one window.

"The place is on fire, Ian," Stephen called out. He rose and started toward the cabin, only to fall into knee-deep snow. Rowand came behind him, following the track Stephen had made. Stephen struggled in the drift. His legs felt like heavy weights. He pushed through the snow with the strength of his knees and thighs. When he reached the other side of the drift, he raced to the cabin and entered.

There was an obscene chaos inside. The smoke blinded him. There would be no extinguishing this fire. He looked about. Angus lay across the bed, his blood-soaked body partially hidden by that of his wife. Stephen went to them. On the floor at his feet, his blank eyes staring at the ceiling, was their ten-year-old, Andrew. The girls lay in a heap in the far corner, the heads of the little ones split open by tomahawks. Stephen started to retch.

"Over here," Rowand called out. "This one's still alive."

He bent over Jamie. The boy had been shot in the shoulder. A bit lower and the bullet would have pierced his heart. Blood flowed from a wound in his head and covered the boy's forehead. His face was pale and lifeless.

Stephen reached Ian's side.

"Let's get him out of here. The smoke is too thick," said the Métis.

"What about the others?"

"Leave them be. This place will be an inferno in minutes. It is for the best. We couldn't bury them. There's too much snow and the ground is frozen."

Ian cradled the boy's head and neck in his arms. Stephen lifted his feet as they carried him outside into the snow.

The flames were reaching high into the sky. The snow on

115

the roof of the house melted and turned into steam. The goats in the shelter some yards from the back of the house were bleating in panic.

"What's that?" Stephen shouted.

"What?"

"I heard a sound. Like gunfire. It was coming from downriver. There's no one at my place. It must be from yours."

"Can you carry him yourself?" Ian asked Stephen.

Miller nodded.

The Métis placed Jamie McAlistair down on the snow. He checked his rifle to be sure it was loaded and then he disappeared behind a snow hill in the direction of his homestead.

Stephen lifted Jamie and placed him across his shoulders, holding one of the boy's legs in the crook of his arm. He bent down again and picked up his musket with his free hand. Bending low, he started at a trot toward the riverbank.

He found the snow-covered depression that in spring, summer, and fall was the Red River. He saw Ian's tracks heading off. He followed along. The smoke from the McAlistairs' home lay heavy in the air. He could still hear the cracking of the burning wood. Suddenly he realized the sound was not diminishing as he moved away. He had a sinking feeling in his stomach. It was not the burning of McAlistair's house that he heard. It was his own.

He had no time to raise his head. He pushed forward. The boy, who was fifteen, was as large as a man and seemed to grow heavier with each step. Stephen followed Rowand's tracks until they swung away from the river.

Stephen straightened up, letting Jamie slide from his back onto the snow. He readied his musket. He heard a rifle crack and an instantaneous scream. He found his musket and fired in the direction of the scream. The rifle shot had come from his house.

He waited for some moments more, then heard Rowand call his name.

"They've gone, Miller. Head toward my house. I'll meet you."

Again Stephen picked up the limp and heavy body of the boy and struggled with him through the drifts. Rowand met him and took half his burden. Together they carried the unconscious Jamie McAlistair to the Rowand household.

Elizabeth rushed into Stephen's arms as soon as he put the

boy's body down on the floor of the cabin. He clutched her tightly to himself.

"Stephen, is the house—" She couldn't finish the sentence.

He looked away from her and she started to sob.

"Cree Woman," Ian called his wife, "the boy, can you do anything for him?"

The Indian woman sent her children scurrying back up into the loft where they had been hiding. Then she went to the boy and tore open his shirt. The wound in his shoulder was red and puckered. She turned the boy's heavily muscled body over onto his stomach as if he were a buffalo calf to be skinned. She smiled when she saw an exit wound. The ball had passed through the flesh, probably glanced off a rib, and passed through the back muscles. He was comatose, more because of the blow on his head. She cleaned his wounds with hot water.

Stephen stayed with Elizabeth while Rowand guarded the door. He jumped nearly a foot when the wind rose with some force and banged closed a shutter that had been open to allow firing.

"I'm going back outside," Rowand announced.

"I'll come with you," Stephen offered.

"I think you should stay with the women and children."

Stephen realized that Ian was more at home in these prairies. He nodded.

Ian opened the door and stepped silently outside. Stephen closed it after him.

The Métis moved cautiously around the drift beside his home. The fire at McAlistair's was almost out but Miller's house was still ablaze. Smoke reached high into the heavy black clouds. The snow had begun to fall again. Frozen ice pellets stung his face. He did not expect to see any sign of the raiders. He was sure he knew who they were but he wanted to find real evidence.

He crawled to his horse dugout. The animals were safely inside. His and Miller's horses were untouched. That convinced him. No Cree would have left three horses, even in a winter raid. No Cree would have left the scalps on the heads of the McAlistair family. Nor would a Cree fail to attack the third of three isolated farmhouses after burning the first two. The fact that a Métis owned and lived in the third farm would have stopped only a Métis. And only a Métis of this region,

117

Fort Garry, would have known that the third farm was owned by one of their own.

He worked his way back toward the Millers'. Then he found his evidence. The footprints in the snow showed not only moccasined feet but several booted footprints as well. All that evidence would soon be lost in the fresh snows. He stood watching the flames consume the precious wood of his neighbor's home. Ice pellets accumulated on his black hair. At first he had felt pangs of guilt. Perhaps his raid for horses had brought the Cree down upon them. But no, this raid had not been aimed at him. The Métis community at Fort Garry had picked on the McAlistairs and the Millers. But why?

Jamie McAlistair regained consciousness the next morning. Cree Woman had spent the whole night by his side changing the compresses on his head and shoulder. He woke up screaming, "Indians! The house is filled with Indians. Daddy, Mum."

Cree Woman stepped back into the shadows so that the boy would not be frightened by her appearance. Elizabeth left her spot on the buffalo robe next to Stephen and came to calm the boy down. She placed her hand on his warm face.

"It's all right, Jamie," she called out to him. "You're safe with friends."

The boy's eyes began to focus in the dark. "Is that you, Mrs. Miller? Am I at your place?"

"No, at Rowand's. Cree Woman, his wife, is nursing you."

The Indian woman stepped back into his line of vision. His eyes darted from her to Elizabeth in fear.

"Where are my folks?" he asked softly, his adolescent voice cracking.

"You've been hurt." Elizabeth tried to avoid the question. "Don't ask any more questions until you're stronger."

"I want to know where my parents are, and my sisters and my brother." His voice was rising in panic.

Elizabeth knelt on the floor at Jamie's side. She took his head to her bosom and held it tightly.

"They're dead," she whispered in his ear.

He was silent for a moment, then a great sob escaped from his lips. It was muffled in Elizabeth's breast. The first sob was followed by a second and a third.

"It's not true!" he cried out in anguish.

Elizabeth continued to hold the boy, rocking his head and

wounded shoulder back and forth as she clasped him to herself.

"But why?" he asked her. "What did we do to them?"

She could not answer. She did not try. She just continued to hold him until he fell back into a troubled sleep. Then Elizabeth laid his head back on the bunched-up Indian blanket that served as a makeshift pillow. She watched him for some moments, then crawled back next to Stephen, who lay watching her, his head resting on his arm.

"That was nice, what you did for the boy," he offered.

"It was very little," she said, "and he needed much."

He put his arms around her and drew her tight against him. In a few moments they were both fast asleep. From out of the shadows Cree Woman approached the restless form of Jamie McAlistair. Once again she placed warm water compresses on his wounded head and shoulder.

VIII

Red River, Winter 1821 and Spring 1822

Christmas and New Year's came and went unnoticed in the Rowand cabin. They were crowded now, four adults and a boy large enough to be an adult and three children—all in one room and a loft. Cree Woman hung a blanket to divide Stephen's and Elizabeth's sleeping quarters from hers and Rowand's. Jamie was sent up into the loft with the Rowand children. Special provisions of meat, sugar, and flour were sent out from the fort by sled to assist the survivors of the "Indian attack." Chris Douglas sent a jug of whiskey along with a wagon full of pemmican for them.

Stephen and Ian enjoyed the whiskey. Even Elizabeth felt a gulp might help her get warmer in the depths of the January freeze. But Cree Woman would not indulge. Only Douglas's note wishing them the best for the new year made them realize that they had entered 1822.

"We should have a little celebration anyway," said Ian, looking at the jug and laughing.

Jamie sat staring at the flames in the stove. He said very little but followed Elizabeth around like a lost puppy. He could not bring himself to look at Cree Woman.

"Here," said Stephen, offering an earthenware cup of whiskey to the boy, "I think you can use some of this."

Jamie looked at the whiskey and then sniffed it. The boy's hair was long now, and the dark lines on his upper lip, chin, and sideburns indicated he would soon be shaving regularly.

Stephen remarked to Jamie that he bore a strong resemblance to his father.

"Angus was a handsome man—even at fifty."

Jamie gulped the whiskey down in one swallow. His face turned a brilliant red. The boy's insides felt that they were aflame. But he would not give in to it. He kept the whiskey down and soon felt a warm glow.

"Want another?" Rowand asked.

Elizabeth signaled the Métis not to offer, but Jamie nodded and another cup was poured for him. This time Jamie sipped it but even the slower consumption added to the glow.

Cree Woman picked up the jug from the crude wooden table on which it sat and placed it on the shelf above. She then walked back to the stove to stir the pemmican stew she was cooking.

Jamie was feeling more a part of this new family with each passing moment. He looked over at Cree Woman. She was the only one out of place. Even her children were being raised as whites rather than devils. Jamie looked at Rowand for some moments.

"Why do you keep that squaw around?" he asked finally. "Aren't you afraid that some night while you're asleep she'll unbolt the door and let the devils in to murder you and your children?"

He shocked himself by the question. Cree Woman, who knew English well enough, did not even look at them. But the spoon with which she stirred the stew suddenly came to a halt.

Rowand eyed the boy and said nothing. It was Elizabeth who intervened.

"Don't paint everyone with the same brush, Jamie. The British murdered Stevie's father but he doesn't blame all Englishmen and hate them. Cree Woman didn't kill your parents. It's unfair for you to blame her."

Stephen thought her analogy a poor one. In fact, he did dislike almost all Englishmen and he did blame them for his stepfather's death. It would have been better if she had told the boy that his natural father had been burned to death by Indians and that he did not blame anyone for that.

"In fact, Jamie, it was Cree Woman who nursed you back to health," Elizabeth continued. "You shouldn't fault her. You should be grateful."

Jamie was slightly drunk now. It was clear that he grew resentful as they lectured him. Finally Rowand rose from his chair. He walked to his wife's side and placed his arm about her. He spoke softly to her in Cree. She smiled to him and responded, shaking her head. Then he turned to Jamie.

"I've asked her if she wanted a tender young tongue for the

122

stove. There's been one that's been pickled and wagging in this room for some minutes now. Boy, the only time this woman will open the barred door at night is when she decides she's had enough of you and she decides to throw you out of her lodge."

Jamie grew angry. It was clear to Elizabeth that the boy had drunk enough and that he was prepared to challenge Ian.

"Jamie, Ian is right," she said. "Cree Woman is a fine and good woman. Right now it is you who behave like a savage."

She winced as she spoke. Stephen started to laugh.

"I think we have another savage in the family," he said. "The one in your belly jumps around and kicks just as any wild . . ." He was about to say "Cree" but he changed it to "Blackfoot."

But the look of real distress on Elizabeth's face stopped his joking.

"What is it, Liz?"

"I don't know," she said gasping. "I've this terrible pain in my back. It just moved around to the front."

Cree Woman handed her spoon to Ian and came over to Elizabeth. She placed her hand on Elizabeth's belly.

"It's her time. The baby."

Stephen looked panicky. Ian laughed aloud.

"Well, there's no place to hide, gents. It looks to me that we'll be up this night once the yelling starts."

Elizabeth bore down just as Cree Woman insisted. She wanted to lie down. Instead the Indian woman made her walk and walk. How many hours had this been going on? The men on the other side of the blanket had turned in hours ago, although she was sure they did not sleep. But she had not cried out as Ian had predicted she would. Cree Woman gave her a piece of folded rawhide to bite down on when the pains came. And how they came! She was consumed by them. She had to hold onto Cree Woman, who had led her to a straight-back wooden chair.

"Bear down," she yelled at Elizabeth until the pain passed. Then she let her rest a moment. But inevitably she would pull Elizabeth to her feet again and she would begin to walk. This was not how Jessica had described this moment to her. She should be lying in bed, except that her bed lay in the smoldering ruins of her cabin. The Rowands had no beds. She should have a doctor, preferably Father Eli, attending

123

her. Instead she had this horrible woman who would give her no peace. She gasped as the pain started again. Cree Woman shoved the rawhide into her mouth. She started to bite down and bear down at the same time.

The Indian woman bent down and touched her where she thought only Stephen should touch her. She was consumed by the pain.

"Not long now," said Cree Woman. She led Elizabeth to the chair. Elizabeth sucked in a breath and exhaled heavily. She was sweating. The shift of white cotton, which was pulled up above her waist and which was all that she wore, was soaked clear through. If only Stephen could be there when the baby was born. She wanted to hand him their child. It was funny, she had always thought of this baby as their child, not Charles's. Yet this son or daughter would in reality have been her husband's, not her lover's. But really it did not matter to her. Both Stephen and she felt this child was to be theirs, and in her mind it would always be.

Cree Woman was hauling her to her feet again. She was tired. So weary. This couldn't go on much longer. Her strength was leaving her. She could feel it ebb. She rose and leaned on the other woman. Again they walked about the cabin on their side of the suspended blanket. Again the pains came. They came quickly now, taking away the brief periods of respite. She took the rawhide again but this time Cree Woman pushed down on her shoulders, forcing her to squat. She touched Elizabeth again.

"Push," she hissed.

Elizabeth grunted with the effort. She wanted to scream but instead she bit down harder. Then suddenly she felt as if she would split apart.

"Here it comes," said Cree Woman. She now had the baby's head and shoulders. The rest would slip out easily now.

Cree Woman looked up into Elizabeth's face and smiled at her.

"You have a son. May he be the warrior his father is."

The irony of her remark struck Elizabeth.

"May he be as brave as my Stephen."

Cree Woman nodded in agreement, not knowing that she had been corrected.

The afterbirth had been expelled and Elizabeth collapsed at last on her sleeping mat. The Indian woman tied the cord with thread and then bit it close to the tie with her teeth. The baby began to whimper and then cry. Cree Woman washed the child in warm water, then placed him on a backpack she had last used for her youngest and gave Elizabeth her child. She pulled back the blanket and saw the two men, Stephen and Jamie, sitting up waiting. Ian was sound asleep.

"You have a son," Cree Woman said to Stephen.

He smiled back at her and kissed her on the forehead Then Stephen went to Elizabeth and lay down next to her She was pale and sleepy. He bent over and kissed her on the lips. She smiled contentedly and pulled back the covers so that he might see their child. He looked at the angry red face and the clenched fists. He kissed the baby and the baby looked annoyed at the touch of his lips.

Elizabeth started to laugh. "I think he's already at war with his poppa," she said.

"He looks an awful lot like Eli," said Stephen. "I think you should call him that."

"I'd like to," she responded, "but Mother Jessica always told me it was wrong to name a child after a living person. If I named him Eli, it would imply that my father was gone."

"I do believe that you've taken on a lot of Jessica's strange Hebrew customs."

"I guess I have," said Elizabeth, "so our son must have a great Hebrew name. How about Moses?"

Stephen started to laugh. "Moses Miller sounds funny to me."

Elizabeth smiled. "Me too."

"How about Joshua? He was Moses's right-hand man. My mom used to read to me about the walls of Jericho."

"Joshua Miller." Elizabeth tested the name for the first time. She liked the sound of it. "Josh," she said looking down at her infant. "You've got yourself a name."

Jamie watched them from his mat, which he had brought down from the loft for this night. He was awed by the introduction of new life into the world, and he was overjoyed that Elizabeth had come out of her ordeal well. He saw Cree Woman go to the stove and begin to wash her hands and face in the water she kept there.

He rose from his mat to go over to her. She had scrubbed her face with soap and water. She reached around for a towel to dry her face, not daring to open her eyes for fear of getting soap in them. He put the towel into her hands. She dried her face and when she opened her eyes she searched his face quizzically. He looked at her sheepishly. Finally he was able to get the words out.

"I'm sorry."

She smiled at him and patted his cheek.

The river had finally begun to recede. It had come to within a few feet of Rowand's cabin. Stephen looked at the ruins of his old homestead. They were also dry. He would rebuild in the spring after the hunt, and he would plant. Ian, Jamie, and he had agreed to try to plant and harvest two of the farms together and to rebuild his house. But first they would have to kill a season's meat.

Spring came late to the Red River. But as the snows melted and soaked into the prairie sod and the sun warmed the earth, the endless blanket of white was slowly replaced by a green rich grass carpet dotted with myriad gold-and-white wild prairie flowers.

Jamie was readying two large Red River carts. Along with his father's land, they were his sole worldly possessions. Stephen and Ian Rowand would provide the horses, but Stephen knew it pleased the boy to be able to provide a means of hauling the kill home.

Stephen watched him grease the wheels of the cart, which had been buried under the snows at Miller's farm. Just about everything was in readiness. Cree Woman and her daughters, whom Stephen called Jane and Mary because he could not pronounce their Indian names, wanted to ride in the wagon. Her son, called Jack for the same reason, would ride atop the wagon horse. Elizabeth would ride in the second wagon with Jamie and Joshua. Stephen and Ian would ride their own mounts. Stephen was not comfortable on a horse and would have much preferred to ride in the wagon, but he had to maintain his dignity. The goats were turned loose on the prairie. They could feed off the new grass for the month or so the families would be gone. Ian, dressed in buckskin and wearing an old felt hat with an eagle feather in it, came out of the house and joined Stephen.

"As soon as the boy is finished we can all start out for Fort Garry," he said.

Stephen nodded. Elizabeth and Cree Woman had been preparing for the hunt for days. They had baskets of pemmican and potatoes. The children were rushing about the house, shouting with anticipation about the great event of the year. Ian had chased his son about the cabin and up into the loft with the promise of a good spanking if he did not calm down. Only Joshua in his cradle or strapped to his mother's back was oblivious to the excitement.

"Jamie," Stephen called out. "If those wagons aren't ready now they never will be."

"We're all set, Mr. Miller."

"Let's hitch up then and start loading."

They rode along the river trail downriver toward the fort, which was located at the junction of Red River and the Assiniboine. Wagons were coming to the fort from farms along both rivers. The trails were clogged with wagons. About the fort were clustered at least a thousand men, women, and children, the entire white and Métis population of the settlement.

Stephen shook his head in wonderment. How would this rabble ever organize itself, much less move out and hunt buffalo? Stephen and Ian's party, loaded into the two wagons, inched their way through the congestion in front of Fort Garry until they found a spot where they could bring the horses to a halt.

Ian and Stephen left the wagons and walked through the congestion of wagons to the gates of the fort. Inside on the campground about three hundred men had congregated before the company store. The door of the store swung open and five men stepped out onto the porch. The only one Stephen recognized was Christopher Douglas.

Douglas raised his hand. The men grew silent, but in the background outside the walls the pandemonium of the encampment continued without pause.

Douglas began to yell above the noise.

"Men, the situation outside there gives you an idea of what it is going to be like on the prairie if we don't get ourselves organized. This hunt has grown too big. We've got to have rules and we've got to have leaders."

"And you've got to be one of them, ain't I right?" yelled a Scotsman from the Red River settlement.

Some men laughed, but others, particularly the Métis, glared at the Scotsman.

"No, I don't got to be one of them. And you don't got to come away with anything but a sore ass after chasing buffalo all over the prairie never seeing even one."

Everyone laughed at that.

"I nominate Cuthbert Grant to be the captain general of the hunt," one of the men in the crowd called out.

A buckskin-clad Métis standing next to Douglas waved acknowledgment to the cheers of some in the crowd.

"Shit," said the Scotsman who had called out against Douglas. "He's the worst of the lot. He was the one who led the North West Company men in the Seven Oaks massacre. I'd rather have that bastard Douglas lead."

Someone in the crowd called out, "The Scotsman nominates Chris Douglas."

The men started to laugh again.

Stephen was startled. He recognized the heavy French accent that had called out Grant's name. He stepped away from Rowand and started to make his way through the crowd. The voice had come from the group that stood near the Scotsman and across the yard from where Stephen had been standing. Then he saw him. He waved. The priest's eyes acknowledged him and his face broke into a grin. He came toward Stephen and threw his arms around him, kissing him on both cheeks.

"My friend, I had hoped to meet with you but not so soon. I've just arrived."

"What brings you to Fort Garry, Father André?"

"Not so loud, here I am just Pierre. No priest. Nothing."

"But certainly you're known. If I recognized you, dozens of others will. Douglas for one. He even warned me that the Hudson's Bay Company men were looking for you."

"They found me," said the priest smiling, "working for Mr. Astor across the mountains. They won't find anybody else— ever." He patted the large knife at his side. "But the Astor people had no sense of humor. They asked me to leave. Well, I've always wanted to join the Red River buffalo hunt, so here I am."

"I hope you can ride a horse better than I can."

"I despise horses. Filthy beasts. They drop their shit wherever they walk. The canoe is the only way to travel."

"Not on a buffalo hunt."

Both men started to laugh.

"Really . . ." Stephen hesitated, "really, Pierre, are you sure a certain Métis can be trusted?"

"No, I'm not sure that either of us can trust him. But I am sure that you are safer now that I am here. Ah, we're about to vote. Those for Grant are on this side. Those for Douglas are on the other. Let's vote for our old friend."

Père André walked across the yard in full view of the candidates on the storefront porch. André waved at Douglas as he went by. The Métis watched them and a smile crossed his face. As they reentered the crowd, Rowand grabbed Stephen's shoulder.

"I don't want to vote for Douglas. Grant is the better man."

"Who is this fellow?" André demanded.

"This is my neighbor and friend, Ian Rowand. Ian, this is . . . Pierre."

Stephen looked at the priest to furnish him his last name. "Just Pierre."

Rowand greeted André in French.

"You can, of course, walk across the yard like we did but I wouldn't. I've known Chris Douglas for most of his life. He's a mean fellow. Voting publicly allows him to count his friends—and his enemies. I wouldn't want to be listed among his enemies if I could help it."

"From the look of the division he has more enemies than friends. Grant has clearly won the election," said Stephen.

Douglas came away from the porch after the vote had been counted. He shook hands with Grant and then walked among his own supporters.

"You ride with me," he said to specific individuals. "Grant has named me one of the ten group captains."

When he came to Stephen and Ian he shook their hands.

"Thank you for your support. You ride with me, eh?" Then he looked directly at Père André. "Your friend, he can come too."

"You mean Pierre," Stephen responded with a smile.

"Yes, Pierre."

The carts had been out on the prairie for three days. The cloud of dust they left behind them rose into the sky like a long mud-brown cyclone that inched along the prairie without wind to move it. The wagons had been subdivided into groups of fifty each. Each day, half an hour before departing, a flag was raised. The children were searched for and hauled up into the carts by their mothers. Horses were hitched and the camp broken. Ian was chosen as one of the scouts. He and his compatriots scattered out looking for signs of the great herd. So far none of the scouts had returned. The days were hot. Stephen rode his horse beside the cart that carried Elizabeth and Joshua. His rump was sore from the riding. He offered to change places with Père André, who rode with his family. The priest merely laughed at him and patted his behind.

Elizabeth handed Joshua to the priest. "I'll change places with you," she said.

Stephen hesitated. But the look of expectation on her face was enough to make him relent. He climbed down from his mount and held the horse steady while she swung her leg across the horse's bare back. She grabbed the reins from Stephen, kicked the horse in the ribs with her heels, and went racing through the line of march at breakneck speed. She broke from the long line and rode out onto the open prairie, her hair blowing behind her. She felt free of the dust at last.

Stephen watched her ride off with some concern. He removed his shirt to wipe his perspiring body. The priest handed him the baby with a look of disgust on his face.

"I had forgotten, *mon ami*, babies are like horses. They too shit whenever and wherever they please."

Stephen held Joshua against his chest while he searched the prairie with his eyes for signs of Elizabeth.

Joshua began to suck at the matted blonde hair on Stephen's chest.

"Whoa, little fellow," Stephen laughed. "That's mighty poor fare compared to what you've been used to."

Again he looked for Elizabeth, who had passed over a hillock and disappeared.

Chris Douglas rode back in among his wagons until he came to Stephen's cart.

"Was that your woman?"

Stephen nodded.

"Damn, never saw a better woman rider, but she's not supposed to do that. She's supposed to stay in the line of march."

Stephen barely heard the group captain. He continued to search the surrounding hills for signs of Elizabeth.

Douglas winked at André.

"How are you doing, you old reprobate?"

"Waiting for you to make your move," said André.

"I don't know what you're talking about." Douglas kneed his horse and rode away.

"What was that all about?" Stephen asked.

"That's one man who is not happy to see me and who will breathe some relief when I'm no longer breathing, especially now that he works for the Hudson's Bay Company."

"I know what you know about him. I can understand why he might want to get rid of you, but I know as much as you do."

André smiled and nodded.

The look of surprise that crossed Stephen's face gave way to one of anger and then concern. He looked back toward where he had last seen Jamie walking behind the cart. The boy had disappeared.

"Damn it," he cursed, "everyone is taking off."

Then Elizabeth appeared on the knoll off in front and to the right. She was silhouetted against the setting sun. The horse reared on its hind legs. Elizabeth gave the steed his head and they plunged down the side of the knoll and charged toward the advancing caravan. When she arrived, her exhilaration was contagious. Cree Woman hugged her and Père André laughed and kissed her hand.

"Beautiful riding," he said.

"What would you know?" Stephen asked in annoyance. "You barely know one end of a horse from another."

He was annoyed because he would now have to rub down the horse, which had worked up a lather.

The signal gun was fired and the flag was raised. The carts were drawn into a wide circle and the horses were unhitched and hobbled in the center. Each family pitched a tent or tipi near its wagon and lit its fires. Cree Woman and Elizabeth cooked the pemmican stew and Stephen threw several potatoes directly into the fire.

Elizabeth opened her blouse and offered Joshua her breast. Jamie, who had turned up at the last moment, morose and silent, turned away in embarrassment. It was clear the boy had a crush on Elizabeth, but everything involving the body, especially when it was her body, mortified him.

He was strangely silent this evening, and when Stephen asked him where he had been, he refused to answer.

Père André played with Jane and Mary, Cree Woman's daughters. He held a coin in his hand and turned his wrist over and it disappeared. Both girls gasped in awe. Then he pulled the coin out of Mary's ear. She giggled. The coin disappeared and then it was Jane's turn. The boy, Jack, looked on wide-eyed but he would not carry on like the girls.

After eating, the children were hustled off to the bedrolls in the tipi that Cree Woman had set up. Jamie yawned and then he followed the young ones. Père André still played with the coin.

"Do you wish to pull a coin out of my ear? You may, as many times as you like, so long as I may keep the coins," Elizabeth joked.

André laughed. He called Stephen to sit by Elizabeth. Her baby had finished nursing but she continued to nestle him in her arms. Stephen sat down beside Elizabeth and took Joshua from her. Then he looked across the fire at the priest.

"Why did you come here, André? There were a dozen safer places for you."

"The Hudson's Bay Company controls all the places where I would be comfortable. One place is as good as another."

"Do you really trust Douglas?"

"No, he would kill me and you to protect himself or if he were paid enough. But there are always men like Douglas around. Remember the white cutthroat at Lachine and the assassin at Manitoulin Island. They come in all colors—red, white, and mixed."

There was a commotion on the far side of the camp. Sentries gave the word that riders were coming across the prairie at some speed. Shouts were heard all over the camp.

"It's the scouts returning. They've sighted the herd."

Ian Rowand was in the lead. His horse leapt over the low spot in the cart barricade, and as Ian pulled in the reins, the horse rose on his hind legs and came to a stop. He asked for Grant and the captain general came to him.

"A large herd of buffalo, less than a half day's ride to the west," Ian reported.

Those men within hearing of the report gave off war whoops and shot off their rifles.

"We leave at dawn," Cuthbert Grant said. "Call the group captains together. We have some organizing to do tonight."

Ian took his horse to the center of the camp, where the animal was staked with the others, and then he looked for his own campfire. Cree Woman watched for him. When she caught sight he went back to the fire and prepared a bowl of stew. He sat down before the fire and acknowledged his friends and Pierre. Then he took a bowl from his wife's hands and began to eat.

"Well," said Elizabeth finally, "what news?"

"I wouldn't be here if I had not sighted buffalo. The hunt will be tomorrow."

Cree Woman broke into a smile.

"Tomorrow we will have roasted tongue," she said. "And we will gorge ourselves on fresh meat. It is almost one year since we've had anything but pemmican or fish from the river. My husband will fill my lodge with fresh meat and I will make clothes for my children and my man and we shall be warm for another winter. The spirit of the buffalo has been good to us again, directing the herd into our guns."

It was more like a prayer of thanksgiving and more words than anyone around the fire had ever heard her speak at one time.

Elizabeth sat closer to Stephen. "What she says is true," she whispered in his ear. "And it worries me."

"Why?"

"Because, Stevie, although you're good with a rifle, you're one of the worst horsemen I have ever seen. Yet our winter is going to depend on how well you do on the kill tomorrow. We can't afford to purchase pemmican again for next winter. We have to shoot buffalo and make our own."

"We could raise some crops on our farm."

"Another thing you're not too good at."

He was growing annoyed. "I'm a fur trapper and I'm good at that."

"I'm sure you are," she responded. "I know you're getting angry and you're going to be even more angry after I make a suggestion. I want to ride in the hunt tomorrow."

"Are you mad? The hunt is dangerous. Even experienced hunters get gored. Women, especially those nursing infants, shouldn't take those kind of chances."

"Stevie, I'm a better rider than you and just as good with a rifle. I want to ride tomorrow."

"No, we don't have an extra horse. We need two to pull the carts and two for riding."

"I know," she said.

He looked at her, his eyebrows arched.

"You expect me to stay behind with the women and the children, don't you?"

"Pierre will be here, and Jamie also."

"No, I'll not be unmanned."

"She's right," interrupted Ian. "If your future depends on your skills tomorrow, you've got no future. You're a good

133

man, Stephen Miller, but you'll be a stupid one if you let pride interfere. I say your woman ride with us."

Stephen glared at Ian. He looked over at Père André. The priest shook his head.

"It's not proper for a woman to carry on in that fashion. You should ride yourself, or maybe that equipment you used to carry between your legs has shriveled up."

Rowand looked quizzically at the priest.

"A priest should never call into question another man's manliness."

Stephen felt the tension but he couldn't help the laugh that came to him.

"You don't know this priest."

"No, I don't," said Ian. "How well do you know him?"

"Well enough." Then he turned to Elizabeth. "I know it's dumb but I can't bring myself to sit here like a dunce while you ride off with the men and shoot buffalo."

"You won't sit here," interrupted Ian. "You can bring the carts right behind us and start to butcher the carcasses with our markings."

Stephen was still troubled.

"Please, Stevie. We need the meat and we have Jamie to feed too."

"All right," Stephen said finally. His whole body seemed to slump with resignation.

André made a disgusted sound.

"I risked good men's lives to save your balls from the Ojibwa once, boy. I guess it was all for nothing."

He stood up and walked away from the campfire.

Elizabeth laughed. "Priests don't know how to deal with women, especially women who wear pants and ride horses and shoot straight. Father Thomas could not deal with me either. Only Father Eli understood." She spoke softly and there was a note of wistfulness in her voice when she mentioned the old man.

Stephen put an arm about her shoulders.

"You miss him, don't you?"

"It's just that he's so old and these would be the last days we could be together and we're missing them."

Joshua began to fuss, and Elizabeth picked up her son and began to rock him in her arms.

*   *   *

The signal flag was raised as soon as the eastern sky began to turn gray. The camp was up. Breakfast fires were lit. The women led horses to hitch them to their cart while the men checked their rifles and muskets to guarantee that they were in perfect working condition. A misfire would not only rob them of a fine kill but it could also cost one his life.

Elizabeth was excited. Stephen could see it in her face. Her cheeks were flushed and her eyes seemed to sparkle. She had tossed a great deal during the night and this morning seemed to exude nervous energy.

Stephen checked his musket completely. He had already cleaned it thoroughly and now he aimed down the sights to check on them. As he did Ian walked into them and raised his hands above his head.

"I surrender," he joked. "I didn't know that siding with Elizabeth would make you that angry."

Stephen started to laugh. "I should be more angry with the priest. He was kind of rough."

"He was impossible," Elizabeth chimed in.

"I suspect that anyone who attempted to stand in your way would have earned that label," joked Stephen.

"I don't know what you mean," she said defensively. "I wanted what was best for all of us. It was the priest who raised selfish emotional issues. I am still angry with him and I have not seen him this morning and I think that is for the best."

"That's right. Where is the good Father?"

"Licking his wounds. There's little place to go. It's the camp or nothing."

Cuthbert Grant rode into the center of the camp on an Indian pony.

"Hunters," he shouted, "mount up. We ride ahead. Group captains, make sure your riders maintain the pace. Make sure your carts get under way."

Stephen fetched his roan horse and walked the animal back to the cart. Ian was already mounted and Cree Woman was hitching the other horses to the two carts.

Stephen handed the reins to Elizabeth. She leapt onto the back of the horse like the expert that she was. She smiled down at him. He had never seen her look more beautiful. She had untied her hair and let it fall down to her shoulders and the first rays of the early golden sun struck her face.

Stephen handed her his rifle and extra pouch with powder and ball.

"Ready?" Ian asked.

She nodded.

"Good hunting!" Jamie called out; his adulation now knew no bounds.

Cree Woman reached up and touched Ian's arm. He smiled at her and at their children.

Stephen said nothing. He merely looked at Elizabeth. She maneuvered her horse next to Ian and then rode with him to where Chris Douglas was gathering the riders under his command. The Métis looked at Elizabeth in amusement, then his eyes went back toward the camp to find Stephen's.

Stephen resented that look. He wished he could wipe it off Douglas's face.

The group captain turned. Grant gave the signal and the whole force of hunters moved slowly as a group, about four hundred strong, out of the ring of carts.

Stephen watched them disappear over the first knoll, then went about the camp loading their possessions into the cart.

"Come on, Jamie," he called out in annoyance. "I haven't got all day. Give me and Cree Woman a hand."

The boy tore his eyes from where Elizabeth had finally disappeared. He wished he was with her. It would give him the opportunity at last to do what had to be done.

Elizabeth was surprised that they moved so slowly. She looked at Ian quizzically.

"We will have plenty of opportunities to race ahead when we are among the herd. The buffalo are in no hurry and we should be in no hurry to get to their vicinity."

She rode quietly then. The sun was fully up now. It was going to be a warm day. There were no clouds whatsoever in the sky. Rolling grassy hillocks blocked their view of what was directly ahead until they reached the top and could see more hillocks.

"How much farther?" Elizabeth asked with impatience.

Ian smiled. "There's a stream still running off spring ground water. It flows into the river a few miles further on. There's plenty of grass and water and that's where the buffalo are—only a few more miles now."

They continued the slow pace for a few minutes longer.

Then Grant, standing in his stirrups, raised his hand in the air.

"Spread out," Douglas called.

The riders, who had been bunched together, veered to the right or the left to make a long single line. When Grant was satisfied that his four hundred riders were spread out abreast he dropped his hand, and all the riders broke into a trot.

Elizabeth started to smile. This was more like it. Now they would cover the remaining ground quickly. The horse underneath her sensed her relaxation and began to move ahead even more quickly.

"Hold that roan in check," Ian called out. "Don't break ranks. We all come in on the herd at the same time."

Elizabeth reined her horse in. "It's hard to keep this discipline. All I want to do is race ahead and charge into the herd."

"That way you get your shots off and the rest of us chase a scattered herd."

He opened the pouch at his side and placed three lead balls in his mouth. She followed his example. That would help in reloading at a dead run.

Again Grant raised his hand and dropped it. All the riders increased their speed. The line became ragged, with some riders slightly ahead of the others. Ahead of them was a ridge.

Elizabeth wanted to be the first to reach the top of the ridge. To the left she could see the group captain, Douglas, pull ahead of her. She gave the roan more slack on the reins and she surged ahead. The horse was a natural racer and didn't like any other horse ahead of him.

Elizabeth had reached the top of the ridge. Below, the prairies opened before her and a shallow creek flowed to the north toward the Assiniboine. Everywhere in the valley there were buffalo. Some of the shaggy beasts lay in mud puddles they had created. Others chomped on lush grass that grew between the creek channels. There were thousands and thousands of them. Now the whole line of riders had reached the top ridge. They charged at full speed toward the herd.

The calves were the first to panic. They raced for their mothers' sides. The cows began to huddle together. Finally the bulls, aroused from their lethargy, began to paw the soft ground. They shook their great shaggy heads. Their horns reflected in the sun. Then all at once they too panicked and the whole herd began to race away from the oncoming hunters.

Elizabeth had never been more excited in her life. The roan ran at full speed and she was in the lead. Now she was among the herd and the animals eyed her and swerved away. Their panic was complete. They no longer followed the herd leader but rather whatever animal was immediately in front of them.

Elizabeth knew she must pick her kill. A calf cut in front of her. She could see its eyes wide with fright. She did not want a calf. A young bull was racing directly ahead of her. Elizabeth bent down closer to the roan's neck and urged him forward. She heard rifle shots behind her. Slower, more experienced hunters were already making their kills. She was alongside the bull now. He shifted his head to the side and his horns flashed by her boot and just missed the leg of the roan. Elizabeth knew she could wait no longer. She rose in the stirrups and brought the gun to her shoulders. She had no time to aim. She fired as the gun came up.

At first she thought she had missed. The bull kept right on running. In fact, he pulled ahead of her. But then, as if someone had cut him down at the knees, his front legs collapsed and he went tumbling, his giant head crashing into the ground. His right horn hooked into the earth and his body was twisted completely about and landed with a thud. The buffalo coming up behind him veered out of his path. The bull attempted to struggle to his feet but then collapsed with a shudder. His bladder emptied itself onto the ground, creating a small puddle at his side.

Elizabeth reined in the roan. There was chaos all about her. Ian came up behind her. He had already loaded. He spit the remaining bullets into his hand and called out to her.

"Keep going. Reload. I'll mark the kill."

Elizabeth acknowledged him with a wave of her hand. It was dangerous even to slow down in this stampede, much less dismount. She took the next lead ball out of her mouth. It was a wonder to her that in the excitement she had not swallowed one of them.

She gave the horse his head again. She reloaded as she rode. The trick was new to her and she fumbled with the powder twice before she had the gun ready to fire again. Most of the herd was ahead of her now, but she was surrounded by stragglers. She kicked the roan and moved toward a

138

panicked cow that had a terrified calf racing at her side. The cow stopped short and turned to face the attacker. Elizabeth swerved at the last minute to avoid the cow's horns. She raised the musket and shot downward into the cow's shoulder. The cow collapsed instantly. The bullet had pierced its heart. The calf immediately panicked, nuzzled its mother, but then ran off a short distance. More stragglers came racing by and the herd instinct of the calf took hold. It ran with them.

Elizabeth breathed a sigh of relief. She had not wanted to have to kill the calf. She looked around for Ian but saw no sign of him. She stayed with her kill until she saw him coming toward her. He was holding his shoulder and she saw that he was bleeding.

She kicked her horse to meet him.

"What's wrong?" she called out after spitting the remaining lead ball into her hand.

"He only grazed me. A stray bullet. It's a wonder someone doesn't get killed every year in this mess."

"Can you mark the cow for me?"

He nodded. "Can you hunt for yourself? Three kills already and I plan to get me one more."

"How many more do I need?" she asked.

"You probably have enough meat already. But no harm is done if you get more."

"Good." She took her last bullet and reloaded. She again kicked the roan into action. She had to race across the valley to catch up with the herd. She could hear shooting ahead. Off to her right she saw a horse lying prone, half its body in the creek, half on the bank. Its leg was bent at an impossible angle and it was clear that the horse had tripped, broken its leg, and then been put out of its misery by the rider.

The roan leapt across a stream and raced on after the other hunters. This was the part she liked best. The chase. The sense of freedom with the wind blowing in her face—the exhilaration. She felt a joy she had not known before.

The herd came into view again amid a cloud of dust. They were in the dry part of the valley now. Some of the herd had moved over the far ridge onto the open prairie again. She followed them over the ridge.

The buffalo were stampeding mindlessly now, racing across the prairie away from the hunters and their merciless rifles. Elizabeth gave the roan his head. The horse's ears bent back and his neck strained forward as he tore after the lumbering beasts.

Elizabeth heard a rifle fire off to her right. She saw a great bull crash to the ground in a gigantic cloud of dust. She recognized the painted horse of Christopher Douglas. The group captain was catching up to her. She didn't want to fire. She doubted if her party could haul more than three buffalo even after they had been butchered. Her next kill would be her last. She didn't want the chase to end.

She heard a man shout. She turned in her saddle and saw Douglas's horse down and Douglas himself sprawled on the ground. His rifle was gone and the herd stragglers were closing in on him.

Elizabeth swerved to the left and began to race toward Douglas. Even at a breakneck pace she would not arrive in time. She rose in the stirrups and fired in one motion at the stragglers. She missed but the lead buffalo was frightened by the bullet that passed over his head and he swerved further away from the charging roan and away from the hapless group captain. Those that came after the lead buffalo followed after him.

Elizabeth rode up to Douglas. She dismounted and knelt by his side. He sat grasping his shoulder, his whole face contorted with pain. Elizabeth knelt beside him. Without saying anything she tested his shoulder and neck for broken bones, as Dr. Eli Stoddard had taught her when she had served as his nurse. No bones were broken, but when she touched the shoulder joint Douglas gasped.

Elizabeth turned to look at his horse. The paint was dead. She commented to distract him. Then without warning she grabbed his arm and jerked. The dislocated joint snapped back in place as Douglas screamed in pain.

"Damn you, woman," he shouted at her. "What are you trying to do to me?"

"Move your arm," she ordered.

He moved the shoulder gingerly, then tested the arm itself. "It's all right," he said in genuine surprise. "It's sore but I can move it."

He looked up at Elizabeth with obvious admiration. "You're an unusual woman. You ride like a Cree, you shoot better than most men, you saved my life, and then you fix my shoulder."

"You cost me my last kill," she responded gruffly, although his compliment had touched her.

"Please accept one of mine. I have far more than I can use."

Several other riders came up from behind. Elizabeth recognized one of them as Ian Rowand.

"Rowand," Douglas called out, "you know my mark. Have your people butcher one of my beasts for Mrs. Miller. I owe her that much at least."

Cuthbert Grant rode over to join the group about Douglas.

"It was a good hunt," he said as he dismounted. "I estimate about a thousand kills. The carts are coming up. Now the dirty work begins. I have no intention of staying around here. The stench will be unbearable. I'm going back to the old campsite. I have a keg of whiskey that needs opening."

Several of the men grunted assent. Douglas smiled at Elizabeth.

"You're welcome to join us, madam," he said, rising to his feet and making a mocking bow. "I assume your man will be doing the butchering along with the other squaws."

Elizabeth was silent. She climbed back on the roan. She started to move off but then turned to face Douglas.

"My man proved his manhood in more significant ways than killing dumb beasts—beasts so dumb you could walk up to one if you stayed downwind and hit him on top of the head with a club to kill him. Stephen Miller doesn't need to do that. He proved he's a man in better ways. In ways you could never match," she said smiling shyly.

"How will you know that's true if you don't try anyone else?" asked Douglas.

Some of the men started to laugh rudely.

"But if you think so little of the hunt," offered Grant, "why did you join it?"

"For the chase," she said, her face breaking into a smile at the mere memory of it.

Rowand joined Elizabeth as they rode back over the ridge and down to the stream.

"You should not flirt with a man like Douglas," he said softly. "He is a dangerous man."

Elizabeth looked into Ian's face.

"I will flirt with any man I want, including you."

Rowand laughed.

"Not me, Liz. Cree Woman would . . . I don't even want to

141

think about what she would do to me. I just better get you back to Stephen Miller right away."

He kicked his horse and broke into a gallop, and Elizabeth followed his example.

Elizabeth and Ian met the horse-drawn two-wheel Red River carts just as they entered the valley. Ian pointed out the kill to Cree Woman and she went to work on one with her enormous knife. The children helped her but the younger girls kept holding their noses at the stench and ran behind the cart. The Indian woman first cut the tongues out of the buffalo and built a fire of buffalo chips. The tongues were placed over the fire to roast while she continued to work. Jamie, Stephen, Ian, and Elizabeth, their bodies starving for fresh meat, watched the fire with growing impatience and anticipation. Elizabeth nearly choked when Cree Woman sliced open the great belly of the nearest beast and with both hands pulled the intestines and offal from the gaping wound. The huge stomach bags were cut out of the cavity and the rancid-smelling contents were spilled onto the prairie grass. With expert strokes she began to skin the beast. She turned back to the fire, her arms dripping with gore, and started to take the tongues off the spits.

"Let me do it," offered Stephen after taking one look at Elizabeth's green face. He grabbed the meat and cut it into slices with his knife. Ian and his children devoured their pieces.

"God, that's good," Ian said, laughing.

"I want some more," demanded Jack.

Jamie gulped his down without comment. Elizabeth looked at Stephen and he at her.

"Well, here goes," he said, sinking his teeth into the sliced tongue.

Elizabeth overcame her squeamishness and bit into her slice. Her eyes widened in surprise. It was delicious. Soon the whole party was devouring slices of buffalo tongue. Stephen's moustache, normally so yellow, was dark with meat juices. Jamie's shirt was covered with drippings from his mouth. He held out his sticky hands and then sheepishly wiped them on the seat of his pants. He looked about, waiting to be corrected. His mother would have shouted for that, but then sadly he remembered that he hadn't a mother any longer.

Cree Woman had grabbed an end of the buffalo intestine and handed the other end to Ian. The two began to eat the intestine raw. When the woman had eaten enough she turned her end over to her son, but Ian kept on devouring. Soon the liver appeared and was placed over the fire to be roasted, although Cree Woman preferred it raw. She sliced the meat from the buffalo hump into long strips and hung them high over the fire to dry, while other strips were laid out on the prairie grass to dry in the sun.

Cree Woman ordered Jamie and Elizabeth to look for berries—Saskatoon berries—which would surely be growing wild here in the valley. The best pemmican was made with the berries. They would be several days drying and powdering meat into jerky and then mixing it with berries and buffalo grease. Once her pemmican was prepared, she would pack it in the stomach bags and load it in the carts. In the meantime, her children and friends would gorge themselves on fresh meat. After all, it might be another year before they would again have the opportunity to taste fresh meat.

She continued to work on the carcass well after all the choice meat had been devoured or dried. She was not like the wasteful whites or even the Métis. The hides would provide lodging when they traveled. The brains would help tan the hides. The hides would become robes for the winter's cold. Even the chips that covered the valley could be collected and dried for burning in the stove next winter.

They stayed in the valley for four days. Occasionally the buffalo herd would stray back to the place of slaughter, drawn by the water and good grass. It was possible, given their poor eyesight, to walk up to one and shoot it. As it fell bleeding to the ground, other buffalo, as if fascinated by the scent of blood, would come closer to watch their late companion being slaughtered. Then suddenly and nervously they would run away again.

The Rowands and Millers made no more kills. Their two carts were heavily loaded, so heavily loaded, in fact, that all four horses would be needed to trek back to the Red River.

On the morning of the fourth day after the hunt they were ready to return to Fort Garry. Little groups had already set out on their own, although the leaders advised that several parties should travel together for protection. No Cree or Assiniboine had been sighted, but Grant warned all that it was never wise to take foolish chances.

143

When Stephen suggested to Ian that they travel with Douglas and his band to reach the fort, he was surprised by the Métis's instant rejection of his idea.

"Stephen, my friend," said Ian, "there are no Cree about. I scouted the prairie not only for the herd but for those who follow the herd. There are no Cree for at least three days' ride west of here. I think we take no chances by finding our own trail back home."

Stephen had no choice but to accept Rowand's evaluation. But the vehemence with which he presented his arguments surprised Miller.

They set out before sunrise to cover as much territory as possible before the June sun was too high in the heavens. The two carts groaned under the weight of the fresh meat and the pemmican. There was no room for passengers this time. Everyone walked, except Joshua, who was strapped to Stephen's back.

"Has anyone seen 'Pierre' since the hunt began?" Stephen asked as they started out.

No one had. Stephen finally shrugged.

By the time the morning sky had turned from golden pink to blue, they had covered many miles of open prairies.

"How about some breakfast?" Jamie called out to Ian.

Ian looked at Stephen in annoyance.

"Growing boys need their food," Stephen responded to Ian's look.

"We eat on the move, then," Ian ordered. "Cree Woman, cut some pemmican and give everyone a cup of water."

He climbed up onto the wagon and searched the horizon in all directions.

To the north and south there were clear signs of prairie travelers. Clouds of dust hung over the hills in both directions.

"Elizabeth," Ian called out, "you come lead this horse for me. Jamie, can you shoot a rifle?"

The boy's eyes lit up. "You bet."

"Then come with me. Cree Woman, get my rifle. I'm going scouting on foot with the boy."

Stephen brought his wagon to a halt alongside Ian's and waited for Elizabeth to take the front.

"Rowand," he said, "we left early before anyone else. You're as jittery as a mother cat yet you insist there are no

144

hostile Indians about. Now you go out scouting. This isn't a military party. We're going home from a hunt. What's wrong?"

"Not all hostiles are red," the Métis responded. "Come with me, Jamie. Stephen, keep heading due east. We'll catch up with you at noontime."

Ian waited until the wagons were out of sight over the first knoll. Then he began a leisurely walk with Jamie at his side.

"This ain't much of a scout," the crestfallen boy complained after some moments of walking.

"We don't need to scout, boy. If there's any danger, I know from which direction it will come. It will come from our rear. We left before anyone else. Besides, I need to talk to you."

"What about?" Jamie said defensively.

"I saw your face when you met Chris Douglas. What do you know about him that you ain't telling?"

Jamie looked away and didn't answer.

Ian grabbed the boy by his shirt collar and began to shake him.

"I'm not asking you politely. I want to know what you know."

Jamie was frightened of the Métis. His father had told him that you couldn't trust half-breeds. He was frightened but he had no intention of providing this man with the knowledge he wanted. Why should he trust him? It was the Millers he trusted. He would confide in Mr. Miller and he would do anything for Mrs. Miller, but this Métis would get only silence.

"Well, then, McAlistair, you're dumb. You're as dumb as your father was and you deserve to share his fate."

"You leave my father out of this, Rowand," Jamie shouted, his voice quavering.

Rowand sighed in exasperation.

"Look, boy, I know you know something. If I was the one who wanted to silence what you know, you'd be dead right now. I saw what went on at your parents' cabin. You weren't attacked by Cree. Cree would have made mincemeat of the bodies. And if anyone had stayed alive, as you did, he'd be walking around without any scalp on his head. It was no Cree who murdered your father and mother and burned out the Millers. I hoped at first that Cree Woman's presence kept them away from me, but I knew all along that it wasn't her—it was me they protected. That's because it was Métis who did you in. You didn't know that at first because they dressed like Cree. But I knew the minute you saw Chris Douglas's face that he had been the one. It was Douglas, wasn't it, who slaughtered your family?"

Jamie continued to look away from Rowand.

"I'm right, ain't I?" Ian continued, his voice rising to a shout.

"Yes, damn it, and I'm a damned coward. I should have faced up to the bastard and stuck my knife in his gizzard." Jamie started to weep as he shouted.

Rowand held Jamie's head and pulled it to his shoulder. He patted the boy on the back.

"It's a damned good thing you held your peace, boy. If Douglas knew you had pointed him out you'd be buzzard food and so would my family and the Millers. Your guts would be ripening up there with the buffalo carcasses."

Jamie sniffed and wiped his eyes and nose on his sleeve.

"So you and I know who killed your folks but what we don't know is why. Come on," Ian said finally, "we can't let them get too far ahead."

They started to walk slowly. The carts were clearly visible at the top of the knoll. Ian walked with his rifle cradled in his arm and searched the horizon to the north and to the south and to the rear. More and more his attention was drawn to one large dust cloud that seemed to trail off into the sky but whose source was clearly getting closer.

"What makes you think Douglas won't attack us right out here in the open?" Jamie asked Ian.

"He has no reason to. Not unless he knows something more than I do. Did he recognize you?"

"I don't know."

"Even if he did, the important question," said Ian, "is did he think you recognized him?"

Again the boy merely shrugged his shoulders.

Ian glanced to the northwest. A force of at least twenty men was moving swiftly toward them.

Ian decided to take no chances.

"Come on," he called to Jamie as he broke into a trot. "Let's catch up with the others."

Ian ran with the graceful lope of one who could run for days across these same prairies. Jamie ran like the boy he was, with a burst of speed followed by the loss of wind. But they did not have far to go, and it was Jamie who called out first to the Millers and Cree Woman.

"Wait, hold up," he called out, waving his arms.

146

Stephen was walking ahead of the cart horses. He brought them to a halt when he heard Jamie's call. He stood in place and waited for Jamie to approach. Behind the boy he saw Ian Rowand. The look of concern on the Métis's face gripped his attention far more than the boy's arm-waving. Stephen handed the horses and reins to Elizabeth and walked to meet Ian.

The Métis, without speaking, pointed to the column of brown dust that trailed out to the west behind them.

"Trouble?" Stephen asked.

"I think so," Ian warned.

"Are they after our meat, our horses?"

"Us, more likely. More precisely, I think they want Jamie."

"Jamie, why?"

"Because he recognized Chris Douglas as the leader of the men who murdered his family."

Stephen was not totally confused, but then the argument McAlistair had with Douglas in the store came flooding back into his memory.

"There was bad blood between them, I know, but I didn't think it was strong enough to lead to murder, especially to the murder of children. And why me too? My place was burned too."

"I don't have any answers, only worries right now. We are out in the open. The country is very flat here. That's just as well. Anyone approaching us will be without cover the whole time. We've got to fortify ourselves, Jamie, grab the bridle of those wagon horses and pull them around. Then unhitch the horses and hobble them. Stephen, you and I and Elizabeth and Cree Woman have got to start unloading that pemmican. I want to make a square of the carts and the pemmican bags."

Cree Woman was already hefting the dried pemmican bags out of the cart and handing them to Stephen. Elizabeth checked Stephen's musket to make sure it was loaded.

"Put some of that meat under the cartwheels and make a safe place for the children. Jamie, you get under the wheels with them and take care that they don't raise their heads."

"Why me?" asked Jamie. "I've got my knife."

"Don't argue with me, you bloody fool. The women can both shoot and they will be needed to take up the slack if we're attacked and Stephen and I get hit. Now get under the goddamned wagon and be man enough to take care of my kids."

Within five minutes they had constructed their little fort.

Stephen knelt at the back of the now empty cart, his musket pointed in the direction of the oncoming strangers. Ian lay prone on the ground behind the meat barricade. His rifle was pointed in the same direction. Since his weapon had far greater range, much would depend on his judgment and accuracy.

Cree Woman searched the horizon in all directions for signs of other intruders. Elizabeth held a long line that ran to the hobbled horses, which fed without concern on the grass beyond the square.

They could hear the horses of the approaching troop. There were no wagon noises. Stephen concluded that the armed force had moved ahead of their women and children, who would bring the carts along later. They were well within long rifle range now. Ian counted twenty-three horses. The men were shirtless and wore the leggings and loincloths of the Cree. Ian knew instinctively that they were his own people. He could not yet make out any faces. He looked for the paint mustang that Chris Douglas had ridden, but then he remembered the accident and the death of that horse.

"That's far enough," he called and fired his rifle high above the head of the lead rider.

The oncoming troop came to a halt. Then the first rider came forward at a slow walk while the others fanned out. The lone rider came within hailing distance. Ian was looking into the glare of the midday sun and it was difficult to see the rider's face.

"You don't need to come no closer," Rowand called out in French.

"You're right," was the response. It was Douglas.

Stephen glanced down below the wheels of the cart and caught sight of Jamie's face. The transition that took place was startling. Jamie was scared but not so scared that he didn't recognize the sound of his enemy's voice. His lips tightened and his eyes seemed to change from those of a child to the narrow, hard slits of an angry man. Someday, maybe today, Chris Douglas would pay for the deed of last winter.

"What do you want, Chris?" Rowand called.

"Why, just passing through on our way to Fort Garry. Thought we might share a little bit of fresh meat before the fire tonight if we rode together."

"Cowshit, Douglas," Stephen yelled out. "Why do you need twenty men riding ahead without women and children?

Whose meat are you planning to enjoy? I guess it would be ours since you haven't any of your own with you."

"It would be neighborly of you to share some meat, Miller," Douglas called out. "I wouldn't mind sharing a lot of what you've got."

Elizabeth remembered the exchange between them after his fall from his horse and she winced. Had she caused all this by flirting?

Ian hushed Stephen. "I'll do the negotiating." Then he yelled out, "You're welcome to share our pemmican with us, Chris. Come on into our little camp here. Send your boys home and we'll make it real cozy here for you."

Douglas's cheerful tone changed. "You got something we want, Ian Rowand, and you're one of us. Give us what we want and yours can go home in peace."

"All I got is buffalo meat," Ian responded.

"Give us the whites, that's all we want."

"You start murdering whites out here on the prairie, Douglas, and you'll ruin it for all of us. Lord Selkirk may be dead but it seems to me that all those fellows you work for at the Hudson's Bay Company are white. I don't think they'd take kindly to any killing."

"I want Miller!" Douglas said emphatically.

Ian turned and looked at Stephen in surprise. Stephen himself was shocked. Elizabeth went rigid with fear.

"Why you?" Ian asked Stephen. "Why not Jamie?"

Slowly the truth began to come to Rowand. Douglas had never been after the McAlistairs. The attack on Angus and Flora was meant as a cover for the raid that Douglas had planned for the Millers. But even though he now knew who the real intended victim was, he was no closer to understanding why Douglas wanted Stephen dead.

"Why do you want me, Douglas?" Stephen called out.

"I want to have some fun with your wife after I get you out of the way."

Stephen raised his musket and fired. He was too far away for a musket to be accurate. Douglas's horse shied away from the sound and he had to steady her.

Suddenly, from all sides, horsemen charged at the little fort.

Ian swung his rifle around and aimed at the closest assailant. The rifle barked and the horseman flew off backward to the ground. Stephen had reloaded his musket. He fired and a second horseman fell into the dust, dragged along by one foot in the stirrup of his panicked mustang. Ian was reloading as fast as he could. There was not enough time. A horseman leapt over the narrow barricade and slashed the air with his tomahawk.

Elizabeth felt the line running to their horses first grow more taut and then slack as it was grabbed and cut.

Ian's rifle went off and the attacker inside the barricade stared dumbly at the hole in his chest and then slumped to the ground. His horse panicked at the smell of blood and reared and kicked out his hooves.

Stephen yelled at Elizabeth to get under the other wagon out of the horse's way, but as he yelled the words the wagon's giant wheels began to move. Another horseman had grabbed the hitch and was pulling one whole side of their tiny fort away with him.

Stephen had no time to reload. He grabbed the tomahawk from the dead man's hands and jumped onto the cart as it was being pulled out of line. He threw the tomahawk and it struck the rear of the horseman's skull with a terrible thud. The horseman slumped forward, then fell from his horse. The cart stopped moving.

Next, Miller grabbed his victim's loaded rifle and turned to face another assailant. But two men already held Ian down on the ground. Another pulled Mary out from under the wagon by her hair. The assailant screamed when Jamie's knife plunged into his lower belly and Cree Woman simultaneously pierced his back. Elizabeth had Stephen's musket now. She fired at one of Ian's assailants and removed the back of his head, splattering hair, bone, blood, and brains all over Ian, who wrestled with a large swarthy Métis, naked except for a loincloth.

Stephen was standing above them now. He brought the stock of his captured rifle down mercilessly again and again, crushing the head of Ian's opponent.

Suddenly the attack was over. All the horsemen were gone. There were no sounds except for the heavy labored breathing of the defenders and the pitiful wail of the baby, Joshua, from under the cart.

Stephen and Ian, their chest and arm muscles bulging with exertion, hauled the cart back into position.

Jamie and Cree Woman hauled the bodies of the Métis assailants as far out into the prairie as they dared. Jamie was smiling and his eyes were alive with excitement when he returned.

"We sure as hell showed those bastards, didn't we?" he said.

Ian looked at Stephen and Elizabeth both. Both of them stared grimly at the loose restraining line that lay on the grass at their feet.

"We have no horses, Jamie," Elizabeth said. "We can't move. All we can do is sit here and wait for them to pick us off." She pointed off in the distance. Beyond rifle range a man on horseback appeared. Douglas was not going to go away.

IX

Spring 1822

They heard the carts join their attackers' encampment. Soon wails from mourning women filled the night sky. Several women came to within rifle range of the little fort and hurled oaths at these destroyers of their men.

Cree Woman served some cold pemmican. She gave them nothing to drink. They had to conserve their water. Ian ordered the group to come together for the night. He assigned watches for the four adults. Then seeing the look of disappointment on Jamie's face, he assigned the first and earliest one to the boy.

They gnawed at the meal in silence. Finally Stephen could stand the silence and the unanswered questions no longer.

"Ian, are we going to get out of this?"

Before responding, Rowand waited until Cree Woman had tucked her children into their bedrolls underneath the cart and returned to the group.

"Chances of getting out of here are slim," he said with brutal honesty. "For some reason Douglas wants you dead."

"I think I know why," offered Elizabeth. "It's his brother, my husband. He wants Stephen dead and I believe he wants me dead along with him."

"You mean you two ain't married?"

"No," said Stephen.

"And you run off with your brother's wife? That can produce a powerful lot of hate."

"His brother ordered him killed before anything happened between us. He thinks something happened between us and he wants Stevie's money."

Rowand merely stared at Elizabeth and Stephen. He knew they spoke the truth. Whites would murder for gold. He could have understood and even sympathized with Miller's

153

brother if he sought revenge for the seducing of Elizabeth, but to kill your own brother for money. He was glad he was Métis and was only half corrupt. And he blessed Cree Woman. Because of her, his three young ones would be even less corrupted.

Stephen sat quietly for some moments, pulling absent-mindedly at his moustache.

"Mr. Rowand," Jamie asked, "what are we going to do?"

"We're going to sit right here and let them sit over there. If they come after us we're going to kill the bastards. And when they get either tired of sitting or tired of dying, they're going to move on and go home and so are we."

Stephen smiled. He knew that Rowand was cheering the boy up. He was well aware the noon battle had been close, and that Douglas's people far outnumbered them. The next charge would be the last one, and this little group would be the victims.

Ian handed his rifle to Jamie. "We're going to get some sleep now, boy. Keep your eyes open."

Jamie took his gun and the responsibility that went with it solemnly. No one would be more alert than he. All their lives depended on him.

Elizabeth spread their bedding underneath the cart. Cree Woman and Ian slept out in the open space between the carts.

Stephen could feel the tension in Elizabeth's body when he put his arm down for her to rest her head on it.

"Tomorrow could be the end, couldn't it?" she said softly.

"I won't try to fool you," he responded in a whisper.

She opened her blouse and allowed Joshua to suck hungrily. She stroked the back of the baby's head as he nursed.

"What will become of him?" she asked as her eyes filled with tears.

"Elizabeth, they won't kill you or Cree Woman and the children."

"I know what Douglas wants from me, Stephen. That would be death. I would rather give Josh to Cree Woman and face your fate."

The baby had fallen asleep. She gently put him back into the backpack and laid him down next to her. Stephen placed his mouth lovingly in the spot vacated by her son. She stroked his head as she had Joshua's.

"Stephen" she whispered in his ear, "I want you to make love to me."

"But the others may still be awake," he protested.

"I don't give a damn about what the others hear, Stephen Miller. This may be our last time together and I want you."

He moved his arm and drew her head to his chest. She began to unbutton his shirt. She bit at the hair on his chest and teased his nipple with her tongue. He undid the buttons on his pants and slid them down to his knees. Then he began to work on her clothing. She was soon lying completely naked in his arms. He twisted his body and pushed her down against the bedding. She reached him and stroked him until he became hard. Looming above her he looked huge and indestructible. She needed to have him looking that way. She cursed the darkness. She wanted to memorize every detail of him. How often had she seen him like this—beautiful, powerful—and had concerned herself only with her own feelings? Now she wanted this to last forever, if not in time at least in memory. She reached for him again. He groaned with pleasure as she held him. He pushed his heavily muscled body toward her and she guided him into her. A wave of contentment spread from the point of their union up her stomach and chest. Her face was flushed, although he could not have seen that in the darkness. She did not want him to move. She wanted him to remain as he was, filling her and spreading warmth from her thighs to the nape of her neck. He kissed her shoulder and he began his motion and she knew it could not last forever.

Stephen felt a hand touch his back. He awoke with a start. It was Rowand.

"Your watch," the Métis said, handing him his rifle. Stephen was instantly alert. Elizabeth slept on her back. The baby was at her breast again. Clearly she had risen in the night to feed him and had fallen asleep as he nursed.

Stephen slipped silently from out of the coverings. As he watched, Ian joined Cree Woman in the far corner next to the cartwheel behind which their children slept.

He took his post behind the barricade, searching the night for signs of motion or noise. The moon had already risen and set. The only light in the heavens came from the twinkling stars. The dome of the sky was alive with them. He had never seen so many stars at one time before. He forced his

155

attention back down to the blackened prairie. Off in the distance he heard an animal. Maybe a dog, more likely a wolf.

"They should attack us now, before sunrise," he said aloud. He heard the whirring of wings and a tiny bleat. Some bird of prey had sunk its talons into its victim. He listened carefully to the night sounds, trying to recognize any that were unfamiliar. That would be the signal that men approached. He felt a hand touch his arm. He jumped in fright. It was Cree Woman.

"I could not sleep, Miller," she whispered. "I will keep your watch with you."

He smiled at her and nodded.

They remained silent for some minutes.

"They will not come until dawn. They still retain many of the fears of my people. It is ingrained in their souls. They will attack at first light."

That was little consolation to Stephen.

"In either case we'll probably die," he responded. "I'm sorry. This whole thing seems to be my fault. That all our lives should be taken is unacceptable—Elizabeth's, Joshua's, yours, Ian's, your three little ones'. I won't let that happen, you know. I'll not let all of you die if I can help it."

The Indian woman said nothing. She stared into Stephen's face. Her normal impassive expression, however, changed to a smile of compassion. She understood his suffering and his feelings. She would not blame him even for the death of her children.

"You are a remarkable person, Cree Woman," he said finally and touched her hand.

He turned back to search the night and his soul some more.

They appeared again at dawn. They were mounted and totally surrounded the tiny fort. When they charged this time they would charge together from all directions. This time there was little chance that rifles and a musket could hold them off. Ian and Jamie were awake. It was time for a decision. The woman he loved more than life itself lay sleeping. Their child at her breast. Yes, he thought of Joshua as their child. Charles Miller be damned. He wanted them to live—even if the price of their lives was his life. Stephen put down Ian's rifle and hopped over the barricade.

Ian called out to him but he walked straight ahead toward

the Métis horsemen. He heard Elizabeth call out. His step faltered but he continued forward again. When he reached the point halfway between the camps of the Métis and his own people he yelled out.

"Douglas, if it's me you want, I'm here for the taking, but let the others go."

Between the horsemen in front of Stephen, Chris Douglas appeared. He signaled to two men to go forward to bring Stephen to him. The Métis kicked their horses and charged directly at Stephen. He thought they intended to trample him and that would be the end of it. If that was the case he was determined not to flinch. But at the last moment the horsemen veered around him. They pointed their rifles at him and came up behind him.

Rowand called out from the fort.

"You bring back our horses, Douglas."

Douglas said nothing.

Stephen walked toward him, and several of the horsemen rode forward to surround him. One dismounted. He approached Stephen from the rear and pulled his arms behind his back and tied them tightly together.

Douglas urged his horse forward. "Mr. Miller," he said mockingly, "it was a generous gesture, but so much for generosity."

He raised his hand in the air. The horsemen let off yells and charged from all sides at the little fort.

Ian was the first to react. He fired his rifle, striking one horseman directly in the face and dropping him backward from his horse. Elizabeth fired Stephen's musket and a second rider was down. Ian had already handed his rifle to Cree Woman to load. He and Jamie, with a knife and a tomahawk, stood back to back to face the onslaught. The first horse to leap the barricade lost its footing and went crashing into the cart under which the children were hidden. The cart went flying onto its side and the horse collapsed, his massive flanks crushing the screaming children of Ian Rowand and Cree Woman.

Cree Woman screamed their three names and leapt at the rider, who had collapsed to his knees after breaking his leg in the fall. She pulled the trigger of Ian's rifle and nearly blew the attacker's head from his shoulders.

A second horseman charged through the gap. His mount crashed into Cree Woman, knocking her off her feet. She landed with a terrible thud amid the thrashing feet of the downed horse. His hooves slashed at her body. She screamed and then lay perfectly still. The horse struggled to its feet, and Cree Woman was dumped on top of the silent and crushed bodies of her three children.

Elizabeth fired from beneath the cart. Her bullet struck a horse in the neck. The beast reared its head in agony and then collapsed and threw its rider headfirst over its neck. The rider's head struck the prairie and his neck collapsed with a sickening snap. Then Elizabeth covered Joshua with her body and lay still awaiting her chance to scramble from cover, seize a loose horse and escape with her son. Any fate was preferable to lying inert awaiting death. She saw her chance. A free horse stood over its fallen rider. A brief dash from cover and she and Joshua could escape. She stuck her head out from under the wagon's cover. A bullet whistled past her. She ducked back under. Someone had targeted her. There was no escape.

Ian and Jamie stood alone facing the circling horsemen. Ian had seen what had happened to his family and not even a facial muscle had twitched. He merely glared at his attackers. Now he suddenly charged forward, his tomahawk raised high. From his mouth came a scream that rose above the sound of the horses and the men. He leapt at one horseman and knocked him from his mount. He grabbed the horse's mane and pulled himself on the run onto the horse's back. His tomahawk was raised high above his head. Holding the mane and guiding the beast with the pressure of his knees, he crashed into another rider. Ian's tomahawk came crashing down into the man's neck. He turned the horse, looking for another victim. A rifle barked. Ian swayed in the saddle, his eyes wide with panic and pain. He saw his attacker beyond the remains of the near cart, which was now aflame. He could feel the strength leaving him. He let go of the horse's mane. His assailant was madly attempting to reload. The horse, frightened by the smell of blood that poured out of Ian's belly, charged at the rifleman. With what little strength he had left Ian hurled the tomahawk. It struck the rifleman's horse a glancing blow on the nose. Ian fell from his mount and was dead before he hit the ground. The injured horse threw the rifleman off his back, then bolted.

Jamie stood by himself. The riders circled him. He backed away toward the cart under which Elizabeth and Joshua hid.

He wanted to run. God, with all his soul he wanted to bolt, to grab one of the loose horses and ride away, back to the Red River, anywhere away from here. But he would not abandon Mrs. Miller and her baby. Suddenly the circle of riders parted, and Chris Douglas, dragging the bound Stephen Miller, entered the circle.

Stephen's eyes took in everything. A moan escaped his lips when he saw the motionless Cree Woman and her children. He saw Jamie, knife in hand. Panic possessed the boy, but he would take several Métis with him before they got to him unless they shot him down in cold blood. Douglas turned back to Stephen.

"Tell the boy to surrender."

"Like Rowand and his family?" Stephen spat out.

"Rowand was a traitor. He sided with the whites against his own people. He paid the price."

Elizabeth called out to Jamie. "Put down the knife, Jamie. Save yourself."

The boy looked confused. Douglas raised his rifle and aimed it at Jamie's heart. "Drop it!" Stephen yelled out.

The confusion in the boy's face turned to resignation and then defeat. The knife dropped with a clunk onto the hard ground.

Douglas dismounted and stepped to the cart. He reached under and offered Elizabeth his hand. She ignored it and crawled out by herself. She held Joshua and started to move toward Stephen. Douglas blocked her path.

"You're mine now. You have no more to do with him."

Stephen strained against the cords that bound him. But Jamie, whom Douglas had ignored, leapt at him. Several of the Métis blocked his path and grabbed him.

Douglas turned around. "No, let the nipper go. He thinks he's a man."

The Métis stepped aside and Jamie lunged. Douglas's foot went crashing into the boy's crotch. Jamie doubled over in pain. Douglas stood over him, laughing. Then he grabbed Jamie's head in both hands and sent his knee crashing into the boy's jaw. Jamie collapsed onto the ground.

"Little piece of shit," Douglas said, still smiling. "He doesn't deserve a quick death. Strip him and leave him out here on the prairie. You, Gabriel, you're about his size. You can have his things."

The smallish black-bearded man whom Douglas addressed

grinned with delight at the offer. Like a vulture he had soon stripped Jamie of his shirt, pants, and boots. He even took his undergarments. The boy was bound, then grabbed by the shoulders and feet, and tossed on top of the motionless Cree Woman.

"Now let us take the prisoners back to camp."

Douglas pulled Elizabeth up behind him on his horse. She did not resist. Her first instinct was to protect the baby, whom she held in her arms. Then Douglas kicked the horse into motion. The rawhide line that was tied to Stephen's hands went taut and he was almost jerked off his feet. He caught himself, however, and broke into a loping run behind Douglas's horse. Elizabeth turned around to look at him but his eyes were on the ground so that he might avoid any obstacle that would trip him to be dragged behind the Métis.

They camped about five miles away, dragging their twenty carts into a large circle. They were a sullen crowd. Too many of them had fallen victim to the defenders. Their women and children picked up clumps of sod and hurled them at Stephen as he was led into the camp. One Métis woman and some Cree squaws in the crowd had already sharpened their sticks for the torture. The white man had to be burned.

Douglas halted in the middle of the circle.

"We'll wait out this day here. There's pemmican to be divided among the families of those who died. We must send out burial parties. Leave the bodies of the enemy for wolves and the birds. The prisoner here, his cart and horses are mine."

He leapt from the back of his horse and pulled Elizabeth to him. He grabbed her milk-swollen breasts in front of the entire encampment.

"Chris has taken more than his cart and horses," someone yelled.

The men laughed.

"But now for the prisoner. I'm afraid this is his last encampment. Pierre," Douglas shouted.

The flap of the tipi was pulled aside and Père André emerged. Stephen watched the priest cross the circle and approach him. He was surprised that his friend had joined forces with his enemies. But he was too exhausted to register that surprise.

–"*Mon ami*," the priest greeted him. "I am sorry."

"He's all yours," said Douglas. "Take him."

Some of the Métis women growled in disappointment.

"He should burn," a squaw yelled out in Cree.

"Come with me," the priest said as he took the rawhide that bound Stephen and began to lead him through the angry crowd. A man with a scraggly beard spit tobacco juice into Stephen's face. The foul mixture of tobacco and saliva ran down his dusty and sweat-stained cheek, leaving a wet brown streak.

André brought him into the tipi. He took a cloth and wiped Stephen's face.

"You've got to help us," Stephen pleaded.

André pulled out his knife and cut the rawhide thongs that bound Stephen's hands. Stephen collapsed onto the furs that were piled on the tipi floor. André stuck his knife back into his belt.

"How can I get Elizabeth and Joshua away from Douglas?"

"You can't!" the priest responded.

Stephen remained silent, searching the priest's face.

"Are you going to help me?" he asked finally.

"You don't really understand, do you? You never did. You are a dead man, Stephen Miller. You should have died at Lachine, and if it hadn't been for your stupid cousin, Marc Stiegler, you would have died right there and that would have ended it."

"What do you mean?" Stephen said in confusion.

"And then at Manitoulin. I paid good money to that Ojibwa. But he got too involved with his own squaw and turned the whole tribe against all of us."

Stephen stared at him in silent amazement.

"You are a big lovable dunderhead, Stephen Miller. It is a wonderment to me that you are smart enough not to piss your own pants. I had orders at Lachine from the company that you were not to return from the voyage. I tried twice. I missed twice. I think you are blessed by the saints. Then you make the gesture with my son. I couldn't bring myself to do you in after that. I send you to Red River so no one would ever hear of you again. How do I know that the Hudson's Bay Company gets mad that I take a little for myself? They hunt me down. They tell me I can keep some of the fur money if you die. I send to Douglas. I tell him to kill you. Again the saints work for you. He kills the wrong people to cover your death and the Métis, Rowand, interferes. Again you escape. This time I must come and do the job myself."

Stephen listened to the priest. Several times he wanted to interrupt and ask questions, but he remained silent. He didn't need the details. Charles had hired Père André to kill him and had hounded him until he did it.

"I suppose Elizabeth and Joshua are to be returned to York?"

"I have no instructions about them. Besides, *mon ami*, I do not think I could take them away from Douglas. From now on she is his woman."

"How am I to die?" Stephen asked.

"That has not been determined. It is not really up to me anyway. I do know it will be tomorrow morning. For old time's sake I promise you I will try to make it quick. Some of these savages wish to burn you but Douglas has big ideas. He thinks he has the civilization. I will talk him into shooting you quick in the head."

Elizabeth drank the bowl of water that had been placed in front of her when she entered the tipi. It was Douglas's lodge and she knew why she was here. She was exhausted, yet she had fed and changed Joshua. Now he cooed contentedly as he lay by her side. She tried to put everything together. The priest was obviously working with the Métis. Stephen was to be killed. She did not know how to stop that. Douglas would be coming to the lodge tonight. Perhaps he would rape her if she refused him. Perhaps she could bargain with him. Her body for Stephen's life.

The screams of Cree Woman and the sickening sound of her children's bodies being crushed kept flooding back into her mind. She shook her head. She would not allow today's horrors to take control of her. If she did, her mind would snap. She had to remain in control of herself. If any life could be saved it must be saved. She was determined that Joshua at least would live.

It was growing dark outside. It had been gloomy in the tipi all along, but now she could feel the cool air of the prairie night enter from the many openings around the ground pegs.

The tent flap was pulled back. The entryway was filled by the frame of Christopher Douglas. He carried a bowl of fresh roasted buffalo meat. He offered the bowl to Elizabeth. She shook her head.

"Come on, lady," he smiled. "It's choice meat from the hump. You've got to keep your milk flowing for the little one."

She took the bowl from him. She felt sick at heart. He

already knew how to bend her to his will. He could use Joshua against her.

"Now you make yourself nice and pretty for your man, little lady. I'll be back after I've had a few snorts of whiskey. The bridegroom has to do a little celebrating with his friends before he comes to his own lodge. When I get back, missy, I expect to see you lying there without them duds on and I expect to see your pretty little legs spread wide apart."

Elizabeth felt helpless and sick to her stomach. She watched him leave. She loathed him, yet when he returned she knew she would have to accept him for Joshua. God knows, nothing could help Stephen now.

Jamie came to slowly. The night air was chilly and he was naked and his arms and legs were tied. He opened his eyes and stared into the sorrowful face of Cree Woman, who stood over him, cutting the thongs that bound him. He stood up groggily. His jaw ached and his nakedness embarrassed him. He looked around for his clothes but they were gone. The Indian woman moved slowly. There were bruises on her face and arms and she limped badly. Nevertheless she had enough strength to build a fire from buffalo chips and grass and wood. She led him to it. Off to the edge of the fire's glow he saw four fresh graves, one large and three small ones with stones piled atop them to keep out the wolves.

Jamie recognized some of the wood on the fire. It was the hitch from his own cart. He sat with his hands covering his nakedness, but the Indian woman seemed not even to look at him. Instead she stared off into the darkness.

"What do we do now, Cree Woman?" he asked her.

She spoke to him, not in English but in the slow rhythmic Cree. She sang her death song.

"What are you doing?" he asked her.

She stopped her chant and looked at him.

"I prepare to die and join my little ones."

"Don't do that," he said. Tears filled his eyes and his chest started to heave with sobs. "I don't want to be left all alone out here. I lost just like you did, Cree Woman, and we lost our kin to the same man, that son of a bitch Douglas. You've got to come with me. I'm too scared to do it alone."

She stared at the boy and then nodded her head.

"First we kill the Métis and then Cree Woman dies," she said.

She handed him her skinning knife. He hefted the huge blade in his hand. He didn't know where Douglas was. He was as naked as the hour of his birth. All he had was a wickedly sharp butcher knife. He shrugged.

"Why not," he muttered. Maybe there was more than revenge at stake. The fact that no graves existed for Elizabeth and Stephen might mean they were still alive.

He rose to his feet. The Indian woman smiled at him.

"Let's go," he said. "We have to track them in the dark."

"I can do that," she said, and slipped away from the fire. Jamie followed her into the darkness.

Douglas had taken too many shots of whiskey. One more, he knew, and he'd be drunk. But he did not wish to be drunk. He wanted to savor what lay ahead. Almost everyone was drunk tonight, even the women. They consoled themselves with whiskey. There would be no burning of the white man. The priest had persuaded them to give the man a quick death. But there had to be a ceremony. Too many of his band had died at the hand of this Miller and his traitor friend, Rowand. They would tie the man to a cartwheel and then shoot him. Then he would turn the body over to the women to do with as they wished.

"Watch the priest's tent," Douglas called out to the sentry, who was even more drunk than he was. "But you leave mine alone. There may be some yelling from mine tonight. That woman will feel a real man inside her for the first time. She'll do a bit of screaming."

The sentry laughed and had to hold onto a cartwheel to keep from falling. Douglas crossed the camp unsteadily and came to his own tipi. He pulled back the flap. It was dark inside.

"The bitch let the fire go out," he muttered. "Where are you, my little bitch?" he called out softly. "Have you got them wide open for me like I told you to?"

He saw her dark outline lying on her mat. Her knees were propped up but that was all he could make out. Her legs were naked and he assumed that the rest of her was also. This was going to be easier than he had thought. The bitch was horny for him. Well, he wouldn't disappoint her. He unbuttoned his trousers and pulled them off. He wasn't too drunk. The very thought of her lying there waiting for him had started to get him hard. He flopped to his knees and moved forward to touch her. His hand rested on her knee. It was bony and the leg was too muscled. Too late he realized his mistake. Jamie drove Cree Woman's skinning knife with all his might into Douglas's full belly. Then with both hands he pulled up on the handle, opening a cavity in the Métis's abdomen. Blood, intestines, and their contents spilled out and fell on Jamie's naked lap.

Douglas stared wide-eyed in disbelief. His bladder emptied itself. He moaned, then fell toward Jamie. The boy caught him and ripped the knife from his belly and plunged it a second time into the Métis, this time into his chest. Air seeped from Douglas's lungs and blood gushed from his chest. The boy was beyond control now. He wanted this man to know what was happening to him. With a vicious slash of the skinning knife he cut off the man's sex and stuffed the bleeding organ into Douglas's mouth.

Elizabeth sat huddled in the corner of the tipi in terror. She had been dozing when Jamie had clamped his hand over her mouth and awakened her after cutting his way through the buffalo hide of the tipi. She had no idea where he had come from or how he had gotten there. He told her to get into the shadows and attempt to keep Joshua quiet. Her heart pounded away as the minutes had passed, fifteen or twenty, she couldn't be sure, and then Douglas had entered and died.

Jamie smelled of blood and waste when he came crawling over to her. He had picked up Douglas's discarded pants and slipped his legs into them. He pulled the boots from the Métis's feet. They were tight, but it was better than running barefoot.

"Cree Woman waits at the edge of the camp. She will have horses for us."

"How?" Elizabeth questioned. "I thought she was dead."

"They left her for dead but she is tougher than any one of us."

"What about Stephen?"

"Is he still alive?"

She nodded.

"Good," he responded. "I'll show you the way out of camp and send you on your way to Cree Woman and the horses. Then I'll come back for him."

"Jamie," she said softly, touching his face, "no matter what happens I want you to know that I am grateful and proud. You're no longer a boy. Few men could have accomplished

165

what you have done already. Your father would have been proud of you."

The words sent Jamie's heart soaring. He crawled through the slice that he had made in the tipi wall and reached back to help her through. But she was not there. He stuck his head back in and saw her making a bundle of things that they would need, some pemmican, flint and, most important, Douglas's rifle. He felt ashamed that he had not thought to salvage these things before leaving. She strapped Joshua to her back and finally took his hand and stepped out into the night.

Several fires blazed in the camp. Jamie and Elizabeth kept to the shadows. Drunken men lay where they fell to sleep off the effects of the whiskey. The sounds that came from the tipis indicated that those who were not drunk were making love. Camp discipline had broken down completely.

Jamie reached the ring of carts that were the outer boundary of the camp. He crawled under one and waited again for Elizabeth. Then he walked deeper into the night shadows.

"Cree Woman," he called softly. From the darkness ahead the Indian woman emerged leading four horses. Elizabeth went to her and wrapped her arms around her. Tears came to her eyes. But the Indian woman's eyes remained dry.

Jamie left them with the horses and returned to the camp. He had to find where they kept Stephen. He was confident that no one would come to look for Douglas until morning. If he could get away with Stephen they would have a good head start.

He was startled when a man stepped from the shadows directly in front of him. He was unbuttoning his pants.

"Get out of my line of fire, boy. I've got to piss mighty bad."

The man was too drunk to have recognized him. Jamie decided to use him.

"I've got to go too," he said and stepped alongside the Métis. He suddenly became frightened that he could not go. The man next to him farted.

"By God, next to screwing, pissing with a full bladder is one of nature's joys."

Jamie finally started to urinate. He pretended to sigh with contentment.

"See what I mean?" said the other man.

"Yeah, it's been quite a night. What have they decided to do with that Miller fellow?"

"They shoot him tomorrow morning just as soon as the boss finishes with his woman. He wanted the poor bastard to know what was happening for the night. Kind of an extra torture."

Jamie nodded. "Where are they keeping him?"

"About five lodges up the camp from mine. This one here's mine. Why?" He looked over at Jamie and his bleary eyes barely focused.

Jamie didn't know if the man recognized him, but he did not want to wait to find out. Cree Woman's knife flashed in the moonlight, and Jamie's companion grunted as the blade tore into his stomach. Then Jamie clamped his hand hard over the man's mouth and nose. The man fell to his knees. Jamie yanked the knife free and drew it across the throat of his victim. Blood spurted from the jugular. He would be dead shortly.

Jamie buttoned his pants and moved quickly. His victim may have been with a woman or companions who might come looking for him. He counted the lodges. There was a drunk lying in front of the sixth. Jamie was sure he was a sentry. This had to be the right one. He went to the back and again slowly cut his way through the hide. There were hot coals glowing in the fire. They cast an eerie reddish tint in the darkness.

Someone was sleeping not far from where the fire had been. Jamie crept closer, his knife in his hand. He leaned forward to get a look at the man's face. A hand shot up and grabbed him by the throat. The grip was incredibly strong. He raised the knife but a second hand grabbed the knife hand. Suddenly the grip loosened.

"Is that you, Jamie?"

It was Stephen Miller.

"How the hell did you get away?"

"They left me and Cree Woman for dead. She's helping me. I've rescued Mrs. Miller and Josh. They're waiting for us now. All we've . . ."

The hand reached up again and clamped over his mouth this time.

The skin of the tipi glowed orange. Someone with a torch approached them. Stephen rose to his feet and shoved Jamie toward the side of the entryway.

"Son of a bitch," said a voice outside, "damn drunk. If Miller's escaped..."

The skin of the entryway was pulled back and Père André stuck his torch into the tipi. He saw Stephen on his feet, his hands behind his back. He twisted his body to allow both himself and the torch to enter in.

"Well, *mon ami*..." He never got the rest of the sentence out of his mouth. Jamie's knife struck a vicious blow. The boy had intended it for his chest but the priest's twist with the torch saved his life. The knife pierced André's left arm, severing muscle and veins. The priest screamed. He thrust the torch at Jamie's face. The boy jumped back and the torch fell to the floor of the lodge. The priest ran from the tent screaming in French.

"Let's go," Stephen yelled.

He picked up the torch, touched the skins of the tipi with it. Flames leapt up. The tent would burn quickly.

They ran out the back of the lodge through the hole Jamie had made. Several rifle shots were fired in the air. Stephen touched the torch to the next tent and then to the third. He left it lying against the fourth. Pandemonium had erupted in the camp. Men, still drunk, staggered to their feet and called out. More rifles went off.

Jamie and Stephen raced to the carts. A bullet slammed with a dull thud into the pemmican on the cart above their heads. Both of them scurried under the cart and out into the night. They ran around the circle of carts until Jamie came to the place where he had first entered the Métis camp. The fires in the camp were burning brightly now, illuminating the night.

They left the carts and moved toward the open prairie. The noise coming from the camp drowned out Jamie's call. He began to panic. What if someone had discovered Cree Woman and Elizabeth? What if something had happened to them? He called out loudly this time.

"Cree Woman!"

Still there was no answer. The frustrations and the fears were finally taking hold of the boy. He started to tremble. He turned to Stephen. Tears came streaming down his face.

"This is the place. I know it is the place," he cried. "They'll find us here without horses. We're dead."

"So are they," said Cree Woman as she emerged from the darkness. Behind her, astride a mare, sat Elizabeth with

Joshua. Stephen reached up and took her into his arms. Then he pulled himself up onto a stallion that Elizabeth had behind her.

Jamie mounted the horse Cree Woman was leading.

"We can travel at a good pace. They will not follow us for some time. I have scattered their herd," said the Indian woman.

"Let's get the hell out of here," said Stephen.

Elizabeth kicked her mare and the horse bolted out onto the prairie. Soon the five of them were cantering across the grassy hills, crossing the moon-drenched plains.

X

Red River, Spring 1822

The four stood looking at the junction of the two rivers. The horses bowed their heads as they tried to get a few mouthfuls of grass while their riders rested. Stephen looked at Elizabeth. There were dark shadows beneath her eyes from lack of sleep. He knew that he could not look his best. He hadn't shaved since the hunt had begun. Cree Woman was silent but otherwise seemed strangely unchanged by her recent sorrows. Maybe they were all in shock. Jamie had killed brutally, yet he still seemed to be calm. His calmness almost frightened Stephen.

"You are still determined to seek the Hudson's Bay Company's help?" Elizabeth asked.

"What else can we do?" Stephen responded. "Chris Douglas's people will be back at Fort Garry within a week. They will come looking for blood, Elizabeth, especially yours and mine." He turned to look at the boy and the Indian woman. "They might not have figured out yet that we had help. But it won't take them long if Cree Woman and Jamie go back to their homes. They're supposed to be dead. I think it folly for any of us to stay here."

"I'm staying," said Jamie. "I got me a horse, I got me my land. I intend to plant it and to harvest it. I'll trade some potatoes for pemmican."

"You haven't got a house," objected Elizabeth.

"If Cree Woman stays, I'll live in her cabin."

The Indian woman nodded in agreement. "The boy can live with me. I'll look after him. I will need someone to look after." The brief look of pain they noticed on her face flittered away as fast as it had first appeared. "The Métis will behave when it comes to the boy and me. I will visit my father and brothers among the Cree. Word will be passed to our enemies not to bother Cree Woman and her friend. Rowand had friends among the Métis. They will be angered by his death and the death of his children. My father will be more than angered by the death of his grandchildren. He will admonish the Métis."

"I don't fear the Métis," said Elizabeth. "I believe your father can frighten them into behaving themselves. It is the priest who still lives and who hunts us down that I fear."

Stephen smiled wanly. "He'll not come after Cree Woman," he said, "and I doubt if he even saw who it was who attacked him. No, he had only one intended victim—me—and there is no escaping him. But I don't want to cause the rest of you any more grief. I'll leave. If André follows me I'll try to kill him before he gets to me. Then we'll all be safe."

"You're wrong," said Elizabeth. "You ignore the real cause of our problem. He sits in an office in York and pulls strings and makes little men like Père André jump to do his bidding—his murders, his mayhem. The real killer of Ian and his children is named Charles Miller. He is your brother and my husband. As long as he is determined that you and I must die because his sick mind formulated a liaison between us and because he needs your money, as long as we do not confront him, we are at the mercy of his vengeance. Oh, it might not come right away. We might have some peace—even be lulled into security—but then some night, out of the darkness, a Père André or someone like him will step out of the black and kill me or you or even Joshua."

"You're suggesting that we go back to York and put an end to my brother?"

Her face twisted into a grimace. "I don't know, Stephen. He was never an evil man. Something has snapped. Something happened in the war to twist him up inside."

The horse Stephen rode raised his head and pawed nervously at the ground.

"He hears," said Cree Woman. "Carts are returning from the prairie. By afternoon many of the hunters will have returned."

"Elizabeth," Stephen interrupted, "André warned me once before. The return route to York would be a death trap."

"There is another way," said Cree Woman.

Stephen, who had been staring down at the prairie grass, looked up at her in surprise. "Which way is that?"

"You could leave the Red River by going north—the way

172

the Hudson's Bay Company men go and the way all the furs leave here now."

"Where would we end up?"

"On the Great Ice Sea to the north."

"Hudson Bay?" said Elizabeth. "Yes, there will be ships bound for England there."

"We don't need to go to England. We need to go to Upper Canada," said Stephen in annoyance.

"Maybe we could find something sailing for Montreal, Stephen. Anything is better than sitting here waiting for the priest to come."

"It will be dangerous, Elizabeth. I don't know the route. If we take too long, the ice will have formed on Hudson Bay and we will be snowed in for the winter."

She smiled at him. "All these risks are worth taking."

"All right, let's do it," he said. "First we'll take our companions back to their home and then I'll go to Fort Garry and get us a boat. We can trade one of the horses for a canoe, some supplies, and maybe even some cash for a trip by ship to Montreal."

Later that same day the fort was surrounded with Red River carts loaded with pemmican. Most of the hunters had returned. Stephen worked his way through the yard without catching sight of any of the faces he had seen with Chris Douglas. He went into the Hudson's Bay Company store. Several of the group captains sat drinking in the corner. As Stephen walked to the counter, the captain-general, Cuthbert Grant, stepped away from the drinkers and approached him.

"Mr. Miller, you were with Chris, weren't you? You're the first of his party to return. I'm surprised because you all left early. How did your hunt go?"

Stephen did not know why he should trust the man. The whites hated him for a clash between the Selkirk Scots and his North West Company men years earlier, but Ian Rowand had trusted and respected him and Stephen had come to love Ian.

"It was a disaster. So bad, in fact, that I must sell out, get a canoe, and get to Hudson Bay right away."

Grant listened patiently to Stephen's story. The only time he interrupted was to question him about his brother and Père André. When Stephen finished, Grant was silent for some minutes. It was clear he was angry. A tiny nerve just below his right eye was twitching.

"Ian Rowand was my friend," he said. "Douglas was not. I will protect Cree Woman and the boy. This should not have happened on my hunt. Métis killing their own. We are not savages, Mr. Miller. This is our land. Some day we will govern it. But if we murder and behave little better than the Cree, the whites—and by that I mean the Canadians—will come and take it from us. Men like Chris Douglas will destroy us. But I'll not let them. You shall have a canoe and directions to York Factory, some pemmican, and even some salt pork. How good is your horse?"

Cree Woman loaded the canoe carefully. She wrapped the pemmican in the sailcloth that Stephen had received from Grant. She knew the lake they would travel and she knew it would need careful wrapping. Elizabeth already sat in the front of the canoe, Joshua strapped to her back.

Elizabeth held out her arms and the Indian woman returned her hug. She kissed the baby atop his head wistfully and a look of sadness dominated her face.

Stephen walked to the riverfront side by side with Jamie McAlistair.

"You have the paper renting my farm to you for one pound of pemmican a year until I can return and reclaim it?"

Jamie nodded.

"You don't need three horses, not for the two of you. Trade one to Grant for a cart and some more stores for the winter."

The boy was impatient with the instructions. He loved these two friends who had taken care of him since his family's murder, but he was a man himself now. He had rescued them. He didn't appreciate Stephen's treating him like a child. Had he forgotten already what he had done to André and to Christopher Douglas? Cree Woman certainly thought of him as a man. She had already indicated that he could come to her bed this very night. God, how he wished his father had told him about these things. He would have liked to ask Mr. Miller, but surely that would bring on a lecture far more long-winded than the present one on horses and carts.

They reached the canoe. Stephen picked up his paddle. He bent over and kissed Cree Woman on the cheek. "Take care of yourself and the boy," he admonished her.

She looked at him sadly and nodded.

"Jamie, aren't you going to kiss me good-bye?" Elizabeth asked him.

Jamie blushed and bent down and kissed her on the cheek. He was sure he would never see her again. He loved her but he was confused. He was looking forward to tonight. Nevertheless, it seemed like a betrayal of his love for her.

Stephen pushed the canoe's bow out into the Red River and hopped into the stern. He arranged his legs more comfortably, then dug the paddle into the river. The current picked up the craft and it moved quickly down the river.

The boy and the Indian woman stood on the riverbank watching as the canoe receded from sight. Soon it disappeared altogether beyond the small bend.

They came to the mouth of the river quickly. Suddenly, amid marshlands and heavy reeds, they entered Lake Winnipeg. The wind was at their backs—coming out of the south.

"It's like Lake Ontario or Superior," Elizabeth called out in awe at the size of the lake. She strained her eyes to see the eastern shore, but the rugged coastline disappeared off into the horizon.

"It's about twenty to thirty miles wide here but it gets as wide as sixty-five miles," Stephen said. "Grant says it's shallow, mostly ten to twelve feet deep and never more than thirty-five. It's treacherous."

Stephen stayed close to the west shore. He paddled strongly and steadily but without great exertion. As the sun rose higher in the sky, the wind shifted to the west, then swung against them, coming from the north. The waves grew short and choppy. Heavy clouds moved directly down the lake and the winds grew to squall strength.

Stephen headed for shore. He saw a sandy beach directly to the port side. He steered for it. Now he had to work hard heading directly into the offshore wind. The canoe started to ship water. The winds started to howl and so did Joshua. The baby screamed louder than at any time in the past.

"The little fellow doesn't like the water," said Elizabeth, turning around to look at Stephen.

"Can't say he takes after his father then," Stephen responded.

The smile left Elizabeth's face. "Bad joke, Stephen," she called out.

He had reached shore by now. He hopped out of the canoe. The water was thigh-deep. He pushed the craft onto the white sand and began to unload it.

He turned the canoe over and they crowded under it together, the baby in between them. The rain beat against their birchbark roof. Stephen covered their legs and feet with the sailcloth, but the embankment behind them could not hold all the water that soaked into the earth. It collapsed sending mud down to the beach, which oozed under the canoe. The sand became damp and then saturated. It stuck to their clothes. Elizabeth and Stephen were soon just as miserable as Joshua.

The rains continued throughout the afternoon. They had no fire; everything was wet, too wet to burn. They lay under the canoe and prayed for the wind and rain to stop. They both knew the night would be spent in misery. Maybe their second day on Lake Winnipeg would prove better.

Jamie brought water from the river for Cree Woman. She was roasting the buffalo meat that Stephen Miller had brought from Fort Garry as a gift from Cuthbert Grant. He entered the cabin. She had set places for both of them at the wooden table. He put the bucket of water down by the hearth. She turned the meat on the spit without looking at him.

She doesn't say much, he thought. But he liked it that way. His father had been a man of few words at home, but his mother more than made up for it. She had never closed her mouth. Her talking must have been painful to his father.

Cree Woman took the meat from the fire and put it on a wooden platter. Then she brought it to the table and set it in front of him. She drew her skinning knife from its sheath at her side. It was clear that she intended him to carve the meat.

Jamie blanched when he saw the knife. He had blotted it from his mind as much as possible. How he had used it last was something he did not wish to recall. The slaughter, nevertheless, poured back into his mind. He saw the horror of what he had done to Douglas. But the bastard had deserved that and worse. He regretted deeply that he had only wounded the priest. If he had finished that job, Elizabeth and Stephen might still be with Cree Woman and himself.

Cree Woman saw the look on his face. She picked up the knife and handed it to him.

"Slice the meat," she said. "Or do you only play the man?"

He looked at her in anger. He took the knife from her and stabbed viciously at the roast.

She smiled.

They ate in silence. It was a tender piece of meat and Cree

176

Woman had cooked it with care. He should have complimented her on it. His mother would have scolded him for not praising her.

When he finished, she removed his bowl from the table and washed it in the river water he had hauled for her. Then she washed herself and removed the braids from her hair, letting it hang straight down her back. She stood naked but with her back turned to him. The boy had never seen even the naked back of a woman. He knew that if he tried to rise he would be embarrassed. He continued to watch her. She walked to her mat. He glimpsed the profile of her body and if possible he became even more aroused. But when she lay down she faced the wall and turned her back to him. He felt suddenly let down. She was going to sleep. Nothing was going to happen.

He could rise now without risk. He walked over to the mat.

"Cree Woman?" he called out softly. "Don't you want to . . . to do anything?"

She turned and looked at the crestfallen boy. It was too soon to take another man, especially one so young—one who among her people would just be graduating to wearing a loincloth. Her heart ached for her man. They had shared so much in this very room as little as two weeks ago. Did she betray that love if she took this boy to herself? Her body yearned for the feel of Ian inside her. She should have died out there on the prairie with him and with her children. She had started her death song but the boy had brought her back to life. She did not really thank him for that. But at least she was not alone. For that she did thank him. She examined him with her eyes. He was big for one so young. He would have broad shoulders and a big chest once he became a man. His cheeks were still smooth like a little boy's, but he grew chin whiskers. They made him look funny. His ears were too big for his narrow face, but his eyes were a beautiful hazel, calm and sad. She loved his eyes.

She raised the edge of the covers. He sat down on the edge of the mat. He is such a baby, she thought, he doesn't even know enough to take off his clothes. She reached over and began to unbutton his shirt. He looked the other way, too embarrassed to look into her eyes. She slipped the shirt off of his shoulders and ran her hand across the muscles of his chest. He shivered, but she knew he was not cold. His chest

177

was hairless like Rowand's. She closed her eyes and Ian's body was under her touch. She shook her head and opened them again. She would not submit to that temptation.

The boy was very aroused now and did not know what to do. Her hands went to his waist and the buttons of his pants. When she touched his stomach he closed his eyes and sucked in his breath sharply. He stood and quickly unbuttoned and dropped his pants to the floor. She touched him. He gasped.

He looked at her and at himself in mortification. "It was just too much," he said. "I couldn't hold it any longer. I guess I've ruined it all."

She rose from the mat and went to the washstand for the cloth that she kept there. She washed her hands and dried them and then she gave the cloth to him and dropped back onto the mat. When he had finished he lay next to her. She reached over and touched his chest and then ran her hand down the length of his back. She took his hand in hers and brought it to her breast and allowed him to touch her there. She reached out for him again. She smiled when she touched him. He was a boy. He had not ruined everything and it was not all over.

The moon flooded into the one-room cabin through the open windows. It was warm and the breeze that entered was welcome. The boy lay sleeping on his side, facing her. He had one leg bent and his knee had stabbed her in the back several times. In fact, she found herself pressed against the wall of the cabin. To Jamie, who had slept only with his brother, sharing a sleeping mat was obviously a form of warfare. The winner would be the one who occupied the most territory.

His face had relaxed in sleep. The embarrassment had disappeared, but so had the look of pure pleasure when she had done things to him that were clearly beyond his ability to imagine, although not to enjoy. He would stay with her now. Maybe she would bear new children. She did not love this boy as she loved Rowand. But she would remain with Jamie at least until he became a man and knew what he wanted.

She needed to sleep but she needed more room. She took Jamie's knee in her hands and gently straightened it and moved him to his side of the mat. He moaned in his sleep and mumbled something. She turned on her side facing him. She wanted to fall asleep staring into his baby face.

Sleep came to her at last. She could feel herself sinking

down into it. It was like falling without hitting any bottom. She saw herself riding the prairies next to her father. The village had moved from the Red River west to hunt buffalo and to fight their enemies, the Blackfoot. Her father's face was painted black and white, with lightning streaks on each cheek. She reached out to touch his face. He smiled at her. But then suddenly he was not her father. The black-and-white streaks turned red. They were blood running down from wounds. The face was deathly pale. It was Ian, her husband. He moved his lips but nothing came out. She called out to him to ask him to forgive her and this boy, Jamie. But then his face began to fade also. The air was filled with the smell of death and of putrefying flesh. Then the face reappeared. It was not Ian. The face that stared at her from across the mat had bloodshot eyes and gray-black hair. His breath smelled foul and his face was full of pain. She opened her mouth to cry out when a hand clamped down firmly to stifle the sound.

She was instantly awake and terrified. The hand was still there. It was real, and so was the face.

The dueling pistol's muzzle was resting directly on Jamie's temple. He was awake and his eyes were wide with fear.

"I ought to blow your fucking head off, *mon petit*," the voice said to Jamie. "And I will jam this pistol up your whore and fire if you move a muscle."

Then the priest backed away from the mat and brought both of them under the fire of his gun. The stench that came from the wound in his arm was horrifying. It was the smell that had penetrated Cree Woman's dream. Her knife in Jamie's hand had killed him. But she doubted he would admit it even to himself. The wound was infected, and he was in a rage like a wounded bear and just as dangerous.

"Now, my little lovers, out of bed. And make it quick. Tell me where Stephen Miller is. Then, I let you go back to your fucking."

"He's gone," said Jamie nervously. He did not believe the priest would let them go. It was clear he knew who had attacked him.

"Where?"

"I don't know. He wouldn't tell in case you tried to follow him."

André reached over to Jamie as he got to his feet. He grabbed Jamie's arm and twisted it up behind his back. Then he dragged him to the hearth where the evening's cooking

179

fire had been reduced to hot embers. He stirred them with his foot. Sparks flew up the chimney. He dropped some twisted hay on them, which soon caught fire. The blaze cast shadows all around the darkened room.

"Now, *mon ami*," André said. "You will tell me where Miller is or I'll shove your bare ass into the fire. I'll hold you there until you tell or until that puny little thing you call a cock burns right off. Now where is Miller?"

Jamie was terrified. He knew André would carry out his threat. Already the heat of the fire was blazing hot on his thigh. But he could not betray Stephen and Elizabeth. He had to try to get the gun away from this man. André held it in his limp arm, vaguely pointing it at Cree Woman. His powerful right arm held Jamie. His strength was prodigious. When Jamie failed to answer he was shoved closer to the hearth. He smelled the hair on his legs singeing. The pain was growing stronger. He pushed forward to get away from it and André took another full twist of his arm, turning Jamie completely around in his agony. Now his front faced the fire.

"Stop it," Cree Woman called out. "I will tell you where the Millers are."

André shoved Jamie even closer to the fire. He cried out in anguish.

"I will not lie, I promise," she repeated.

Reluctantly the priest allowed Jamie to back away from the flames. He collapsed to the floor. Cree Woman bent down and helped him to his feet.

"Come on. Where are they?" André said, his face contorted into a smile. "Or maybe we go back to roasting the ham."

"They left three days ago for Montreal." André grabbed Jamie's hair and shoved him sprawling into the fire. He screamed as the flames bit into his flesh. He jumped out of the fire. Cree Woman picked up the bucket and splashed river water over his body.

"You said you wouldn't lie. Stephen Miller was seen two days ago purchasing a canoe from Cuthbert Grant in Fort Garry. I've no doubt he's left within the last twenty-four hours but I need to know the direction. I don't think he'd try the lakes to the Ottawa. He knows I have too many friends along that route."

Jamie searched his hips and thighs for burns. There was no serious damage. But this had to come to an end. His eyes searched for Cree Woman's knife.

"If you're looking for this," said the priest pointing with his pistol to the knife that was sticking in the waistband of his pants, "I took the precaution of pocketing it as I entered. It was careless of you to leave the house wide open. But, *mes amis*, it saved the house. I would have set it ablaze to force you out if I had to."

He took the knife out and approached the naked Indian woman. "Now, little one," he addressed Jamie with contempt, "you will tell me the directions."

André saw the look of defiance in her face. This one could die in the fire bravely. Even the knife work he planned for her would draw nothing from her. But the boy would collapse. Pain had frightened him. He was desperate for escape. Fear for the woman would drive him to take the easy way out and talk. He was right.

"They're heading for York Factory by Lake Winnipeg," Jamie blurted out. He could not bring himself to look at Cree Woman after he spoke. All the confidence built up in him was drained by the humiliation he suffered at the hands of the priest.

"Well, little boy, I believe you this time. Miller would be good enough with a canoe to try that way out. Now just to insure that you have told me the truth I'm going to take you with me. I've hired two of Douglas's best men. If you lie, I'll turn you over to them and tell them who you are. If they can't have Miller, I believe they would be satisfied with his mascot."

Jamie was relieved that André didn't know it was he who had killed and mutilated the Métis leader.

"Get dressed," André ordered. "And, squaw," he said, turning to Cree Woman, "if you wish to see this little boy again, you'll not follow me or warn anyone."

The cabin grew darker as a bank of night clouds covered the moon. There was a flash of lightning. André sat down at the table. He was in great pain every time he moved his arm.

"Squaw," he yelled at Cree Woman, "pack pemmican for your boy and for me and my men. Enough for fifteen days. It should take no more than that to chase Miller all the way to Hudson Bay. I'll catch him before that. I know the route. I've traveled it before, but he hasn't. I hope this storm is making him uncomfortable out in that stinking murky bog of algae they call Winnipeg."

* * *

181

Stephen and Elizabeth were miserable. Only Joshua seemed happy. His belly was full and he gurgled and cooed admiringly at his hands and toes, which he had discovered not long ago.

As soon as the storm passed, Stephen had reloaded the canoe. The winds from the north still blew violently down on them. But with any luck at all they too would pass, and they could be on the lake before four in the morning.

It would be difficult to travel at night, but Stephen had a compass and he knew he must travel north until they came to the narrows. The swells on the shallow lake turned up by the second storm were still high and crashed against the narrow beach on which they were camped.

Elizabeth stood at his side. The baby was strapped to her back again. Her wet hair was hanging down in her face. Like his, her clothes were soaked through.

The rain started to fall again.

"I suppose we should wait," Stephen said. "But we're already as wet as we'll ever get. Grant warned me about this lake. If you want to make a full day on it, you leave at night and make camp at noon, he said. Forget about the afternoon and never try to cross it except at the narrows."

"Let's go," Elizabeth answered him. She moved into the bow of the craft and picked up her paddle. Stephen shoved off. They bounced on the waves and immediately started to ship water. Elizabeth stopped paddling and started to bail.

Stephen, when he calculated that they were in deep enough water to avoid any reefs, turned the bow to face north into the wind. The bow began to bounce on the swells with a loud noise. He was working hard now. The paddle dug deeply into the water and he pulled backward and twisted at the end of his pull to get the bow pointed straight. He could not see the shoreline and had no way to estimate his speed. But against a head wind of this strength, he knew he would be lucky to make five miles' distance in an hour's paddling. In his own mind doubts were beginning to form. If this weather continued, he would be paddling forever. The lake was two hundred and eighty miles long and he had covered a mere thirty the first day. But now thirty miles of paddling seemed a prodigious feat. If he made twenty today it would be miraculous. He wasn't much on figures, but he didn't have to be in order to figure out how long he would be on the lake at this rate. If he could make Norway House on Playgreen Lake—a northern bay of Winnipeg—on time, he might intercept the

York boats of the Orkney men coming with the Hudson's Bay Company furs from Fort Edmonton on the Saskatchewan River. They could lead him through the maze of rivers and lakes to the Hayes River and York Factory on Hudson Bay.

It was getting lighter in the east. Dawn was not too far off. He needed to rest a minute. His muscles already felt as if he had been paddling for half a day, not half an hour. But if he delayed he would actually lose ground. He continued to paddle. They were not shipping water any longer. The swells were diminishing in size. Elizabeth stopped bailing, picked up her paddle again, and started to aid him.

They worked together for another hour. The sun made a brief appearance on the horizon and was quickly swallowed up in black clouds. A gray light descended on them. Stephen knew that they could not expect much more than that from this day.

He detected, along with the lessening of the winds, a shifting from the north to the northwest. If this was the case then luck was with them. The long jetty of land of which Grant had warned him, Hecla Point, would have to be rounded either this afternoon, if possible, or tomorrow in the morning. At Hecla the lake narrowed to five miles before opening up again. There he would have to make a decision. If he crossed the five miles to the eastern shore, he would be safe traveling on the eastern shore to the second narrows at Dog's Head. Then straight up the widest and longest part of the lake to the northern reaches. But if he could not cross and he stayed on the west shore, he would have a twenty-mile open traverse to the north because of the deep bay on the north side of Hecla.

Again he noticed the lake was becoming less choppy. His spirits began to brighten. They were making better speed now. He called out to Elizabeth.

"You and I seem to be forever doomed to paddling canoes."

They both instantly recalled the rescue of Eli Stoddard from the gruel of Mistress Bridges.

"It will be good to see the old man again," she said, turning her head about to look at Stephen.

"On the way to Upper Canada we must stop at Quebec and see my mother. God knows what Charles has told her about us, but I know we could obtain her blessing if we could only speak to her."

"Your mother is fond of me."

183

"And of me," said Stephen laughing. "Even when I was a little boy she always praised Charlie for his good deeds and scolded me for my bad ones. But I got most of the hugs and kisses."

"Maybe that's Charlie's problem. First your mother and then I preferred Stevie to Charlie."

"Not fair," said Stephen. "He had you and he lost you. I didn't become involved until after he lost you."

"That's not what he thought."

"No, Elizabeth, you and I can't be held responsible for the twists of his mind."

"When we go back we'll be held responsible for the way we live," she offered.

"That's something we'll face when the time comes and we'll face it together."

For the next hour they remained silent, paddling rapidly and making good distance. Ahead of them from out of the gray loomed Hecla Point and the Grassy Narrows. Here Stephen would have to decide whether or not it was safe to cross to the eastern shore.

Beyond Hecla the sky blackened again. Stephen watched it carefully. At first he could not be sure. He only sensed a change in the choppiness of the lake's swells, but after five minutes he was certain. The wind had shifted again to the north. A storm would be upon them again within an hour.

Stephen called to Elizabeth and pointed at the sky beyond Hecla.

Elizabeth grimaced.

"We'll make camp before it hits," Stephen yelled over the wind.

Stephen found what he was looking for—a sheltered cove. He straightened the bow into the wind again, and with a few quick powerful strokes of his paddle he brought the canoe into the sheltered water of the cove. The craft came gliding to a halt on a muddy bank on the shore amid a tangle of bushes that grew there.

"Grant told me about this place," he said as he jumped out of the canoe into knee-deep water. "It is a resting place for those who decide not to try Hecla until the next day." He offered Elizabeth his hand and helped her from the bow. He pushed aside some bushes and they entered a grove amid the lakeshore shrubbery. There before them was a crude lean-to built of wood and enclosed on three sides with only the south end exposed. Within it there was a stone fireplace and next to it a small bin filled with dry sticks, twisted hay, and some very dry buffalo chips.

"Tonight," Stephen said cheerfully, "we will have a fire."

Elizabeth flopped onto the dirt floor of the lean-to. She swept her damp hair back off her face and began to unstrap Joshua from her back.

"This poor fellow," she said as he fussed and complained, "hasn't been changed since this morning." The baby shoved his fingers into his mouth again and began to suck on them.

"I don't think it's changing that's prime on his mind right now, Liz," Stephen said, smiling at the baby.

"You're right," responded Elizabeth. "Like a typical male he's concerned with his stomach."

"No," responded Stephen in much seriousness. "Once he gets older the 'changing area' gets used for better things. Why, I suspect even this little fellow's priorities will alter. Even I've been known to skip a meal or two for concerns that could be described as below the belt."

"I'll give you a concern below the belt, my dear," said Elizabeth, "if you don't get that fire you promised started. God, I want to get dry."

They sat naked before the fire in the stone fireplace. The heat kept them warm. Their clothes were strung on a line behind them in the lean-to. The bedrolls they sat upon were dry tonight as well. Even Joshua lay naked, sleeping on his belly. His tiny rump was raised in the air. He had tucked his knees under him to sleep. Stephen noticed the peculiar position and pointed it out to Liz. They laughed together.

The storm from the north crashed down upon them. Yet the lean-to was solid. It kept them dry and warm.

Stephen ate the pemmican stew that Elizabeth had prepared for them. Although he wolfed it down, he was growing deathly tired of dried buffalo meat.

"You know," he said, as he laid his head in her lap after they had finished eating, "the finest thing about returning to Upper Canada will be fresh vegetables from the garden."

She stroked his blond hair.

"I would like raspberries," she said, "with sugar and cream all over them."

"I don't like raspberries," he said, looking up at her. "They've got those damn little seeds that get caught in your teeth. In Amherstburg when I was a boy, my mother grew strawberries in her garden. Now that's a berry for you."

"They give me the hives," said Elizabeth.

They both started to laugh.

"Maybe we can only get along when we have to eat pemmican," said Stephen. "As soon as we get real food again we'll start to hate each other."

She looked down into his face. His eyes were soft and warm, his nose straight. His lips were covered with an untrimmed long moustache, but behind it was the mouth whose taste she cherished. She bent down to taste him. His mouth opened and she entered it, exploring those teeth that flashed so whitely when he smiled.

He reached up and touched her milk-swollen breast. He pushed himself up onto his elbows and took her nipple into his mouth. He looked so calm, almost blissful. She withdrew her breast from his mouth.

"I need that," she whispered to him.

"I'm jealous," he said.

"I can tell. But I have better charms for you," she teased.

He flopped over onto his belly and teasingly buried his face in her stomach. Then he kissed her. She lay back and waited for him to pleasure her.

The north winds blew through the night and the rain kept up a steady beating on the roof of the lean-to until well past dawn. There was no point in trying to make headway around Hecla with such a wind. Stephen lay with Elizabeth, their arms and legs entwined. Joshua fussed once but he too, as if observing the weather, decided to go back to sleep.

At about seven the rain stopped. Although the winds still drove the low-flying clouds through the sky, there were now occasional patches of blue interrupting the gray and the black.

Stephen rose refreshed. The wind blew his and Elizabeth's clothes on the line in front of them. He noted that immediately. The wind was shifting. It was beginning to enter the shelter, which could only mean that it was swinging away to the south. Their luck was changing.

"Get dressed," he called out to Elizabeth. "It's time to get started. Today we cross this goddamn lake. From then on it's a straight paddle to Norway House and safety."

He loaded the canoe in the quiet of the cove. The sun

broke through the clouds and bathed them in gold. Even the waters of the lake did not look quite so murky in the sunlight.

They paddled through the quiet water out onto the lake. There was almost no swell and the wind came from the south. It was warm enough for Stephen to remove his shirt. He felt joyful that the last big obstacle to reaching Norway House in time to meet the York Boats—the traverse of Lake Winnipeg—would be accomplished this morning. He scanned the eastern shore of the lake, which lay only six miles ahead of them.

It was Elizabeth who first noticed it. "Stephen, what's that?" She pointed off toward the south.

Stephen turned quickly. His heart sank. There was no doubt in his mind about what it was or what it meant for them.

"It's a sail," he responded.

She looked at him for further explanation.

"Only a trade canoe would carry a sail like that. It's André. He's found us."

He could see the fear in her face. He looked again to the south. With a breeze blowing from that direction, the giant canoe would gain rapidly on them. If he continued to attempt to cross the lake they would pass him on the western shore and cut off his route to Norway House. He could not let André get ahead of him.

He twisted the paddle in the water and faced to the north. They would pass through Grassy Narrows on the west shore and attempt the twenty-mile traverse to Dog's Head. It was their only chance and it was a slim one.

"Paddle," he said to Elizabeth. "Paddle like you've never done before. We once gave our all for Eli. Now let's do it for Joshua."

"I love you," she responded. "Just in case you weren't sure."

"I'm grateful that you do. Until you my life was a waste," he said, just loudly enough for her to hear.

She dug the blade of her paddle into the water. On Lake Ontario she had given out halfway through the struggle. Not this time. Life on the prairies had toughened her. Her hands would not blister and render her useless.

The canoe seemed to fly across the water. Stephen started to call a stroke to synchronize their paddling and to set the pace that he knew he could meet for hours. He hoped she could do the same and he hoped it was good enough to keep them ahead of André.

They rounded the Narrows point. Islands stretched out like giant stepping-stones toward the eastern shore. Stephen cursed their timing. If only they had started a few hours earlier. They could have crossed the lake and begun the race northward from there. But he kept the bow pointed to the north once they cleared the headland. On the west the land fell away, leaving them now in the center of a giant bay. There was no land closer than twenty miles on any side of them except to the rear, and to the rear was death.

Stephen kept calling the pace. He glanced behind. The *canot du nord* had not yet cleared the headland. He would not look back again. Ahead lay miles of open water to cover. He determined he would concentrate on that alone.

The sun was hot now and the breeze was falling off. That was an advantage. With a following wind, the sail-rigged canoe would be on top of them in a matter of three-quarters of an hour.

The sweat poured off Stephen's torso. He could not see Elizabeth's back because Joshua played happily upon it. But the sweat stains spread from her armpits down the length of her sleeves.

After fifteen more minutes of work Stephen could no longer resist the temptation. He turned around once again. He was shocked to see that he had actually gained on the pursuers. Then he realized why. André was so confident of overtaking them that he had taken advantage of the favorable breeze and was crossing Lake Winnipeg at Hecla Point. Then he would race up the eastern shore and attempt to beat Stephen to the Dog's Head Narrows. Without some change in the weather he would probably succeed.

Stephen renewed his vow not to look back. He could see the vague outline of land on the horizon directly ahead— maybe fifteen miles away. His muscles were growing tired, but he realized that before long he would fall into the rhythm that would keep him going until he fell on his face exhausted. It was the pace he had to set. He did not think about tomorrow. If he failed today, there would be no tomorrow— not for him, not for Elizabeth, not for Joshua.

The baby squinted at Stephen from his position on his mother's back.

"Liz," he called out. "Why don't you lay Joshua on the floor of the canoe? He's getting the sun on his face and it would give you a rest."

She stopped paddling and followed his suggestion. She kissed her son before laying him down in the shadows. The back of Elizabeth's shirt was sopping and she had soaked the baby's carrying pack as well. Or perhaps Joshua had contributed some of the wetness, himself. Joshua looked up at Stephen, who loomed over him. Stephen could have sworn that the baby smiled.

They went back to paddling. Elizabeth seemed to have increased her pace now that she was free of the weight of Joshua. Another hour passed. The land was clearly visible ahead of them now. Several times Stephen stole glances behind him. Soon it would no longer be necessary to look behind. André's giant canoe was almost even with them on the opposite shore of the lake.

The wind was now directly from the west. The hot air and dust from the prairies were blowing out onto the lake. Now the wind helped him. He steered his canoe more and more westerly, following the shore of Dog's Head Point, but Père André could not sail directly into a west wind. The wind would blow him more and more toward the eastern shoreline. He would have to break out his paddles shortly.

The swells on the lake grew large and choppy once again and the bow began to bang into the cresting waves. With amazing suddenness the weather on Lake Winnipeg changed from its morning placid quiet into a churning dangerous afternoon squall. The hot winds striking the cool humid air of the lake created miniature cyclones. A gust swirled from the west to the north and struck the canoe broadside, nearly capsizing it. Stephen called to Elizabeth to strap on Joshua again for safety. Nothing could move on the lake when it was like this. He turned the bow to shore. There were several white sandy landing beaches. He picked the closest and drove the canoe up onto it. They had been lucky. Had the squall come up an hour earlier while they traversed the twenty miles from Hecla to Dog's Head, they would never have made it.

He found some shelter for Elizabeth and Joshua in the bushes a few yards from the shore. He left her to begin unloading the canoe's essentials. They were about a half mile from the narrows. He had to find out what happened to André. There was a pile of rocks halfway to the end of Dog's

Head. He ran to them. The waves slapped against them, sending up spray. Stephen climbed the largest of the boulders. He cut his hands and knees and tore his buckskin pants, causing his knees to bleed. But he got to the top of a rock. He stood and tried to find André. There he was, still out on the lake. His rigging had come loose in the wind and flew straight out behind the canoe. As Stephen watched, a giant tear appeared in the sail and it came crashing down into the canoe.

André had been more reckless than Stephen and he had now paid the price. Stephen knew that André was an expert at ripped sails and that by morning he would be ready to take advantage of any breeze coming from behind them. He could tell now from the angle of the fallen rigging that André was putting in on the eastern shore. He and Elizabeth were safe for another night, as long as the squall lasted.

Stephen went back to Elizabeth. She lay sprawled on her stomach. Joshua was at her side, crying.

"My love," he said bending down and kissing the back of her head. "We have one more task before we rest."

She looked at him. The dark shadows under her eyes and her almost colorless complexion told him how exhausted she really was. He could not be sure she had another day like today in her. He lifted her to her feet and took her into his arms. They were both wet with sweat and lake spray. He kissed her on the mouth.

"One more task," he said to her.

She nodded wearily to him.

He picked Joshua up in his arms and placed him in the canoe. He hefted the back end and she strained with the front. They carried the bark craft for about a quarter of a mile down the beach toward the rock observation point that Stephen had used earlier. Then he told her to strike through the bushes away from the water. A few hundred yards later they emerged onto another beach. Ahead there was nothing but water.

"We are now past the waist of Lake Winnipeg. We are on the other side of Dog's Head. If we strike due west we cross the narrows. We've still got to cross, but at least this way a northern gale won't trap us south of Dog's Head unable to round it."

Elizabeth really didn't care. All she wanted to do was rest. Stephen unloaded the canoe and set it on its side to provide them with minimal shelter. Elizabeth took Joshua to her breast. He sucked hungrily. She fell asleep, and not long afterwards the infant's tiny slurps grew fainter and then ceased altogether.

Stephen was left alone with his thoughts. Tomorrow was the day. André would repair the sail tonight. If the winds were favorable, he would intercept them as they crossed the narrows. If not, his superior paddle power would bear down on them and intercept them as they traveled north. He had to have at least three canoe men with him.

If he were André, he would repair the sail and get a good night's sleep. He could have his prey tomorrow. But the mental picture of André asleep gave Stephen his idea. The wind had settled down and the night would be a calm one. If Elizabeth were rested and if he were not half dead on his feet, he could get his head start north tonight. But he could not do it. Elizabeth would collapse and probably so would he. They needed a night's rest and a head start.

There was one chance for both of them. It was bold, but he was desperate. Once darkness had descended, Stephen reloaded the canoe. He placed the semiconscious Elizabeth on the bottom and strapped Joshua to his own back.

Elizabeth mumbled a complaint but she was too exhausted to do much more. The storms on the lake had subsided and the wind blew from the west. Stephen crossed the narrows with very little effort. He had finally reached the eastern shore of the lake. He found a landing beach. Once again he beached the craft and lifted Elizabeth out and laid her gently amid the brush. He placed Joshua in the crook of her arm. He covered them with the overturned canoe. He left his rifle by her side. The powder was wet. He would need only his tomahawk and his knife.

He followed the beach southward until it disappeared into a natural jetty of stone. He crawled out into the waters and crept around this point. The water came only to his waist. There was another beach on the other side of the jetty. He climbed ashore and went on. The land was rising here and the water was now below him at the base of a bluff. He had come at least a mile south of where he had left Elizabeth and still there was no sign of André and his men.

Then he saw their fire. The land sloped down again to another beach. André was so confident that he had not tried to conceal his camp.

Stephen dropped to all fours. Now he was in his element. This brush was poor compared to the giant woods of his youth, but he could move as silently as any Indian in the underbrush. He crept to within a few yards of the camp. He smelled not only the brush fire but a strange, sickeningly sweet odor.

The giant *canot du nord* lay on its side on the beach about twenty feet away from the campfire. There were three men. Two of them slept; the large man lying on his side, tossing and turning almost as if in anger, had to be André. The third man, a Métis by the look of him and the dress of him, sat beside the fire, keeping it going. It would be suicide to attack the camp, but then that had never been Stephen's intention.

He crawled as silently as possible through the night. He had to find the sentry who guarded the canoe. Luck ran with Stephen. The sentry was a voyageur and no voyageur could be without his pipe. If Stephen had not seen the glow in the dark, the strong pungent odor of tobacco would have led him to his prey.

The voyageur was seated beside the canoe looking out toward the darkness of the lake. Stephen crawled to within ten feet of the man. He could have killed the sentry but he could not afford to have his murder, or even disappearance, detected. His main victim was to be the canoe. He slipped around in back of the voyageur and approached his victim from the rear. He pulled out his knife and pushed its razor-sharp edge into the bark. The noise of the bark tearing sounded like nails grating on a slate to him. He stopped cutting and stared at the dark smoking form in front of the canoe. He had not moved. Maybe the waves lapping at the beach covered the noise of the bark tearing. Stephen made at least ten slices in the hull. He lost count. He hoped that none would be noticed until they launched. He took no big gouges out of the bark. Instead he made neat incisions.

When he felt he had done enough damage, he crawled away from the canoe. He had a choice of skirting around the encampment or taking the quicker and most dangerous way, the way he had come, slipping between the shore and the camp. He had been so successful he decided to take no new chances. He crawled around the brush, making a large semicircle around the camp. It brought him closer to the sleepers. Again the smell of something rotting struck his nostrils. He was no more than ten feet away from his enemy now. The

192

temptation to rise to his feet and dash the remaining distance and fall on the priest with his tomahawk was enormous. But he had to resist it. He would no doubt kill André. But the others would cut him down. If he made it safely back to Elizabeth and they launched the last part of their trip tonight, they could get away safely. This had to be his goal.

The Métis sentry stirred by the fire. Stephen froze. The man rose to his knees. Stephen could make out no details. He heard the form mumble in French about pissing. The Frenchman came in his direction. Perhaps a fight and his own destruction would be forced on him by someone else's weak bladder.

He decided he would not move. He lay motionless and prone in the bushes. Still the man came toward him. Stephen clutched his knife. He would take at least two of them with him. God knows what would happen to Elizabeth and Joshua. His heart pounded. Why hadn't he awakened her and told her about his plans. She would think he had abandoned her and the baby.

The feet of the man appeared not far from his left. Stephen held his breath until they passed him. Then he lay there motionless awaiting the sentry's return. If he followed the same route back, could he avoid stumbling onto Stephen? He heard the sentry curse. He had stubbed his foot on a fallen log. There was silence again. Then the sentry returned to his fire by a wider circle to avoid the dense underbrush and another aching toe. Stephen started to breathe easy again. He waited until he was sure that the sentry had left and then he moved cautiously forward. Soon the campfire was in back of him. He made his way up the incline to the bluff. He would be back at his own fire in time to sleep for a few hours and then to begin again on the last leg of the journey.

Elizabeth complained bitterly when Stephen awakened her. By his best estimate it was about three in the morning. The lake had calmed down again and there was a mild breeze blowing from out of the south, perfect weather for the run of a hundred and fifty miles to Norway House.

As soon as Elizabeth was awake enough, however, she caught on to his cheerful mood.

"What has happened, Stevie?" she asked.

"We have a chance now. It's slim, but we needed a head

start and now I think we have one." He told her what he had done.

Her first reaction was fear for him, but then she became angry that he had done it without telling her. But nothing could dampen his mood. He kissed her. She started to strap the baby on her back, then in her annoyance she loosened the rawhide bindings.

"You carry him today," she said in annoyance. "I've got sores on my shoulders from the rawhide."

Stephen tried to put his arms through, but it was clear that his shoulders were too broad.

"We'll lay him down in the bottom like last time," he said.

He helped Elizabeth into the canoe and handed Joshua to her. Then he shoved off again. He started off with a strong stroke. Elizabeth lagged a bit, but he knew she would get into the rhythm as soon as she woke up a bit more.

He would not take it easy. Every stroke of the paddle was a stroke away from danger and closer to safety. He knew the crucial moment would come at dawn when he could see to the south of them. He knew he would not see that dreaded sail, but until that moment he could not feel that his adventure of this night had been successful.

Now Elizabeth's stroke grew stronger. The canoe, with the wind at its back, was surging across the waters of Lake Winnipeg. If only the weather of this wretched lake would hold off, he thought. He was doing it again—searching the eastern skies for the signs of light. He was sure it had lightened from black to gray. He turned around once, knowing full well he could see nothing.

When the sun did break over the horizon, it took him by surprise. He had concentrated so on the paddling that the passage of time had eluded him. He took a deep breath and turned around. Lake Winnipeg stretched behind him, totally free of any other craft. He let loose with a war whoop that startled Elizabeth and set Josh to crying. He threw his head back and started to laugh with joy.

"I'll bet their goddamned boat sank with all of them sitting in it."

"Does that mean I can rest?" Elizabeth asked.

"For a minute," he responded.

She brought her paddle inboard and turned around to face him. He could see the tears stream down her face.

"Are we safe yet, Stevie?"

He wanted to tell her yes, but he could not delude her.

"Soon," he responded. "We have the lead time we needed. It all depends on how soon André can make repairs. He is a voyageur. He will have a supply of pitch and he will repair and relaunch soon. But last night he had us in his web and we escaped. Now he will have to weave a new one and now time is running out on him."

She sliced some pemmican and handed him a piece. He made a face.

"Just pretend it's strawberries," she said, laughing. Then she cut one for herself.

"Raspberries?" he said.

She nodded and smiled at him. Then she turned her back and started to paddle again.

They kept the pace going all morning. The wind blew from the south and the sun beat down on them. Just after they ate their lunch, Elizabeth fed Joshua while Stephen continued to paddle alone. Then the wind died altogether. For the first time since they had entered its waters from the Red River, days before, the surface of the lake was quiet. And the gusting of winds gave way to silence. But Cuthbert Grant had warned him never to trust the moods of this treacherous lake.

"I have a feeling it's saving itself up for something," he said to Elizabeth. "I'm going to stay close to the shore."

He steered the canoe to the right, closer to the eastern shore, and searched the lake behind him.

"It has taken them longer than I thought it would to repair," he said to Elizabeth as she laid Joshua back down and covered her breast.

Again he filled his mind with the thought that every stroke brought him closer to Playgreen Lake.

The hours passed. Then, at midafternoon he caught a glimpse of the sail. It moved toward them rapidly. The wind picked up from the south and André and his crew had the advantage of it.

Stephen again began to search the sky. Clouds were forming to the southwest. Hot winds would again churn up an afternoon squall. Stephen was determined to stay on the lake until he actually saw the *canot du nord* put into shore. And then he would stay out even longer to make up the lead time he had lost.

The breeze cooled him off. He watched Elizabeth's back and shoulders for any sign of collapse. She sagged, but like some spring-wound machine, she kept going stroke after stroke. Her reserves of strength amazed him. Last night she had been completely exhausted and yet she had paddled today with almost no breaks for twelve hours. And they had covered a mighty distance. He estimated that with any luck and an early start they could make Norway House by tomorrow night, even if they had to trudge the last miles on foot.

The winds grew strong again and the shallow waters started to churn. The gusts swung from the south to the southwest and suddenly from the west and then back off again to the southwest. The high cresting waves started to send up a spray. Heavy clouds came rushing in from the prairies. Stephen knelt higher in the small craft. The sail canoe still came on.

"Damn him." André was taking risks.

Joshua began to fuss and Elizabeth turned around to help him. She wanted to stop paddling, to strap him to her back, but Stephen objected.

"Don't let up," he called to her. He covered Joshua with some of Elizabeth's bedding to keep the spray off.

Now the lake was almost like a boiling cauldron. The winds swirled in all directions. The bow of the canoe crashed with such force into the waves that Stephen's eyes began to search the seams of the craft for splits. The afternoon sun disappeared to be replaced by an early dusk. Lightning streaked through the skies behind them and was followed by a crack of thunder. That was enough for André. Stephen saw the sail come down and the *canot du nord* angle for the shore. Again he threw his head back and let out a whoop of joy. The voyageur had given up. But his family would push on, just a little bit longer now to get beyond their reach.

He didn't see the cresting wave that struck the canoe on the left side. It poured over the sides and swamped the floor of the canoe. Elizabeth screamed in panic for Joshua. Without thinking she rose to turn around and grab him. Stephen had already picked up the child in his arms. Elizabeth rose to her feet.

"Get down, Liz," Stephen screamed at her. "You'll swamp us."

The canoe struck another wave head on and flipped over. The water was shockingly cold to Stephen. He held Joshua's head above water. Another wave struck him and he kicked his feet to ride with it.

"Elizabeth," he screamed over the crashing of thunder and the roar of the churning maelstrom of water. But he could not see her, nor did she answer him. It was too dark, too wild. Joshua was gagging.

Stephen knew that he was not far from shore and that the lake was shallow. He stretched his feet down while holding Joshua above his head. He could not touch bottom. He was numb and he was terrified. He had to get to shore and get Joshua to safety.

Keeping the baby's head above water as best he could, he struggled against the waves to make it to the shore. The effort was almost too much for him. He could feel the strength seeping out of his body as the cold entered it. Then his hand cracked into a submerged rock. The pain was barely noticeable. He was near land. Again he lowered his feet. He touched and rose in the waist-deep water. He struggled ashore as the waves slapped at his body. He collapsed on the ground. Joshua sneezed and gagged and then started to wail. Stephen was grateful for the sound of his cry. He stood up. He cupped his hand and yelled "Liz," at the top of his lungs.

"My God, Elizabeth, answer me," he called out in anguish. "Goddamn you, Elizabeth, don't leave me. Don't die on me!" he screamed into the night.

Still there was no answer. He started to wail in despair. He fell to his knees. There was nothing he could do. He would never find her in the storm. In any case, he could not abandon the child. Maybe she had made it to shore as he had. The lake was shallow and they had paddled close in. Maybe she was already ashore. He remembered he had placed the flint in his pocket that morning. He felt for it. It was still there. He would have a signal fire going in minutes and she would come to it. She had to. The baby was hungry. Soon she would have to nurse him.

Stephen fed anything dry he could find into the tiny fire. He was desperate to make it bigger so that Elizabeth would see it and find her way back to him and to Joshua. But the storm continued and the rain soaked everything. Joshua was hungry now and fussed continuously in his arms. He held onto the boy. Joshua was his sole link with Elizabeth. He was sure she would come back and feed her own son. If he stayed with Joshua, they would be reunited. He put his head in his hands and began to sob.

They found him like that about midnight. It was not the puny little fire, nearly burned out and smoldering badly, that led them to him. It was rather the cries of the baby.

André could barely stand. The pain had moved from his arm and shoulder to his neck, purple veins of infection had spread to his chest. He knew he was dying.

"Miller, *mon ami*," the priest said to Stephen.

He received no answer. He pointed a rifle at Stephen's head and walked closer to him. He pulled Stephen's head back by a handful of his blond hair. Then he slapped him in the face. The pain he caused himself was greater than his hurt to Stephen.

Stephen's eyes slowly focused on the priest.

"You smell like shit," he said.

"I'm dying," said the priest.

"Go find a priest," Stephen said with contempt.

"I'm going to kill you slowly, Stephen Miller."

"If you do it too slowly, you won't be around to finish it yourself."

The voyageur whom Stephen had seen guarding the canoe pushed Jamie McAlistair into Stephen's view. His arms were tied behind his back. The sentry's face was a mass of bruises—presumably the price he had to pay for Stephen's success had been heavy.

"Stevie, I'm sorry," Jamie said.

"Grant couldn't protect you from the likes of André. No one could have. I should have known that. I should have stayed and faced him. If I had, my Elizabeth would still be alive."

Jamie's knees almost buckled when he heard Stephen's words.

"But it doesn't matter any more. Nothing does."

"Oh, yes," interrupted the priest. "It matters that I get even with you for what you did to me. Mario, Jean-Claude, strip him. I want to work on him with my knife so that he can feel the pain that grips me."

"André," Stephen said as the Métis and the voyageur grabbed him and began to remove his clothes. "You are scum. The bishop in Quebec was right all along about you."

Stephen could see the rage build up in the man. He had little chance of escaping. He just hoped that if he made him angry enough André would lose control and make it quick.

"I'm going to remove every inch of hide off of you, Miller, before I touch even one vital spot. The pain you will feel will be exquisite."

"Priest," Jamie called out. "It wasn't Miller who stabbed you in the tipi. It was me."

André ignored him. Mario and Jean-Claude had spread-eagled the naked Stephen out on the ground. André knelt down next to him and pulled out Cree Woman's skinning knife and flashed it in the firelight.

Jamie could not let this happen. His hands were tied but he could still run. The two henchmen were too fascinated by what André was contemplating to pay much attention to him. André slipped the knife an inch into Stephen's thigh and began to slice. A gasp escaped Stephen's lips.

Jamie tore across the clearing. His speed caught the guards and Père André by surprise. With all of his strength Jamie slammed his foot into the priest's festering arm. The wound broke open, sending blood and a stinking pus in all directions. André screamed in agony. His eyes rolled backward and he fainted. Jamie kicked at Andre's head again and again, striking him with terrific force. Jean-Claude, the Métis, moved to stop Jamie but he dropped to the ground—a knife in his back. Mario, the voyageur whom André had brutalized, wanted no interference with Jamie's punishment of the priest.

The boy's rage poured out now. He dropped to his knees again and again from a standing height crashing his knee caps into André's fast-disappearing face.

"Jamie," Stephen called out, "put an end to it quickly."

The boy hesitated. He saw the butcher's knife lying on the ground. He dropped to a sitting position and picked it up with his bound hands. Mario was already removing the belt that André wore about his middle. In it would be all that was left from the theft of the North West Company furs.

Jamie had sliced through his bonds. He picked up André's rifle and pointed it at Mario.

"I'm on your side," said the voyageur.

Jamie fired. The bullet nearly tore Mario's head off. Jamie put the gun down and cut Stephen's bonds. Then he went back toward the prostrate form of André. He held the skinning knife in his hands now.

"Jamie, enough," said Stephen.

Jamie looked at the priest. He put his head against André's chest.

"It won't be necessary to finish him off," the boy said. "He is already dead."

Stephen went over to where Joshua lay. The baby had

grown silent amid the screams of agony and death that had surrounded him. He picked the boy up and cradled him. The baby made sucking sounds with his mouth.

"I'm sorry, son," he said to the child. "I'm sorry for all of this." He went to the spot where they had first found him. He held the baby to his chest and wept for the baby's mother.

In the morning the storm stopped again. Stephen picked up the desperately hungry baby and offered him some water from a cup. Most of it poured out of the sides of the baby's mouth, but he swallowed just enough to satisfy him temporarily. With the first light, Stephen in desperation searched the shoreline as far south as André's camp. There was no sign of Elizabeth. By now, Stephen hoped he would not find her, because if he did, he would probably find her body and he could not face a lifeless Elizabeth. When he and Jamie reached the priest's camp they had to make a decision.

"I think it's pretty well determined what I do," Stephen said, looking down at the child in his arms. "I can't go back to Red River. This little one won't make it that far. The wind is blowing from the south. We raise the sail of the canoe and we will be at Norway House before sunset. There will be someone there who can help us."

Jamie agreed. Joshua's needs must be satisfied first. They carried the giant canoe to the waterfront. Jamie handed André's money belt to Stephen. Stephen opened it. It contained about a thousand dollars in American gold coins. Stephen handed half of them to Jamie.

"Take care of all our farms while I'm gone. Rebuild my house and plant my acres because some day I'm coming back."

Jamie took the money and smiled wanly. He had grown almost frighteningly silent since his outburst the night before.

"Are you all right?" Stephen asked.

Jamie ignored the question. "Come on, Stevie. Let's get this canoe launched and the sail raised. I can't wait to get going again."

Stephen watched him quizzically. It was almost as if he were trying very hard to be only a boy again.

The wind held all the rest of the day and for once Lake Winnipeg was unruffled by storms. The sun was hot and Joshua cried from hunger the whole way. As they entered the quiet protected waters of Playgreen Lake, Stephen made out the giant structure—half fort, half trading post—established there by the Hudson's Bay Company.

They beached the canoe and walked up the path to Norway House. The storekeeper came out to greet them. It was unusual that a *canot du nord* came here. This was York boat country and the Orkney men were due any day now.

When Stephen showed his American gold no questions were asked of him. A wet nurse was found among the Indian women who lived near the house. He bought passage for himself and Joshua to York Factory when the Orkney men arrived.

The storekeeper's Métis wife began to feed Joshua with finely ground oatmeal cooked in water. He took to it instantly and swallowed it from a spoon. The journey to Hudson Bay would be arduous but they would make it, and from there they would go on to Upper Canada—somehow. He was determined to confront his brother with the consequences of his deeds.

He watched Jamie leave Norway House in a small two-man canoe. He would retrace their path back to the Red River alone. Without pressures it would only be a slow and uncomfortable trip, not a deadly one.

Jamie was anxious to get back to his farm. From hints he had dropped it was clear that something had happened between Jamie and Cree Woman. Yet Stephen found the boy's calm after so much violence disturbing. Well, if anyone would be good for him, it was the courageous Indian woman. If anyone could help him, she could.

As Jamie's canoe disappeared from view, Stephen turned his back on Lake Winnipeg and walked back to the fort.

Elizabeth awoke with the sun beating down on her and with water from the bottom of the canoe lapping at her mouth. It tasted foul and brackish. She raised her head and looked about. She could see no land whatsoever. The paddles were gone. She was at the mercy of the winds.

She groaned when she thought of yesterday. Or was it yesterday? It had to be. For one thing, she wasn't terribly thirsty yet. She remembered her panic as the water entered the canoe. All she could think of was to protect Joshua. She remembered her surprise at seeing him already in Stephen's arms. The next thing she realized, she was in the water. She had gone under and then resurfaced. She heard Stephen call her. She answered but had heard no more of him. She could only assume that the man and the boy had drowned.

She sat up and wept bitterly for her dead lover and her dead child. It had all been her fault. Her panic had caused it all. She lay back down in the water of the canoe. She didn't care what happened now. This canoe could be her coffin for all she cared. Nothing mattered anymore.

It was ironic that she should be back in the canoe. She remembered seeing it looming above her as she swam in the water. Somehow or other it had righted itself. She had grabbed for it and hauled herself into it, almost tipping it over again. She remembered throwing up some of the lake water she had swallowed. Then she lost consciousness. She had drifted, not into shore as she had hoped, but into the middle of the giant lake. Today the winds blew from the southeast, driving her further and further onto the western shore.

She lost track of time. It was night again and the lake was rough. Then dawn came. The canoe finally came to rest on a rocky beach where some Cree were fishing. They could hardly believe their luck when a totally intact canoe washed among them. They were even more surprised when they looked into it. One young warrior, Steals a Horse, immediately claimed the squaw as his captive. After all, he'd been the first to see the canoe. Some of the other young men disputed his claim. They demanded that the chief, Thunderhorse, be called in to settle the disagreement.

XI

York, Summer 1825

York harbor seemed to welcome Stephen Miller. Its entry opened like arms embracing him as he returned. But he knew that it was a false embrace. This was Charles's town, and neither Charles nor his town would like what Stephen schemed in his heart.

Joshua stood by his side. The boy was large for three; his hair was a brilliant yellow, and his eyes were green. For all his life he would be marked by that coloring. It would always be "the white-haired boy did it" when Joshua was in trouble. And Joshua was always in trouble. His ability to get into things from laundry baskets to jam jars never ceased to amaze Stephen. Stephen was sure that many an accusing finger would be pointed at this obvious and vulnerable young target.

He lifted the boy in his arms as the Kingston packet boat reached the dock off Front Street in York.

"Look, Josh," he said, pointing out the town. "That's where your grandma lives, that's York."

Josh tried to repeat the words but it came out "yuk."

"Well, I don't think much of it either," Stephen joked.

The gangplank was already in place and Stephen walked off the vessel onto the dock and dry land. He was glad to be ashore, even if his legs were like rubber and his gait wobbly.

The journey from York Factory to London, England, had been the worst journey of his life. He had been seasick the whole way. When they left the waters of Hudson Bay and the straits and entered the North Atlantic, he progressed from miserable to desperate.

In London he had contacted the agents of the firm of Nowell and Ferryman. There was no one from the family still involved in that company, but Stephen was amazed to meet the dark-skinned, black-and-silver-haired William Vaughan Ferryman, who ran the company. He was the only son and heir of Josiah, friend and associate of his grandfather and Stephen Nowell. Mr. Ferryman obviously had some African blood in him, judging from his complexion and his features, but his accent was the clipped speech of the British. He had helped Stephen arrange a settlement for Joshua out of the gold he had taken from the priest. And he helped Stephen to find lodgings in the city. Stephen had wished to return instantly to Canada but Ferryman had convinced him that it was better to wait until the child was older.

That delay had extended to two and one-half years, until the spring of 1825, when Stephen felt himself ready to return and extract his vengeance. He had written to no one. He wished to warn no one of his arrival.

His first task was to find Joshua a home. Then he would seek out the boy's father. He walked to Bay Street and turned left. Joshua was not at all impressed with the bustle of the town, not after London. Stephen, who had seen York in its infancy, was surprised by its growth.

He knew Michael Brant's law offices had been on Bay Street. He saw the name Brant painted on the sign where it had always been and knew that at least some things were constant. He opened the door of the building. The outer room was occupied by two clerks dressed well but all in black. One of the clerks came across to the wooden railing that divided the work area from the waiting room. The clerk had a sallow complexion and rubbed his hands down the sides of his trousers. Shaking hands with this one would be like holding onto a wet dishrag, Stephen thought.

But the clerk had no intention of such familiarity. "May I be of assistance to you, sir?"

"Mr. Brant, please."

Joshua reached out and tried to grab the spectacles that sat propped on the tip of the clerk's nose. The man pulled his head back. His hand shot to his face to protect his possession from so forward a child. But his hand knocked the glasses from his own face and he was forced to trap them against his chest with his arm, showing quicker reflexes than Stephen would have believed the man possessed.

"Oh, my," the clerk said, stepping backward to make sure he was beyond the child's reach. "Mr. Brant, I'm afraid, can't see you now."

"I'm sure he would be willing to if he knew I was here. Tell him it's Stephen Miller."

"I can't do that," said the clerk. "Mr. Brant is in court and won't return until this afternoon."

"I see. Could you tell me where I could find Mrs. Brant, his mother? My understanding was that she used to live right here."

The clerk looked at Stephen in surprise. It was clear to Stephen that he had hit upon a topic of great embarrassment to this poor gentleman. Something he did not care to remember.

"That was some time ago, sir," the clerk said finally. "Mrs. Brant lives in Mr. Brant's new home on Bay Street. It is one of the finest houses in all of York."

"I'm happy for her. Where can I find it?"

"Oh, that's quite simple. You walk to the next block from here and then turn right. It's a good walk. It's on the right-hand side of the road. You can't miss it. It's the largest house on the block and Mr. Brant's name is on the door—that is, Mr. Brant, Senior, Mr. Aaron Brant."

Stephen smiled. He remembered the brass nameplate. He wondered that Charles had let her take it off the door of the old Bay Street house.

Stephen turned to go, much to the clerk's relief. The gold-haired little chap was sure to go with him.

"Oh, by the way," Stephen asked as he was about to step outside, "does old Mr. Eli Stoddard still live with them?"

The clerk lowered his eyes in a clearly insincere look of sadness. "Just barely, sir. Mr. Stoddard has been ill for over two years. They say he can't last very much longer, but as you seem to know him, sir, you must also know that he is very aged. Some say he is well over a hundred years old."

"Not unless he's been counting by twos over the last few years," Stephen laughed. He was relieved to know that the old man was still alive. He would like to present his foster grandson to him.

Stephen took Joshua's hand for the first part of their journey to Bay Street. Then at the corner, as the horses and wagons noisily crossed without much concern for anyone's right of way, Stephen picked him up in his arms.

He turned one corner and walked at a faster pace. He thought he recognized the woman who came walking toward him. She looked a bit older and he remembered her only as a girl, but he was sure she was Jessica's maid, Mary.

He walked more slowly as he approached her. She, in turn, searched his face. She seemed embarrassed at seeing him and cast her eyes down.

"Is that a way to greet an old friend, Mary?" he asked.

She blushed. "I'm not supposed to talk to you, sir. I've orders from me mistress."

Stephen only then realized that she thought he was Charles. "But it's me, old hairy-face Miller, not my weak-livered brother."

At that moment her face went red with excitement and then white as she collapsed at the knees and fell to the ground.

Stephen placed Joshua on his feet hurriedly and rushed to pick Mary up off the ground before a wagon splashed mud onto her from the street.

He raised her head and slapped her sharply on the cheeks, shocking the two or three bystanders who had crowded about her.

"Is it really you, Mr. Miller?" she asked as soon as she opened her eyes.

He raised her to her feet and the small crowd dispersed.

"How could you confuse me with the other fellow?"

"Well, you two be twins, after all," she protested. "And your brother has grown himself such a lovely piece of hair on his lip, just like yours."

Stephen ignored her comment about Charles, although it angered him that his brother should look now more like him than earlier. Never had they been more alienated than now.

"I want you to take me to your mistress," he said. "Lead me to the Brant house."

Mary had been severely charged by Jessica to pick up a freshly killed chicken at the market and she feared her mistress more than anyone else in the world. But Stephen Miller's return was the most exciting thing to happen in the family since his brother had kicked them out of the old Bay Street house three years ago, and she had no intention of missing his return.

For the first time she noted the boy.

"Is the lad with you?" she asked.

"Like glue," answered Stephen. He intended to tell her no

more despite the fact that he could see she was dying of curiosity.

"Lead me to the Brant house, woman," he said pinching her cheek hard enough to draw a yelp from her. She began to scurry back down the street in the direction whence she had come.

Stephen took Joshua's hand. "Come, little fellow," he said to the boy. "You're going home at last."

Mary had alerted the whole household well before Stephen began the walk up the flagstone pathway to the front door of the house. Jessica, a bit grayer, but not much more changed, stood in the doorway. The look on her face was one of mixed delight at seeing Stephen, curiosity about the blond little imp who clung to his leg, and deep-seated fear—fear for Elizabeth, a terror that gripped her insides. Why had she not returned with Stephen?

Stephen threw his arms about Jessica and held her to his chest. He bent down and whispered in her ear, "We've lost her, Mother Jessica. She's gone."

Jessica sagged at the knees. The strength of his hug was all that kept her on her feet. She gripped his arms with her hands. Then her strength began to return. Stephen could feel it in the grip. Her fingers dug into his biceps until she actually began to hurt him. But he did not pull away or complain. He knew she needed someone to hold onto.

He waited for her to draw away from him. He touched Josh on the top of his hair. "This is your grandson, Joshua," Stephen said.

Tears were flowing freely down Jessica's face. She bent down to look at the boy. But her eyes could barely focus. She drew the boy's body into her arms. Stephen was amazed. Instead of pulling away from her as he did from all strangers, Josh allowed himself to be hugged. He looked up at Stephen with an almost resigned look on his face. Stephen in turn smiled down at him through the tears that were welling in his eyes.

Jessica rose up. "How did it happen?" she asked.

Stephen told her the whole story—of Elizabeth's flight to Fort William, their farm on the Red River, Joshua's birth, the buffalo hunt, the slaughter of the Rowands, his and Elizabeth's escape, the chase on Lake Winnipeg. He could barely speak when he came to the part where Elizabeth was lost in the storm.

Finally, when he had finished, she put her hands on his face and wiped away the stream of tears with her two thumbs. She sighed and there was a quiver in her voice as she spoke to him.

"I'm sure you lived as husband and wife while you were together in the wilderness, Stephen, and I am so happy for you both that you did. At least you and she knew the happiness that I shared with Aaron. I knew Elizabeth had nothing like that with Charles. Now that we've lost them both, my boy, we share a common sorrow."

"I know that one love can never replace another," he responded, "but it brings me joy to present her son to you, Mother Jessica."

The woman smiled at the child but then her face hardened. "And it is your belief that Charles caused all of this—the assassination attempts, the pursuit?"

"Directly and indirectly I can trace everything to my brother and I will confront him with that knowledge."

"You do what you must," she said, the hardness still in her expression and in her voice. "But if his goal has always been to destroy you, take care you don't play into his hands by any rash actions."

Then she led him out of the hallway and sat both of them down in the parlor.

"We must bring the boy to Eli," she said. "But you must sit here. He is not strong. I will have to try to break the news to him gently."

Stephen sat in the Brant parlor watching Joshua play on the floor. The house was clearly unaccustomed to children his age. At least half a dozen times in the span of half an hour Stephen had to stand to remove some expensive and delicate object from the boy's grasp.

Finally, Jessica came down the stairs. She descended slowly. Her eyes were red from crying. When she reached the bottom stair, she smiled bravely at Stephen.

"He'll see you now," she said. "But don't stay with him too long. He is very weak."

Stephen started up the stairs. Jessica stopped him with her hand. "He wants to see the boy too."

Stephen retraced his steps to the parlor and scooped Joshua up into his arms. The boy had wet himself.

Stephen reached the head of the landing. The door to the old man's room was open. Stephen and Joshua entered.

Eli was propped up in his large four-poster bed. At least three large pillows held him in an upright position. His face was almost skeletal. His long hair, which formerly had grown from the sides and back of his head, had been cropped and now he looked truly bald. He squinted at Stephen when he entered.

"Is that the traitor?" he asked, his voice cracking like a teen-aged boy's.

"No, it's your champion, old man, and if you have any challengers for me I hope you have your cane handy."

The old man coughed and put his handkerchief to his mouth. The first cough was followed by a spasm of hacking and spitting. When he had finished, he leaned back against the pillows.

"Now, you necromancer, they tell me you have provided a child with no mother. It is a feat that you need not have attempted. In fact, its reverse would have filled my liver with contentment. Did you know, traitor, that the ancients saw the liver as the seat of all the emotions—not the heart? So that you might address your love as your sweet liver."

He started to laugh and the laughing gave way to coughing.

"Where is the child?" he asked finally.

"Right here by my side," said Stephen, lifting Joshua up in his arms.

"Why do you dress him in pants? Do you try to emulate the behavior of the mother of this child?"

Stephen looked quizzically at Eli.

"Eli, this is Joshua, Elizabeth's son."

"Nonsense, it's Ann, her daughter. I told everyone she would have a daughter and that the child would be named Ann after my mother."

Stephen chuckled. "Well, this time you were wrong, old man."

"Bring the child to me," Eli commanded.

Stephen sat Joshua on the bed next to the man.

The old doctor groped for Joshua with his hand.

"Well?" said Stephen.

"The child's wet," said Eli irritably.

"Is that all?"

"Damn you, Miller. I've been a doctor all of my life. I know penis and testicles when I touch them, even if they are only slightly bigger than the poor specimens you possess. He's a boy."

Then he leaned over and stared into the wide-eyed face of Joshua Miller.

"And let me tell you something, you little pisspot. You are indeed fortunate—nay, blessed—that I am not long for this vale of tears. For surely as my name is Elisha Stoddard, nephew of that great bag of flatulence—the Reverend Jonathan Edwards of unhappy memory—your name for all your years, despite your equipment, would be Ann as I intended it to be if I had lived. God damn it."

The boy stared into the old man's face, but instead of fearing him, he started to giggle and finally to laugh.

"Ah ha," exclaimed Eli, "you have comprehended me and your show of mirth is a paean of self-congratulations over my demise. You are, indeed, a delightful little snot. Now, traitor, take the child from me. Through him my Elizabeth lives on and I am contented. I hung on hoping for her return. But it seems that it was not to be. It is sufficient that a child of her body should come in her place and release me from my vigil. Like chained Prometheus, I am released by the son of the girl to whom I did a kindness."

Stephen gave Joshua to Jessica, who had remained in the hallway. Then he returned to the bedroom.

"Now tell me," Eli's voice croaked. "What are you going to do to that filthy scoundrel of a brother of yours?"

"I will confront him with all of this—the murders, the pain he has caused."

"Confront? What kind of punishment is 'confront'? I want pain, I want blood, I want that spineless worm hanging on a hook wriggling. I want to see him mess his breeches in terror. I want his gonads—his stones—on a plate to serve to the family canine."

"Calm down, Eli. You'll do harm to yourself."

"Are you mad?" asked the old man, his eyes bulging. "I've been dead for two and a half years. How do you harm the dead?"

He fell back against the pillows again. His face turned a bright red. Stephen grew alarmed and called Jessica. She came into the room, took one look at Eli, and went to the table by his bed. She poured a tablespoonful of a foul-smelling liquid. She held Eli's nose until he opened his mouth and then she jammed the spoon in.

He gagged once and then swallowed. His eyes fluttered open.

"Where did you get that elixir from, my dear?" he asked her.

She looked at him somewhat startled.

"Why, you prescribed it for yourself."

He gave off with another hoarse laugh.

"Oh, yes, now I remember, loaded with laudanum, you know, old girl. Terribly habit-forming drug, but it does have its compensations."

His eyes seemed no longer to focus on anyone.

"You should have married me, Jessica," he said, after some moments of silence. "No disrespect meant for your Thomas, who was my good and cherished companion. But a respectable woman should not live in the same abode as a gentleman outside the encompassing arms of nuptial bliss. Again no disrespect to Thomas."

"I understand, Eli." Jessica soothed him. "And you're very right," she said stroking his forehead as he seemed to drift off to sleep.

Suddenly one eye shot open.

"There's still time, you know," he said and laughed once again.

"You are an old reprobate," she said, joining in his laughter.

But soon he had drifted off to sleep. Jessica rose from the bed and stood next to Stephen.

"What did the doctor say?" he asked her.

"I haven't been able to bring any in. He'd throw him out if he even saw one. For a doctor he has very little respect for men of medicine. I've talked to a few and they tell me that the symptoms show his heart is gradually giving out. There's no reversal possible. It can't be long now. But at least he has an answer about Elizabeth. Not knowing what had happened to her was worse than knowing, I think."

"I'm sorry," Stephen said. "I should have written to you."

"No," said Jessica. "It was better hearing it from you. At least I could hold onto the man she loved as I heard of her fate."

Stephen put his arms around Jessica. She looked over at Eli.

"He'll sleep now," she said. "Let's leave him be."

They walked out of Eli's room together. Jessica closed the door behind her. Stephen waited for her at the head of the stairs.

"I would like you to take care of Joshua for me," he said. "By the way, where is he?"

"Listen." Jessica laughed.

He heard squeals of laughter coming from below in the kitchen.

"Mary and the cook have him. I think it would be very difficult for you to win him away from us."

Stephen felt relieved at her comment. "I want him to have this," he said, removing the gold Nowell locket from around his neck. "My sister gave it to me. It passes from generation to generation. Aaron wore it once and so did my mother. Joshua is the first of the next generation. He should have it."

"I don't remember seeing Aaron wear it." Jessica responded.

"It was when he was a boy—a Mohawk boy—Grandfather Nowell gave it to him. Then he returned it. My mother wore it then and she gave it to Margaret Nowell as her first born. Now it's Joshua's."

Jessica took the worn gold medallion from him. The gothic N had all but disappeared and the chain was wearing thin and clearly it had once snapped.

"It will need a new chain," she offered. "But I will see that he wears it." And now he had to get to his other business. "Does Charles still have the same offices?" he asked.

"You're going to confront him so soon—this early in the morning?"

Stephen nodded.

"I suppose he does. I have not laid eyes on Charles Miller since the day he stole Aaron's house from me. But I think I would have heard talk of any move out of the Front Street offices."

"I'll be back," said Stephen. He walked briskly down the stairs and out of the house.

Bay Street was even busier now than it had been when he first arrived. He retraced his steps to the corner of King and Bay and walked on Bay back toward the lake. When he came to Front Street he saw some boys swimming naked in the lake. He was reminded of Charles and himself swimming in the Detroit River despite their mother's warnings. They had been friends then. Now he went to confront his brother with the charge of theft and murder.

He remembered the office as soon as he stepped into it. It had not been long ago that he had first entered the same door while Eli proclaimed the prodigal son returned.

There was a new clerk sitting in the outer office. He looked up and his mouth opened in surprise. But before he could say anything the door to Charles's office opened and John Sutherland stepped out. He too looked at Stephen in surprise.

"Mr. Miller. I was not expecting you today," Sutherland said.

"I'll bet you weren't," Stephen responded.

Sutherland stopped in his tracks. He took a more careful look and his face went white. "You're not Mr. Miller...you are..." he stuttered.

"All my life I've been a Mr. Miller."

"You're the brother. We thought you were..."

"Dead?"

"Missing," Sutherland corrected him.

"I knew where I was the whole time, as did my brother. May I see him?"

"He has not arrived from home yet," said Sutherland. The man's complexion had turned from white to green. He looked as if he were about to be sick.

"I'll tell you what I want of you, Sutherland. I want you to go to my brother's home and tell him I want to see him right away."

"Mr. Miller is a very busy man. He doesn't just drop things and come running because someone demands it."

"I'm not just someone, you goddamn little twerp. I'm the brother he's been trying to kill for four years and I'm the brother that's going to make him pay for what he's done to me and mine. I'm coming back in an hour, Sutherland. And if my brother can't come here," he shouted, "I'm going to take it out on you. I'm going to kick your ass so hard my boot is going to sink to my shin up your asshole. Do you hear me?" He grabbed Sutherland's jacket and pulled his face roughly toward him.

Sutherland grimaced in fear. Then he exhaled. His breath smelled stale and sour. Stephen let him go and the man sank to his knees. Stephen turned away and walked out of the office. He had little time to waste on such a pitiful creature.

Charles Miller had grown older. It was clear to him every morning when he looked in the mirror to shave himself. He lathered his face and stropped his razor. He could not ignore the lines about his eyes. The moustache he had begun to grow just after Elizabeth left was coming in more gray than blond, just like the hair on his sideburns.

He was forty-seven years old and he was alone. Initially, there had been concern among his business associates: "Poor lonely Charles, his wife has left him." At first, everyone had blamed Stephen. His friends had rallied to his side, especially the women. Secretly, they were delighted by the scandal. Elizabeth and Stephen Miller were on every gossip's lips.

But gradually, all of that had changed. Michael Brant was every bit as important among the York elite as Charles Miller. Soon, Brant's associates, the lawyers, judges, and politicians of Upper Canada, were spreading the story of Miller's loss of the family money and his eviction of his mother-in-law, Dr. Stoddard, and the Honorable Michael Brant. Sentiment swung against him. No one excused Elizabeth—her behavior was regarded as shocking—but all concluded that Charles had sought revenge on the innocent, and for that he was soon universally condemned.

He cared not at all what they said of him. He liked the solitude. He didn't care about his business any longer; he had turned that over to Sutherland to run completely and he ran it well enough.

Now Charles had time to return to his projects. The development of Canada, the independence of Canada, was his prime concern. He had been a consistent supporter of the construction of the canals at Welland to bypass Niagara and at Lachine to circumvent the rapids that had halted Jacques Cartier in the sixteenth century and every western traveler on the St. Lawrence ever since. He took pride in these achievements and they had been completed none too soon. The Americans were finishing a major canal connecting the Great Lakes with the Hudson through New York State. If Canada did not have its own system, then the great West would fall by default to the American republic.

He was proud of his work. That it had helped western trade—the source of all Charles's wealth—was incidental to him, although not to Sutherland—John, as Charles now called him. He was, after all, a business associate. Charles was contemplating rewarding him with the title of general manager or even vice-president of the firm. It would be wise to offer it before it was demanded. It annoyed him that John still refused to call him by his first name. He was always "Mr. Miller." Well, old habits were hard to break. John Sutherland was a good businessman, and the firm of Charles Miller, Merchant, was prospering.

Charles sneered in his mirror: Yes indeed, John Sutherland was a good businessman in every sense.

Charles also spent many days at home in his study reading. Elizabeth's departure and his estrangement from his family (even his mother had ceased to write him after the Jewish bitch of a mother-in-law wrote to her) had given him solitude. He had time to read and time to think. And then there was Ginny. She had stayed on in his employ, even though there was talk of her past in her father's long-ago boarded-up saloon. He had no real feelings for her and he suspected that she loathed him for the things he had her do, or rather do to him. But he didn't care about what she thought either. Most times he did not think about what they did, but then the pressure would build and he would need release. He accepted now that he would never have a normal relationship with a woman. He had loved Elizabeth. He suspected he still did. But he had been no match for his brother.

The very thought of Stephen raised his ire. He believed he truly hated his brother—his stronger brother. Stephen had always been first; he had even been born first. Charles had spent hours figuring out his feelings toward Stephen. He realized intellectually that Stephen had never meant to harm him, yet his very existence, his every action, had mocked Charles's weaknesses. Charles had struggled for years to father Elizabeth's child. Stephen had succeeded with only one effort. Charles had been the dutiful son returning to his mother's home after each voyage on the lakes. She always praised him and gave him a peck on the cheek. Yet Stephen, who stayed away once for a solid year trapping in the north country, was inundated with kisses and hugs on his appearance in Amherstburg. It was almost as if he was rewarded by her for his indifference. The one act that displeased her, his own failure to help Stephen rescue their stepfather, had turned her against him forever. He doubted she would have turned on Stephen for the same action or lack of action. Yet deep within him, he knew that Stephen would not have failed to act. There was a generosity in his brother's nature that he totally lacked. He was a hard, unbending man.

But he had still done nothing wrong. Was it wrong to try to bring the proud Brants under his control? They had a destructive influence on his wife. They were totally undisciplined.

215

Stoddard—the old man was impossible. He had caught only a glimpse of him in the three years. He heard he still lived but was bedridden. Jessica, the Hebrew woman, had never raised her daughter correctly. How could an infidel and a pagan, her husband, Aaron Brant, raise a proper daughter? He never should have married Elizabeth. But still, he loved her and Stephen took that love from him. He was not wrong to squander their money. It was their independence of him— Eli, Jessica, Michael, Elizabeth, yes, even Stephen—it was their independence that had threatened him. He had never stolen anything. The family money lost in the North West Company had been regained in his own name after investment in the Hudson's Bay Company ventures. John Sutherland had placed all of that in the private account to be restored to the family members when they came back to their good senses. And Stephen's gold was still in the safe where John had put it. He had taken the others' money with power of attorney. Since he had nothing from Stephen he had touched nothing. It did not belong to him.

He slapped some witch hazel on his cheeks. It stung slightly but he liked the smell.

He left his bedroom and walked down the stairs into the dining room. Ginny, as usual, was still in bed and had failed to make him a breakfast. He was used to her lack of attention. He went into the kitchen to make himself some coffee. He found the tin in which Jenny kept the ground, roasted beans. It was empty. He searched the kitchen for bread or rolls, anything he might eat. But there was nothing.

"I've a good mind to go upstairs and kick her lazy ass out of bed," he mumbled half aloud. But he didn't. He knew that she would threaten him with leaving, and the thought of not having her when he needed her frightened him. Better to leave well enough alone and not initiate such a futile exercise.

There was a knock on the front door. "Who could be calling so early?" he said aloud. He found he talked to himself frequently since Elizabeth left.

He walked out into the hall. The glass panes on either side of the door revealed the form of John Sutherland, pacing on his front stoop. Charles opened the door and Sutherland removed his beaver hat and stepped through the doorway.

"Mr. Miller," he said. His voice was raised in tone, indicating his agitated state, a very rare phenomenon for him.

216

"What is it, John? You don't make the walk from my offices to my study nearly so often as you used to."

"Someone must see to the day-to-day operations, sir, and since you seem to prefer staying here with your..." he seemed to struggle for the right word and, failing, he uttered the word *woman*, with utter contempt oozing from his mouth.

"I presume you've not come here to lecture me on my morals."

Charles was startled by the look of fear that crept into his associate's face. His head twisted to look behind him almost as if he expected pursuit.

"It's your brother, Stephen, Mr. Miller. He's returned."

"Why should that shock you? You knew he must return someday," Charles said nonchalantly. Nevertheless, he had to struggle with himself not to ask the next obvious question. Surely Sutherland would mention it if Elizabeth had returned to York as well.

"He's been to our offices, sir. He made a threat against me and you, sir. He demands to see you at once."

Charles stepped from the doorway. "I suppose you should step into the house, John. I don't think we should conduct our business on the front portico. Come into my study."

He walked down the hall. Sutherland closed the door to the house behind him and followed Charles down the heavily carpeted hallway. He stopped in front of a large leather-bound book sitting on the oak table. Charles turned and waited for him to catch up before he entered the study. He saw Sutherland's eyes search the book.

"The old family Bible, John. It records all our vital statistics. It belonged to my great-great-grandfather, a gentleman from Charlestown, Massachusetts, by the name of Breed. I'm in it. So is my much-feared brother—feared by you at least. It was sent to me by my mother just after Grandmother Nowell passed on. She thought me the most stable family member and she didn't want the Stieglers to get their hands on it. None of them are really descendants of Mr. Breed." Charles chuckled. "I wonder what dear mother thinks of my stability now? But come, John. Sit in here. I'll pour you a glass of port and you can tell me how Stephen has frightened you."

"Not at this hour, sir."

"I presume you mean the drink," said Charles, smiling. He was proud of himself. He was holding his nerves in check. He went to the cut-glass decanter on his desk and poured himself a full glass of port. He raised it to his lips. His hand trembled only slightly.

"To your health, John. I think that an appropriate toast, since my brother seems to have threatened it."

"When are you prepared to see your brother?"

"I see no reason for hurry. Stephen can make an appointment just like anyone else."

"I don't think he'll wait, sir."

It was clear to Charles that his brother terrified Sutherland.

"He was a raving maniac, sir. He hardly made any sense at all and he threatened me with bodily harm."

"He's best with his fists. I hope he didn't wave a knife or gun in your face. What did he say to you?"

"I'd rather not repeat it, sir."

"Come on, John, you can tell me."

"Well, sir, it was some extremely indelicate remark. The man is no gentleman."

"Ah," said Charles, smiling, "there you are right."

"But his anger was directed at you, Mr. Miller. His anger with me was because you were not there."

"So you're telling me that he has threatened me as well."

"Precisely, sir. I believe we should notify the authorities and have him arrested."

Charles merely smirked. He finished the rest of his port in one large gulp. "Perhaps I should see him. Arrange for him to see me tonight here at the house, won't you, John, like a good fellow?"

"Yes, sir."

"You may go now, John. Unless you wish to share a glass with me after all."

"No, Mr. Miller." He turned to leave the study.

"Oh, John, by the way, did my brother happen to mention anyone else?"

"What do you mean, sir?"

Damn the man, Charles thought. He knows what I mean. He's going to force me to ask.

"Did he mention . . . Elizabeth . . . my wife?"

"He didn't mention her, but my understanding is that as soon as Miller left Mr. Brant's home, Mr. Stoddard slipped into a coma. The maid informed me that the man, your brother, brought him very bad news."

Charles sat down softly at his desk. He could feel the nausea coming over him. A cold sweat broke out on his forehead. He again struggled to regain control and maintain his dignity.

"Well, that will be all, Sutherland," he said.

Charles's associate turned to leave and halted at the door. "Oh, by the way, Mr. Miller, your brother has a child with him—a boy. The maid said it was his son—his bastard, I guess, since he was never married. The maid told my man that the child is about three years old."

"Thank you," said Charles coldly.

"Any time," said Sutherland. Charles waited until he heard the front door close. His fingers gripped the wineglass so tightly that the stem snapped in his fist.

The rains came in the early evening. The thunder had rolled in off Lake Ontario and lightning lit up the dusk sky so frequently and for such long durations that momentarily it almost seemed as if time had rolled backward and the afternoon had returned. Soon it rained and the sheets of water slashed into York, turning the dirt streets into rushing brown muddy creeks. Then, as quickly as it had come, the rain abated, to be replaced only by a slow, drenching drizzle.

Charles lit the oil lamp on the desk in his study. He had taken everything off his desk except the lamp. He sat back in his high-back leather swivel chair. A clean desk meant only one topic to think about—his brother, his wife, and the boy. He was actually looking forward to this confrontation. There was so much stored within him that he wanted to get out—so much hatred of the twin brother who was so unlike him.

He heard the knock. He wanted to pour himself a glass of wine to steady himself. But he resisted the temptation. He didn't need anything.

Ginny went to answer the door for a change. He saw her walk down the hallway just as he was about to rise from the desk to answer the door himself. He sat back again in the chair. He heard sounds in the hallway but not his brother's loud, obtrusive voice.

Ginny came into the study, followed by John Sutherland in his rain gear.

"John? I did not expect you tonight. I don't think it's necessary for you to be here. This is a personal meeting. It has nothing to do with the firm or with my finances."

"I took the liberty of waiting by the Brant residence and following your brother on his way here to make sure the

219

timing was right. He is almost here." As he said this he approached Charles. He placed his hand on the back of Charles's chair and turned it away from the desk and came around to face his employer.

"Timing? Timing for what?"

"For this," Sutherland said, removing a large knife from under his rain gear and stabbing Charles viciously in the chest.

Miller's body stiffened with pain and shock. His eyes bulged as he stared down at the growing red stain that spread across his white shirt. He looked at Sutherland's emotionless expression and his lips formed the word *why?*

Charles's body went limp in the chair. In a flash he saw it all. His jealousy of Stephen had blinded him. All along it had been Sutherland. How foolish I've been to have trusted anyone, he thought, as the darkness descended upon him.

Stephen had reluctantly agreed to meet Charles at his home. He had little choice. He needed to see his brother and Charles had no great need to see him. If he could have smacked the smirking grin from Sutherland's face when he announced the appointment, it would have pleased him immeasurably. He looked for some kind of gear to keep off the rain but Jessica had little or no men's clothing in the house except for Aaron's rather dated suits. Eli had an old greatcoat. It too would have been more at home in the past decade but at least it would keep the rain off. He knew his arms and shoulders would never fit into the coat and so he merely draped it across his back. He stepped out into the drizzle and retraced his steps from the Brant house to the Miller mansion on Bay Street.

It was a dark night. No moon or stars could penetrate the cloud cover and there was little or no wind to drive the clouds away. The night air was heavy with moisture and patches of fog. Tomorrow was likely to be no better.

Stephen walked rapidly. There were very few others on the street. The wise folk were in the comfort of their homes, not walking along getting soaked in the drizzle.

He suddenly felt a strong sense of someone's presence. He turned around to look. The street was empty. He shivered from the cold rain dripping under his collar. He turned back to face the long length of Bay Street. The fog was thicker as he approached the lakefront.

He stopped. His footsteps echoed or someone was imitating his start-and-stop walk. Again he turned to look behind him; again there was no one in view. He continued to make his way down Bay Street. He thought he saw shadows off to the side and then to the front of him, but then he realized his imagination and the fog were playing tricks on him.

Now he was only a few steps from Charles's home. He laughed at his own sense of unease. There were lights burning in Charles's study. Stephen could see them from the street. He went up the pathway and used the brass knocker on the door.

Again he shivered. The fog was almost impenetrable here. He shrugged down deeper into Eli's old coat. A drainpipe leading from the roof poured rainwater onto the ground off to his left. The sound of the water splatting against stones blurred out any other sound from his mind.

Stephen raised the knocker and let it drop a second time. Then he tried the door. It swung open and he entered.

The hallway was dark except for the light that streamed from under the door to Charles's study. Stephen called Charles's name. There was no answer. He tried the study door. It swung open and he stepped inside. Charles sat with his back to Stephen in his large leather swivel chair.

"Charles?" Stephen called out. He walked over to the chair and spun it about. Charles's chest was covered with blood and the swinging of the chair sent him sprawling to the floor.

Stephen cried out in horror. A razor-sharp knife lay on the desk. It too was covered with blood.

Stephen dropped to his knees and placed his head next to Charles's chest. Again he sensed someone behind him. He looked up and saw the raincoated figure of John Sutherland, pistol in hand. The muzzle was pointed directly at Stephen. Behind him stood a woman whom Stephen vaguely remembered from his stay at the old saloon on Front Street.

"Ginny, please run and get the constable," said Sutherland, his demeanor quite calm. "I believe Mr. Miller here has murdered our employer."

"What are you talking about? I just came in here and found him like this. And if you run for anyone it had better be a doctor. My brother is still alive."

"Make it a stroll for the constable, Ginny. It's a dark and

treacherous night out. We wouldn't want anything to happen to you on your way. You try to bluff me, sir. No one could survive that thrust. If, by some miracle, old perverted Charles does survive the wound you inflicted on him, sir, then surely he will bleed to death before Ginny returns with the constable."

"You did this, didn't you?" Stephen asked.

Sutherland chuckled. "It is a novel twist—this last piece—isn't it? I've been trying to get rid of you for so long. But all my agents failed. First, as Mr. Miller's trusted right arm and associate, I worked through contacts in the North West Company. Your death was ordered for the good of the organization, to say nothing of the good of John Sutherland. Then the company failed but Mr. Miller became very influential in the Hudson's Bay Company, which meant that I became very influential. I was even placed in charge of the investigation of the theft of the North West Company furs of the last rendezvous. I found out about those chums of yours, André the priest and Christopher Douglas the half-breed. Certain pressures were placed on them to do company bidding."

"In fact, they were doing your bidding."

"Precisely. You learn quickly, sir, once everything is laid out for you. Your brother never understood. He was too busy getting spanked by poor Ginny. But then, *poor* is probably not an appropriate adjective for Ginny. She has been paid large sums of money for her services over the years by your brother, and I have taken care of her as well. My tastes are somewhat more delicate than your brother's, but in both cases her fees are high."

"I still don't understand why?" said Stephen, stepping from behind the desk where Charles lay. The oil lamp stood on the desk. He inched closer to it.

"Don't come any closer to me, Miller. I don't want any tricks."

"Why did you have to kill me? Why did so many have to die just so that you could finish me off?"

Sutherland became agitated. "I never meant anything to happen to anyone else but you. I certainly never wanted to cause the death of Mrs. Miller. Even if she was a slut. I planted the seeds of jealousy in his mind," he said, pointing his pistol at Charles. "I hoped he would be mad enough to protect his rights as a husband and to do to you what should have been done."

"But I don't understand. What did I ever do to you to earn your hate?"

"I don't hate you, at least not at first I didn't. I only came to hate you when you continued to thwart my plans and to threaten me."

"I threatened you? How?"

"By continuing to live. You see, Mr. Miller, I never put your gold in your brother's safe."

"I had a receipt," said Stephen stupidly.

"Worthless paper. I had it all figured out. Your gold bought me influence and power of my own. I was no longer someone's right arm unless I wanted to be. I was someone in my own right. But to keep it I had to get rid of you. You might return and demand it back. I could have paid you off but it would have left me broken—someone's right arm forever. And since I could never pay it back with enough gold but only paper and securities, I could never be Charles Miller's right arm again. My employer would have known what I had done, that I had made use of your assets to my own benefit. He has a strange sense of morality, Charles Miller. He can let some silly girl smack his ass black and blue to get his thrills. He can throw his whole family out of their house and steal their money using power of attorney, but he would throw me out on my ear, despite all my years of service, for using funds without authorization."

"But it makes no sense. If you had succeeded in killing me, Charles would have inherited my gold. He would have discovered it missing just as soon as word of my death came to him."

"I'm not a fool, Miller. You seem to forget the influence and power I have had over your brother. For all practical purposes I have run this business since you and Mrs. Miller ran away together. He would simply have told me to take care of it as he has told me to take care of everything else. But I could not 'take care of it' if you were standing there demanding your damn gold in person. I could have handled it all but for you. All the paper work would have been in good order. He would have signed for all of it after a mere glimpse, if he knew I had prepared it and I would be free. Just as now I will be free, free of you and free of him."

"So you compounded stealing with murder."

Sutherland's face contorted with rage. "You had no right to be so wealthy, a stupid lout like you. You didn't earn it. I can understand your brother's wealth. He worked for it. You got it because some ancestor left it to you. I was doomed to spend the rest of my days working for a pittance caring for an insipid, sickly old lady. I was the smartest boy in my class. I was the star pupil in school. What did you ever do? Why should you have the damn gold and not me? You didn't even know what to do with it."

Stephen inched closer to the oil lamp. "Yes, Sutherland, you have the brains," he said, "but I have the muscle. It does come to that, you know. All your plans had to be carried out by others, hired cutthroats, Ojibwa Indians, unfrocked priests. They all failed you, Sutherland, and you've been forced to do your own violence now and you'll fail too. My brother is still alive. If he survives, he'll tell who assaulted him and it will all be over for you. And I'm going to see that he lives because I'm going to break your body in two with my bare hands. You're a weakling, Sutherland, and you're going to fail again."

"Don't come any closer to me. I can kill you too. I'll just tell the constable that I caught you in the act of stabbing your brother." Sutherland's hand shook as he pointed the pistol at Stephen.

Stephen knew he could not wait much longer, if only for Charles's sake. With a sweep of his arm, the oil lamp went flying off the desk and crashed into Sutherland's chest. The pistol went off, but the ball went screaming over Stephen's head and pierced the plaster ceiling. The glass lamp shattered on impact, spreading oil and flames all over Sutherland. He screamed and then panicked. He raced out of the study into the hallway. Flames burned through his clothing and seared into his flesh. He ran for the door and pulled it open, screaming in panic. Once outside, he ran down the walk into the street—a human torch lighting up the dark foggy night. He raced for the harbor, perhaps hoping that the lake would quench the agony that gnawed at him. He never made it. The flames seared his lungs and he collapsed in a Front Street alley. Some street boys discovered his charred body the next morning.

Stephen didn't bother to chase Sutherland. He stamped out the small fires that had begun on the carpeting, then picked up Charles's limp body and carried him into the parlor. There was an upholstered divan there. He stretched his brother out, then lit the lamp on the table by the divan.

Blood still trickled down Charles's chest. His breathing was rough and labored but his heartbeat was still strong.

The front door of the house was swung open, and Ginny, followed by two constables, came into the hallway.

Ginny was the first into the room. "He's the one that did it," she cried out. "Arrest him."

Stephen stood up from bending over his brother. "Gentlemen," he said, "I am Mr. Miller's brother. Would one of you please go to Mr. Michael Brant's house and fetch him and tell him to bring a doctor immediately? I believe my brother's life can be saved."

Ginny's face turned white from fear at Stephen's words. If Charles Miller lived, he would tell who had attacked him. She started to back toward the door, but one of the constables grabbed her wrist.

"Not so fast, missy," he said. "You'll have to answer some questions."

His partner disappeared out the front door, heading down the street.

Stephen and Michael sat in the kitchen of the house, where they had moved Charles so that the family might care for him. Jessica was upstairs with the doctor. Stephen paced the kitchen while Michael sat sipping coffee. The cook, thoroughly annoyed at this invasion of her domain, was taking it out on Mary, the maid, sending her on a series of useless, never-ending missions throughout the house.

"Stephen, sit down," Michael said finally, his patience wearing thin.

Stephen collapsed onto the same wooden bench that Michael occupied.

"The doctor said yesterday that he didn't think the wounds were fatal. As long as there is no infection or pneumonia Charles should live, Stephen."

"But they have been up there for so long. I hate the waiting. It reminds me almost of waiting for a woman to give birth."

"I know nothing about that, but if it's a fact, it is another reason never to marry."

"I've mixed feelings, Michael," Stephen said. "It's hard for me to forget years of pent-up anger against Charles overnight. But he is my twin."

"It's hard for us also, for mother and me. After all, it was not Sutherland who squandered our money. It was Charles. I have always felt it was deliberate—to gain control over us and most especially over my sister."

Mary came racing into the kitchen down the back stairway. "It's a crisis, the doctor says," she practically screamed. "He needs a kettle of steaming hot water, something to ease his breathing."

It confirmed Stephen's worst fears. His brother was not going to survive his ordeal.

Mary grabbed the teakettle that always sat on the stove and ran back up the stairway once again.

Michael touched Stephen's arm. "Perhaps, if he is slipping away, we should go upstairs and join my mother."

Stephen nodded assent. The two men rose from the bench and walked out into the hallway. To their surprise Dr. Baker was descending the main stair. He shook his head.

"He's gone."

Stephen felt his stomach sink. "It's my fault," he said, almost choking on the words. "Maybe if I'd stayed in London, none of this would have happened."

Michael patted Stephen's shoulder.

"Perhaps you're right," said Dr. Baker. "The excitement may have been too much. He was very old and very fragile."

Suddenly it dawned on both Michael and Stephen that the doctor did not mean Charles. It was Eli who had slipped away from them.

It was a strange feeling for Stephen. He could feel no elation that his brother still lived because that elation would mock the memory of one whom he truly loved—a far better man than Charles, or for that matter, he himself, could ever hope to be.

Michael looked as if he had been struck in the stomach. Eli had been foster father to Elizabeth, but he had also been confidant and confidence-builder to a young boy in awe of his own father's strength. Michael climbed the rest of the stairway alone. Jessica came out of Eli's bedroom. She held back the tears. Michael put his arms around her.

"He couldn't breathe," she said to her son. "Then suddenly he was at ease. He asked me to come sit beside him. He raised my hands to his lips, and as he kissed my hand, he died. It was so peaceful, his going, just like your father's, Michael." She started to weep finally and he held onto her.

226

Stephen climbed the stairs to the top of the landing. "I'll go make the arrangements," he offered.

Jessica shook her head. "Dr. Baker said he would take care of that. You go see Charles. He is conscious."

Stephen left Jessica and Michael clinging to each other. He walked down the hall and entered the room where Charles had been placed. The shutters were drawn and the room was dark even though it was close to midday.

His brother's eyes were closed, and Stephen tiptoed across the room and sat in a chair placed by the bed. When he sat down, Charles sensed his presence and opened his eyes.

"Stevie," he said weakly.

Stephen reached over and touched his hand.

"I'm sorry for everything. Jessica told me all that Sutherland had done. I was so careless with those I loved. I allowed it all to happen by carelessness. Your money will be restored to you. So will the money I took from Jessica, from Michael, and from Eli."

"Eli is gone, Charles. He died this morning. His money should go to Joshua, Elizabeth's son."

Charles bit his lip when he heard the news. "It will be done," he whispered.

"Joshua is a good boy, Charles," Stephen started to say, but Charles raised his hand to stop him.

"I don't wish to speak of Elizabeth or her son, Stevie. They stand between us. They always will."

"They are the only thing we have ever had in common, Charlie," Stephen corrected him. "Our love for her."

"I don't believe I am capable of loving anyone but myself, Stephen. I am a very selfish man. I warn you. If you come into my business with me, you'll earn a handsome wage but it will be Charles Miller's business and I'll never give you or anyone else the satisfaction of management. I want those satisfactions for myself again."

"Wait a minute," interrupted Stephen. "I have no intention of going into your business."

Charles looked at him; the keenness of his disappointment was hidden by his weakness. "What are your plans?" he asked after a long, solid pause.

"I'm leaving Joshua with Jessica. She needs her grandson and he needs a woman's love and care for a while. I'm going back to the Red River. I have a farm there and I've got neighbors who are working it for me. I'm going to get established there, get my farm working, my barns filled, and then I'll send for Joshua."

Charles was silent again. "You hate to farm, Stephen. You always have. Both of us hated it so much that I went to sea and you went to fur trapping."

"Things have changed with me," Stephen said unconvincingly.

"You were happy there on the prairie, weren't you?"

Stephen nodded.

"You were there with Elizabeth, weren't you?"

"I've got to get back, Charlie. It's the only place I can call home now. It won't be the same without her but the memory of her will linger on there. Even that is better than anything else I've ever known."

"You've come to say good-bye then, brother."

"Yes, I have."

"You can have free passage on my next ship to Fort William. I doubt if we will ever see each other again, Stephen. If we don't, please know that I've hated you and loved you at the same time. The hate I could not help. I didn't want it. It was just there. I've always wanted only to love you."

Stephen bent down and kissed his brother on the cheek. There were tears in Charles's eyes.

"Get well," Stephen said as he rose from the chair. He walked across the room to the door. He turned around to say good-bye again but he could see from the even movement of Charles's breathing that he had fallen asleep once more.

The journey from Fort William had been filled with sad memories for Stephen. At Rainy Lake he recognized the place where the pemmican-eaters had met with the pork-eaters and where Douglas and Père André had hatched their plot to steal the company furs—a plot that would lead to their violent deaths and to the deaths of so many others, including his Elizabeth.

Paddling across the Lake of the Woods restored peace to him, and the descent of the rapids of the Winnipeg River was actually exhilarating. But as that river entered the lake of the same name, a depression settled on him. He would never be able to see Lake Winnipeg without thinking of her. He hated the fickleness of its storms. As if to mock him, the lake's surface was almost mirrorlike when his canoe left the river and entered it.

He paddled west on the lake without incident until he

reached the mouth of Red River, and for the first time since leaving Rainy Lake he paddled upstream against the current.

He would find his farm before evening came. The river curved a bit here. He saw the smoke rising from Cree Woman's stove first. Another slight bend in the stream and her cabin would come into view. There it was. The sun was setting to the rear of it, bathing everything in red and gold. He beached the canoe and climbed up the slight incline to the grass-covered prairies. He looked upriver to where his old house had stood. There it was, still unrestored, and beyond it, bathed also in the golden light of the dying sun, were acres of growing wheat. A horseman, rifle slung across his back and shoulders, was riding through the wheat field.

Jamie saw Stephen. He reached for his rifle and fired a shot into the air for the joy of it and to warn Cree Woman to set another place for dinner—Stephen Miller had returned home.

ABOUT THE AUTHOR

A Canadian citizen since 1976, ROBERT E. WALL draws on his love for Canada and his native United States in creating the saga of *THE CANADIANS*. He perceives the histories of the two nations as deeply entwined and, influenced by the writings of Kenneth Roberts, seeks to teach those histories through the historical novel. *Blackrobe*, the first in the series, is Wall's first novel, followed by *Blood-brothers* and *Birthright*.

Robert Wall is married, has five children (one is an adopted Cree Indian, the most authentic Canadian in the family), and divides his time between New Jersey, where he is provost at Fairleigh Dickinson University, and Val David, Quebec, where his family lives.

Coming early in 1984 . . .
The stirring culmination
of an epic saga

THE CANADIANS
BOOK SIX

DOMINION

by Robert E. Wall

From the rebellions of the 1830s to the formal
Confederation of Canada in 1867, the sweeping
story of the descendants of Stephen Nowell and
Aaron Brant unfolds.